Long-Distance Memories

~

J. Robert Thompson

PublishAmerica
Baltimore

First printing

ISBN: 1-60441-495-2
PUBLISHED BY PUBLISHAMERICA, LLLP
www.publishamerica.com
Baltimore

Printed in the United States of America

Long-Distance Memories

~

J. Robert Thompson

Regina,

Thank you for having more faith in me than I had in myself
And not allowing me to just put this book on the shelf.
Thank you for finding all my mistakes and making corrections.
And thank you for understanding my need for perfection.
Thank you for all the time and effort you put in with me
And thank you for being my eyes when I couldn't see.
This book would have never been written if not for your push.
Okay, I know you're right; it was really more like a kick in the tush.

—Rick

DISTANT MEMORIES

Distant memories coming through
A look at life the things we do
Where I have been what I have done
My distant memories remember the fun
Each distant memory from shore to shore
Is meant to see the life I explored
Of what I remember some borrowed, some true
The distant memories of my life with you
Whether you're my town my school or just a friend
My distant memories carry me to the end…

—J. Robert Thompson

Prologue

I've never been big on reading, especially stuff like How-To books, technical manuals, and those little help windows you find on every computer program ever written. Now give me a good James Bond thriller or some other form of reading entertainment; I might stay up all night reading it to its conclusion. So it's safe to say if I read, I read to be entertained.

While I've never a big reader I've always felt like I wanted to write. I just never wanted anyone telling me how. Somewhere along the way I heard it said that in order to write anything you needed a beginning, middle, and ending. As a high school dropout from a small West Texas town that made sense to me. But over the years I've discovered that isn't always that simple. It has always been that middle part that gets me all wrapped around the axle. You can begin with just an idea, but after spending hours sitting and staring at that great idea and not coming up with another word you say, "Screw it," and quit; so much for being a writer. That same guy said to be a good writer you should write about something you know. That made sense to me too. It's amazing what happens when you pay attention sometimes. You really learn a lot of good stuff.

After giving it some thought I have come to the conclusion that what I know most about is myself. I've never considered my life much more than ordinary; certainly not extraordinary. In fact it has probably been a lot more boring than most folks'. But what the hell? What may be dull and boring to me might give someone else a laugh or two or just make them think and recall their past, the way it was or the way they wished it had been. As I think about it, my life consist of a little of this and a little of that and a whole lot of nothing. So here is what I know nothing about most: my life.

MY HOME TOWN
Chapter 1

If you're going to talk about your life, where better to start than with the town you grew up in. I never considered Abilene a city but the sign on the side of the road said you were either leaving or entering the city limits so maybe we were. I always just thought we were a pretty big small town. The thing that sticks out in my mind when I look back on the "good old days;" no matter whether it was a city or a town, it was a friendly place and a good place to grow up. You could ride your bicycle, if you had one, to or from school and pretty much anywhere in town you wanted to go.

I don't remember much about the first five or six years of my life. I do remember that my parents were nomads and traveled between Texas and California several times in my early childhood. When I was about six years old they left me with my grandparents and went back to California.

My granddaddy was my early father figure, and I thought he was a pretty smart man. When I was eight years old he took me down to get my social security card. I had no idea what a social security card was or why I needed one, but if Granddaddy said I should have one then I knew it must be important.

We walked into the office and the lady behind the counter looked at me and said, "What can we do for you today, young man?"

"I came to get my social security card," I said.

"Well, good for you. I need to know your name before I can give you one, though."

"My name is Ricky!" I proclaimed.

"Hold on a second there, son," my granddaddy said; "that's what we call you, but that isn't your Christian name."

I was totally confused. *What's a Christian name?* I wondered. I listened as Granddaddy told the lady what my Christian name was. To that point in my life I can't ever remember being called by either of those names. All I knew was Ricky.

When we left the social security office I asked my granddaddy, "Why does everyone call me Ricky if that's not my name?"

Granddaddy patiently gave me the following explanation: "Your mother always wanted to name you Ricky, but she never told anyone, not even your daddy. When you were born you were a really big baby, and things didn't go real well for your mother. When it came time to put a name on your birth certificate; it was up to your daddy to give you a name. Since your mother hadn't told him to name you Ricky he just named you after your mother's favorite uncle and himself. Later on when your mother found out she wasn't very happy with your daddy, and she said, 'Well, we are still going to call him Ricky.' So that's why everybody calls you Ricky."

To this day if you ask anyone left in my family what my name is they will tell you it's Ricky. If you ask one of them for me by my Christian name; they'll look at you and say, "Who?"

Abilene was probably pretty much like the town a lot of ya'll grew up in. If you were brought up in a small Texas town there was probably a church on every corner, and in all likelihood it was a Southern Baptist Church. Those things are like ants, they're everywhere. I pick on the Southern Baptist a lot because I was brought up by my grandmother who was a staunch Southern Baptist and she made sure I got to church every Sunday when I was in her charge. Even after I moved away from my grandmother I continued to go to a Southern Baptist Church during my teen years but for totally different reasons none of which my grandmother would ever approve of.

As I got older I used to wonder about all those non-fun loving believers sitting in church on Sunday morning all red eyed and nodding off every time the pastor let you sit down. The Baptist do a lot of getting up and sitting down as I recall. A few years later when I was old enough to go riding with boys looking for girls I learned about Charlie Blanks Night Club and it all became perfectly clear. Charlie Blanks was a BYOB type of place from what I understood and all those red-eyed, nodding off believers sitting in the front row of church on Sunday morning had been out at Charlie's the night before dancing and drinking and sinning up a storm. Seems my mother and daddy and a few friends of theirs were regular customers too.

When I was eight I started playing little league baseball at Cobb Park. By this time my parents were back and my daddy had opened a barbeque café downtown but he always managed to make my baseball games. I think he really wanted me to be a professional baseball player. After every game there was always a critique; I could have done this better or I could have done that differently. Even though I made the all star team every year it never was enough. By the time I out grew little league, I had pretty much lost my interest in baseball.

By this time it was the early 1950s, and there couldn't have been a greater time to be a kid; especially in a small town like Abilene. On Saturday mornings we used to ride our bikes down to the Paramount Theater and for about 50 cents you could get your ticket, a coke, some popcorn and get change back. They always had a double feature starting early Saturday morning with a bunch of cartoons in between features. If you were lucky enough to have as much as a dollar; after you left the Paramount you could go down to the Queens Theater and watch another double feature. It was always fun going to the Queens; in between their features they had Yo-Yo contests. I finished second once but I never could beat this kid named Joe Eddie at doing loop de loops; but more about Joe Eddie later.

Abilene sat in the middle of a "dry" county in West Texas. This meant there was probably a bootlegger within walking distance of your house. For those of you that don't know or remember bootleggers; these were guys that would drive to the nearest "wet" county and stock up on beer and liquor and bring them back home and sell them to you at a much higher price. Actually it was the Southern Baptist that kept the bootleggers in business for years because they kept voting the county dry. They finally lost out somewhere around 1960 when someone got smart and incorporated about ten acres just outside the city limits and got a liquor license; which meant there was no need for bootleggers anymore.

I tried bootlegging once myself. One summer when I worked as a bellhop at the motel, a guest called me over to his room. "Can you get me a bottle of gin or vodka?" he asked.

I thought about it for a minute and said, "Sure, I can do that if you don't mind waiting a little bit." The guest agreed, and I went back over to the desk and told the desk clerk I would be gone for about 30 minutes.

I jumped in my car and drove straight to my house; I knew neither of my parents would be home so there was no need to be sneaky. I walked in the house went straight to the bathroom my daddy used, lifted the top off the toilet and grabbed the new bottle of gin he kept hidden there. I wiped the bottle off, stuck it in a paper bag and took it back to the man at the motel. He gave me $25.00 for it. That was a pretty good tip for a 30 minute deal.

One thing about us Texans: we love our high school football. Some of ya'll probably saw the movie *Friday Night Lights.* I didn't live in the town the movie was about, but we played them every year. But that was before that particular high school existed, and before them there was us. We won three straight state championships in football, 49 straight games. We won two state championships in baseball, and a couple of state titles in track and field. One year we were regional finalist in basketball. Basketball was our weakest link, probably because I played: just my luck.

A year or so after I graduated, they built another high school and I think that kind of broke up, not just the athletic programs Abilene High had going but split up the closeness among the kids as well as the people in the town.

One year when I went back to visit, my cousin, who was five years younger than I was and went to the new High School asked me if I wanted to go to a football game. I was expecting to go to the same old stadium at Fair Park. The stadium where Abilene played high school football and held track and field meets for as long as I could remember. The same stadium where I ran into a pickup truck and broke my collarbone trying to get in the stadium in time to see the opening kickoff when I was 9 years old.

Instead my cousin took me to some new stadium they had built way out on the edge of town. She also didn't tell me that the team her school was playing was my old alma mater. I can't tell you how weird it felt to sit on the opposing team's side of the stadium. I felt uncomfortable and out of place. It didn't seem right; there should only be one team representing Abilene, and that was my team, the Eagles. Abilene won that day; but Abilene lost. It's a shame sometimes what growing up does to a town and its people. But I guess Abilene is no different in that respect; that's just the way it was in my old hometown.

MY HOME TOWN
Chapter 2

My home town was really a pretty peaceful place I think. We didn't have a lot of crime, it seemed, for a town of around 20-30 thousand people you didn't hear or read a lot about drugs or guns or murders or things like that. Of course back then I only read the sports page in the local newspaper and the only time I listened to the radio was to try and pick up a professional baseball game or listen to the Lone Ranger or the Green Hornet and sometimes The Shadow.

The police didn't wear body armor or carry riot gear in their cars. Of course that could be because they hadn't invented body armor yet and the closest thing to a riot was a conga line in the parking lot after the home team won a football game. You could walk down Main Street at 1-2 a.m. and no one would bother you. Actually we didn't have a main street. We had a Pine Street and Cedar street, and a Cypress Street and Palm Street. Somebody was big on trees I guess. The town was divided in half, the Union Pacific Railroad ran right down the middle of it from east to west and you either went under the tracks or over 'em.

Of course we had our ritzy part of town and our not so ritzy part of town. The ritzy part of town consisted of houses that cost in excess of at least $50,000.00. I don't think you can buy a double wide with all vinyl interior for that these days. We had our segregated parts of town too. The African Americans had their portion and the Hispanics had theirs. The first Hispanic male came to our school while I was there. He and I became friends as much as society would let us back in those days. We had played little league baseball together. He never came to my house and I never went to his but he was a great guy and a hell of a quarterback. He was a starter our senior year and he had a lot guts and character to take the crap he put up with from opposing teams. We served together later on in the Army. Actually he was my commanding officer for a short period.

I mentioned in Chapter 1 that we had a great athletic department when I was in high school. That was because we had three junior high schools feeding one high school. It was a great plan, all the junior highs ran the high school offense and defense; by the time we moved up to high school we knew the offense and defense inside and out.

One of the most traumatic moments of my young life came the summer of '53 before the new high school opened up. The old high school was going to become the third junior high school, which I would have attended along with all my friends that I had gone through elementary school with; but we moved and that put me in the South Junior High School District. I thought my world as I knew it had just ended. I thought of running away from home but the only place I could think to go was my grandparents' place and that wouldn't do me any good. That would put me in the hated North Junior High School District and that would never work. But I had all summer to figure out what I was going to do.

So where are all the girls you may ask? Well, so far they hadn't really been discovered as yet. Well, that's not exactly true. They were discovered during the summer after sixth grade, it was just that we or at least I hadn't figured out what to do with 'em yet. Bobby Mitchell, Duane Jones and I had arranged to have a semi-chaperoned date/party at Bobby's house. Talk about awkward, it was like Richie Cunningham, Potsey, and Ralph trying to figure out what to do next. Finally we came up with a bold plan. We would go for a walk around the block and somewhere long the way, at some point during that walk, we would get kissed. I can't speak for the other guys, but I got mine. Afterwards, I thought Doris was a great kisser; but then I really didn't have anything to compare it to.

That was a big moment in our lives, I remember the next morning, Bobby and I went over to the little neighborhood store across the street from Bobby's house and got our usual Little Debbie's Chocolate Cup Cakes and a Dr. Pepper and sat out on the curb and reveled in our conquest of the evening before. We were now men of the world....well at least in our little part of the world.

Having failed to figure out how I could keep from going to South Junior High. I finally accepted my fate and enrolled and got my class assignments. Actually things weren't as bad as I thought they might be. Some of the kids I thought I would never see again were already in the South Junior High School District so I didn't lose all my rowdy friends.

It was a great time to be a teenager. Rock and Roll was becoming the new music of the age, and everybody wore an "I like Ike" button, but not because we were Republicans; we didn't even know what a Republican was. We just thought it was a cool button. Things, they were a-changin', but I settled in with my old friends and made some new ones at South Junior High School, and life continued on and actually got better in my home town.

MY HOME TOWN
Chapter 3

I had a great three years at South Junior High. I lived less than a block from the school and my dad had bought a hamburger joint just up the street and turned it into a barbeque place. My dad was a chef of sorts and barbeque was his specialty, and I gotta admit the old man knew his way around a barbeque pit. Of course it took him awhile to forget about me dropping that brick on his head when I was helping him build the pit. It was an accident! I swear! The name of the place was Rick's Bar-B-Q. What else would you call it? And it made me really popular at school when the guys got hungry and didn't have any money. Of course the old man wasn't too happy when I brought the guys in for lunch.

Going to South Junior High was about to open my eyes when it came to girls. It was like a dream just walking down the halls between classes. It seemed like something happened to all the girls over the summer between sixth grade and junior high; they were the same girls but different. We had two sets of twins; just having one of each was enough to drive a guy blind. I didn't have one class that didn't have at least one very pretty or sexy girl, some even had both.

Suddenly, without realizing it, guys started finding themselves more and more interested in cars and girls. Not necessarily in that order. The girls in their poodle skirts and bobby sox and their hair all done up in a pony tail were getting a lot of second looks.

Guys wore their jeans down low around their hips with the legs turned up at the bottom to make a cuff, along with a white T-shirt, under a leather jacket. They combed their hair back in a Duck Tail style with the help of a lot of greasy kid stuff; unless you were a jock then you had a flattop hair cut. James Dean and Elvis were fast becoming our idols.

Even though we were too young to have a driver's license and drive a car; the '54 Mercury, the '54 Chevy Corvette and the brand new 55 Chevy convertible were hot cars and everybody was going to get one…next year.

I particularly remember my seventh grade math class which just happened to be taught by one of the football coaches. The class wasn't crowded and I sat on the back seat of the third row from the far wall away from the teacher's desk. Sitting in the very last seat in the very last row was a girl named Wanda something or other; we never got around to last names. Basic math came relatively easy for me so the class didn't really hold my attention; not nearly as much as Wanda did. It was obvious that Wanda cared even less than I did about math. She used to wear tight, straight and short skirts to school and during class she liked to prop her feet up in the seat of the desk between us. Wanda was a very careless girl. Wanda didn't always wear panties.

I know Wanda failed that class; if I hadn't needed to pass to stay eligible to play sports and the coach hadn't been the teacher I would have failed just to take the class over again with Wanda.

Junior High was kind of rough in the dating department. We weren't old enough to have a driver's license yet so dates were either chaperoned with a parent driving or you just went to the movies on Friday or Saturday nights with a group and then paired off after you got to the movies or whatever particular function you were going to.

The 8th grade was pretty boring really. I had decided I didn't want to play football anymore but since basketball season was about ready to start; they let me stay with the team and I was designated as a coach's assistant. Basically, I was an errand boy but when there was nothing to do I was allowed to go in the gym and shoot some hoops. The only time I couldn't practice was when the cheerleaders were decorating the gym on Thursday afternoons; getting it ready for the Friday morning pep rally.

I kind of had my eye on one of the cheerleaders named Janice but she was really out of my league so I had never really talked to her much other than to say hi. I remember this particular Thursday I was asked if I could give them a hand with the decorating and naturally I said I would. So here I was the only guy in the gym with eight cheerleaders running around in short shorts and blouses tied in a knot at the waist and unbuttoned most of the way to the knot. Who could ask for anything more?

Janice was up on a ladder near one of the baskets trying to tie some colored streamers as high up as she could reach on the backboard when she dropped her tape and asked me if I could get it for her. I got the tape and climbed up the ladder to hand it to her. I climbed up as high as I could on the ladder with her and when she turned around to reach for the tape her blouse popped open. At that point it was more than obvious that Janice wasn't wearing a bra. I was just at the right height that if I had to lick my lips we would have both got licked. I'm not sure who was the most embarrassed. I tried to look away and she tried to turn away and one or both of us dropped the tape again.

I got down and got the tape and headed back up the ladder while she adjusted her blouse. I just stuck the tape up in the air without looking up and let her take it out of my hand and as soon as she had it I was outta there. I don't think any of the other girls noticed what happened. Of course Janice and I never talked about it. But every once in a while if our eyes met when we passed in the hall or something we would both kind of smile and just keep on walking.

There is a provision in the Texas Law or used to be that allows someone 15 years of age to get a driver's license under special circumstances. I don't know what his circumstances were but Stephen managed to get a driver's license so when I could scare up a date I could usually count on Stephen to let me and my date double with him and his girl. That made the 9th grade a little more tolerable.

In September of '56 we entered the now three year old high school. It was the first time I had been to a school that big. I remember the first day I walked into that school. The main building had the Administrative Offices and classrooms on the first floor and two more stories of classrooms on the floors above.

There was a music hall and auditorium in a separate building. Behind the main building was the cafeteria, which also served as the detention hall, a place I became quite familiar with, but it wasn't from all the meals I ate there. The gym, both boys and girls, was in a separate building across the parking lot behind the auditorium. Behind and surrounding all of this was a practice field for the football team, a baseball diamond, a full track and field layout including a high jump pit, a broad jump pit, a pole vaulting pit and of course a track for the runners. All that and more is pretty standard for schools these days but back then it was pretty awesome for an almost 16 year old. I remember wondering how I was ever going find my way around in all this maze of buildings, rooms and hallways. Would I ever make it from one class to another on time?

This was only a three year high school so the first class for the new sophomores was an assembly in the auditorium. I remember walking in to the lobby of the auditorium and running head long into Duane Jones. This was sort of awkward because Duane and I had gotten into a fist fight a few days after that night we had our "date" with the girls and since he stayed at Central Junior High I had not seen him since. It was the only fist fight I ever had. Actually it wasn't much of a fight. I think I got in one punch and then spent the rest of the time trying to get out of a head lock or get Duane in one. Finally we both just got tired and quit; besides it was time for supper. If I remember correctly the fight was over a girl but not one that had been at the party. We looked at each other, both took a step back and then shook hands and laughed about our childhood antics.

This was a day of coming together. All the friends I had made over the past three years at South Junior were there. It was a reunion for many of us with old friends we left behind at Central Junior and the arch rivals from North Junior were rivals no more. We all came together as the new sophomore class of 1956; ready to take on all challenges and challengers that we may face for the next three years. It was a good day in my old home town.

MY HOME TOWN
Chapter 4

My sophomore year was the beginning of a whole new life for me. Some of the things I had only dreamed about before were actually coming true. I got my driver's license and my home town suddenly became a lot smaller and a lot bigger at the same time. I made the basketball team, now I could play with the big boys, and I met Charlene.

Getting my drivers license and making the basketball team were goals that I had set for myself long before I actually got to high school. My parents weren't too excited about me getting a drivers license and were less than cooperative in giving me practice time behind the wheel. But I managed to get enough to feel reasonably sure I could pass the test. Since both my parents worked, I got my friend Wayne to take me to the Department of Public Safety Office to take my drivers test in his car. Wayne had a lot of faith in my abilities. I passed, and needless to say my parents were surprised when I showed them my license.

Getting my drivers license was exciting but making the basketball team was even more exciting. I was the only sophomore to be moved up to varsity. That gave me some instant credibility with the upper classmen. I remember the day we got our letter sweaters. I have to admit that my head probably got about two hat sizes larger. Of course that didn't last too long; the coach had a way of bringing you back to reality.

But no matter; life was getting good around my old home town and bound to get better.

My class schedule never worked out the way it was supposed to. If you played a sport other than football, you were supposed to have 6th period PE and a 7th period study hall. Then when your sport began it was just an easy swap from one to the other. When it came time for basketball I ended up in a 6th period Spanish class. It wasn't all bad; two of my best friends were in that class; and so was Charlene. As I learned later on she was an 18-year-old senior. I have no idea what she was doing in a sophomore Spanish class and it really wasn't something I was concerned with at the time.

It's funny how you can remember some things so specifically and some you can't recall no matter how hard you try. For the life of me as I sit here now I can't remember our Spanish teacher's name. I want to say Ms. Hayes but I think she taught Spanish at South Junior. Oh, well, it really isn't important except that whatever her name was, she used to let us step out in the hall and get a drink of water, two rows at a time.

About the third day of class my row and Charlene's row got to go to the water fountain at the same time. As was my custom I hurried out to the fountain to be up towards the head of the line to get a drink. Then I would hang out in the hallway until everyone else had finished then go back for a second drink. Somehow I felt like this was one way I could postpone having to go back and sit there in that class any longer than I had to.

After finishing my first drink of water I walked over and stood leaning up against the locker behind the door to the class room. This way the teacher couldn't see me just standing there. Suddenly there was this little short blonde haired, blue eyed girl standing in front of me. It was Charlene. I stood there looking down at the top of her head when she stuck her hand inside my shirt and started tweaking the only two hairs growing on my chest, which I was so proud of.

She looked up and said, "How do you like our Spanish Class?"

Of all the really cool things that I could have said, the only thing that came out of my mouth was, "It's okay."

You have to remember now I was just 15 going on 16; knew nothing about older women and had absolutely no experience to draw from. Okay, so I didn't know anything about younger women back then either. Sue me. She just stood there looking up and smiling up at me, rubbing my chest, and I just stood there like an idiot. We finally realized we were the last ones in the hallway and went back to class. As I sat down behind Wayne I hit him on the back so hard he swallowed his bubble gum. He turned around and looked at me like I was crazy.

I nodded towards Charlene's row and whispered to Wayne, "Who is that girl behind Gloria?"

He looked over there, not so casually and broke out laughing. He leaned over to Stephen sitting next to him, whispered something and Stephen broke out laughing. I could have killed 'em both right then but the teacher was giving us that stare only a teacher can give.

I didn't get a chance to talk to either of them before class was over but before the bell rang, Gloria gave me a signal that she wanted to talk to me after class. I walked Gloria to her next class and she told me that Charlene wanted me to call her, then handed me a piece of paper with a phone number on it. That was probably the worst day of basketball practice I ever had. Well, maybe the second worst but the other one hadn't occurred yet. As soon as I got home I called Wayne and asked him what was so funny. He said he had heard some talk about Charlene. I asked him where he heard it, and he said from Stephen. Now I liked Stephen, we were friends, but I didn't always have a lot of trust or put a lot of stock in what Stephen said. I spent the next couple of hours locked in my room rehearsing what I was going to say to Charlene when I called.

I remember that whatever I rehearsed never made it out of my mouth when I finally got up the courage to call. I did manage to stumble around and ask her for a date on Friday night.

She replied, "I can't go on Friday."

That certainly took the wind out of my sails, and all I could say again was, "Okay."

But the wind picked up again when she said, "But I can go Saturday night."

I remember this fleeting thought flashing through my mind that now would be a good time to play hard to get but I didn't know how.

I just blurted out, "Great, I'll pick you up at seven," and hung up. I forgot to ask her where she lived. That was Thursday, so I still had Friday to get an address.

The first five classes on Friday were the longest I ever spent I think. I didn't know where Charlene's locker was and didn't have time to look and never saw her in the hall ways. We flirted in Spanish Class and afterwards I walked her to her next class and got her address.

I picked Charlene up at seven. We drove across town to the newest drive-in movie. All the way over there people would have thought there was a two-headed person driving that car. Charlene was practically sitting in my lap, which was fine with me. I'm glad I grew up before cars had bucket seats and consoles. After I got married I was glad they did. But that's another story.

I found a place on the very last row and after rolling down the window and getting the speaker in the car; to my surprise I found Charlene sitting all the way across the seat next to her door. I had no idea what I was supposed to do or how to react. So I just sat right where I was.

A few minutes passed, and then she said, "I don't like to sit behind the steering wheel. Why don't you slide over this way?"

She didn't have to say it twice I think that was the last time we saw what was on the big screen in front of us.

I don't know how but I managed to drum up enough courage that night to ask Charlene if she wanted to "go steady." That was a big leap for me, all things considered. I mean she was a senior, and I was just a lowly sophomore. I think two more hairs on my chest popped out when she said yes.

After the drive-in we drove around the Dairy Queen so everybody could see us, then headed straight for lover's lane, which happened to be a new sub-division full of half-finished houses. I pulled over to the side of a road in the back of the sub-division that hadn't even been paved yet and before I could get the ignition turned off Charlene was pulling me down in the seat on top of her and that tight skirt was about as high as it was going to get.

Somewhere in the recesses of my mind, as she was helping me pull her panties down, I seem to recall hearing her say, "Oh, no please don't; you'll hate me in the morning."

My only response was, "No, I won't. No, I won't. I promise. I won't hate you."

That's one promise I never will have to worry about not keeping. I have never hated Charlene. Not one day, one hour or even one minute.

I think two more hairs popped out on my chest again after I drove Charlene home. I couldn't wait to strut around the locker room with my shirt off when I got back to school on Monday.

Charlene and I went "steady" for about six months, and we never missed a night. She used to take my car home when we played out of town basketball games and then come pick me up when we got back in town and we headed straight for the sub-division. While other guys were waiting on their parents to come pick them up or sharing rides with other guys that had cars, I was driving off with Charlene. I was the envy of them all because they all knew where we were going. But at sometime and somewhere along the way I guess she got bored and lost interest because she found some guy that rode a Harley. But of all the girls I loved before and since Charlene will always be a special memory.

I was heartbroken, for about 30 minutes then Cindy walked by and said hello. Cindy was just the opposite of Charlene as far as looks went. She was a dark haired, dark eyed girl with an olive skin complexion. We went together for a few months then she moved out of town and took my letter jacket with her. I was really pissed about that. But I guess you had to give a little to get a little sometimes; back in my old home town.

MY HOME TOWN
Chapter 5

My junior year in high school was significant, if for no other reason than because it was evidence that I survived my sophomore year. By this time I was feeling pretty comfortable with my surroundings and the people I spent the majority of my days and weeks with.

I can only recall one incident of any significance during my junior year that could possibly have could have gotten me in a wee bit of trouble in school. But fortunately Mr. Kurkendahl wasn't the type of teacher that liked to get involved in trouble. And when you get right down to it; it wasn't really my fault to begin with.

Paula Douglas sat in the seat right behind me in Algebra. Go figure another math class; I wonder if there is a correlation between me, a girl and a math class. Maybe someone better at math than me could figure that out.

Our desks in that particular class were sectional, in that three or four desks were linked together. And every time someone moved, they could shake the other desks that were linked to theirs.

Algebra definitely did not hold my attention and I never could sit still. I was a fidgeter. I must have fidgeted once too often one day because Paula jabbed in the back with her pencil and told me to be still. Well, naturally I had to get even so I began to throw spit wads over my shoulder at her. One of them went down the front of her blouse. She jabbed me in the back again, harder this time, I had to bite my tongue to keep from letting out a howl. Paula leaned forward and whispered in my ear that I had to get that nasty spit wad out of her blouse because she wasn't going to touch anything that had my spit on it.

I could understand her feelings and who was I to be so unfeeling or uncooperative. I reached back to retrieve the nasty spit wad just when Mr.Kurkendahl happened to look up from his desk.

"Ricky!" he hollered.

I knew I was caught. I froze with my hand down the front of Paula's blouse and the rest of the entire class looking right at us and all of them snickering or just out right laughing.

"Would you please remove your hand from Paula's blouse and continue to work on your assignment?"

Did I have a choice? I moved my hand, turned around and attempted to pretend I was working on my assignment.

Paula jabbed me in the back again and whispered, "You didn't get that nasty spit wad, and I still expect you to get it."

"When am I gonna do that?" I asked.

"After class; follow me," she said.

Now my curiosity was dying to know how this was gonna work so I nodded my head, "okay," and couldn't wait for the bell to ring.

When the bell finally rang I let Paula go first and followed her out of the classroom and down the hall. She stopped in front of her locker which was right next to a janitorial room. Paula stepped back between the lockers, reached behind her to see if the door was unlocked. It was; she slipped in and I followed her in.

She turned around and looked at me and said, "Get it."

If I said I was not more than a little bit nervous I would be lying. I pulled Paula's blouse away from her body so I could peek down and see if I could see the nasty little spit wad. It was nowhere to be seen.

Paula said, "We don't have all day here."

She began to unbutton her blouse down to about the third button. I still didn't see the spit wad, not that I was really looking for it. Paula pulled down the left side of her bra exposing her breast and stood there as if to be saying, "Well?" Finally I saw it. It was just above the nipple.

I reached up and removed that nasty little spit wad. Paula covered herself back up and buttoned her blouse.

"The next time you wanna play with my tits, just say so," Paula said, as she turned and walked out the door.

I just stood there stunned, thinking hell lady it wasn't my idea but before I could say anything she was gone. The bell ringing brought me back out of my trance. I hurried out the door and down the hall to civics class. Somehow I got the feeling that was not the first time Paula had used that janitorial room. I didn't throw anymore spit wads at Paula, but I did take her to a school dance a couple of weeks later. There was a new sub-division under construction on the way to her house.

I said there was only one incident that could have possibility got me in trouble in school. There was one other incident that I really never talk about much, it was and still is kind of embarrassing but now I can look back on it and laugh.

In my junior year I had a date with Mary Jane Bradbury and we went to the Drive-In Movie over on North Treadway. Mary Jane was a senior and a cheerleader; I still never have figured out what possessed her to go out with me, but she did. And I felt blessed. That was the year I was diagnosed as being near sighted. My folks couldn't afford expensive eye glasses so I got horn rimmed glasses. Besides Buddy Holly I was the only guy in the world who wore horn rimmed glasses but Buddy could get away with it. I was a geek.

I refused to wear mine except under the most critical circumstances and I didn't consider a date with a senior cheerleader as critical at least as far as wearing my Geeky horn rimmed glasses. Besides I had already managed to break one of the ear pieces and I definitely wasn't going to wear them on a date with Mary Jane.

We made it to the Drive-In movie all right; it wasn't quite dark yet. I made it through the movie without my glasses. I mean who needed glasses at a Drive-In movie anyway.

After the movie was over we left and I turned right on to Treadway. As we drove down Treadway I am sure I was running my mouth trying to impress Mary Jane.

All of a sudden she started shouting, "LOOK OUT! LOOK OUT!"

But it was too late. I had already run over one of the concrete dividers in the middle of Treadway and was now proceeding down the wrong side of the road. Fortunately there was very little traffic, and I didn't face any on coming traffic. I was desperately trying to correct my path and even more desperately searching for my glasses above the sun visor.

Suddenly Mary Jane started screaming again, "LOOK OUT! LOOK OUT! OH, MY GOD!"

I had corrected my direction but in doing so was about to run over two more dividers and narrowly missed a sign that said, "Wrong Way." I finally got my glasses on and got on my side of the roadway.

I had no idea what to say or what to do and was scared shitless to look at Mary Jane. I finally glanced her way and to my surprise she was sitting there laughing her cute little butt off. I joined her in attempting to laugh it off but I know my face was red as a beet. We went on to the Dairy Queen and grabbed something to eat. I could have easily done without going to the Dairy Queen; I was sure Mary Jane would be telling the world of our little adventure. But to my relief she didn't say a word.

After we ate, I figured lovers lane was out of the question so I just drove her home. I walked her to the door she gave me a kiss good night; funny though she said she was busy when I asked her out next weekend. Go Figure. But I guess a girl only wants to put her life in the hands of a blind guy once in her life time.

I was sure I would be hearing all about my driving expertise come Monday morning but surprisingly I never heard a word. Mary Jane was a good gal; if you're out there, Mary Jane, thanks for not sharing.

If you ever saw the movie *Grease* or watched *Happy Days* on television then you can relate to growing up in the '50s. Those could have been filmed in any high school in any town in America I suppose. I don't think there was a scene or an episode that I couldn't find something to relate to.

There were the same little cliques in my school that you saw in the movies and TV programs. The Jocks, the Nerds and the Bad Boys; I never really locked in to any of those groups. I was kind of on the fringes of all of them. I wasn't smart enough to be a real Nerd but they had a couple of things going for them and I went to the same church as a lot of the more popular Nerds.

I got interested in bowling when Wayne, Stephen and I went bowling one Saturday afternoon. I remember the manager of the bowling alley coming down to our lane and telling us if we intended to join the Junior Bowling League we needed to learn to stay behind the foul line.

I didn't have anything else going on since basketball season was over and joining a bowling league sounded challenging so I signed up after we finished bowling. Stephen and Wayne decided bowling wasn't for them.

When I showed up that first Saturday morning to start my league bowling, there they were, the Bad Boys. They all smoked, drank and wore their hair in a duck tail. They were the last people I expected to see at the bowling alley. Who woulda thought guys like that would have been interested in bowling? As it turned out all of them were very good bowlers, except one, he was an excellent bowler. I didn't know most of the others but I knew this one, his name was Joe Eddie. He was the only one that still wore a flattop, the last signs of his days as a jock.

Joe was a year older than I was and we used to play on the same little league baseball team. Joe was probably the most naturally gifted athlete I had ever known. And one of the luckiest persons you would ever meet. At one time he was the starting quarterback on the high school football team and the starting catcher on the baseball team. He could handle a basketball like a Harlem Globe Trotter. He was drafted by the Pittsburgh Pirates right out of high school. But he never graduated and never played for the Pirates. To this day I don't know anyone that knows why Joe gave up such a promising career in sports. But whatever the reason, Joe just basically dropped out of the high school sports scene.

I took to bowling, it was a challenge and having Joe down there made it more challenging. I set an average of 144 to start the league. By the time that league was over it was up to 182. Not bad for a first-year bowler, and it got the attention of the Boys. It seems they had their own thing going inside and outside the league. They bowled in pot games. For those of you that may not know a pot game is for money. Of course that was against Junior League rules but nobody really paid attention. I soon learned that bowling wasn't limited to the Saturday morning bowling league. The Boys were full-time residents at the Bowling Alley it seemed.

This was the beginning of a side of me that I didn't even know I possessed. I became addicted to bowling and bowling for money. But the gambling didn't stop there; it went from the bowling alley to all night poker games in some smoke filled motel room. I got good at it all. I could beat all of the Bad Boys at their own game. All except Joe Eddie; it seemed no matter how good I bowled or how good my cards were, Joe's were always better. I would win one every now and then but somehow Joe always ended up with the money.

I remember one night I was in a pot game against this guy named John something or other. Joe Eddie and some of the other Bad Boys were watching. I was about 20 pins down going into the 10th frame. Unbeknownst to me Joe bet one of the other guys that I would strike out in the 10th and win the game, and I did. That's just the way Joe Eddie's luck went. He had more confidence in me than I had in myself; I would never have made that bet.

That wasn't the only surprising thing that happened at the particular time. As I turned around to walk off the lane after I threw that last strike, I was stopped dead in my tracks. Standing there in front of me on the approach next to the ball return was this very familiar short blonde-haired, blue-eyed girl. Charlene was back.

She walked up to me right there on the alley; stood on her tip toes, and whispered in my ear, "Your pants are unzipped." She stood there in front of me while I zipped 'em up and then turned around and walked off, back to the guy she had come with, which was not the guy with the Harley. I couldn't help but wonder how she was the only one in the whole bowling alley that noticed my pants were unzipped.

I was spending more and more time with the Bad Boys, but I didn't completely desert the other groups. We had a spring practice for basketball which kept us in 7th period PE and while not mandatory you knew you better participate if you planned on staying on the Coach's good side. I went to church on Sunday morning, mostly because the Nerds met at the café across the street from the church. They swapped stories about their activities over the past weekend. You found out who was dating who and why, details were mandatory. Can't you just picture Ralph and Potsey trying to goad Richie for details about his last date? And Richie caught between the devil and the deep blue sea, knowing nothing happened but not wanting to admit failure to his friends but not wanting to lie either, trying to just bluff his way through the interrogation.

It was getting to be that time of year when school was almost over and we were making plans for the summer, including summer jobs. I always had a job; both my parents and two of my aunts worked at a local motel. It was kind of a family affair and there was always an opening for a dishwasher, pot washer, PBX operator bell hop or life guard. I had been doing these kinds of jobs for the past couple of years, but this year, I could tell this summer was going to be different. I had more spending money in my pocket from bowling and playing cards than I could make in a month at the motel. In my teenage mind, life was good in my home town.

MY HOME TOWN
Chapter 6

I knew the summer between my junior and senior year was going to be different than summers past. But I don't think even I knew just how different it would be. I remember feeling this sense of rebellion growing inside me but felt helpless to stop it.

The bowling alley became my home away from home with the rest of the Bad Boys. The bowling in pot games and playing cards pretty much consumed my days and nights. I had gotten a job as dishwasher at the motel on the night shift, but every day I was getting to work a little bit later.

One day while I was bowling I looked up, and there stood my dad. I didn't have to look at my watch to know what time it was. I could tell by the look on his face I was in big trouble. I knew there was only two ways I was going to leave there; one, on my own two feet or two, flat on my back. I always preferred to walk.

The walk to my car must have been two miles long; at least it seemed that way. My dad was in my ear every step of the way. I got to "my" car and was instructed to drive straight to work and he was going to follow me to make sure I didn't go anywhere else.

Needless to say there was a rather large stack of dishes waiting on me when I got to the kitchen and everybody was just getting ready for the supper run. I knew it wouldn't take me long to catch up but I got busy right away so I wouldn't have to look across the kitchen. My dad was working as the night chef and for some reason it seemed hotter in the kitchen than normal that evening.

While I was washing dishes my feelings were stirring and that feeling of rebellion was growing more and more. I can look back now and see how much of an embarrassment I was to both my parents; but right at that time my thoughts were more on my own feelings. I had been totally embarrassed in front of all the other guys and anyone else that was in the bowling alley at the time; and I lost money. I didn't know what I was going to do right then; but I knew this wasn't over.

As it would happen, we got paychecks at the hotel that evening, so before I left that night I got the hostess to cash my check. I was formulating a plan and knew I was going to need money. I followed my dad home. I wanted to be sure my car was the last one in the driveway. We got home around midnight; I went straight to my room and started to pack a bag. I was going to run away from home.

I waited until around 2 a.m. then slipped out the front door, pushed the car into the street and down a couple of houses before I started the engine. I didn't want to get caught before I even left, destination: Tucumcari, New Mexico.

Now, why would anyone run away to Tucumcari New Mexico you may ask? It's like this, the summer before; Wayne, Stephen and I had gone to Glorieta, New Mexico, with the rest of the Nerdy Church goers to a Baptist church retreat in the mountains, and had met some girls from Tucumcari. Need I say more? I stopped at the local truck stop, gassed the car up and got a road map and planned my escape route. I drove all night, and when the sun came up the next morning I found myself in the barren waste of the Texas Panhandle. If I had been able to see that vast area of nothing at night I may have turned around and gone back.

I don't know what that area of Texas looks like these days but back then it was pretty desolate. I drove through Lubbock and on into Amarillo before I stopped and got some rest. I drove on into Tucumcari the next day.

I've been sitting here trying to remember the names of the girls I saw while I was there; the one I was most interested in was June; and I think the other girls name was Darlene. I know the strange thing about them was that both their parents owned Funeral Homes. Dying must be a booming business in Tucumcari. I stayed there a couple of days, playing the big shot and Bad Boy role the best I could. I called Wayne and told him where I was and swore him to secrecy under the threat of castration if he told anyone where I was. He said my mother had already called a couple of times.

I started my return trip home not having any idea what I was going to do when I got there, but I was running short on money and instinctively knew I had to be or should be, okay, preferred to be closer to familiar surroundings. I didn't get any further than a place called Muleshoe Texas. The Chevy threw a rod and busted the oil pan and probably did some other damage I don't remember anymore. I managed to get to a gas station that had a mechanic and he told me it was going to take a lot of money to try to fix it and I would probably be better of just selling it for whatever I could get out of it.

This presented a problem; the car wasn't in my name, I didn't have the title and I didn't want to be drawing anymore attention to myself than I already had. I checked into a hotel and pondered my situation. I decided the only thing I could do was swallow my pride and call home. My mother answered the phone and put on this I-was-so-worried-about-you act. That may sound callus, but you had to know my mother. She put Daddy on the phone, and I asked him what he wanted me to do, sell the car or try to get it fixed. He asked if I had the money to get it fixed and I said no. He told me to stay where I was and they would come get me.

Bright and early the next morning there was a loud knocking on my door, and there they were, both smiling and grinning like nothing ever happened. We stopped by the gas station where I left the car. I'm not sure but I think Daddy sold the car for what he could get for it. Anyway we drove home, not much was said about my little excursion; but they asked me about this bowling thing and I just told them I was pretty good (by this time my average was up to around 195) and I enjoyed it and I was making some money from it. I casually mentioned there was a tournament that afternoon I was scheduled to bowl in.

When we got back in town they dropped me off at the bowling alley and told me to call them if I needed a ride home. Go figure, they dropped me off right back in the place that I got in trouble in; in the first place.

The Bad Boys welcomed me back with open arms, Wayne and Stephen had to have all the details, not about me just about the girls in Tucumcari. I noticed some of the kids looking at me with a little different look. I didn't know if that was good or bad but it didn't seem to hurt my image any. After a couple of months had passed things were pretty much back to normal around the old home town.

MY HOME TOWN
Chapter 7

It was only a couple of weeks after my return home from Muleshoe until the final year of life as I had known it for the past two years was about to begin. The sophomore class of 1956 was now the graduating class of 1959.

I was still bowling and playing cards when I felt like it. The key phrase there is "felt like it." It wasn't an all consuming thing for me anymore. Maybe running away from home was the best thing that I could have done. The Bad Boys were breaking up, a couple were moving and the others didn't seem to be interested in finding new blood to join the group or keeping the image they had created in tact. Joe Eddie was still the leader of the pack, even though there wasn't much of a pack left; and he had bigger plans.

Having shed my addiction for pot games and poker, I put more concentration into my basketball. The team had a winning season and my personal game showed some improvement. The last game of the season the coach started all five seniors on the team. We played well but needed the help of some of the better and taller underclassmen to win the game. With only five seniors on the team they had a good nucleus of returning sophomores and juniors, three of which were starters already.

I didn't have a steady girlfriend during my junior year, but I dated a few different girls. That pattern continued through my senior year, for the most part. But then there was Eva. She was a sophomore. Now things were reversed; when I was a sophomore I went with a senior. Now that I was a senior I was dating a sophomore. Eva and I never committed to that going-steady thing. But we kind of dated exclusively there for a while. She was one of the little rich girls that lived in the ritzy part of town. There were no sub-divisions around her place but we managed to find an area they were clearing off and had some of the hard gravel roads laid in. I made the mistake of pulling off the gravel road a couple of feet one night. After an appropriate amount of time had passed and the steam had cleared off the windows, we were ready to leave but I found out the car was stuck in the soft sand and the more I tried to get it out the further it dug in.

Now we were really between the preverbal rock and a hard place. I couldn't leave Eva there and go for help, and I certainly couldn't let her go by herself. To make things worse it was getting close to her curfew time. We finally decided to leave the car and we would both walk to the nearest gas station or whatever and call for some help. Actually it wasn't that far to a gas station just ahead of us. I called Wayne and told him of my predicament. His step dad drove a tow truck, and I figured Wayne could get some chains from the truck and come pull us out.

It took about 20 minutes before Wayne and his dad pulled up at the gas station in the tow truck. I didn't even give Wayne the evil eye or question why he brought his dad along. We hopped in the truck and headed back for my car. Actually I was glad Wayne had brought his dad he had us outta there in just a few minutes.

Eva and I raced to her house we were about an hour late and thought we had got away with it since there were no lights on in the front of the house. Unfortunately as we got to the door, the porch light came on and her father opened the door. That was the bad news; the good news was he was drunk as a hoot owl. I gave him a quick story about a flat tire and how it was my fault I didn't have a spare in the car and had to call a friend to come help. Hey, it wasn't all a lie! He seemed to believe me and just said I should always carry a spare. I said, "Yes, sir, I would get a spare right away and put it in the car.

Eva and I had known each other for a long time. She used to go with Bobby back when we were still in junior high. We used to have our ups and downs, and an on again off again type of relationship. But when we were on we were on. She was only about four feet eleven inches tall; we looked like Mutt and Jeff walking down the hallway together. But for a little girl she had muscles in places I never even thought about.

We fought like cats and dogs sometimes. I guess we had what you might call a love/hate relationship. She loved to hate me sometimes. Little did I know that our paths would cross again some fifteen years later.

Despite all the activities going on and all the excitement the seniors were going through I think the closer graduation day came, the stronger a sense of reality began to set in. I can't count the number of times I heard someone say, "When I graduate I'm going to...." Now that day was fast approaching and the realization that maybe they weren't really ready or prepared to do all the things they thought they would be doing was beginning to surface. I didn't have a clue as to what I was going to do. I had a chance to go to a small two year college on an athletic scholarship but I didn't want to do that. I was tired of schools, books and classes. Looking back now, maybe I should have done that. I wonder how much my life would have changed if I had.

The day after the '59 annuals were handed out; the seniors had an annual signing day. We were sitting all over the floor in the foyer in front of the Administrative offices and outside on the covered walk and any place else you wanted to be. Despite all notes of, "We'll always be friends," and all the, "I'll never forget you," that were written in your yearbook, somewhere inside you knew that for the most part that wasn't true, but at the time you didn't doubt the sincerity of the person that wrote it.

Two weeks after graduation the Nerds had a going away party for yours truly. Most in attendance were on their way to one college or another. A good many were headed for Baylor, a good Baptist school. Stephen was going there to play football and be with his long time girlfriend. Wayne was going to the University of Texas on an

Academic scholarship. Despite his carefree attitude and seemingly dimwitted sense of humor, Wayne was one smart fellow. He had the highest GPA every year I knew him and was President of the National Honor Society for a couple of years, as I recall. I saw him twelve years later on Jeopardy. He was a returning champion. I was on R&R from Vietnam visiting with friends in Honolulu when I saw him on TV. I couldn't believe it was him.

Besides being a going away party for me there was something else really special about that night. It was the only time I got to kiss the one girl that I ever really had a teenage crush on from the first time I saw her six years earlier. I couldn't say anything; she was one of my best friend's girlfriends. I made the most of it and everyone got a big kick out of it but I wore that kiss for a long time, at least in my mind.

Since I was the guest of honor at the party that night when the party ended and everyone was leaving; all the girls lined up and gave me a kiss goodbye. The next morning, the 15th of June 1959, along with about 50 other guys I took the oath and said the pledge of allegiance and joined the US Army. I left that same day for Fort Carson, Co. As the train chugged along down through the middle of town I sat quietly staring out the window. We passed Mrs. Baird's Bakery and down the street I could see the high school; the parking lots were mostly empty, only teacher's cars and a few students that were taking summer courses. That was the last time I saw the school. With the exception of going back for funerals of relatives I've only been back one time in the last 47 years to revisit.

Well, that was my old home town as I remember it back in the 1950's. It was a great decade to be alive and to grow up in. If I had my druthers as to which time and place I would live in; I would pick my home town way back when. For all the things we didn't have and couldn't do back then, we got along just fine.

We've come a long way since then but I can't help but wonder how much better off we really are. I see our kids and grandkids with all their cell phones and iPods and other gizmos and gadgets they just can't seem to live without. I think this modern age of technology is going to be the ruin of us all one of these days.

How sad is it that the little girl working at McDonalds can't even make the right change without the computerized cash register telling her what the correct amount is. I remember the girl on roller skates hopping cars at the Dairy Queen making change right out of her little coin changer she wore around her waist and never missing a beat.

Kids today can't work out a math problem without a calculator or write a paper without using spell check. I remember staying up all night working out math problems and writing essays with pen and paper and a dictionary.

I can't help but wish sometimes I could just snap my fingers and take all my kids back to that time and just for once let them see how much fun it was to be able to be a real kid and live at a slower pace when our biggest fears were getting caught sneaking in the house past our curfew or worse yet sneaking out after curfew.

At school the worst thing you could do was get caught smoking in the bathroom or get sent to the principal's office. If you got sent to the principal's office you knew you were gonna catch hell at least twice that day, once from the principal and once from your folks.

If a cop pulled you over, you got out your license, stayed in the car and said, yes, sir, and no, sir, when asked a question. The rules were simple back then and you didn't have to write them down and nobody had to explain them to you. You just knew.

We may not have had all the goodies our kids have today but we had something better, we had each other we talked to each other face to face. We played together, laughed together, cried together but mostly we grew up together. And that's the way it was back in my home town.

My whole life changed after that night. We all went our different directions. I saw a couple of people that were there that night later on as years went by, but I wasn't thinking about that then. My next stop was Fort Carson, Colorado…all aboard!

YOU'RE IN THE ARMY NOW
Chapter 8

I don't know how long I had been on the train or what time it was. We had left about 10:00 a.m. My mother was there to see me off, along with a lot of other mothers seeing their sons off. I was glad to hear them tell us to get aboard I just wanted to get this trip started. Fort Carson, Colorado was our destination for in processing and basic training.

I had found a seat by the window and after passing over Mockingbird Lane and seeing the high school down the street with its almost empty parking lots and passing Mrs. Baird's Bakery, I just kind of lost track of time and distance. I don't remember passing through Sweetwater. Maybe we didn't even go through Sweetwater. I have no idea what route the train took.

A guy I recognized from the recruiting office stood up across the isle from me to stretch and as I looked around it seemed there were more people on the train than what I remembered waiting on the loading platform. Some guys seem to either have known each other or just made some new acquaintance and were carrying on conversations. As I came to find out later the train had made previous stops in Alabama, Mississippi and Louisiana so in fact the train was quite full. They just used the last empty car to put the Texas boys in.

Some sergeant came by carrying a clip board; he looked at the guy across the isle and asked, "What are you doing, Private?" It took him a minute to realize the sergeant was talking to him. I guess he hadn't got used to be called Private yet.

"I'm just stretching," he replied.

"Stretching what?"

I could tell the guy was caught off guard. I was thinking to myself, *What kind of friggin' question was that?*

"I'm stretching my legs, my back and my arms," the guy replied.

The sergeant took one step closer and was in his face. "I asked you a question, Private. What are you stretching?"

By this time every guy in the car was listening to what was going on. My mind was racing trying to figure out what this sergeant wanted in case I was next. Suddenly I remembered our first class of instruction back at the recruiting office. Always address an NCO (Non Commissioned Officer) as "Sergeant" and an officer as "Sir."

The private, now standing at attention and sweating profusely must have figured it out about the same time I did I guess because he suddenly blurted out, "I'm stretching my sergeant, sir!"

With that, the whole car broke up laughing their respective asses off. The sergeant shouted, "At ease!" and quiet immediately fell over the whole car. The sergeant stepped one step closer to the private, and I could see the fear in the kid's eyes. I knew he thought he was about to get eaten alive. Suddenly the sergeant burst out laughing told the private to stand at ease and turned around and walked out of the car still laughing and shaking his head. I think the kid must have peed in his pants because he sat down real quick and didn't move.

At least the incident lightened up the mood in the car, everybody began talking. Those that smoked lit 'em up, and those of us that didn't started cracking the windows. I struck up a conversation with the kid the sergeant had picked on. I found out his name was Shockley and he was from Brady Texas, a small town almost due south of Abilene. We talked a little about everything and nothing specific; until sometime later some guy came through the car passing out ham sandwiches and cartons of milk and an apple. I hate apples. Only one sandwich per person and I was starved.

Time seemed to pass quickly, as Shockley and I chatted the next time I looked out the window it was dark and the chatter in the car had dropped to almost a whisper among only a few as one by one the guys started drifting off to sleep. I squashed up that little thing they called a pillow the best I could and stuffed it between the seat and the wall of the car, kicked off my shoes and tried to get as comfortable as I could. The rhythmic sounds of the wheels of the train rolling over the track became hypnotic and I soon drifted off to sleep.

YOU'RE IN THE ARMY NOW
Chapter 9

It seemed as though I had just fallen asleep when the rail car was flooded with lights and two sergeants, one on each end of the car were hollering and telling everyone to wake up and get on our feet. I glanced out the window and it was still dark out, I checked my watch and it was just about 5:30 in the morning.

I wanted to stretch but after yesterday's incident I was afraid to. The sergeants told us we were about to stop and when they told us to we were to dismount the train on the platform on the right side of the train and form a column of twos. For those of us that did not know what a column was it was a row so form two rows.

The train came to a screeching stop and the sergeants started telling us to move and get off the train. As we stepped off the train there were two more sergeants standing outside our car telling us where to stand and which way to face. I looked down the platform and the same thing was going on in front of the other cars.

Once everyone was off the train cars and apparently in place on the platform, one of the sergeants stepped forward with his clipboard and told us as he called off our names to "sound off" and move onto the bus waiting on the other side of the platform. He began to call off names. He finally got to mine. I "sounded off" and moved out and got on the bus. Once the bus was loaded the sergeant got on, told the driver to close the doors and take off.

I guess we traveled for about 30 minutes and then passed through the gates of Fort Carson, made a couple of turns and came to a stop. The sergeant stood up and said this was the mess hall and we should get off the bus and walk straight in to the mess hall, grab a tray and silverware and go through the serving line and then go find a place to sit and eat breakfast. He said we had 30 minutes to eat and return to the bus and check with him to get our names checked.

I've had better breakfast but at the time cold powered eggs with soft greasy bacon stripes, dry hard toast and a glass of milk tasted like a gourmet meal, I was starving. I gulped my food down and hustled back to the bus. I didn't want to take a chance on missing the bus or being late.

Once everyone was back on the bus we drove down a couple of streets and pulled up in front of some old WWII barracks. The sergeant herded us into the barracks and told us to grab a bunk and stay there until we were called. He said if you smoked, light 'em up and use the butt cans provided, and then he turned around and left. Some guys rolled the mattress down, grabbed the pillow and sacked out, some sat on the edge of the bunk and smoked and some gathered in small groups and talked.

Shockley, or "Stretch," as he had become known was on the bunk next to me. "I wonder what's next?" he asked.

"I don't have a clue; guess we'll just have to wait and see."

"I heard one of the guys say we would be getting our uniforms next," Shockley said.

"Makes sense. I'm sure they aren't gonna let us stay in these civvies very long."

Shockley said, "That was a good breakfast, wasn't it? I went back for seconds."

Somehow that didn't surprise me. "It filled me up. I was hungry but I didn't go back for seconds. It did make me sleepy, though; I think I'll try to get some sleep while we don't have anything else to do but wait."

I rolled over on my side with my back to Shockley and tried to get some sleep.

YOU'RE IN THE ARMY NOW
Chapter 10

I guess I must have slept for a couple of hours. I woke up to one of those clipboard carrying sergeants hollering for everyone to get out and form two columns in the company street. I'm wondering what the hell a company street is?

I rolled out of the bunk and fell in with the rest of the herd and went out side. It appears the company street was the road running between our barracks and the ones on the other side of the street. You learn something new every time one of those sergeants hollers.

"Okay, you people listen up!" boomed a voice from the middle of the rows or columns. "We are going to march down to the Central Issue Point where you will be issued your basic uniforms."

The sergeant with the booming voice was moving up and down in front of us now, as if he was sizing us up.

"Now I know you are recruits, but try not to fuck this up too bad because I am in no mood to babysit your dumb asses this morning."

"Atten Hut!" the sergeant screamed.

We all jumped to a position we considered to be the correct one. The sergeant just stood there, looked at us, and shook his head. I was trying to figure out what a "tin hut" was.

"Right face! Your other right, you ninny!" he screamed at any and everyone that turned to their left.

After he was satisfied that we were all facing the same direction he moved to the center of the formation and said, "Beginning with your left foot…forward march."

Somehow the columns began to move in the same direction but not necessarily in step; apparently some people had two left feet to go with their two right sides. As we moved down the company street the sergeant began to call cadence. "Your left, your left, your left, right, left. Hup, two, three, four…."

As he called cadence other NCOs were moving along the formation with their faces about two inches from your ear, telling those of us in no uncertain terms that were out of step how to get back in step. I think by the time we got to the Central Issue Point we had it down pretty good. I felt pretty good; I made it without anyone yelling in my ear.

Picking out uniforms was not exactly like shopping at Sears. Actually there was no picking. There were a long line of other soldiers standing behind a long counter; each soldier ready to give you a particular item of clothing. The first item was a duffel bag. They might ask you what size you wore but it really didn't matter; you got whatever they had that was close. Except for foot gear, I will say they tried to fit you with the right size boots. I think there was a hint of things to come in there somewhere.

After making it through the line, you exited a door at the other end of the building and fell in formation. As soon as everyone was finished we tried that marching thing back to our barracks. Once we arrived back in front of the barracks we were dismissed and told to fall back in the barracks and get into a fatigue uniform and boots.

I found my fatigues and boots down inside the depths of my duffle bag. Once I got 'em on I felt like a big green olive. Nothing fit. But then there must have been about fifty green olives in the building. Once dressed all we could was sit and wait.

We didn't have to wait too long this time one of the sergeants came and said we were going to the mess hall and to fall out in the company street. So now I knew what a mess hall was and where the company street was. Things were progressing. We marched to the mess hall, fell out and lined up single file at the door to the mess hall and made our way through the chow line. The mess hall was a busy place and while there was a lot of noise there wasn't really a lot of talking going on. You really didn't have time to do a lot of talking one of those clipboard-carrying sergeants were hovering about encouraging you to hurry up and get the hell out of his mess hall.

Once outside the mess hall you were allowed to stand at ease and smoke in place. As soon as everyone was out of the mess hall, we were called to attention and marched down the street to another building with a sign out front that said Personnel. Again we were at ease and the smoking lamp was lit, until told to go inside the building. I must have been outside for an hour before I was called in.

Personnel was a long, barracks-type building that had been converted to an office. There were rows and rows of desks with a soldier sitting behind each one. As you walked in one of the soldiers would call your name and you would go sit by his desk. He would ask you a bunch of questions you had already answered a 100 times before and type up some stuff and start building your personnel file.

At or near the end of the processing procedure the guy asked me one question that probably had an impact on the rest of my military career. It was the first and only choice the Army had given me so far.

"Private, do you want to take basic here at Fort Carson, or go back to Fort Hood, Texas, to take your basic training?"

Being a born and raised Texas boy there was never any hesitation. "I want to go back to Texas."

Texas is nice and flat, and you don't walk up a bunch of hills and shit of course it is also nice and hot, but we natives were used to the heat.

The personnel guy said, "Okay, you'll get some orders cut and be on you way back to Texas within a couple of days. That's it; you're done here."

I got up and left with a smile on my face. I was going home. As happy as I was to be going back to Texas I couldn't help but wonder why they had to transport us all the way to Colorado just to turn around and send us back to Texas? Why didn't they just ask us before we left? Sure didn't make a lot of sense to me.

Apparently I wasn't the only one that chose to go back to Texas, Stretch Shockley and a couple of the other guys I saw getting on the train in Abilene and some that I didn't recognize all chose to go back. In all I would guess there were about a dozen in my barracks that were going back to Texas.

Those of us that were going back to Texas were told to get out a Khaki uniform and were marched down to a one hour cleaners to get the uniform cleaned and pressed. Guess the Army didn't want us looking like slobs on the trip back. There was already a line when we got there. I finally got my uniform dropped off and returned to the barracks.

Over the next couple of days those that were staying at Fort Carson continued their In-Processing and little by little they began to disappear from the barracks. As each completed his processing he was moved to a regular training unit where he would take basic training. Those of us going back to Texas just hung around the barracks and waited for our uniforms and orders. Two days of waiting and finally we had both. We were leaving the next morning for the long train ride back to Texas.

The Army must have had a specific plan for moving troops by train; which includes arriving at your destination before day break, being herded from train to busses and taken directly to the mess hall. This time we "grounded" our gear outside the mess hall and then went in and had breakfast. Finished, we moved back out to stand by our gear and once all were assembled we were marched down the company street to our basic training unit. We were assigned to Company C, 1st Medium Tank Battalion, 66th Armor, 2d Armor Division, Fort Hood Texas; also known as Hell on Wheels. Charlie Company, this was where I would spend the next nine weeks of my life. I learned a little history of the 2d Armor Division while I was assigned there; it was once commanded by General George S. Patton. Of course I didn't know that at the time, didn't even know who General Patton was and really didn't care but I do now.

Back in those days these were very modern barracks to house troops in. The first floor was the administrative offices, the Day Room, Cadre Offices and some other secret rooms that were unmarked and locked all the time. But we also had our own mess hall. No more consolidated mess hall for us.

In typical military logic, things were done by the numbers and it was easier if the numbers matched. I'm not sure who it was easier on the troops or the cadre but anyway; as it turned out I was assigned to the fourth platoon. So it was logical that the fourth platoon be housed on the fourth floor. Just my friggin' luck; they didn't provide elevators in those barracks; so all of us assigned to the fourth platoon had to tote all our equipment up four flights of stairs. I remember my first thought as we all proceeded to carry our duffle bag up those four flights of stairs…I got nine weeks of this shit ahead of me.

YOU'RE IN THE ARMY NOW
Chapter 11

I can look back on those nine weeks now and smile and laugh at some of the things that went on. But at the time I didn't have a lot to laugh about. In those days the normal basic training cycle was eight weeks, but it seem the third platoon of Charlie Company had not received a full compliment of trainees so the rest of us had to wait for third platoon to fill up. We had what they called a Zero Week.

It wasn't exactly a week off. Our platoon sergeant, Sergeant First Class (SFC) John T. Yoder kept us busy. Usually in the mornings we would fall out on to the parade field across the company street from our barracks. Sergeant Yoder was a crusty old sergeant obviously having spent more years in the Army than he cared to remember. And while he could be funny as hell sometimes you knew you didn't want to piss him off. The mornings he and the cadre spent with us trying to teach us basics like proper hand salute, how to fall in as a platoon, the proper way to do a left face, right face and about face and how to dress right dress. That's military talk for getting your spacing right. He even started teaching us how to march as a unit. This was probably his most daunting task. What is it that makes it so difficult for forty or so grown men, well almost grown men, to march as a unit of one? I can answer that in one word….Stretch. More in a minute.

Sergeant Yoder "sized" his platoon from front to back. To begin with if you were shorter than the man in front of you' you moved up until you couldn't go any further. Next he gave us a right face and if you were taller than then in front of you, you moved forward until there was no place else to move. So when all this was done first squad was the shortest and the forth squad was the tallest. After you thought about it....it made sense. This way the guy in the last row, or fourth squad could see over the guys in front of them. And when you marched in column the tallest guys were in front. I'm not sure what the reasoning behind that was. It made the little short legged guys in the back of the column move their little legs a lot faster to keep up with the long legged guys up front. But it wasn't mine to reason why.

There was only one problem with this scenario as far as I was concerned. Stretch seemed to think I was the only friend he had so he attached himself to me which as things turned out probably couldn't have been avoided anyway. We were both tall and ended up in the fourth squad. He was slightly taller than I was so I ended up marching right behind him. This had to be the worst thing that could happen to me at least when it came time to march. Stretch was the only soldier I ever knew that could take off on both feet at the same time. Don't ask me how he did it, but he was out of step on the command of "Forward March." That means I had to constantly change steps to try to get in step with him and he was continually changing steps to get in step with the squad leader. I spent my entire basic training punching Stretch in the back and telling him to "Change step, damn it!" This of course had a chain reaction on the rest of the squad when I was out of step and changing step the guy behind me could be doing the same thing and so on and so on down the column.

After lunch we belonged to anyone that wanted us. It was detail time. Details could be anything from cutting grass to digging holes, to painting or if you were really lucky you got a desk job filing papers. Normally you had no choice in what detail you got. They tell you never to volunteer for anything in the Army. That's usually good advice but sometimes you volunteered and didn't even know you were volunteering. Some sergeant would step up in front of the platoon and say something like; "Hi, fellas, how ya'll doin' today? Hot as hell out here, ain't it?

My name is Sergeant So and So, and I'm from Texas. How many of ya'll are from Texas? Raise yore hand." So like idiots we raise our hands, and Sergeant So and So says, "Great. You boys step out and move right over yonder by that deuce and a half," (That's a two-and-a-half-ton truck for those of you not familiar with the Army lingo.) Trapped again! Damn, I hate it when they do that. Actually it only takes one incident like that if you're smart; you learn not to raise your hand. On the other side of the coin sometimes it's the same Sergeant So and So that comes back the next day, and he remembers who was from Texas and who wasn't. It came to be a lose/lose situation.

After all was said and done, at the end of Zero Week the fourth platoon was definitely the best marching, saluting platoon in Charlie Company.

YOU'RE IN THE ARMY NOW
Chapter 12

When we fell out for morning formation the next Monday morning it was a whole different ball game. The company was in full force, four platoons, and each four squads deep. It was kind of like mass confusion. None of us knew exactly where we were supposed to be but the platoon sergeants and the rest of the cadre got us going in the right direction and they weren't mincing words…or boots; within a few minutes each platoon was formed, and each platoon leader, this was the first time we had seen these lieutenants was standing tall in front of their respective platoons facing the company commander who was also making his first appearance. If we didn't know we were in the army before we knew it now.

The commander barked some orders which were in turn barked by the lieutenants to the platoon sergeants. We just stood there at attention. A few minutes later the commander called for the first sergeant. This was a short heavy set, not fat, sergeant that had stripes running from his shoulder to his elbow with a diamond in the middle. When he came forward the lieutenants disappeared and the platoon sergeants moved forward to the front of the platoon. The first sergeant hollered, "Report," and each platoon sergeant starting with the 1st Platoon responded with an, "All present and accounted for."

A few more commands were barked and then the platoon sergeants turned to face his platoon. Sergeant Yoder barked out his orders, "Open ranks." Back in those days to open ranks the first squad took three steps forward, the second squad took two steps forward the third squad took one step forward and the fourth squad stood fast. I think they do it differently these days. After that was accomplished Yoder barked out, "Dress right, dress!" This was done by looking to your right and extending your left arm out until you couldn't touch the guy on your left. You lined up on the man to your right so your lines were perfectly straight. Sergeant Yoder would go to the first man on the right end of each squad and look down the line and tell whatever man was out of line what to do, such as, "Third man in…move a half step forward or backward. He would do this to each squad until he was satisfied we were perfectly aligned.

The next order was remove your blouses and headgear and ground them to your right. This did not sound good, and it wasn't. In between the 2d and 3d squads was a big platform and on that platform stood a cadre member with his blouse off and grounded. He started talking but I really couldn't hear him, but I did pick up the phrase "daily dozen" and the word "exercise." Then I heard the phrase "demonstrator post." Some guy apparently another member of the cadre stepped forward and as the one guy gave instructions, the other demonstrated. This exercise, as I learned, was called "Jumping Jacks." After a couple of demonstrations the main exercise guy stepped forward and announced that we would do an eight count of eight repetitions. I had no idea what that meant but knew I was about to find out.

They call these the daily dozen for obvious reasons; there are 12 different exercises. And almost all of them are done with an eight-count repetition. Gawd! I was an athlete and used to exercise, but I thought I was gonna die before we got through with all these exercises.

Once we were finished. We were told to redress and as soon as we were all ready we were marched by Platoon up to the outside entrance to the mess hall and lined up outside waiting for our turn to enter the mess hall. And if we thought we were through with PT for the morning we had another thought coming. About ten paces away from the entrance to the mess hall was a chin up bar. There were cadre standing there, and you had to do five chin ups before you could enter the mess hall. If you couldn't do five chin ups you got to go to the back of the line so you could try again. I was thinking, *What the hell? I'm not that hungry anyway,* but fortunately I was able to do my five and was allowed to go eat.

After breakfast it seemed each platoon had a different assignment and each went in separate directions. Our direction was to the little PX that sat in the middle of the parade field. It also had a barber shop in it. It didn't take an hour until all our respective heads were as shaved as a new born baby's butt. One more step in the Army's never ending attempt to keep recruits humble and all looking alike.

After getting our heads shaved the 4th platoon headed for another Issue Point. This time we got issued our field gear; pistol belt, canteen with cup, silverware, poncho, helmet with liner and on and on and on. Every time they throw another item in my duffel bag I'm thinking of those four flights of stairs I gotta carry all this shit up.

When we had all been issued out field gear we toted it back to the barracks and up those dreaded four flights of stairs. We dropped our gear and headed right back down stairs and fell in on the parade field only to be marched over to the mess hall and lined up for noon chow. And the dreaded chin up bar. I was really starting to hate that bar already.

After chow we went back to the parade field and then promptly marched off to Personnel. One by one we were called over to someone's desk and filled out more of the same paper work and asked the same questions we were asked at Fort Carson. I know the army likes things in triplicate but you would think you would fill out all three copies at one place and not one at each place they sent you.

This was a long drawn out process and by the time the last private was through it was time to go eat....again. I was never used to eating three meals a day and I damn sure wasn't used to doing chin ups three times a day! We finished evening chow and fell out on the parade field to be dismissed and told to report to our barracks. We thought we were through for the day....not.

We no more than got into the bay area when in came Sergeant Yoder and two of his clipboard carrying sidekicks. It seems we were not through yet. It wasn't enough to have the 4th platoon on the 4th floor now they wanted us in alphabetical order. So beginning with the first top bunk on the right as you came in the door; whoever had a last name beginning with A, this was your bunk. From there it went down that row and then started up at the back of the next row. Guys who thought they had found a bunk were moaning and groaning because they had to move. As it turned out, Shockley ended up on the top bunk next to mine, below him was a black guy named Thomas, then there was me, and below me was another black guy named Washington.

After we got our bunk and wall locker assignments our orders were to start making our bunks and squaring away our wall lockers according to the diagrams hanging on the inside of the door of the lockers. It was now about 1800 hours (that's 6 p.m. to you civilian types), and we were told that lights went out at 2200 hours (10:00 p.m.), and we best be sure we had showered and shaved by that time.

There was one other thing before the sergeant left. Each squad would be responsible for cleaning up the shower and latrine on a rotating basis starting with the first squad. Sergeant Yoder didn't say we had to do it this way but he suggested that whichever squad was on shower detail shower last so no one else would be coming in behind them to mess up the area again. It all made perfectly good sense to me. I didn't feel like messing around and wasting time, I was tired. I got my clothes out and did the best I could to follow the diagram on the door and even though it wasn't exactly right I figured it would be a good start. I made my bunk as best as I knew how to make a military bunk and then headed straight for the shower.

I got out of the shower and headed for my bunk I climbed up on the top bunk and let out a big sigh. I was glad today was over. I remember thinking, one day down, seven weeks and six days to go.

YOU'RE IN THE ARMY NOW
Chapter 13

During our first four weeks of basic training we learned many useful things. Some men had numerous lessons on the proper way to make up a military bunk. Others had several individual lessons on how to hang cloths properly in a military wall locker; still others had special instruction as to the proper way to set up a military foot locker. All of us had instruction in cutting grass with a pair of scissors from a military sewing kit. But perhaps the most intense instruction came in how to clean a latrine with a toothbrush and a toothpick. We were told these blocks of instruction were given to help build character and a sense of pride. Somehow I never felt that sense of pride after spending all night on my knees scrubbing a tile floor with a toothbrush.

While all this was occupying our time there were other things going on that we were not even aware of: Everyday we were changing. That childish individualism we came in to basic training with was disappearing and there was a sense of unity and teamwork developing among us. There were other subtle changes that went virtually unnoticed.

Physically, skinny kids gained weight and got stronger. Fat kids got slimmer and remained strong. Mentally it was the same. The sergeants knew how to take the kid out of the young boy that showed up to take basic training and replace it with the mentality of a mature young man.

All this was going on right before our eyes, yet we didn't even realize it.

During the time we were under the watchful eye of our sergeants we were all business if we knew what was good for us. At night or perhaps on weekends when we had some time to ourselves the kid that had not quite left us completely would come out. It seemed to be the time to let off steam and relieve some of the stress of the day's training.

The first time it was the 4th squad's turn to clean the latrine Stretch didn't bother to put his boxer's back on like the rest of us and it was apparent that Stretch's nickname could have been given to him for more than just his verbal slip of the lip back on the train on the way to Fort Carson. He became the envy of all the rest of the 4th squad and the rest of the platoon for that matter. Maybe it also explained why he had so much trouble marching in step.

Sometimes on Saturday evenings and Sundays we were allowed to visit the little PX in the middle of the parade field. They had a small beer garden and sold pitchers of 3.2 beer. That's probably about the cheapest, weakest beer you can buy but while we weren't even old enough to vote yet, we were old enough to drink on base so swishing down a glass of 3.2 was a great way to express our ever-growing manhood. Personally I always hated beer and never drank the stuff. I could always back off saying I would rather drink water than that crap. Actually I just drank coke. There were a few of us that were not beer drinkers. We formed our own little group.

Among this group were a couple guys named Marshal and Kingsley. I have no idea how we bonded as friends but we seem to hang out a lot together when we had time off. One Sunday afternoon we had been given free run of the post and the three of us drifted off to the Main Post Exchange. It was like going to Sears or Wal-Mart. They had everything, or so it seemed anyway. Of course we were privates with no money to speak of, so about all we could do was look.

On our way back we passed the post gym with adjoining tennis courts. As we walked around the corner towards the front of the gym there stood a very, very attractive brunette, wearing white tennis shorts and a sleeveless white blouse. We couldn't help but stare and she couldn't help but notice. She was very attractive, I think I said that, but she smiled as we stumbled over ourselves trying to walk one way while looking over our shoulder. Marshal suddenly stopped and said, "I'm going to go back and talk to her."

Kingsley and I both agreed he was crazy.

Marshal asked, "Why not? She is just standing there by herself."

"She is probably waiting on someone," I offered.

"Maybe she isn't," Marshal replied.

"You best mind your own business," Kingsley offered.

Marshal said, "You guys are chicken shits. I'm going back." And he turned and walked back towards the woman who appeared to be in her late 20s or early 30s. Just as Marshal got within hand shaking distance, one of the doors to the Gym popped open and this tall well tanned and muscled man wearing tennis shorts and a white sleeveless shirt came walking out and headed straight towards the woman, Marshal froze in his tracks, Kingsley and I tried to hide in the cracks in the sidewalks.

We knew this man, even out of uniform. He was our company commander. We probably could have gotten away clean but Marshal got so scared he saluted him which automatically gave away the fact that we knew who he was and obviously told him we were assigned to his command otherwise we probably wouldn't know he was an officer.

"Are you men enjoying your time off this weekend?" the captain asked, as he gently took his wife by the arm.

"Yes, sir," Marshal said still saluting.

"At ease, Private," the captain said, and Marshal dropped his salute.

"We got kind of lost on our way back to the barracks," Marshal lied.

"Well, you're on the right track, Private," the captain said, "It's right across the parade field there."

"Yes, sir, we are headed there right now, sir," Marshal stuttered.

"Well, good evening to you then, Private. I'll see you in formation in the morning," the captain said as he turned and guided his wife towards their car.

Marshal turned around and we all double timed clear across the parade field to the barracks. We spent the rest of the night wondering and worrying what lay in store for us at formation in the morning. Our fears were relieved the next morning when there were no officers at the morning formation. Apparently they had some kind of meeting to attend. The three of us couldn't help but wonder if we were one of the topics of that meeting.

YOU'RE IN THE ARMY NOW
Chapter 14

During the next four weeks, when not learning these lessons of character and pride, we were busy learning how to do things like how to assemble all our recently acquired field gear and make a bedroll. As we were to find out this instruction was to become very helpful when preparing for a road march with full field gear and back pack with bedroll.

Somewhere in between these classes they issued us our assigned basic weapon, the M-1 rifle, a gas operated, bolt action, 9.3 lb. shoulder fired weapon. We spent several days learning how to break the weapon down in to about a gazillion pieces and putting it back together again. And oh yeah, as time went on it became a timed exercise.

When we weren't doing that we were learning to march with the damn thing. And of course we had to learn the manual of arms; you know, right shoulder arms, left shoulder arms, port arms, inspection arms, etc, etc, etc. None of this came particularly easy to a bunch of klutz like us. Marching at shoulder arms could be dangerous to the guy behind you if you weren't careful.

In week five we went on a forced march and bivouac. This was with full field gear and back-pack with bedroll. I'm not sure but I think someone said that damn back-pack and bedroll weighed somewhere around 75lbs. If it didn't it felt like it. As we marched out of the cantonment area and got further into the woods they began playing games. Low flying aircraft flew over head and were supposed to be enemy planes shooting at us and we had to duck and cover. Okay, this was fun. But if you ever rolled over on your back and then tried to get up with that pack on your back you could find yourself in serious trouble. It was embarrassing to have to ask someone to help you up.

This was Texas in July and it was friggin' hot. You were warned about drinking too much water because what you had in your canteen was all you got. Some guys heeded the warning....some guys didn't. Some guys got taken back to the aid station, which consisted of a jeep with a couple of medics and an ambulance.

Sometime around noon they let us take a break for lunch. That consisted of cans of C-Rations. Don't ask me what I had, I couldn't describe it then and still can't. We resumed our road march; we seemed to be following this little gulley and were moving in a column of twos and this gulley was barely big enough for a column of one. Finally we came to a wide spot in the road and the commander called a halt. They had a meeting of the minds at the head of the columns and then each sergeant called their platoon together and told us where to set up a perimeter and pitch our shelter half. A shelter half is half a tent, someone else has the other half. So, you find a partner and the two of you share your half of the tent and make a whole tent. Hopefully you like whoever you end up sharing a pup tent with.

After we got our tents pitched and our perimeters had been set we had another cold meal of C-Rations. As dark descended upon us, those who had first watch moved out to their points; supposedly to be relieved in two hours by their tent mate. That was fine in theory but after the sun went down things looked different and you weren't exactly sure where your partner was anymore. Maybe he got relieved and maybe he didn't.

About 0200 it really didn't make any difference anymore. The sky opened up and it became a real gully washer out there. It was raining like a cow pissing on a flat rock. That gulley we marched up was more like the Rio Grande and those of us that were in our pup tents stayed there, those that weren't....tough shit.

As dawn broke over the eastern sky, wet, soggy, muddy bodies began to emerge from under tents that didn't stand up to the hard rain and from under any other object that offered any type of relief from the unexpected downpour. We were supposed to have a hot meal for breakfast but the hard rain had wiped out the field kitchen so once again we ate C-Rations. We did the best we could to clean up our gear and put our back packs in some sort of order and began the march back to the barracks. Needless to say it was a rather quiet and subdued march back in.

We marched straight to the motor pool where they had ample hoses and space so we could lay out our equipment and start cleaning it up. The more equipment we got cleaned and put back where it should be the more our spirits started to rise. Instead of feeling down and out we suddenly felt like we had really accomplished something. We may not have done it very well or by the book but we survived the elements and somehow among the muck and mud and dirty water rushing around us in all directions we made it. In some small way it served as a small victory and a sign of the men we were becoming.

YOU'RE IN THE ARMY NOW
Chapter 15

The weekend following our big adventure in the bush we were given an overnight pass. After Saturday morning inspection we were free to go get dressed in our class 'A' uniform and if we could pass inspection by the Charge of Quarters, (C.Q.) we would be allowed to sign out on a 24 hour pass and leave the base.

The CQ was generally a Corporal, a low ranking NCO but still God as far as we were concerned. Now he didn't like having to pull CQ duty on the weekend and getting past his inspection was not something one did easily. He would look for strings on your uniforms, which if he found one he considered a rope and that was a sure sign you were trying to hang yourself with it. Or if he couldn't find any "ropes" he would check the seams of your shoes around the soles to be sure there was no dirt between the seams. He would also check the backside of your belt buckle to see if it was shined. And his most favorite was to have you either recite the chain of command starting with the President all the way down to your platoon sergeant. Or, to be really difficult he would ask you to repeat one or all of your general orders, all 11 of them. Now there were really only 10 general orders but he had an 11th that he would expect you to know.

Sometimes a fella gets lucky and just happens to be in the right place at the right time. One day during the week before morning formation I had been assigned to empty all the trash cans in the NCO offices and I just quietly moved among them as they smoked and joked back and forth and attempted to draw as little attention to myself as possible. But while I was not drawing any attention to myself I was listening to what the NCOs were saying.

When I stepped in front of the CQ and came to attention all decked out in my Class "A" uniform I felt ready to be inspected. He checked for "ropes" but didn't find any; he checked the seams of my soles but didn't find any dirt. He checked the back of my belt buckle, but it was as shiny as the front side

I could tell he was getting upset; no one had gotten this far past his inspection so far without getting sent back to make corrections. He asked me to recite my general orders. I responded with all 10 General Orders, one through ten. When I stopped at ten I could see a gleam in his eye, now he thought he had me. He took one step forward and got nose to nose.

"Private, there are 11 General Orders. What is your 11th General Order?"

"Corporal, my 11th General Order is: To walk my post from flank to flank and take no shit off any rank."

I could almost see the blood vessels in his eyes pop. Nobody had ever given him the 11th General Order before. The Corporal gritted his teeth, slapped an overnight pass in my face and said, "Have a good time, Private."

I thanked the Corporal, did an about face and got the hell out of there before he changed his mind. As I said, sometimes it pays to be in the right place at the right time; while I was emptying the trash in the NCO room I heard them discussing things to check and questions to ask privates when we went out on pass next weekend.

For all the trouble we went through to get that over-night pass it was really hardly worth it for most of us. Some of us went to Killeen, TX, and some of us went to Temple, TX, a short bus ride down the road. Marshal, King, stretch, and I decided to take a bus ride to Temple and try our luck there. For the most part we just walked around town stopping to get something to drink every once in a while; somehow we felt like we had to do something to make this a memorable event. Since hooking up with a girl was obviously not going to happen and getting drunk and fighting was not our style that only left one thing....a tattoo.

The four of us found a tattoo parlor and went in to see what they had to offer. From the looks of the walls and the books on the table we could go through we could get about anything we wanted. Marshal and King decided on something rather large for the shoulder. Stretch wanted some snake like thing running between his shoulder and elbow. All things considered somehow something long seemed a perfect choice for Stretch. I wasn't that brave. I settled on a little scroll on my right forearm with my initials on it.

After things were all done, it was only about 2300 and we knew that the last bus for Fort Hood left at midnight so we hustled our butts over to the bus station, caught the next bus and was back in our barracks by 0100, along with the majority of the rest of the platoon. We all really had a rousing good time on our one and only overnight pass during basic training.

YOU'RE IN THE ARMY NOW
Chapter 16

In the sixth week of training we began intensive training learning how to make that M-1 shoot and shoot straight. We learned about sight alignment and elevation. We went to a practice range, I think it was called an R.I.C. course but I'm not sure. Anyway we practiced firing blanks to get a feel for what it felt like to fire the weapon. I think the first time I fired mine in the prone position I slid back a foot from the rifle recoil.

I always fired a rifle from the left shoulder. My instructor decided this was not a good thing. The rifle ejects its spent rounds and the empty clip to the right. This meant that each round ejected would fly across my line of sight as would the clip when it was ejected. The only solution was for me to learn to fire from the right shoulder. This was not a comfortable position for me but what choice did I have. I finally got comfortable with it so that I could shoot reasonably well from the right shoulder. By the end of the week the company was ready for the real firing range.

Week seven found us out at the firing range from early morning to mid afternoon. There were only so many firing positions so while one group was actually firing another group was working the pits down at the target area and yet another group was getting additional instruction behind the firing line. They set up a field mess so there was no wasted time going back into the company area for chow. When the noon meal was ready we took a break and ate at the range.

Thursday and Friday were qualifying days, the days you either made it or you didn't. If you didn't qualify they threatened to hold you back for the next training cycle until you could qualify with your basic weapon. I don't know if they would have really done that or not, but personally I really didn't want to find out. I didn't qualify expert, but I managed to get my marksman's badge; that's all that counted. I don't think anyone in 4th platoon failed, but there were a lot of Maggie's drawers flying those last two days.

The beginning of week eight; our last week of basic training; the only thing left now was to pass the qualification courses. These were a bunch of different stations each soldier had to pass through and pass whatever was offered at that station. One was a medical station where you had to give CPR and bandage a wound, one was a weapons station where you had to take apart and reassemble that damn gun one more time. There were about seven or eight stations in all and none of them too difficult if you had paid any attention at all in the course instruction.

Wednesday of that week was the final test. We had to negotiate an obstacle course with back pack and weapon. When we got up Wednesday morning it was raining cats and dogs. They gave us a choice: either run the course in the rain or wait and see if the rain let up. I don't think there was any doubt in anyone's military mind. We had come too far and were too close to graduation on Saturday to wait any longer. We chose to run the course.

It was another one of those character-building moments. We fell out in the rain in our ponchos and weapons at sling arms, muzzles down and marched over to the obstacle course. One of the cadre broke out in a "Jodie Call," and we all joined right in. It made no difference what the weather was doing; we were Charlie Company, and we were proud of it. For those of you that don't know what a "Jodie Call" is...well it's a song soldiers sing as they march. The ones we sang back then you won't hear around military bases today. They would be considered politically incorrect.

Okay, I'll give you a sample of one of the "nicer" ones:

Cadre: "I got a girl on Blueberry hill."
Troops: "I got a girl on Blueberry hill"
Cadre: "She won't screw but her sister will."
Troops: "She won't screw but her sister will"
Cadre: "Sound off."
Troops: "One, two"
Cadre: "Sound off"
Troops: "Three four."
Cadre: "Break it on down."
Troops: One, two, three four"
Troops: "One two…THREE! FOUR!"

Okay, maybe you had to be there to get the full effect, but the point is we were out there in the rain, full of piss and vinegar, and bound and determined to get 'er done.

We returned from the obstacle course the same way we returned from our field exercise, sloppy, muddy and very wet. But we didn't care. We knew what we had to do and went about getting things back in shape.

Friday morning formation, the first sergeant came out with a fist full of papers. We all knew what they were; they were our orders for our next assignment out of basic. Those of us that had signed up for a specific MOS (Military Occupational Specialty) expected orders for that particular school. I expected to get orders for Military Police School at Fort Gordon, GA. Instead I got orders for the 512th MP Company at Fort Huachuca, AZ. I had no idea what that meant.

The rest of Friday was spent rehearsing for our graduation Saturday morning. Friday night I was lying on my bunk with my eyes closed; not sleeping just lying there. Suddenly I got the feeling someone was watching me. I opened my eyes and looked straight into the face of Washington. He had his chin resting on my mattress.

"So you're gonna be an MP, huh?"

"Yeah…looks that way," I said.

"How's a skinny guy like you gonna arrest a guy like me?"

"First I'm going to tell you that you're under arrest, and then I'll ask you to turn around and put your hands behind your back," I said, like I really knew what to do.

"What if I say, 'Hell, no'?"

"Then I'll ask you again."

"And if I still say no?"

I was running out of answers. I only had one left. "Then I'd pull my pistol out and shoot your black ass."

Washington broke out in a big grin and said, "Okay, you da man. I won't be fuckin' with you."

Then he turned around and broke into his version of some song by the Platters and shuffled on out into the bay area.

Saturday morning came and the sun was shining and the skies were clear. We were all excited and anxious to get this ceremony over with. Finally we fell out in the company street. Sergeant Yoder inspected each of us in turn and made sure our uniforms were on straight, and we didn't have any "ropes" hanging off of us.

Finally the company commander came out and took charge of the company. He marched us over to the parade field where the review stand had been set up and brought us all online in front of the battalion commander and a bunch of other people I never saw before. There were a few families sitting around the reviewing stand.

The battalion commander called the company commander to the reviewing stand and told him what a great job he did and then made a little speech to us that nobody paid any attention to. Finally the lieutenants put in their second appearance of the entire eight weeks and started barking orders. The band started playing and we began to march in a circle so we could do the pass in review thing. Upon completion of the pass in review and return to our original spots on the parade field, Sergeant Yoder came about and looked at us all and then gave his last command to this Platoon....Dismissed!!

FORT HUACHUCA
Chapter 17

After basic training I had 15 days before I was due to report in to Fort Huachuca, AZ. I went back to Abilene, but besides my family I really didn't see many of the kids I went to school with. Most of them were still at whatever college they had picked to attend or moved away. Somehow it really didn't bother me, I didn't seem to have much interest in meeting up with that old gang of mine. My mother drove me crazy, as usual; she wanted to show me off to her friends and wanted me to wear my uniform. I enjoyed wearing my uniform but didn't want to wear it around just to show off. My daddy didn't have much time since he worked most of the time. My little sister, was just about 4 years old, I took her to Day Care in the mornings and picked her up in the afternoons while I was there. My family was never close, so there wasn't a lot of interaction there. I left for Fort Huachuca two days early.

I caught a bus from Abilene to Tucson, AZ, and from Tucson to Sierra Vista, a one-horse town just outside the gates of Fort Huachuca. It seems the city of Sierra Vista consisted primarily of a café, a skating rink and a USO. The bus dropped me off at the USO and the driver told me to check inside to get a ride to the base.

I checked with the lady at the information desk inside the USO, she told me I could catch a bus that made the rounds on the base to the USO and back about every hour; or I could get a base cab and they would take me right to the Replacement Depot. I told her I was supposed to go to the MP Company. She told me I would have to go to the Replacement Depot first. All newly assigned personnel went there first. I didn't want to show my stupidity and ask what a Replacement Depot was. She obviously knew more than I did so I said thank you and asked where I could get a cab. She told me to go wait outside by the sign marked "Taxi Stand," and there would be one there shortly.

I didn't wait long before a taxi pulled up. "Where you headed?" the driver asked.

"I'm assigned to the MP company here," I replied.

"You just reporting in to Fort Huachuca?"

"Yes," I replied.

"You need to go to the Replacement Depot first," the driver said.

"Yeah, that's what the lady inside told me."

It seemed everyone around here knew more about what I was supposed to do more than I did and these were just civilians. I got in the taxi and we headed for the base. The Main Gate wasn't very far from the USO and the driver slowed down as we approached. The MP stuck his head in the window and looked back at me.

"He's a newbie," said the driver. "He is gonna be one of you."

The MP took a second glance at me and said, "Welcome to the 512th; I'll see you when you get out of the Replacement Depot."

"Thanks," I said.

Damn, did everybody know about this Replacement Depot but me? *That was a stupid question,* I thought, *obviously they did.* What the hell is a Replacement Depot? The driver pulled away from the gate and headed down the road. We traded some idle chatter but I didn't pay much attention to what he was saying; I was looking around taking in the sights of Fort Huachuca. Finally the driver pulled up beside this WWII looking barracks similar to the ones I had seen at Fort Carson and told me to just go right in that door, pointing to a door with sign on it that said Orderly Room and that someone in there would take care of me. I paid my fare, picked up my duffel bag and went to report in to the Orderly Room.

Some Specialist 4th Class (Spec 4), pointed to a chair and told me to have a seat by his desk. I sat and watched as he pulled out a stack of papers and got them all lined up by his typewriter (Yes, I said typewriter; remember this was pre-computer days). He asked me for my orders, which I presented to him. He pulled off a few copies and gave the rest back to me and told me to hang on to them. He went about typing out the papers in front of him without saying anything else until he was finished.

After he was finished he pushed the papers over in front of me and said, “Sign your full name and put your service number by the x’s.”

“What am I signing?” I asked.

“Just paperwork you’ll need as you process in,” replied the specialist.

Damn! I thought, *how many friggin’ times do I have to process into the Army?* I gathered all the paper work up and stuffed them in a folder. The specialist told me to grab my stuff and follow him. Without further conversation we left the Orderly Room and he led me down a row of barracks until we came to one he seemed to like. Inside it was almost empty.

“Pick a bunk,” the specialist said, “Be in fatigues in the morning. Chow is between 0600 and 0700. After that there will be a police call around the company area. Then report back to the Orderly Room for further instructions. Bring those papers with you, got it?”

“Yeah, I got it,” I said.

“See you in the morning at 0730. Have a good evening,” the specialist said and turned and walked out the door.

As I lay back on my bunk contemplating life as I knew it; a couple of other guys walked in the barracks and fell into a couple of bunks just past mine.

“Hey, you just report in?” asked one of the guys.

“Yeah, just about an hour ago,” I replied.

“Where you going to be assigned?”

“The MP Company.”

“You been to chow yet?” asked the other guy.

“No, not yet. What time does the mess hall open, and where is it?” I asked.

“We’ll be going down in a few minutes if you want to go with us.”

"Sure, I'm hungry; haven't eaten since this morning," I replied.

I lay there quietly; I could hear the other two guys talking among themselves. I was just about to fall asleep when they got up walked past my bunk and said, "Hey, we're going to chow. You coming?"

I got up and fell in step behind them and we walked down the street to the mess hall. Introductions were made all around but I don't remember their names. One was from Chicago and the other was from New Jersey. We fell in the line that had already gathered outside the mess hall door and waited our turn. It was a short line so it didn't take long to get inside. We each filled our trays, found a place to sit and began to eat. Both these guys had taken basic training at Ft. Polk, LA.; neither had anything good to say about the place. One was going to be a mechanic and the other was a clerk, but didn't know what unit they would be assigned to.

I returned to the barracks after chow, the other two guys stopped outside to smoke a cigarette. When I walked in there were some other new guys hanging around; some were going to the mess hall. Others were just sitting around talking. Back in those days the only one with a TV set was the C.Q. and nobody really wanted to hang out with him in his little office. Some settled in and read a book, some sat around bull shittin', some went to the post movie. I got out my fatigues and boots and got them ready for tomorrow like the guy from the Orderly Room had said.

Shortly after dark there seemed to be some noise on the back porch of the barracks and I went out to see what everybody was getting excited about. There were a couple of girls sitting out there in a car. Actually they were more like women than girls. All the guys were trying to get them to come in the barracks but they weren't having any of that. On the other hand if you had some money they would take you for ride if you bought them a beer. I didn't see any of the guys taking them up on their offer either. This was fun for about twenty minutes then I got bored and went back inside. I went to my bunk, stripped to my shorts and T-shirt and climbed in bed. I put my wallet inside my pillow case and under my pillow and drifted off to sleep. I still didn't know what a Replacement Depot was.

FORT HUACHUCA
Chapter 18

At 0530 the next morning the C.Q. came through turning on lights and making noise. "Okay, all you lowlifes, drop your cocks and grab your socks; it's time to get your asses out of bed," he yelled.

I rolled over and sat up on the edge of my bunk. Well, that was different I thought, never heard that one before, and I thought I had heard about all of them during basic training.

I grabbed my shaving kit and headed for the latrine. I took care of two of the three S's. I didn't have to do the third one. I never was regular that way. Back at my bunk I got dressed, and along with the guys I met yesterday and a few others headed for the mess hall.

They had French toast for breakfast. I hate French toast. I grabbed a couple of those little boxes of cereal they have and that was breakfast for me that morning. As soon as we finished breakfast we fell out in the company area and some sergeant broke us down in groups and sent us off to different areas of the Replacement Depot to do police call. For those of you not familiar with a military police call it may not be what you think it is. This is police as in clean up the area. Basically it requires you to line up and walk a specific area and pick up trash, mostly cigarette butts that others threw down. Probably those that weren't responsible for police call in that area.

After police call was over we had a formation and the sergeant in charge called out some names with specific instructions for each. Some were to go back to the barracks get their bag and baggage and fall back out in front of the Orderly Room. Others, such as myself, were told to get the papers we had filled out and report to the finance office; now if I only knew where the finance office was. There were several of us going to the finance office so as a group we asked where the finance office was, got some not so specific directions and headed off in the general direction.

When we found the finance office we walked in and were met by some guy behind a wire cage. He told us all to give him a copy of our orders and have a seat. This was obviously going to be a hurry-up-and-wait situation. There were six of us that went to finance; they took us in alphabetical order, I was the next to last one called. The finance clerk wanted to know if I had any dependents or if I wanted to take out a savings bond; I thought, *You must be some kind of nut, how am I going to afford a savings bond out of that whopping $78.00 a month they were paying me?* I kept my thoughts to myself and just said no.

When I got out the four previous guys were waiting, so I joined them while we waited for the last guy. Finally he came out and we headed back to the barracks. We got back just in time for the noon meal so we went straight to the mess hall. After lunch we wandered over to the barracks and that's where we spent the rest of the day, just hanging around.

My next three days at the Replacement Depot were spent just hanging around. I got up in the morning, went to chow, made police call and returned to the barracks and waited. I wasn't by myself; there were several of us just hanging around waiting. There was some that left and some new ones that arrived. Actually our barracks filled up and I noticed that there were some new people in the barracks next door. About the second day we figured out if they didn't call us out after morning formation we were pretty well done for the day so some of us would take off and go to the main cafeteria and drink cokes and eat doughnuts. Sometimes we went back for noon meal at the mess hall and sometimes we just got a hamburger at the cafeteria.

On Friday, after morning formation I was told along with several others to get my gear and report to the Orderly Room. Finally! I was getting the hell out of there. I had been there since I reported in on Monday. When I arrived at the Orderly Room there was close to a dozen guys standing around. We were told that there would be some transportation coming to pick us up and they would call our names if we were supposed to go with them.

One sedan, a jeep or truck would roll up and call out someone's name and that person or person(s) would take off for their new unit. There were five of us left when a duce and a half rolled up (Ya'll remember what a duce and half is right?) and this crusty old buck sergeant got out and called off all our names. I don't know why it never occurred to us to ask or talk and find out if any of us were going to the same unit but until that moment none of us knew we were all going to the same place, the 512th MP Company.

FORT HUACHUCA
Chapter 19

It was a short ride from the Replacement Depot to the MP Company. Sgt. Koch had put us all in the back of the truck with our baggage and since the truck had a tarp over it we didn't get to see much of the ride. We came to rather sudden stop and Sgt. Koch came around and dropped the tail gate so we could all get out and told us to leave your bags here and go in the company Orderly Room with a copy of our orders.

Once inside the Orderly Room we met the company clerk who took our orders and the first sergeant, Sergeant Passino came out and shook our hands and welcomed us to the 512th MP Company and Fort Huachuca. We didn't meet them, but there was a captain and a major also wandering around in the Orderly Room. While we all stood around with our thumbs up our butts the company clerk fixed us up with a chow pass and a Class A pass, which meant we could go anywhere we wanted to. This was a first for all of us.

Before we left the Orderly Room the first sergeant said, "Since this is Friday you guys take the weekend off and report back here on Monday morning about 0730."

It wasn't that I wasn't grateful for the time off, but holy shit, I had been off since I got there, it seemed. I was really kind of ready to do something. But I didn't know what I would do, and I had already learned about volunteering.

Privates, Smith, Hobart, Pederson and some guy whose name I forgot and myself got our barracks assignments. We were all assigned bunks on the first floor of the first barracks around the corner from the Orderly Room. We each got a bunk and a footlocker, there was no wall locker, and instead there was an open area with a bar under a shelf that we could hang our uniforms and some civilian cloths on, if we had any. And on the shelf we could put our shaving gear.

Private Hobart I believe was from somewhere along the Mid Atlantic, the guy whose name I don't remember was from New York. Pederson I'm pretty sure was from Kansas or Nebraska. I say this because he looked like he had been corn fed all his life. Smith and I were both from Texas. Smith was from the Dallas area.

I don't know about the others but at last I felt like I was in a place where I was going to stay for a while. I was happy to finally stop living out of a duffel bag. Since we didn't have anything else do to right at the moment; the five of us began to unpack and start hanging our stuff up. Actually we didn't get a lot hung up. None of us had any clothes hangers to hang anything on. So, we worked on our foot lockers and tried to get them laid out the way we were taught in basic. Some guy came in, in full MP gear and said welcome to the 512th and told us we could go over to the mini PX just down the street and get some hangers. He also told us we could use the military laundry and turn our clothes in every Monday and get them back in a week, or we could take 'em to the laundry by the mini PX and get our clothes back in a couple of days. He suggested we would be wise to use the PX Laundry.

Seems like everywhere you turn around it's time to eat. The five of us went to the mess hall which was actually inside the Stockade but there was a separate entry and section for the MPs and the inmates. That was the reason for the chow pass. Some of the custodial inmates worked the serving line and pulled KP in the kitchen. That meant that none of the MPs had to ever pull that dreaded duty while they were assigned there.

After we ate we walked up to the mini PX and picked up some hangers and a few other things we each needed and stuck around in the little snack bar area and had a coke. I kind of like this little place.

Actually I liked the lady behind the counter but that was a day dream, she was too old for me. After finishing our cokes we wandered back to the barracks and began to work on getting all our clothes put away.

About 1630, the barracks came alive with the day shift getting off work and coming in and changing cloths or heading right for the mess hall. They all took note that there were "newbies" among them; most came over and said hello. They all had questions like where you from, what's your MOS (Military Occupational Specialty); where did you take basic and did you go to MP School. None of us knew what our MOS was and we all took basic at Fort Hood. It seems Smith and I were both in Charley Company but he was in 1st Platoon and I was all the way down on the other end in 4th Platoon so we never crossed paths. The other guys were in Delta Company. They graduated a week after we did.

Having nothing better to do, we went to the mess hall....again. I'd only been out of basic training about three weeks and already I was gaining weight. When I was in basic I worked off whatever I ate, that wasn't happening now.

Seems like everywhere we went the first question everyone asked most was if we knew where we were going to be assigned. It seems your MOS determined if you were going to be a Military Policeman or a Confinement Specialist at the stockade. But it didn't make any difference since none of us knew the answers. While Pederson looked like he had been corn fed all his life, Hobart looked like he just had a lot of second helpings of potatoes; those two were odds on favorites to work in the stockade. Smith and I and the guy from New York had the MP "look," whatever that was.

Since it was Friday night the barracks cleared out pretty quick; seems everyone had some place to go and something to do. Everybody but us that is; a couple of guys apparently didn't have anything to do and they stuck around the barracks. One of them had a radio and we listened to the radio for a while. He mentioned the Day Room and said they had a pool table over there and a TV set you might get to work, and some other stuff. Smith and I and the New York guy went over to check it out.

We pretty much had the place to ourselves, we shot some pool, played some ping pong and tried the TV but that was a bust. About 2330 the CQ came around and told us we had to clear out the Day Room was closed. We left and went back to the barracks. Having nothing else to do....we called it a night and crashed.

Don't let anyone tell you it doesn't get cold in Arizona at night. I woke up about 0300 in the morning freezing my ass off. It seems that someone had come in...or gone out and left the damn door open and it was cold! I got up and shut the door and tried to get back in the bed before I froze my butt off. And this was only late August!

FORT HUACHUCA
Chapter 20

At 0730, Monday morning, five privates were standing tall in fatigues waiting to see the first sergeant. About 0800, First Sergeant Passino came out of the commanding officer's office and told us to step outside with him.

When we got outside we found Sgt. Koch standing out there smoking a cigarette. Sergeant Passino said, "Men, we are getting ready for our annual IG inspection in a couple of months so we need to get this place shaped up and ready for inspection. There is a lot to do, and I am assigning you to Sgt. Koch's detail to help get this place shaped up." Somehow this didn't sound like it had a lot to do with learning about how to be an MP.

Sergeant Passino continued, "From now until further notice you will report to Sgt. Koch every morning and follow his instructions. When we get through this inspection you will all be given a three-day pass, and I'll see that you all get promoted to private first class," private first class, PFC, something you normally automatically got after eight months in service. I was thinking it would be nice to get promoted early; the few extra bucks would come in handy, but I couldn't help but wonder if what we were about to get into was really gonna be worth it.

Sergeant Passino went back in the Orderly Room and left us in the crusty old hands of Sgt. Koch. Sgt. Koch was apparently a man of few words. "Come on," he said, and turned around and took off around the Orderly Room. We followed Koch to a work like shed at the back of the company area. We walked in the shed and the first thing that grabbed my attention was a toilet seat hanging on the wall that had "Koch's Detail" on it. Somehow I got the feeling we weren't the first to work for Sgt. Koch.

Sgt. Koch opened up a locker at one end of the shed and pulled out five one gallon cans of white paint, actually it was whitewash. He grabbed five brushes off one of the shelves and set everything on a table by the locker. Koch looked at us like we were supposed to read his mind, but when none of us moved to grab a can of paint and a brush he finally said, "Get a can and a brush and follow me." Did we have a choice?

At that time the MP Company covered a huge area and around the entire area and around any tree or flowerbed or down every side of every walk way leading anywhere were rocks; hundreds and hundreds of rocks; and they were all painted white. They were all about to become whiter. Koch dropped us off one by one at different points around the company area and said, "Start here; go that way."

It seemed like every time we finished a section it would rain and we would have to go back and repaint it because the rain would wash off the whitewash if it hadn't dried yet. I know I must have painted one huge bolder at least three times.

We painted huge rocks, we painted large rocks, we painted big rocks, medium size rocks, and small rocks. We painted pebbles. If it didn't move and looked like a rock we painted it. I painted the tires on the company commander's jeep white because they had pebbles in between the treads.

I never saw so many damn white rocks in my life and don't care if I never see another one. But we were in the Army now and that's how we spent our first month assigned to our first unit assignment out of basic training painting fuckin' rocks!!

FORT HUACHUCA
Chapter 21

The one good thing about working on Koch's Detail was you got the weekends off. The bad part was we were so tired we didn't feel like doing much of anything. Besides we didn't have much money to do anything with.

Bobby Ray, that was Smith and I went into town a couple of times and hung out in the USO. There wasn't a lot going on there, but they had free food, and sometimes there were some girls that dropped in. They weren't exactly the kind of girls you wanted to write home about, but they smelled better than Hobart. One thing you learn quickly, if you don't have a car you're not going to score with the few women that were around.

Of the five of us that came in together, Bobby Ray and I hung out together, maybe it was the Texas connection. Hobart pretty much stayed on base and hung out at the unit Day Room or in the barracks. Pederson said he was saving his money to get married to his high school sweetheart and didn't go out much. The guy from New York, I don't know what he did. He seemed to disappear when we weren't working. He said he had found a girl but the rest of us didn't believe it. But what did we know; we certainly hadn't found one or any.

I don't know if Fort Huachuca was just a strange place or if it was just my first assignment out of basic where my life wasn't totally structured seven days a week; but it just seemed to have a strange aura about it. One night Bobby Ray and I went to the little PX. We had been going there a lot after checking out the USO and the skating rink in down town Sierra Vista we found ourselves satisfied to sit around in the snack bar area of the PX, listen to the jukebox and flirt with Marie. That was the gal that had caught my attention when we were in there the first time. Marie was easy to talk to and I think she got a kick out of flirting with Bobby Ray and me.

This must have been the first Sunday night we had ever stopped in there because what we saw was like nothing we had ever seen before. We walked in and moved toward our usual table close to the jukebox and almost at the same time we saw this....person sitting at a table over in the corner. What made it strange was this guy was wearing a tuxedo with a top hat, white gloves and black shoes and carrying a cane. Sitting on the table was a tea cup with saucer, sitting on a cloth place mat and a cloth napkin with silverware on it and sitting in the middle of the table was a small teapot. Now I don't care where you go, or what Army post you're on, this is not something you see sitting around in a small PX every day. Maybe on a Navy base or a Marine base you might but not on an Army base.

Bobby Ray and I slid into our chairs rather gently and just sort of kept looking at the guy out of the corner of our eye. Marie brought us over a coke and just had this silly grin on her face and whispered, "I'll tell you later." Bobby Ray and I ordered cheeseburgers and fries and Bobby Ray played some do-wop on the jukebox. A few other guys came and went while Bobby Ray and I were there, but they mostly wanted to buy some cigarettes and didn't hang around. Apparently this guy in the tux was nothing new to them. They just seemed to ignore him.

About an hour later the guy in the tux got up picked up his stuff put it in a small basket that had been sitting on the floor beside him; tipped his hat to Marie and walked out the door. Bobby Ray and I were cracking up laughing and waving our hands for Marie to come tell us what that was all about.

Marie came over and sat down at our table which she didn't do very often. She leaned forward on the table on her elbows and began to tell us the following story. The man in the Tux was a retired military member who was not exactly what you would call normal. Marie told us that towards the end of his career he had been stationed in England and met this woman and had fallen madly in love and thought she felt the same. They had met in a small PX very similar to this one. Every Sunday night they would stop by the PX and have a cup of tea. They were constantly together when he was off duty and apparently they had plans to get married and return to the United States. This went on for the better part of two years. About a week before he was scheduled to rotate back to the states she apparently changed her mind and broke off their relationship in the same PX they had met in. The guy was so devastated, he refused to board his flight when he was scheduled to depart and had a break down and had to be taken to the hospital. He finally returned to the states and was discharged from the service. But he never was the same and never forgot his girlfriend. He is apparently from around this area and about a year ago he started coming in here every Sunday night for a cup of tea. Marie said he never bothered anyone, never talked to anyone, just sat there, and occasionally he would let out a little laugh and then just drink his tea. She said she got this story from some of the other soldiers that knew him from before.

As I listened to Marie tell the story, it suddenly wasn't so funny anymore. When I looked up at Marie, she had a tear in her eye I guess she kind of felt sorry for the old guy. I couldn't help but feel sorry for the old man too and couldn't help but remember how I felt when I said good bye to Linda that night on Stephen's porch and what an empty feeling I had in the pit of my stomach. I couldn't imagine what it must be like to be so in love with someone that it drove you crazy. I felt sorry for the old man too, but I wasn't going to admit that to Bobby Ray. I told him to go play some music so he wouldn't see me wipe the tear from my eye. Marie must have noticed; she put her hand on my shoulder. She had never done that before.

FORT HUACHUCA
Chapter 22

The next Monday morning we met back at Koch's Corner, that's what they called his shed where he kept all his supplies. We had painted every boulder, rock and pebble in the entire MP compound so we figured things should lighten up now and we should soon be getting on with our MP training. We should have been so lucky.

It seems that sometime during the past week the commander had decided he would like to have a little cactus garden right outside the Orderly Room. He wanted a variety of cacti in the garden including one of those big suckers that look like a stick figure with his arms up in the air. I have no idea what you call them. So this morning instead of paint buckets and brushes it was picks and shovels and hoes and rakes.

We proceeded some what reluctantly to the front of the Orderly Room. Koch surveyed the area and picked out a spot to be the approximate center of the circle, put a stake in it and told us to start clearing out an area around and away from that stake. Koch kept walking around sticking stakes in the ground and telling us to keep digging up to the outer stakes. Eventually a circle began to take shape in front of the Orderly Room. Koch kept walking around and telling us to dig a little more here or fill in a little bit there. I have no idea how he did it but when he was done he had what appeared to be a perfect circle. I guess Koch had some hidden talents to go along with those hidden bottles of gin he had stashed around his shed.

None of us were positive; we had heard some stories and a couple of times when we were waiting for Koch to show up at the shed we did some snooping and found a few bottles of gin stashed around the place. Apparently Koch was an alcoholic but he seemed to hide it well, at least during duty hours and he always showed up for work and always got the job done.

There was something else different about Koch. He didn't seem to care that he was obviously older than others of the same rank; or that he was the "detail" sergeant. If you looked closely at his uniform you could see the imprints of sergeant stripes of a higher rank, which pretty much told you that he had been busted. Nobody seemed to give him any shit about it and he certainly didn't take any from anyone....including those that out ranked him. I didn't know that much about the Army at that point in my young career but I definitely understood that there was a certain amount of respect expected to be given to those that outranked you. We had heard Koch give some of those that out ranked him, including the first sergeant and even some of the officers some responses that without a doubt were less than respectful. A couple of times I was almost afraid for the old man.

After we had cleaned out an area for the cactus garden, Koch sent us to lunch. When we returned he had the deuce and half parked in front of the shed which pretty much told us we were going for a ride. We all piled in the back of the truck and Koch headed for the brush and undeveloped areas around the post. You'll never guess what our first mission was. Rocks! We were out to pick up more friggin' rocks; but these rocks had to be pretty much the same size. We spent the whole afternoon gathering rocks. We didn't get back to the company until late afternoon. Koch had us unload the rocks and place them around the area we had cleaned out and by the time we were finished we had a nice little circle of rocks. Koch excused us all for chow and the rest of the day but we all knew what we would be doing tomorrow.

The next morning when we reported to Koch's shed; the truck was parked out front again. To our surprise we weren't painting that day, we were off to pick out the cactus. Of course if you thought about it, it only made sense to plant the cactus, and then paint the rocks. We loaded up the truck with shovels and picks, Koch gave us each a pair of heavy gloves which we really appreciated later on that day. We boarded the truck and headed back out to the desert.

I'm not sure where we went or if were we even still on the military reservation but eventually we began to see some of these stick looking cactus. Koch pulled off the road and drove a short way into the isolated area. He stopped the truck and got out and began to survey the area; after a few minutes he spotted one of these cacti he liked and told us to get our gloves and shovels and picks out of the truck and bring a tarp from the bed of the truck. The cactus was only about 4-5 feet tall. Koch gave us instructions how to dig around it and get the cactus out of the ground with as much root still attached as possible.

Even with those heavy gloves and your shirt sleeves down you couldn't help but get pricked by the needles on those damn things. We got it out of the ground and loaded on the truck. While Hobart, Pederson and I worked on the big cactus, Bobby Ray and the New York guy were following Koch around digging up smaller and different types of cacti that he pointed out. After spending a couple of hours out there we had a shit load of cacti in the back of the truck and were heading back to the Company.

We didn't waste any time when we got back to the Company area. Koch wanted those cacti back in the ground like right now! We planted the big one in the center where he had put the first stake and then put the other around in the circle where he told us to place them. As soon as they were all in the ground, Hobart dragged out the hose and began to water them all down. The rest of us stood around and pulled those needles out of our hands and arms and other places they shouldn't have been.

We had a couple of hours before chow call and Koch gave us a choice, we could go back to the barracks and clean up before chow or we could go grab the whitewash and brushes and paint those damn rocks. We opted to paint the rocks, we figured with all five of us painting it wouldn't take that long and we would be through with the damn cactus garden.

As we were painting the rocks the company commander, executive officer and first sergeant came out to admire our work.

"Good job, Sgt. Koch," the commander said.

"Thank you, Major."

"Good job, men. You worked hard; it looks good," chimed in the first sergeant.

We didn't say anything, just kept painting. Of course I kept my mouth shut, but I was thinking, *Is this the end of this shit? When do start learning what we joined the Army to learn?*

FORT HUACHUCA
Chapter 23

It was now somewhere in the middle of September. We had been at Fort Huachuca just a little over a month and all we had done so far was paint rocks and dig up cactus. Every time one of us asked when this IG inspection was the only answer we ever got was "soon." I think we were all getting a little antsy and anxious to move on, but there seemed to be no end in sight as to what they wanted us to do. When we finished painting rocks and planting cactus, they sent us to the Motor Pool to help work on the Military Police sedans, Jeeps and other vehicles. Fortunately this only lasted about a week; I have never been mechanically inclined and really had no desire to be back then. As long as I could put gas in the tank and start the engine and drive off I was good.

Finally towards the end of the month we got what we thought was a going to be a break. It seems the MP Corps anniversary is in September and they were planning a Company party. This sounded just like what we needed about this time.

The first sergeant called us into his office one Thursday and told us about the party. He said the party was going to be held some place on some mountain. There are several mountain ranges surrounding the Fort Huachuca and Sierra Vista area and I have no idea which mountain or range this party was going to be on but I seem to recall the Huachuca

Mountains being mentioned but don't hold me to it. It seems they intended to bring a couple of jeep trailers loaded with iced down beer and soda up there so it would be nice and cold by the time the party started and they naturally didn't want anyone stealing the beer. They said we would have sleeping bags and basically just had to be there. But they were going to give us .45 caliber pistols just in case we ran into any wild animals. None of us had ever qualified with much less shot a .45 caliber Pistol in our young lives. Except maybe the guy from New York, I never did really trust him. Since only 4 of us were needed, two man teams they said, Hobart was excused and was given the duty of C.Q. driver and responsible for insuring the changing of the guard. Bobby Ray and I said we were a team leaving Pederson stuck with the New York guy. That was fine but we got stuck with the midnight shift.

After we left the 1st Sgt's Office, Koch told us we would be smart to take our field jackets and gloves with us because it could get damn cold in those mountains at night. Koch gave us the rest of Thursday and Friday off and told us before he let us go, that he would be sure the mess hall had some food for us to take with us when we went to the mountains. Somehow it struck me strange that Koch was the only one that thought to tell us about the field jackets and gloves and now about being sure we would have food to eat while we were out on the mountain; kind of made me wonder who the real sergeant was around this place.

Friday evening about 17:30 (5:30P.M to you civilian types) Pederson and New York came through the barracks with their field jackets, gloves, sleeping bags and a sack of sandwiches from the mess hall. They each had a .45 caliber Pistol strapped on their side. They told Bobby Ray and me to just go check with the night cook when we got ready to leave and he would give us some sandwiches.

Bobby Ray and I just lay around our bunks and listened to the radio and eventually fell asleep for a couple of hours. I woke up about 2100 hours (you figure it out); Bobby Ray was already awake, we both headed for the shower. After our shower we took our time getting dressed and making sure we had all the stuff we were supposed to have. About 2230 we walked over to the mess hall and talked to the night cook. He walked back to the storage locker and got a couple of sacks out and brought them to us.

We walked back to the barracks to pick up the rest of our stuff and headed over to the C.Q. office. Hobart was there waiting on us with a jeep. The C.Q. gave us the once over and said we could take off.

"What about our weapons?" I asked.

"You will get the ones the guys up there have now," the C.Q. replied. "Oh, one other thing. You can keep one clip in the magazine but no round in the chamber."

I understood that only because it was pretty much the same instructions we used to get in basic when we were learning how to fire M-1 rifle. The only question running through my mind was how do you get a round in the chamber if you need to? But I wasn't going to be the dummy to ask that question.

Hobart got the jeep fired up and Bobby Ray and I piled in. Neither of us asked Hobart if he knew where we were going. Maybe we were both afraid to ask. Hobart put the jeep in gear and with a little herky-jerky clutch action he got the jeep moving and we were off. So here I was, off on my first assignment I could at least consider some sort of police duty. Okay, so it was really only a form of guard duty but I never pulled guard duty in basic so it was new to me.

FORT HUACHUCA
Chapter 24

The drive up the mountain was longer than I thought it would be; or maybe it just seemed that way because it was so dark out. The higher we climbed into the mountains the narrower the road got and while you really couldn't see much you got the idea that there was no place to go but down on one side of the road.

I wasn't about to ask Hobart if he knew where he was going I didn't want to distract him from his driving. I think Bobby Ray must have felt the same way because he wasn't talking either. Finally we came to a wide place in the road, a plateau of sorts it seemed since it was on the right side of the road where there used to be nothing. We caught Pederson and New York guy in the headlights of the jeep and saw the two trailers of beer and soda backed up under a couple of trees in the back part of the area.

We got out of the jeep and grabbed our gear. We relieved the other guys of their weapons and strapped them on, adjusted the belt and said goodbye as Hobart took the other guys back to the company. There wasn't much of a briefing between the changing of the guard. Pederson said they saw some raccoons and a couple of deer but nothing else.

Bobby Ray and I took our flashlights and did a recon run around the area to kind of get familiar with where we were. Then we started to try to think like soldiers or maybe just campers, we decided if it rained it might be good if we put our sleeping bags and sack of sandwiches under the jeep and that would help keep them dry and also keep us dry.

I stepped over to a tree a little further back in the woods to relieve myself and as I stepped back into the clearing I heard the very distinct sound of a can of soda being opened. As I got closer to Bobby Ray I saw it wasn't a can of soda but a can of beer.

"Man, we ain't supposed to be drinking that shit. We are supposed to be guarding it," I said.

"You gonna tell?"

"Not unless you get drunk and shoot me."

"How can I shoot you? I can't put a round in the chamber."

"Good point. Give me a beer?" I said, and with that I actually drank my first beer. To this day I have no idea why. I never did like the stuff. Being Texas boys we talked about high school sports, football in particular. I had bragging rights when it came to sports, especially football. His high school apparently wasn't all that great in athletics. He didn't play sports. From what I gathered from what he told me I would put him in a class with Joe Eddie's bad boys I knew back in high school.

We finished our beer and even though there were several large trash cans sitting around the area the thought crossed our minds that maybe it wouldn't be such a good idea to put our empty cans in one of the trash cans. That would be evidence that someone had been drinking beer and that might not go over too well with the powers to be. So, thinking like soldiers or crooks, we walked back in the woods a ways, dug a little hole and buried the evidence.

About 0300 we decided we were hungry and checked out what we had in our sacks. What a surprise, cold ham sandwiches! I think the Army had a thing about cold ham sandwiches that's what we got on the train ride to and from Fort Carson. Oh, well, they filled us up. Actually we got three apiece, I only ate two and I think that's all Bobby Ray ate. We helped ourselves to another beer while we ate.

After we ate we both took a walk down to that tree I had found earlier and relieved ourselves. Along the way we stopped and buried some more evidence. On the way back Bobby Ray thought he heard something in the bushes and drew his gun.

"What are you gonna do with that? Throw it at something?" I asked.

"It just feels good to know I got it, just in case."

"In case of what? Do you know how to get a round in the chamber?"

"No, do you?" Bobby Ray asked.

"No," I said.

"You wanna try?"

"No. I don't wanna shoot myself in the foot," I replied.

"You don't wanna shoot yourself in the foot? What if you shot me?"

"That wouldn't hurt."

"Fuck you."

"Nice talk, GI."

"Let's go get a beer," Bobby Ray said.

"Beats shooting one another," I said.

Bobby Ray put his weapon back in his holster and we went back to the beer wagon. We decided we should get a beer from the other trailer so this one wouldn't look like it had been touched. We popped the top sat down and leaned against one of the trailer wheels. It was starting to get a little cold. I wasn't sure it was the weather or the beer making me feel that way. I still wasn't sure what the hell I was doing drinking beer. I don't even like the stuff. But I said that already, didn't I?

About 0530 Bobby Ray and I buried another four cans of evidence. I seem to remember thinking a couple of hours ago that it was getting cold. The weather sure changes fast up here in the mountains. Around 0600 we heard a truck coming up the road, we assumed it was Hobart coming up to get us so we gathered up our stuff and got ready to hop in the jeep. Instead of Hobart it was the cooks from the mess hall driving a deuce and a half hauling all their kitchen field gear up to the site to set up and get the food started. They backed the truck into the area they wanted to set up in and began to unload their equipment.

"Hey, you guys, come give us a hand," one of the cooks called out to us.

"We been up here all night already; we wanna get back to the barracks," Bobby Ray said.

"Give us a hand, and you can help yourself to a beer, and when we get a fire going we'll fix you some breakfast."

"You mean we can drink a beer now?" Bobby Ray asked.

"Sure, you're relieved of duty now. We're here," the cook said.

Bobby Ray looked at me; I looked at him. "Sounds good to us," we said and walked over and helped unload the truck.

I never had beer with eggs before, but it tasted pretty good. But I think that about then anything would taste pretty good. By the time we got through eating the guys showed up with the portable tables and chairs. They backed their trucks in and started unloading the trucks.

By the time we finished helping these guys another truck showed up with volleyball net and some other stuff to be off loaded. We helped them too. By the time we got through helping everybody; people were showing up for the party, they wanted to stake their claim to a particular area and table. This was obviously something they did every year.

When Hobart finally showed up Bobby Ray and I really didn't give a damn if we went back to the barracks or not, even if we were the only ones there in fatigues. But we jumped in Hobart's face anyway for not coming to get us on time. He said he couldn't they took his jeep away and told him they would have a patrol come pick us up. We didn't bother to put up an argument we really, really didn't give a shit.

Things begin to get a little fuzzy about this time so I'm only going by what I was told later by less than reliable sources. It seems that sometime around 1100 hours the first sergeant showed up with his wife. Now I do remember from seeing her before that the 1st'Sgts wife was definitely a looker. She was about five feet four inches, with dark eyes and the blackest hair I have ever seen. She was definitely Italian and built like a brick shithouse. But I digress.

According to sources the first sergeant and his wife showed up about 1100 and by 1200 hours I was asking her if she wanted to get married this weekend. I suppose the first sergeant was getting a little irritated by this time and had me and Bobby Ray and some other guys that couldn't hold their beer taken back to the barracks to sleep it off for a while.

I do remember that Sgt. Del La Rosa was instructed to take us back to the barracks. I also remember that Del La Rosa had a 1959 Ford Galaxie Skyliner retractable hardtop convertible. That was the coolest car on the whole base at the time.

I recall that I sat in the back seat on the right side, and there were two other guys back there with me. Bobby Ray was sitting on the top behind me with one leg on either side of me and some other guy sitting back there next to him. I remember Bobby Ray putting out a "Yeeehaaa" as we started off down the mountain road.

From here on my memory is pretty fuzzy. I know we met one car coming up the mountain road and had to back up to a spot wide enough we could move over so he could pass us. I don't think the fresh air was doing much to sober me up.

Just before we reached the MP Company there was like a 90-degree turn in the road. The last thing I remember is Del La Rosa missing that turn and taking off across the field and Bobby Ray letting out another Yeeehaaa.

I don't know if I was knocked unconscious or just passed out but I vaguely remember waking up for a second or two on my bunk with a bunch of guys standing around and one saying the ambulance is on the way. After that I think I remember being put on a gurney and taken out to the waiting ambulance. The next thing I remember was waking up in the hospital in a bed next to Bobby Ray. I had a couple of bandages on my head and some scratches on my arms and legs. Nothing seemed to be broken. Bobby Ray looked pretty much the same except he didn't have any bandages.

Bobby Ray was still asleep when the nurse came in to take my temperature. "How long have I been here?" I asked before she stuck that thermometer in my mouth.

"About twelve hours now," she said as she took my blood pressure.

"Am I hurt?" I asked after she took that thing out of my mouth.

"Not bad, we are keeping you for observation. You may have a concussion."

"How about my friend over there, is he hurt?" I asked.

"Not any worse than you are. Apparently you were both very lucky. You rest now. I'll be back later."

That's what I love about hospitals; everybody is just so full of information to share.

Bobby Ray groaned and rolled over towards me and opened one eye. "Hey, man, you okay?" he asked.

"I think so; the nurse said I may have a concussion, whatever the hell that is. How about you?"

"That's what she told me, too. All I know is that I have one hell of a headache."

"Do you know what happened?" I asked.

"Del La Rosa missed that sharp turn down by the company and took off across the field and snapped a guide wire on one of the phone polls and finally stopped about 75 feet or so in the middle of the field."

"Did you get thrown off the back?" I asked.

"Hell, no…I rode that sucker all the way to the end, but when I looked down you were gone. I jumped off the car and just missed jumping on you."

"How did I get thrown out and you didn't?" I asked.

"Beats the hell out of me, but I must have passed out afterwards because the next thing I remember was riding in an ambulance and ending up here."

"Yeah, I remember that too. The nurse told me we had been here about twelve hours already but didn't say when we could leave. Did she tell you?"

"She didn't tell me shit except the doctor would be around later to talk to us," Bobby Ray replied.

"I got one hell of a headache; I think I'll try to sleep some more," I said.

"Me too," Bobby Ray mumbled.

I rolled over and closed my eyes. While I was trying to sleep I was going over the events of the past few hours. Let's see I thought, I attended my first official MP Corp function, got drunk, tired to make out with the 1st'Sgt's wife, got in a car wreck and ended up in the hospital. Not bad for your first party I thought as I drifted off to sleep.

FORT HUACHUCA
Chapter 25

Bobby Ray and I spent the night and the next two days in the hospital. The doctor had come around the first morning and told us both how lucky we were and they were going to keep us for a couple of days just to be sure we didn't have a concussion. Remember this was the old days when they didn't kick you out of the hospital two hours after major surgery like they do these days.

We didn't have anything to do but lie around all day. They had a reading room just down the hall we were free to visit. We would go down and look for something reasonably current to read or at least look at. Back in those days they had the same kind of magazines they have today; some sports magazines, some Field and Stream kind of stuff and a ton of those Teen heartthrob magazines.

Well, when you got right down to it, even though we were in the Army Bobby Ray and I were still teenagers and what are teenage boys most interested in? Why teenage girls naturally. Back in those days Sandra Dee and Annette Funicello were really hot. I must have really been into those dark haired, dark eyed Italian looking women because I thought Annette was really hot! It's funny how your taste changes over the years.

Having nothing better to do Bobby Ray and I decided to have a contest. We would each write to Sandra and Annette and see who got the most responses back first and who got the best response. I seem to recall there was a third girl in our little contest but not sure now who it was. It may have been Dodie Stevens. We asked the candy striper that ran around the hospital for some stationary and a pen and began to write our stories.

We wrote and told them we were in the army and how different it was and how we had just been in a terrible car accident and so on and so on. Of course we didn't mention being drunk at the time. We must have sounded pretty pathetic.

We were released from the hospital after the 3d day with a clean bill of health and told to report back to our unit. When we got back we reported to Koch's Detail only to find out we had been released from that duty. It was now around the first of October and the IG Inspection was nearly upon us. Our job now was to report back to our barracks and help get it ready for inspection and get our own uniforms and personal gear ready for inspection. Cleaning barracks was nothing new; basic training wasn't that far behind us. It was a little different cleaning an old WWII Barracks than those more modern up to date barracks we had been housed in during basic training. We had an NCO named Bannon who was the senior man living in the barracks. He had his own room upstairs, and he was in charge of us and responsible to be sure the barracks was ready for inspection.

Bannon wasn't hard to get along with; he had been through enough of these inspections apparently not to get overly excited. He gave us details and instructions and let us get after it. The big deal was the floor in the barracks. We moved bunks and footlockers every day and buffed the damn floor. But by the time the inspection came along you could see yourself in the shine on the floor.

A couple of days before the inspection we were to stand an in ranks inspection conducted by the Executive Officer, Captain Canfield. Nobody liked Captain Canfield, it wasn't anything he did; he just had a lousy personality and attitude. Word was he had been passed over for promotion for a third time which meant he was on his way out and wouldn't make major.

The day of the inspection we all fell out in our uniforms, hoping we met Cpt. Canfield's approval so we wouldn't get our ass chewed out and could get back to the barracks and out of this uniform. The platoon was sized with sergeants at the head of each squad. As it turned out Sgt. Koch was our squad leader. We were the Second Squad.

No one had gotten through Canfield's inspection unscathed so far. When Canfield got to Koch he looked him up and down and being the second man down from Koch I could hear the conversation between the two.

"How long have you been in the Army, Sgt. Koch?" Canfield asked.

"Almost twenty-four years," Koch replied.

"And in all those twenty-four years all you have earned is one good conduct medal?"

"No, sir," Koch said.

"Sgt. Koch, I want you to fall out of this formation and return to your room and come back when you have all your medals and ribbons on your blouse. Do you understand me, Sgt. Koch?"

"Yes, sir," Sgt. Koch saluted, took one step backwards, did a left face, and moved out to his room.

No one had noticed that Sergeant Koch was only wearing one little ribbon when we fell in for formation, and I doubt that anyone would have been surprised if they had.

Canfield continued his inspection. Everybody had something wrong. You had "ropes" or your shoes didn't shine, or your brass needed work. Everybody had something. Just as Canfield was about to finish up the 4th squad; I caught Sgt. Koch coming out of the barracks out of the corner of my eye. He walked around behind the formation and took his place as the Squad Leader of the 2nd Squad. I tried to sneak a peek at what he now had on his blouse but couldn't tell from my position in the formation.

When Canfield finished with the 4th Squad he returned to Sgt. Koch. Canfield's jaw almost hit the ground when he turned to face Koch. Sergeant Koch had more ribbons in one row than Canfield had on his whole chest. What he saw, we found out later, was a chest full of ribbons and medals on Koch's blouse. Koch had a Silver Star, a Bronze Star, and a Distinguished Service Cross for gallantry or bravery in battle against an enemy of the United States, and two Purple Hearts for wounds received in two different battles; and more medals that I never even heard of. To add insult to injury Koch held out his hand with a bunch of other medals in it and asked Canfield, "What do you want me to do with these medals, sir?"

Carfield didn't even dismiss the formation; he just turned and walked back to the Orderly Room. The platoon sergeant, SFC Rivera, dismissed the troops, and we all cracked up at Canfield's embarrassment and went over to shake hands with Koch. Koch didn't seem to take any pleasure out of our congratulatory antics at embarrassing Canfield and just moved through the crowd and went back to his room in the barracks.

I thought I understood a little better now knowing what Sergeant Koch had really done and been through in his military career why Sergeant Koch had a certain quality about him that despite his quiet demeanor and his drinking he seemed to draw a little more respect without demanding or asking for it. Sergeant Koch was a true Korean War hero. All of a sudden I felt a certain pride to be able to say I worked on Koch's Detail.

FORT HUACHUCA
Chapter 26

The week following our in ranks inspection we had the real thing. The IG Inspection Team was finally here. Every swinging dick was up at O dark thirty, that's like half hour before sun up. Everyone was running around getting their areas ready for inspection. If you had anything you weren't supposed to have you had better get rid of it. Either take it out and lock it up in your car if you had one, or for those of us that didn't they had a deuce and half sitting outside that everyone and anyone could put their illegal stuff on. Illegal stuff could be a record player or a radio, or too many civilian cloths or personal pictures you may have hanging on the wall near your bunk.

Bobby Ray had to take down the little mimeographed letter he had received from Sandra Dee. I had to take down my autographed picture of Annette and my little personalized card from Sandra with her signature on it. I was so proud. I kicked his ass on that contest. Of course I was most proud of the picture of Annette. He had received his letter first and was really rubbing my face in it; until I got my picture.

Hobart was the designated driver of this truck; his job once the truck was filled was to take it away from the company area and not come back until after the inspection was over. The company had a truck also so they could get rid of anything they weren't supposed to have, or didn't want to be inspected. I understood the motor sergeant had one truck all his own; seems he had more tires than Good Year. As I learned later on in my military career this was an accepted practice by almost any unit getting ready for an IG Inspection. Every unit had a junk trunk when it came inspection time.

We had been told we would not have an in ranks inspection but we were to stand by our bunks with foot lockers open and ready for inspection. I never saw so many people jumping through their asses in all my life. It seemed there was one sergeant for every couple of privates, and they were coming around every ten minutes or so to make sure your toothpaste and toothbrush hadn't moved in your foot locker tray since they were there last.

It seems we stood by our bunks forever. Finally about 1130 SFC Rivera came through and told us we could go to chow and that they were only going to inspect one barracks and they were already in 4th Platoon's barracks. We all let out a sigh of relief and headed for the Mess hall. Sergeant Rivera told us after we ate to take off and get out of the area and don't come back until about 1630.

Bobby Ray and I took our time eating and then having no way to go anywhere else we went down to the small PX and hung out. Marie didn't come to work for an hour or so yet so we just played the jukebox and drank a coke. I looked through some magazines they had in the magazine section. I found a picture of Annette and showed it to Bobby Ray from across the room. He shot me the finger.

Marie came in but she didn't seem to be in very good spirits. I asked her what was wrong; she said she thought she was getting her period. Now, I had heard that "term" a few times but wasn't exactly sure what it meant but didn't think I really wanted to go there so I just said, "Okay," and let it go at that. Finally 1630 rolled around, and Bobby Ray and I headed back to the barracks. Several of the guys were already back and were getting things back to....comfortable again. About 1700 Hobart showed up with the deuce and a half and guys went out and got their stuff off the truck.

Bobby Ray, Pederson, New York guy and I all walked over to the Mess hall and had supper and then went back to the barracks. It had been a really long and boring day but everybody was dead tired. The guy next to Bobby Ray put on some records. Some guys just laid back and listened some guys had places to go.

The following Thursday the first sergeant called us all over to the Orderly Room and true to his word he gave us all a three day pass starting on Friday. We didn't have to be back to the Company area until Monday morning. We were free as birds for the next three days.

Fort Huachuca is located not too far from the Mexican border, Nogales specifically. There are a couple of other border towns also near by but Nogales was supposedly "the place to go." Bobby Ray and I decided it was time to find out what the rest of the world outside the small PX and the USO was like. We were going to Mexico. New York guy as usual said he had plans, Hobart said he was going to visit friends in Tucson, a likely story, and Pederson was saving up for his wedding.

Bobby Ray and I decided we needed some new cloths for our big adventure so we spent Friday at the Main PX on post and did some clothes shopping. The Main PX didn't open until 1000 hours, so it was mid-morning before we even got in the store. Of course it didn't take that long to buy a new pair of jeans and a couple of shirts but we were trying to be picky. By the time we finished we hustled back to the Company and went straight to the mess hall for lunch.

When we got back to the barracks we started taking stock of our available funds and decided if we went down there on Friday we might be broke by Saturday. So we decided to just chill and go down on Saturday evening. The MPs provided what they called a "Border Patrol" section. These guys worked the border towns around Fort Huachuca. Their job was to first of all try to keep GIs out of trouble, secondly keep them out of Mexican jails if possible and thirdly bring those that got arrested and in trouble back to the base and release them to their respective units. Bobby Ray and I found out we could get a ride down to the border with them when they left in the evening about 1800 hours. Coming home was a different story, if they had a bunch of guys they had to bring back to their units and their van was full, then we were on our own getting home.

Saturday afternoon before we left New York guy came up to me and handed me $5.00 and asked me to buy him one of those switch blade knifes with a white handle. He said he heard you could get one for about three bucks, and I could keep the rest and have a couple of beers on him. I didn't ask him what he wanted the knife for; I knew several other guys had them so I agreed to pick one up for him. Why I agreed to do such a stupid thing I have no idea; and I didn't know what I would do with the other couple of dollars, I don't even like beer.

The ride down with the Border Patrol was uneventful. The guys were telling us places we could go and places to stay away from. One of them suggested we hide some money in our socks or somewhere just as a precaution. He said you never knew what might happen. We arrived at the Border, dismounted the van, the guys pointed us in the right direction and we headed across the border into Mexico. This was Bobby Ray's first trip into Mexico; I had crossed the border before back in high school but never told anyone about it.

Bobby Ray and I walked around Nogales, checking out the various shops and places to eat. We found a place that served hamburgers so we stopped in and got a burger and a coke. After we finished we continued to walk around the town and finally found El Mercado, The Market. In El Mercado there seems to be hundreds of little booths and shops; you can buy anything your little heart desires in El Mercado I think. Anyway this was a good place to find New York guy's knife he wanted, and you were expected to bargain for the best price. Nobody paid the asking price in El Mercado.

We finally found a little shop that had all sorts of knives and other such stuff for sale. I pointed to a switchblade knife like I wanted but told him I wanted one with a white handle. He didn't have one with a white handle so I turned to leave. He grabbed me by the arm and asked me to wait one minute. He rattled off something in Spanish to a little kid that was sitting there listening to a radio and the kid ran out of the shop. A couple of minutes later he returned with a white-handled switchblade knife.

"How much?" I asked.

"Ten dollars," the shop owner said.

I turned and started to walk out.

"Wait! I give you special deal $7.50," the dealer said.

"Three dollars is my best offer," I said.

"Five dollars." I turned to leave.

"Four dollars," I heard the dealer say.

I kept walking.

"Okay, okay, I give to you extra special deal, $3.50," the dealer offered.

"Three dollars, my best offer."

"Señor, I have family. You let me make a little money today no?"

I hate it when they pull that shit and make me feel guilty. "Okay, $3.50," I said.

The shop owner gave me an almost-toothless smile and said, "deal."

I took the knife and pushed the button a couple of times to make sure it worked and then stuck it in the hip pocket of my new jeans.

Finally the time had come, Bobby Ray and I had been as cool as we could be so far but we both were dying to get to "Boys Town." Please don't tell me I have to explain that to you. We asked a cab driver if he could take us to Boys Town, and he said no problem. We got in the cab and he drove us around a few blocks and as we rounded one corner you came into and area that was nothing but bars. The road was dirt and very wide. It kind of reminded me of riding into an old western town like Tombstone or something. There were some cars and lots of taxis parked along the sides of the wide dirt road. Bright lights glittered at us from every building along both sides of the street.

We gave the cabby a couple of bucks and got out at the first club we came to. There was a sidewalk running the length of the street; most of the clubs had built a porch with steps leading up to the main entrance. Out on the porch were girls; girls of every shape and size and age. There were GIs all over the place on the porch's and walking up and down the streets. Music was blaring out of every club. Occasionally you would see a uniformed Mexican policeman, sometimes you saw some guy wearing a gun and a badge but no uniform. I'm not sure what these guys were but they definitely weren't undercover cops.

Bobby Ray and I stuck our heads in a couple of clubs. Without fail we were greeted by a couple of ladies and I use that term loosely. Some clubs were very busy, with lots of customers and loud music. A couple of places even had a live band. Other clubs were almost dead. We got a lot of attention when we went in one of those places. One girl on each arm was the norm in the quieter places.

After making our way up one side of the street and down the other Bobby Ray and I finally decided on a place to stop, sit and have a drink. It was one of the quieter clubs so we drew a fair amount of attention from the young maidens that worked there. After we turned them all down when they asked us to buy them a drink they pretty much left us alone.

Bobby Ray and I sat there and discussed our options over a couple of beers. Okay, he had beer I drank some rum and coke, I hate beer. It had been a long, long, long time since I had had the attention of a woman but I just couldn't seem to get interested in anything I was seeing around this place. Bobby Ray on the other hand had an eye on this one little señorita that had managed to catch his attention when she was dancing by herself on the dance floor. I have to admit she was an exciting little dancer.

After she finished her dance she sat down a couple of tables in front of us. Bobby Ray decided he was going to talk to her. He finished his beer and ordered another one. He drank about half of that one and then made his move. He got up and walked up to the young "lady" and started talking to her.

There was a slow song on the jukebox and the little señorita got up and put her arms around Bobby Ray's neck and they began to dance. It appeared that everything was progressing rather well for Bobby Ray. Suddenly Bobby Ray gave her a rather hard push backwards and she stumbled and fell and let out a little yelp. Bobby Ray turned and started walking back to our table. He had to walk past me to get to his seat, and the señorita had gotten up off the floor and was headed for Bobby Ray with a small but heavy ashtray in her hand she had picked up off the table in front of us.

Now I have no idea who I thought I was or what I was doing, but I wasn't going to let this broad hit Bobby Ray with an ashtray, so like Wyatt Earp I stood up and whipped out New York Guy's white-handled switchblade knife and stuck it in señorita hot pants's face. She stopped, screamed, and ran out the door hollering, "Policia! Policia!"

They must have all been standing just outside the door waiting for her to scream because before I could do anything there must have been a dozen of 'em coming through the front door with their guns drawn. Most of 'em were those guys in civilian clothes. Obviously I was out numbered, out manned and out gunned and I didn't want a fight anyway and was about to piss in my pants. I took the knife stuck it in the table and broke the blade and put it down to show them I didn't have any bad intentions. Bobby Ray finished his beer.

One of the plain cloths guys who spoke some English came up and told us to come with him. I asked him where we were going, and he kept saying "Carcel," or something like that, but it didn't take much translation to understand he meant jail.

We ended up walking a few blocks down the street surrounded by this brigade of plain cloths cops until we came to a building with a sign out side that said "Policia." Yep. We were definitely going to a Mexican jail. They sat us down in a room with an old wooden desk and a few chairs and told us to sit and wait.

"What are we gonna do now?" Bobby Ray asked.

"How the hell should I know? I guess we wait and see what they do."

"Why did you pull that knife on that bitch?"

"She was gonna hit you in the head with an ashtray from the table," I said.

"Well, that little bitch. I shoulda punched her out."

"Why did you push her in the first place?" I asked.

"She wanted too much money and called me a cheap shit when I offered her less."

About this time, a uniformed officer, apparently with some rank, came into the room and sat down behind the desk and told us to sit. He spoke some English and asked us if we were soldiers at Fort Huachuca. We said we were and said we were being charged with disturbing the peace. He asked us if we had any money to pay our fines. Something in my mind one of the MP Border Patrol guys had told us on the way down clicked when he said that, and before Bobby Ray could open his mouth I said, "No, sir, we don't have any more money. We spent it all over in Boys Town. We were about to leave to get back to the bridge and catch a ride with the MP Border Patrol back to our Company."

The officer looked at us. "Are you both MPs?" he asked.

"Yes, we are, sir," I said.

"Do you have identification?"

"We are new men just recently assigned; we have our Military ID card and our mess hall pass that identifies us as members of the Military Police Company." Bobby Ray and I both presented our ID cards and mess hall passes.

The officer looked at our IDs, then got up and told us to wait here and walked out the door. Bobby Ray and I looked at each other and just waited.

Bobby Ray leaned over and whispered, "Why did you tell him we spent all our money? We still got the money in our socks."

"Didn't you hear what the guy in the van told us?"

"The Mexican police will arrest you and tell you you're being charged with an offense and want you to pay a fine but, actually they just want a pay off to let you go. If you tell them you don't have any money they will probably just hold you for a while and then call us and have us come pick you up unless it is something really serious."

"And you don't think threatening to cut a woman's throat is a serious offense?" Bobby Ray asked.

"Didn't you hear what that officer said when he first came in? We are being charged with disturbing the peace, not attempted murder or some shit. I think they are just looking for a payoff," I said.

A few minutes later the officer came back in.

"I have checked with the Military Police Border Patrol, and they verify your story that you are new men assigned to their company. Therefore I am releasing you to their custody. They will be here shortly to pick you up. In the meantime you will continue to wait here, and I would suggest you stay out of Boys Town; it is not a good place to be."

We thanked the officer for his kindness and understanding and waited quietly for the Border Patrol to arrive.

About twenty minutes later a couple of the MPs showed up, and we were ushered out and put in the back of the van and taken back to the border station to wait until they got off duty so we could get a ride back to the base. Hopefully they were going to have room for us; I wasn't really interested in spending anymore time in Nogales; at least not right now.

Bobby Ray and I sat around until the Border Patrol packed it in for the night and we started the ride back to the base. Everyone was pretty quiet on the trip home. I was wrapped up in my own thoughts. Let's see now, my first MP party I get drunk, try to make out with the 1st Sgt's wife, get in a car accident and end up in the hospital for three days. My first three day pass I go to Mexico, pull a knife on a prostitute, get arrested by the Mexican Police and held over in a Mexican jail until someone comes and bails me out. Not bad for my first four months in the Army. I wonder if they will let me re-enlist when this tour is up.

FORT HUACHUCA
Chapter 27

The boys from the Border Patrol assured Bobby Ray and me we didn't have anything to worry about as far as any punishment from the Company. They would never know anything about us being picked up by the Mexican Police and even if they found out since there were no charges pending they would just laugh it off. Apparently we weren't the first rookies to get their ass in a bind across the border.

The following week after our shortened three day pass we actually began doing some training in police work. We reported to the training NCO every morning in the training room and spent most of our time going over the various forms we would be exposed to while on duty and the proper way to fill them out.

We took one or two forms a week and went over them day after day. As we progressed we were given various scenarios in which we had to determine which forms we needed to fill out to complete the report. It didn't take long to figure out that after going over a particular form for a week that when it came time to work out a scenario you were more than likely going to use the form you just spent the past week on. As I found out; to be successful in law enforcement you had to be able to write a report, it also helped to be a good typist. If there was one course I took in high school that I really did get the full value out of for the rest of my adult working life it was typing. And to think I just took it because it was mostly a girl's course.

Since they were going to curtail training for the week of Thanksgiving; I requested leave over Thanksgiving. The Wednesday morning before Thanksgiving, I got a patrol to take me to the North Gate of the base and drop me off. I was dressed in my uniform and had a small tote bag with me. I stepped across to the other side of the highway and stuck out my thumb. Back in those days a soldier in uniform didn't have any problems hitchhiking around the country, or so I had been told.

My first ride was in a cattle truck headed for Tucson. I had never ridden in a big rig like that before and got quite a lesson in watching that driver shift those gears. I'd never seen anything like that before in my life. Somehow he wrapped his left arm through the stirring wheel and used both hands to shift two different gear shifts on the right. It wasn't the smoothest ride I ever caught, but it was interesting and the stingiest, and it got me to Tucson. From Tucson I got a ride with a nice couple all the way to El Paso, TX.

The couple was heading north out of El Paso and told me to just stay on this road and I'd be on the edge of town soon and would surely be able to pick up a ride on Hwy 80, which is now IH-20. I must have walked for an hour. Finally, I got far enough out of town that I could be seen and a hippie driving an old rag top convertible stopped and picked me up.

Convertibles weren't exactly built back then like they are today. The wind was blowing and whipping that top up and down and I thought it was going to blow completely off the car a couple of times. In addition to that it was getting dark and colder and the car didn't have a heater.

I thought my ride kept smoking these funny-smelling cigarettes to help keep warm and I never understood why he kept offering me a "hit" after I had already told him the first time I didn't smoke. It wasn't until a very long time afterwards that it suddenly dawned on me what that stuff was. Some cop I was gonna be.

About 0600 hours we finally pulled into the outskirts of Abilene. The hippie dude was driving on through to Dallas so I had him drop me off at South 1st and Sayles Blvd. I could walk to my grandparents' house from there. Back in those days we still had a family gathering at my grandparents' house every Thanksgiving and Christmas. That was the only times during the year that the whole family gathered together. My daddy was the oldest of seven children and with all of his brothers and sisters bringing their kids, my cousins, we had quite a turn out. Somehow my grandmother always managed to have enough food to feed us all. When I think about those days now I'm always amazed at what my grandmother could do in the kitchen. Maybe that's where my daddy got his kitchen skills.

I was one of the first to arrive at the house, which was not surprising since it was so early in the morning. I surprised everyone by being there; nobody was expecting me to be home. We spent most of the day at my grandparents', and then I went home with my mother and daddy. My old room was still there, only now it was more of junk room than a bedroom. I cleaned a spot off the bed to sleep in and didn't have a bit of trouble falling to sleep that night.

I spent the next couple of days driving around and seeing who was still in town. I saw Wayne and a couple of others that had come home for the holiday. They each brought me up to date on someone else. A couple had gotten married. One of our classmates had committed suicide. That kind of knocked the wind out of me. Even though I didn't know the guy very well; I don't know if you're ever ready to hear something like that when you're that young.

I stopped by the bowling alley and to my surprise there was Joe Eddie and a couple of the other guys. Joe Eddie had married some gal he had been dating when I was still in school, but I can't remember her name. It didn't take long to get in a pot game but I wasn't much competition having not bowled in so long and bowling with a house ball. I made a mental note to visit the base bowling alley more often when I got back and thought about taking my own ball back with me.

Joe Eddie told me they were planning a poker party at one of the local motels later on that night and invited me out to play. I told him I'd think about it. I really would have loved to have gone to play but I didn't think I could afford it at the time. Even though I was planning on hitchhiking back to Arizona I wanted to be sure I had some money on me just in case.

The next day my mother asked me when I had to take the bus back to Arizona. I had never told her I hitchhiked home. She didn't ask so I figured there was no need to tell her. When I told her I hadn't planned on taking a bus; I was going back the same way I got here by hitchhiking. She had a conniption. She said I was forbidden to hitchhike back.

I may have still been just an eighteen boy in her eyes but I was a soldier in the Army now and I wasn't living by her rules anymore. That was one reason I joined the Army to begin with. I turned to leave but before I could walk out the door she realized what she had said and asked if she could buy me a bus ticket back. I thought about it and decided that would be okay; I could stay in town another day and still get back to the base on time. Sometimes it's okay for an eighteen-year-old solider to compromise.

FORT HUACHUCA
Chapter 28

I got back to Fort Huachuca Sunday evening and took a base taxi to the Company area. All the guys were there; they asked how my leave was, and I gave 'em a quick rundown of my activities while I was gone. I could tell they were all expecting me to tell them about the girls back home. Unfortunately I didn't have any such stories to tell.

The next morning we all reported for duty in the training room. To our surprise they had five .45 caliber pistols lying out on our desk. Our class that day was to familiarize ourselves with the weapon by learning how to assemble and dissemble the .45 pistol. It didn't take long to learn, as I recall there were only about five pieces that you had to dissemble and put back together. We spent the week taking it apart and putting it back together again.

The following week we actually went to the firing range and fired the .45 caliber Pistol. Since there were only five of us qualifying we were able to take our time and got to fire more rounds than normally is fired by each individual during an annual weapons qualification. We spent two days on the range. This was the most exciting thing we had done since we got at Fort Huachuca, if you don't include Bobby Ray and me getting thrown in a Mexican jail.

Our next bit of training included standing inspection arms with the .45 caliber Pistol. We must have gone through the procedure for standing inspection arms with the .45 caliber Pistol a couple of hundred times. It's a very precise procedure and must be done in a definite order.

The procedure is for the MP being inspected to remove the weapon from his holster, raise the weapon to point it in an upward position by bending his right arm at the elbow. Then eject the clip from the magazine, place the clip in his waistband with his left hand. Then reach across with his left hand and pull the slide back, locking it in the open position this is to insure there are no rounds in the chamber of the weapon. Then remove the clip from his waistband and hold it in the palm of his left hand for the inspecting officer to inspect if he so desires. The MP will hold the weapon in his right hand about shoulder high with the open slide resting between his thumb and the fingers. The inspecting officer will remove the weapon from the MPs hand, inspect the weapon and then return the weapon in the same position he got it from the MP.

Now this is where things can get tricky if the MP is not paying attention to what he is doing. When you do enough of these inspection arms with a .45 they get to be automatic or should and since the MP is looking straight ahead during the time all this is going on he, as well as the other MPs in the detail get used to hearing rather than seeing the procedure. Each movement has a sound all its own. Perhaps the best way to describe it is to relate it to a music scale. When the MP receives his weapon back from the inspecting officer his first movement is to release the slide forward which would be like Do on the musical scale. The second movement is to pull the trigger and let the hammer fall forward, that would Re and the third movement would be to return the clip to the magazine that would be Mi. If you don't hear Do, Re Mi….hit the ground, because chances are the next thing you will hear will be a round going off. Usually the MP will get confused or just not think and place the magazine back in the weapon first and then release the slide, which automatically loads a round into the chamber. As soon as the MP pulls the trigger he will discharge a round. Hopefully the round will be shot straight into the air; but if the MP has lowered his arm or turned his hand there is a chance that round could hit someone standing in front or near the MP. Because of this possibility it is not a good idea to have inspection arms when you have an indoor Guard Mount.

After three days of practicing inspection arms and going over how to break the weapon down and cleaning our weapons and turning the weapons in to the armorer; the training NCO told us that tomorrow night we would all be going on duty with the midnight shift for On The Job Training (OJT). At last we were going to see some real MP duty. The training NCO told us to take the time between now and the time we were to report for duty and get our uniforms squared away.

Bobby Ray and I went to chow and then went down to the little PX and picked up some shoe polish and Brasso to clean our brass with and give Marie the good news. She was excited for us; she knew how long we had wanted to get to do something besides pulling company detail. She was in a good mood; apparently she had gotten over that period thing she was complaining about before.

Two nights later, the five of us reported to the parking lot behind the Orderly Room where they held Guard Mount. SFC Rivera was the Patrol Supervisor that night. We fell in formation in two columns since there were an extra five people standing Guard Mount tonight. SFC Rivera announced some assignment changes and told us who we would be paired with for the evening. I was paired with SFC Rivera. I wasn't sure if that was a good thing or a bad thing. He also announced that Captain Canfield was the MPOD and he would be conducting inspection, and there would be arms inspection. You could hear the guys moaning and groaning. I wasn't sure if it was because Captain Canfield was the inspector or because there was going to be a weapons inspection.

Captain Canfield came out of the Orderly Room; SFC Rivera called us all to attention and reported to Captain Canfield. Canfield stepped around Sergeant Rivera and moved to the first man in the first column followed by Sergeant Rivera. You could hear the movements of the MP preparing his weapon for inspection. As Canfield moved away you could hear the first MP recovering and putting his weapon back in the holster Do, Re Mi and the second MP preparing his weapon for inspection. I was the third man in the second column, Bobby Ray was to my left which made him second and Pederson was on my right, the second man in the column. When Canfield got to Pederson he did like he had been taught and had the weapon ready for inspection when Canfield turned to face him. Canfield took Pederson's weapon; Pederson dropped his hand and when Canfield was finished Pederson raised his hand and Canfield set the weapon back in Pederson's hand. That was the last thing that went right for Pederson. There was no Do, Re' Mi.

Pederson did exactly what you're not supposed to do; he put the magazine in the weapon and let the slide go forward but before he pulled the trigger he realized he had made a mistake but instead of keeping the weapon in a raised position and removing the magazine and returning the slide to the open position he dropped his hand slightly to look at the weapon and that's when the weapon discharged. We all hit the ground face down and covered our heads. Sergeant Rivera told Pederson to freeze and do not move. Rivera went over and pried the weapon out of Pederson's scared hands and cleared the weapon and gave us the all clear signal. We all got up off the ground, except Captain Canfield. He was lying flat on his back just behind Sergeant Rivera.

Rivera rushed over to look at Captain Canfield; we all went over to look. There was no blood or anything that we could see. Canfield stirred and groaned and sat up and reached for his head. One of the guys saw Canfield's saucer hat (that's what we called them) and picked it up and showed it to Sergeant Rivera. There was a small hole in the hat; if Captain Canfield had been two inches taller he would have had a hole in his head.

Sergeant Rivera helped Canfield up and gave him his hat. Canfield said he wanted that man relieved and for him to report to the Commanding Officer's office at 0800 hours in the morning and walked off towards the Orderly Room. Rivera told Pederson to turn in his weapon and return to the barracks and be in the commander's office at 0800. A very shaken and scared Pederson said, "Yes, Sergeant," and moved out to turn his weapon in. Sergeant Rivera kept the ammo clip with the rest of the rounds in it. Just as a precaution.

I think the rest of us were as scared as Pederson was initially but as the tenseness of the moment began to wear off, the guys started moving towards their sedans and you could hear some of them laughing and talking. You knew there were going to be stories flying all over the company before morning.

Sergeant Rivera, as the Patrol Supervisor wasn't restricted to where he went on base as other patrols were assigned to specific patrol areas; so I got to see the whole base. As the Patrol Supervisor, Rivera was only called to scenes when a patrol needed help in some way. We spent a lot of the night in the station as Sergeant Rivera went over reports his patrols had initiated and worked on other things he was responsible for such as the duty roster for the men assigned to his platoon.

Before we were relieved Sergeant Rivera took me down to a five way intersection on post. It was a regular four way intersection with one additional road leading into it. We pulled over to the side of the road and parked. There is or was a place on Fort Huachuca that was some kind of Intelligence building. It employed a large number of civilian and military personnel. The rush hour traffic was tremendous. One of the duties performed by the Military Police back in those days was traffic control. Shortly after we arrived another unit showed up and parked on the other side of the road. I recognized the MP that got out of the sedan, his name was Jones, and everyone called him Jonesy. He was a sharp looking MP. His uniform was tailored and his boots were highly shined. His white hat had what we called a "saddle" in it. A very deep saddle. (Think of a horse saddle to get the idea). Jones picked up what appeared to be a large barrel cut in half and painted yellow and black and carried it to the middle of the intersection. He stepped up on the drum, put on his sunglasses and his white gloves and with his whistle stuck in his mouth; took control of the traffic passing through this five way intersection.

As I was later to learn, even a regular four-way intersection can be difficult to direct traffic at, so after watching Jonesy direct the traffic at this five-way intersection during a rush-traffic hour I was very impressed. Sergeant Rivera told me that Jonesy was the best there was at directing traffic through this intersection, and there were only three or four MPs that they let direct traffic at this intersection, and if I could ever handle this traffic I could direct traffic anywhere. I kind of got the impression that SFC Rivera wanted me to be one of those guys he could use here.

We watched until we got the call on the radio that the new shift supervisor was at the station. We drove back to the station and Sergeant Rivera briefed the new Patrol Supervisor and then we drove the sedan back to the company area. Sergeant Rivera had me drop him off at the Orderly Room and told me to take the sedan down to the motor pool wash it off, turn it in and come back to the Company, turn in my weapon and then I was relieved.

By the time I got back to the barracks, everyone else was already back and getting ready to sack out. I noticed Pederson's bunk was made and he was nowhere to be seen so I assumed he was in the commander's office. I got undressed hung up my uniform and crawled in bed. So now I had actually pulled my first tour of duty as an MP. With the exception of Jonesy's display of traffic control and Captain Canfield almost getting shot it was really a pretty boring tour.

Pederson got off with a written reprimand from the Commanding Officer. Everybody who had anything to say about the incident agreed it was a rookie accident and that Pederson knew the proper procedures and just blew it. Captain Canfield wasn't too happy from what I understand but other than having to buy a new hat he wasn't hurt and even he understood the risk. I know from that day on as long as I was there he never had inspection arms at Guard Mount again.

It was Christmas time already. During the Christmas, New Year holiday period the Company was divided; half got off over Christmas and the other half got off for New Years. I asked for and got Christmas off. I went home for Christmas, this time I took a bus because it was cold and I didn't want to get stuck out on the road in bad weather.

I reported back for duty two days after Christmas and was on duty the next day. We worked every day until about the 3rd of January and then Sergeant Rivera got the schedule back to normal. The whole post had been pretty dead during the entire holiday period, so there wasn't a lot of action as far as police work was concerned. A few drunken soldiers to deal with; that was about the extent of our activity plus some items reported stolen; mostly from people's cars.

One of the many papers you fill out when you do all the in processing is called a "Dream Sheet." If you're stationed in the states you list your top three choices of overseas assignments; and visa versa if you're stationed overseas. I remember that my first choice for an overseas assignment was Germany; I think my second was France and I don't recall what the third one was.

Just after we got back to normal shift rotation in January I got called over to the Orderly Room and the Company Clerk told me that I had orders for Germany and my reporting date was in February. I was authorized 30 days leave and seven days travel time to Fort Dix, NJ for further processing to my next duty assignment overseas. If I was going to take 30 days leave I should have been packing my bags the day they told me I had orders; but I didn't have 30 days of leave on the books so I opted for 15 days leave plus the seven days travel time. As it turned out all five of us eventually got orders for Europe but we didn't all leave at the same time. Bobby Ray was scheduled to leave about a week after me. After that I don't remember who left next or exactly where they were going except we were all going to Germany.

About the middle of January I signed out of the 512th MP Company. After being assigned there for approximately six months I had pulled approximately six weeks of MP duty. I really didn't feel too comfortable or prepared in going to another unit with no more training than what I had. But I was excited about going to Europe; one of the reasons I joined the Army was to travel and see some of the world. Despite my reservations about my training I was looking forward to seeing another part of the world.

IN TRANSIT
Chapter 29

I spent my leave at home before departing for Germany. My mother wasn't happy about me leaving the country. My daddy as usual didn't have much to say one way or the other.

Just as I had done before I went around looking for kids I had gone to school with or hung out with. Not surprisingly Joe Eddie and his crew was the one that was there to hang out with. We bowled. I did better this time than I did the last time I was home. I got in some practice and had my own ball to bowl with.

Bobby Ray and I talked on the phone a couple of times after he got home. He was anxious to get started he wanted to get on over to Germany. I was getting kind of antsy about it too and was ready to get on with it. My two week leave was about up and all I had left was the seven day travel time to Fort Dix, NJ. So I had to be seriously thinking about moving out and getting to Fort Dix anyway.

I had told Bobby Ray in passing conversation that we were going to have a poker party at a place called the Thunderbird Lodge out on highway 80 later on this evening and it would probably be an all night party. Since a good majority of my family worked there, and I spent most of my summers and other times working there, I would get us a room for the game. If we played at the Thunderbird I always got the room when I was home because I could get it for nothing. In jest I told Bobby Ray he should drive down and join in.

I got us a room that evening after everyone else in my family that worked there had gone home. I could get the desk clerk to give us a room and not have to register. There was Joe Eddie, a kid named Bennie, Mousey, I'm not sure I ever knew his real name, Jerry and some guy I really didn't know. That made six of us, a good number for a poker game. We used the bed for the table and pulled up whatever chairs were available and a couple of us would sit on the bed.

Joe Eddie's girlfriend, now his wife, and a friend of hers went out and got us some food and drinks, and there was an ice machine right down the hallway, so we were all set. The game started around 7:30 p.m. and was well under way at midnight, when there was a knock on the door. Everything and everyone just stopped; no one was expecting anyone. Since I was technically the occupant of the room I was designated to answer the door.

I opened the door, and in walked Bobby Ray and a friend of his. I know I had invited him down but didn't really expect him to show up. Actually Bobby Ray hadn't come to play; he had come to pick me up. We had already decided we were going to hitchhike to Fort Dix and it made sense to start from Dallas rather than Abilene.

I figured this was a good way for me to get out of the game a winner. Usually if you played all night you had spurts when you win and lose and if you were losing just before the game was to end; chances are you were gonna leave a loser. Just before Bobby Ray had arrived I had been on a winning streak so it was a good time for me to leave.

I told the rest of the guys what the plan was and that I was on my way to Germany. They all shook hands and wished me luck. I told them to be sure and clean up the room some before they left or we would never get another one. They assured me they would...yeah right.

Bobby Ray and his friend drove me to my house. I went in and grabbed my duffle bag and other little tote bag, woke up my parents and told 'em I was leaving, and I was gone. While his friend drove Bobby Ray and I talked until we got tired and fell asleep. We got into Dallas about five in the morning and got to Bobby Ray's house about 0530.

We unloaded my stuff from his friend's car. His friend whose name I don't remember shook hands all around and took off. Bobby Ray and

I went inside and washed up a little bit to get the sleep out of our eyes; then Bobby Ray grabbed his sister's car and we went to some café not far from his house and had breakfast. After breakfast we went back to Bobby Ray's house and it wasn't long before we were both sound asleep.

We slept most of the day away. I think we both woke up about 1700. Bobby Ray figured we would hit the road in the morning and he wanted to go out tonight and say goodbye to some of his friends. We showered and shaved and slipped into some civilian clothes probably for the last time for a while and headed out the door. This time Bobby Ray had someone else's car, I didn't bother to ask whose. We stopped and got a burger and fries and a large Dr. Pepper.

After we ate, Bobby Ray headed to this club he knew where most of his friends would probably be. It was pretty much a honkytonk joint; there was a live band playing some crying in your beer music and a few couples on the floor doing some two stepping, or something close anyway. Bobby Ray and I weren't exactly dressed for that kind of place but it didn't seem to matter. Bobby Ray found a few friends and we joined them. He talked to his friends and I watched the dancers and chatted with some gal sitting in the booth next to ours. When they played a slow song I asked her to dance and she accepted. After the dance I bought her a beer and we moved to a table so we could sit and talk. She was a pretty nice girl but today I can't even remember her name. I know it was something Jo…Betty Jo….Billie Jo…Mary Jo….or something like that.

Bobby Ray and I didn't stay out too late; we were back at his house by 2300. We re-packed our duffle bags, checked our dress greens (that's what they called 'em back then, I don't think the Army even has that uniform today.) to make sure they were all ready to go and made sure we had our long johns out and our overcoats on the top of our duffle bags. Shortly after midnight we were both in bed. I didn't fall asleep right away, my mind was already in Germany and I was really looking forward to getting there.

The next morning Bobby Ray's friend came by and picked us up and by 0900 we were standing on the side of the road of I-40 with our thumbs sticking out in the air. We weren't there 10 minutes before some guy headed for St Louis stopped and picked us up. St Louis wasn't on our map but the guy said he had to make a stop in Memphis first and that worked for us. The guy was some kind of sales rep. He was a friendly sort and talked and talked and talked. He said he was in the Air Force and wish he had stayed he would have been retired by now. He was trying to talk his kid in to going into the military but the kid didn't want any part of it. We stopped to eat around Little Rock, AR and the guy bought Bobby Ray and me some lunch. Traveling in uniform did have its benefits. And at least it wasn't a ham sandwich he fed us.

We got into Memphis about 1530 that afternoon. The guy was going to push on to St. Louis but dropped us off on I-40. We only waited about 30 minutes and a truck driver stopped and picked us up and said he was headed for Nashville. We hopped aboard and were headed for Nashville.

By the time we hit Nashville it was getting late. Bobby Ray and I decided we would find a motel to spend the night in and get started again the next morning. The truck driver was headed south out of Nashville so he dropped us off on IH-40 just outside of Nashville at a truck stop and there were some motels in the area. We went in the truck stop got something to eat and then picked out a motel, checked in; played a few hands of gin rummy and then sacked out.

Bright and early the next morning, Bobby Ray and I were up, showered and shaved and sitting in the truck stop eating breakfast. The truck stop surprisingly was pretty empty we were hoping maybe to pick up a ride with another truck driver. But fate had other plans for us that day I guess. Since there were no rides we got back out on IH-40. Our plan was to catch a ride to Knoxville and then on up through Virginia and West Virginia then into Philadelphia then on over to Fort Dix.

But like I said fate had something different in mind for us that day. As we stood out on the highway with our thumbs stuck in the air; this brand new 1960 Cadillac pulled over and this pretty little brunette stuck her head out the window and asked us where we were headed. Bobby Ray and I both knew right then we were headed wherever they were going as long as it was in a basically east by northeast direction.

We told them we were headed for Fort Dix, NJ and really didn't care how we got there as long as it didn't take more than three days. They said they were headed up through Kentucky and into Ohio on their way to Albany, NY. Without consulting our map, Bobby Ray and I decided that was close enough so we threw our duffle bags in the trunk and piled into the back seat of the Caddy.

The little brunette was named Jenny. Emily was the driver; she was also Jenny's mother. I would have never taken them for a mother/daughter team. To me they looked more like sisters. But then what the hell did I know. This trip started off being fun from the beginning. Both Jenny and Emily were very talkative and asked a lot of questions. Not only was it a fun trip, I learned something that I found to be true for the rest of my life. Women have very tiny bladders and have to stop about every fifty miles to go to the bathroom.

We passed through Louisville, KY and Cincinnati, OH and rolled on in to Columbus, OH. Somewhere between Cincinnati and Columbus Emily let me drive the Caddy. Back in those days that was one smooth ride. Somehow she ended up sitting in the front seat with me while I was driving and Jenny ended up in the backseat with Bobby Ray. There were periods that things got kind of quiet in the backseat and I couldn't help but check out the rear vies mirror. Now I know Emily couldn't help but notice that too but she didn't seem to mind. She just kept talking to me asking me about my home town, if I had a girlfriend waiting on me back there and so and so and so.

We finally pulled into Columbus and found a little motel with a restaurant right next door to it. And we decided to spend the night there. Bobby Ray and I got a room and Emily and Jenny got their own room. We agreed to clean up and meet at the restaurant in about an hour. I couldn't help but notice Bobby Ray had this shit-eatin' grin on his face the whole time we were getting ready for dinner.

When we got to the restaurant the girls were already there at booth, Jenny on one side and Emily on the other. That was a surprise but not the only one to come during the evening. Bobby Ray slide in beside Jenny and that only left a place left next to Emily for me to sit. Not that I minded, I was just a little nervous. The girls had already studied the menu and knew what they wanted, it took Bobby Ray and I a minute to decide. As it turned out we all ordered the meatloaf with mashed potatoes and choice of veggies with ice tea.

We ate slowly and enjoyed our meal. When we were finished Emily and I sat and talked about anything and everything. While we were talking Emily put her hand on my leg and I gotta tell ya...I really didn't know what I was supposed to do about that...so I just decided to do nothing. After a spell Emily said she wanted to go for a walk around the pool area and walk off some of what she ate and asked me if I would go with her. I said sure but had to take a few sips of my water first until I felt comfortable standing up. I finally got up and Emily slid out of the booth. Jenny and Bobby Ray were going to stay and have some dessert. Emily put $40.00 on the table and said that should cover everything, and she took my arm, and we walked out.

We walked around the pool area of the motel for a few minutes then she said she was getting cold and needed to go get a sweater and asked me to come with her. Who was I to argue? We got to her room which was just a couple of doors down from mine and Bobby Ray's. As we entered the room she excused herself to use the bathroom and I just sat down on the edge of the bed. When she came out of the bathroom that blouse she was wearing wasn't there anymore, and there was no sweater either. In fact there was nothing but bare skin...lots of nice soft, smooth, sweet-smelling bare skin.

I didn't see Bobby Ray until the next morning. When I woke up Emily was on the phone but she hung up before I could hear anything. She leaned over and gave me a kiss and said I probably should get back down to my room and put my cute little uniform back on. So I got up slipped on my jeans and headed for my room. I passed Jenny on the way; she was headed back towards her room.

Bobby Ray still had that shit-eatin' grin on his face when I got back to the room; he had already showered and shaved so the bathroom was open for me. I did my shower and shave thing and got dressed. We met the ladies back at the restaurant and ordered some breakfast. As soon as we were done we were on the road again.

Things were kind of quiet for a while, but eventually things got back to being fun again. This time I sat up front with Emily and Jenny sat in the back with Bobby Ray. It was hard to keep from looking in the back seat. But then as the temperature in the car got warmer that skirt Emily was wearing kept working its way up her legs and that helped keep my eyes out of the back seat for the most part. Except for that one time when I happened to glance back and all I could see was the top of Jenny's head. Emily must have been checking out the rear view mirror, she had a little smile on her face and I suddenly realized she wasn't wearing any nylons or anything else that I could see.

We stopped somewhere in PA. and got some lunch.... Emily said she was tired and asked Bobby Ray if he wanted to drive for a while. Of course Bobby Ray agreed, so he and Jenny climbed in the front and Emily and I got in the back. I thought Emily was really tired; we had only gotten down the road a few miles when she lay down and put her head in my lap. Suddenly I knew she wasn't really all that tired after all. Bobby Ray stayed on 76 clear across the state right into Philly. It was about 1930 when we hit the outskirts of Philly. The original plan was the girls would take us into Philly and we could take the bus on over to Fort Dix. By the time we got to Philly they had decided they had time to take us on over to Fort Dix which suited the hell out of Bobby Ray and I.

We stopped somewhere in Philly and got some gas before we crossed over into New Jersey. Emily got back behind the wheel, I climbed in the front next to her and Bobby Ray and Jenny got in the back. Emily didn't have any trouble finding Fort Dix. We arrived at the main gate; Bobby Ray and I showed the MP our orders and he gave Emily a Temporary Pass and directions as to how to get to the building for overseas arrivals.

Emily drove us down to the building pulled up in front got out and opened the trunk for us so we could get our duffle bags and other stuff out of the car. Both Emily and Jenny gave us a kiss good bye and Jenny had given Bobby Ray an address he or we could write too. We stood out front of the building and watched the girls drive off. When they were out of sight, Bobby Ray and I picked up our bags and walked in the building. Neither of us said anything, whatever thoughts we were having; we were keeping them to ourselves for the time being. Next stop...Germany.

IN TRANSIT
Chapter 30

Once again we found ourselves in a processing/holding pattern while Bobby Ray and I were at Ft Dix. There are two processing centers; one for those returning from overseas and those going overseas. Actually there wasn't much you did on an individual basis as far as processing to go overseas. Bobby Ray and I reported in and handed over a couple hundred copies of our orders. (It really wasn't that many, it just seemed like it). Then we were given a barracks assignment and told to change into fatigues. We were also told there would be three formations a day after each meal and we had better not miss a formation otherwise we might miss our flight.

There was a senior NCO assigned to each barracks. His job was to assign us to various details between each formation. We might be assigned to the shipping and receiving section which required loading and unloading baggage and/or crating up baggage to be sent wherever it was headed. You might be assigned Fire Watch Duty. This was not a good duty to be assigned. You didn't just watch for fires. It was a night time detail and required you to go around to each barracks on a routine basis and stoke the coal burning heaters that provided heat for each of the barracks. If you were on Fire Watch Duty you were assigned to a special barracks just for those that pulled fire watch. This was so we could sleep during the day since we were working at night. I had this duty for exactly one night then they transferred me out I kept letting the damn furnaces go out. That's one way to get out a detail.

I was put back in the barracks with the regular detail guys still awaiting my flight schedule. This was the place Bobby Ray had been assigned when we first reported in two days ago. Bobby Ray told me after our first morning formation together that he was assigned to the shipping and receiving section and that is where he was to report. I also learned that the barracks NCO had received his flight schedule and was leaving the following day; which meant when he left a new barracks NCO would be assigned. It occurred to me that the new barracks NCO would not be familiar with who was assigned where. I had a plan.

The next morning after those that were shipping out had been notified when and where to be the new barracks NCO started calling out names for assignments. If you already had a permanent assignment you were supposed to tell him. So when he called my name which was right after Bobby Ray's I said the same thing he did and started walking off behind Bobby Ray. Bobby Ray turned around and looked at me like I was crazy.

"What the hell are you doing?" Bobby Ray asked.

"I'm getting out of any other shit details, I hope."

"But now you have to report to Shipping and Receiving."

"I don't have to. I can duck out and go up to the main cafeteria and hang out. Why don't you come with me?"

"And then what happens when Shipping and Receiving calls asks where I am?"

"I'm betting they don't call. I bet they just assume you got your orders and left," I said.

I told Bobby Ray, "Look at all the guys they got around this place. They can't possibly keep up with 'em all; that's why they have three formations a day so they can be sure you'll get your flight instructions."

"Okay...what the hell? Let's go to the main cafeteria," And away we went all the way up that frozen ass hill to the main cafeteria.

We made the noon formation and they told me I was to report to a Sergeant Somebody at some building at 1400 hours. So after the formation I started asking around if anyone else had ever had to go see this guy. I couldn't find anyone who had ever been told to go see him so I didn't have a clue as to what I was going for. All they told me it was for an interview.

At 1400 hours on the dot I reported to this sergeant whose name I don't remember. I walked to his office door, knocked and when he looked up I said, "Private Shepard reporting as directed, Sergeant." He motioned me in and just looked at me for a long time. Then he got up out of his chair walked around the chair beside it and then walked around me. "How tall are you?" he asked.

"I am about six feet two, Sergeant," I replied.

"And how much do you weigh?"

"I weigh about 165 pounds, Sergeant."

"That's good, very good. Have you ever had any drill-team experience?" he asked.

"No, Sergeant," I replied.

"You think you could learn?"

"I think I could, Sergeant," I said.

"You have been sent up here for this interview because you meet the physical criteria we are looking for in your MOS (Military Occupational Specialty) for assignment to the 529th MP Honor Guard Company at Heidelberg, Germany. This elite unit provides security for the commanding general of USAEUR. You will be performing honor guard duties at various functions for visiting dignitaries. Do you think you can perform these types of duties?"

Saying no didn't seem like a wise option at the moment; so without hesitation I said "Yes, Sergeant."

The sergeant dismissed me and said he would notify the proper people in personnel to insure that I got orders for the 529th MP Company. I was dismissed and told to return to my unit.

I returned to the main cafeteria and met up with Bobby Ray and some other missing in action personnel we had met up there the day before. I told Bobby Ray about my interview and he was wondering if he would get interviewed since we both have the same MOS. I told him I didn't have a clue. But I was pretty sure by the questions the sergeant had asked me about my height and weight that Bobby Ray wasn't what they were looking for, Bobby Ray was about 5-6 inches shorter and kind of stocky.

At the evening formation, Bobby Ray got his flight schedule. He was flying out the next morning. He was told to report right back here at 0500 in the morning where he would be put on a bus and taken to the air terminal for departure for Germany. Bobby Ray was excited he was leaving even though he still didn't have a specific unit assignment in Germany. I was hoping I would get my orders the next morning.

Two days later I was still dodging the barracks NCO waiting for orders. Finally at the next morning formation I got my notice. I was leaving that very evening and was told to report back here at 1800 hours with bag and baggage. Now I was excited. I went to the barracks and began repacking my duffel bag again and getting my dress green uniform ready to wear. I really wanted to take a nap but I was afraid I would miss my formation and I certainly didn't want to do that.

Finally 1800 hours rolled around and I and several others were standing outside the Orderly Room when a big 36 passenger bus rolled up. We were told to load our gear in the compartments below and be sure we got our names checked off the list as we boarded the bus. About 1830 we were all on the bus and the driver closed the doors and we were off to McGuire, AFB for departure to Germany. It was only about a 12 mile ride but it seemed longer. Once we got there we went straight to the plane boarded along with some other folks that obviously came from some place else because they weren't on the bus with me. I grabbed an isle seat next to a guy I had been talking to at the cafeteria. When the plane was full, they closed the doors and we taxied out to the runway and without much delay we were in the air.

Back in those days you could still smoke aboard an aircraft once it was in the air so when the smoking light came on everyone that smoked didn't hesitate to light up, and when the kid next to me offered me a Salem cigarette I made the biggest mistake of my life and took it.

IN TRANSIT
Chapter 31

The flight was alive with conversation initially. Guys getting acquainted with each other and generally smoking and joking. The guy next to me was from somewhere in Georgia and was going to be assigned to an infantry unit. I told him I was going to the 529th MP Company and what the sergeant back at Fort Dix told me about the unit. Tommy, that was the guy's name, ask me how I got an assignment like that and I told him I had no idea, this sergeant just had me report to him for an interview and asked me some questions and said I was going to this unit.

The chatter settled down some as time passed. About 2100 hours they came through offering us a snack. Somehow I knew what it was they were offering and sure enough I was right….a friggin' ham sandwich! The only difference was this time you had a choice of milk or a soda. Just to be defiant I took the coke. After we ate, Tommy offered me another cigarette and I took it. We pretty much sat in silence and smoked our cigarette and after I finished I drifted off to sleep.

Sometime before daylight we landed in the Azores Islands which are located in the northern Atlantic Ocean. The plane had to refuel and we were allowed to disembark the aircraft and move around the small terminal. I bought a coke and stepped outside. It was still too dark to really see anything but I got the impression that there must be mountains around us. Tommy found me and we had a cigarette and drank our cokes before we got back aboard the plane I figured if I was going to smoke I might as well have a pack of my own so I went back is side the terminal and bought a pack of Salems. The addiction was on.

We re-boarded the aircraft and were in the air and on our way again within minutes. Most of the guys settled in and went back to sleep. I was awakened by a gentle nudge on the shoulder and the stewardess was asking me if I wanted breakfast. I still wasn't awake but I looked out the window and noticed we seemed to be flying into day light. I looked back at the stewardess who was still asking me if I wanted breakfast. I should have known better but I was hungry and I said yes. She reached down put my tray down and set a little plastic thing of scrambled eggs, which I just knew were powdered, and some limp-dicked-lookin bacon that I wasn't even sure was cooked; and some soggy toast. But again I had a choice of beverage, coffee or milk. I never did and still haven't learned to appreciate the taste of coffee so I chose the milk. Tommy was already awake and had a look on his face like a Georgia bulldog that hadn't been fed in a week.

I put all the salt and pepper I could get out one of those little packs on my eggs and even used Tommy's pepper since he wasn't using it. I managed to get the eggs down but I was having a problem with the bacon. The milk wasn't bad if you didn't try to taste it and just poured right down your throat. After breakfast, I lit up the first cigarette out of my very own pack. I couldn't help it the cigarette was best part of the whole breakfast.

Somewhere along the way we flew over the coast of France and I couldn't help but wonder if we were over Omaha Beach or Normandy Beach or one of those other beaches that had been made so famous in war movies of WWII. It seems like it only took minutes before the pilot was announcing we would be landing at Rhein-Main AFB outside Frankfurt, Germany.

We touched down in Germany and the plane taxied up near the terminal. We disembarked the aircraft and were loaded directly onto waiting buses. I'm not sure where we went after we got on the busses but I'm positive we left the confines of the base and were in or near downtown Frankfurt, Germany when we finally got off the busses.

We were ushered into a large auditorium and given a welcome orientation and briefing on things to do and not do while in Germany. This must have lasted over an hour. After the orientation we were given a ten minute smoke break out in the hall way and then told to walk down to the end of the hall and around the corner wait to be called by one of the Personnel Specialist who would continue our in-country processing. Just what I needed more processing. What I really needed to do was find a latrine.

After my smoke break and on my way down the hallway I found a latrine and took a short detour. Now that I felt better I continued on down to the end of the hallway and took my place in line. It didn't take long and I was called into the processing room. A Sp4 (Specialist 4th Class) called my name, pointed me to a desk and told me to have a seat. He sat down and asked me for copies of my orders; looked at me, looked at some paper work he had and filled out a couple of forms and told me to report to building such and such which was out the back door and to the right. I would stay there for tonight and then after chow in the morning report back to him by 0800; I would probably be moving out to the 529th tomorrow sometime.

I walked out the door with my bags and found my way to the building he told me to. There were already other guys in the barracks so I just grabbed the first empty bunk and sat down and lit a cigarette. I was looking forward to getting this trip over with.

I didn't go to the Mess hall that day; there was a small snack bar and PX across the courtyard from where we were staying and a bunch of us went over there and grabbed a hamburger and some fries. Somehow it seemed funny to be eating a hamburger and French fries in Germany. I guess I was expecting sauerkraut and Bratwurst or something.

The next morning we were awakened about 0530 and told the Mess hall would be serving at 0600 and if we had appointments that morning we had better get on with it if we wanted to eat. We climbed out of our bunks and headed for the showers. Naturally there weren't enough showers for everyone at one time so while some showered others shaved or otherwise took care of business. It reminded of basic training all over again.

The Mess hall was not inside this little compound we were in but down the street a couple of blocks. Several of us headed in that direction together; it was a foggy morning and not being familiar with German driving customs and so forth it was an interesting little trip to the Mess hall. When we came to the first intersection the light was red so we all stopped to wait for the light. We didn't notice that we, the GIs were standing a couple of feet in front of all the German Nationals. As far as we knew we were standing behind the white line. What we didn't realize was that the white line we were standing behind, defined the outer edge of a bicycle lane. We weren't there long before we heard this Zing! Zing! Zing! Zing! Coming from our left and before we could get out of the way we were surrounded by a million bicycles, okay, maybe it wasn't a million but it sure as hell seemed like it....they just kept coming and the best alternative we had was to just stand perfectly still and hope we didn't get run over. Some of the bicyclers had to stop to avoid hitting us; and the next thing I knew we had a multiple bicycle wreck. I think I was glad I didn't understand a word of German yet. The German Nationals back on the curb where they should be were laughing their ass off. Finally the light changed and we beat feet across the street and didn't look back.

It was another consolidated mess hall, and there were a lot of people being fed at this facility. We got through the line and found a place to sit. We didn't linger longer than one cigarette; we had to get back to the barracks, field strip our bunk and keep our appointments if we had one. Getting back to the barracks was safer than the trip to the mess hall; we knew where not to stand this time.

I got back to the barracks, field stripped my bunk and tossed the linen in the bin they had marked "used linen" at the end of the barracks. I grabbed my duffel bag and headed for my appointment. It was only about 0730, but I definitely didn't want to be late. It was about a fifteen-minute walk, and when I got there the Sp4 motioned me right in. He gave me some papers and told me to give them to the Company Clerk at the 529th when I got there.

"Now here are your tickets; do NOT lose them. You will have to have them when you get to the Bahnhof," the SP4 said.

"What's a Bahnhof?" I asked.

"That's the train station. You'll be taking a train from here to Heidelberg."

"I'm gonna take a train to Heidelberg?" I asked.

"Yes, that is correct."

"How do I get to the Bahnhof and how do I know when to get off at Heidelberg?" I asked. I was getting a little nervous here.

"You can take a taxi to the Bahnhof. It will cost you about four marks."

"What's a mark?" I asked

"A mark is German money. Four marks is about a dollar; if you don't have any German money just give the taxi driver a dollar bill. That will be enough," the SP4 told me.

"Okay, so how do I know when to get off the train?" I asked.

"When you get on the train the conductor will come around to check your ticket, just tell him then you need to get off in Heidelberg; he will tell you when you get there."

"Okay, I just have one more question; when I get to the Bahnhof, how do I know what train to catch?"

The Specialist took my ticket and showed me a number and told me that was the number of my train; all I had to do was check the schedule they had posted in the Bahnhof and find out what track it was leaving on, and I would be on my way. He also pointed to the time next to the train number and told me that was the time my train left and I had better not be late. I found out during my tour in Germany that was one of the best pieces of advice I ever got. You could set your watch by the German trains; they leave on time, every time.

"Okay, you got it all now?" the Sp4 asked.

"I think so," I replied.

"You have about four hours before your train leaves. So just watch your time and remember, do not be late. It's about a twenty-minute ride from here to the Bahnhof."

"Oh, I have just one more thing. Where do I catch a taxi?"

"Just step out on the street. They are all over the place. They hang out around here a lot because they know GIs need a ride."

"Thanks," I said.

"You're welcome. Have a good tour."

I grabbed my duffel bag and walked out to the front of the building. Not that I didn't believe the Specialist but I just wanted to see all these taxis for myself. I leaned my duffel bag up against the building lit up a cigarette and observed. The specialist was right; there were taxis all over the place.

After I finished my cigarette I grabbed my bag and walked back to the little snack bar, since I had a few hours to kill I figured that would be as good a place as any. Besides I needed another pack of cigarettes. As I sat in the snack bar sipping on a coke and smoking cigarettes it occurred to me just how far I was from Texas and home. I joined the army to travel and see the world and be out on my own. Well, I got my wish; here I was, clear across the world in a foreign country. Actually it was a little scary, I didn't know a soul in this whole country; except for Bobby Ray and I didn't have any idea where he was or how to get in touch with him. It wasn't like I could just pick up the phone and call him. I wondered if Bobby Ray had gotten an assignment and where. I wondered if Pederson, Hobart and New York guy were on their way and would I see any them again. It dawned on me that outside this compound was a whole world I knew absolutely nothing about, I was in a foreign country, (I said that already didn't I), I didn't know the language and was about to get on a train and go to another part of this country all by myself and all I had to rely on was a train conductor that I was hoping spoke enough English to tell me where to get off. And what was I supposed to do when I got off? That SP4 didn't cover that part of this trip.

GERMANY
Chapter 32

I stepped off the curb with my duffel bag over my shoulder and hailed the first taxi I saw. I threw my bags in the back seat and climbed in and told the driver to take me to the Bahnhof. He nodded and off we went. I must have been in awe or shock or something about what I was going through right now, my mind kept drifting back over the past three or four weeks and how I got to where I am right now. I had hitchhiked across three quarters of the United States from Fort Huachuca, Arizona to Fort Dix, New Jersey; spent four days processing out of America. Then flying 8-10 hours to a foreign country and spending two days processing into it. Germany, I was finally here. Well, almost I still had to get to my unit.

I arrived at the Bahnhof an hour early. I gave the taxi driver two dollars in US currency since I didn't have any German money. He took it and said thank you, I think. He could have called me an asshole and I wouldn't have known the difference.

I hustled into the Bahnhof and immediately started looking for where they might have this schedule posted. Just to the left of the ticket booths I saw what I presumed to be a schedule of train departures and arrivals. Now all I had to do was figure out which was which; one said, "Ankunfte," and the other said, "Abfahrt." Okay, I had no idea what either of those words meant and that "Abfahrt" looked a little like it should be on a bathroom door or something.

I must have looked totally confused and lost standing there because this rather attractive German lady walked up and said, "Sprechen Sie Deutsch?" which was about all the German I knew yet.

"No, ma'am, I just speak Texan."

She laughed and said, "I believe that is similar to English, no?"

"It is similar yes," I said.

"I notice you are looking at the train schedules. May I help you find your destination?"

"That would be a great help," I pointed to the number on my ticket and said, "I am supposed to catch this train number to Heidelberg."

She stepped closer to me and more in front of Abfahrt schedule and said, "You leave from track 12."

"Thanks, now how do I get to track 12?" I asked.

"My train leaves from track 14; I will walk with you to your track 12 if you would like."

"That would be my pleasure, ma'am."

She smiled and asked, "What is the meaning of, how you say, "ma'am?"

"That's a Texas expression of respect," I said. Not having a clue how to really explain it.

She smiled again and said, "I will have to remember that in case I ever meet another Texas cowboy."

We walked through a set of double doors to where the train tracks were. The tracks were laid out so that a train pulled into the station between two concrete walkways on either side of the train. At the back of the train was another walkway that passengers used to walk down the line of train tracks until you found the number of the track that corresponded with the track number on you're ticket. Once you found your track number you could walk down the walkway between the trains to board your train.

"So now you know where I'm going. Where might you be going?" I asked.

"I am going to Münchener Stadt," she said.

I looked at her and my face must have said, "*Huh*?"

She laughed and said, "Most Americans refer to it as Munich."

I still didn't know what she said, but I said, "Oh, okay then. Going to visit or do you live there?"

"I am going for a short holiday. I will be back here next week. Here is your track number. When the train pulls in you may walk down this path between the tracks and board your train."

I stopped and set my bags down and told the lady thanks for all her help. She smiled and said, "You're welcome. Perhaps we will meet again sometime. Have a good trip to Heidelberg, auf wiedersehen."

"If you ever get to Heidelberg look me up. I'm assigned to the 529th MP Company, and my name is Rick," I pointed to my name tag for her to see the last name. She waved and went on down to her track. Her train was already there. After she rounded the train and disappeared I thought, *Jesus, you dumb shit, you didn't even ask her for her name. What an idiot.*

My train pulled in just before her train pulled out. As soon as the train had come to a stop and passengers had disembarked I climbed on and found a seat. Apparently this was not a rush-hour train; there were very few people in the car I was in, and from what I saw there weren't many people in the cars ahead of me.

My train was supposed to leave at 1300 hours. At 1300 hours on the dot by my Mickey Mouse that trains wheels began to roll. I understood what the specialist meant about German Trains leaving on time.

I leaned back lit up a cigarette and kept my ticket in my other hand waiting for the conductor to come by. I didn't have to wait long about 10 minutes into the trip the conductor came by and said something which I took to mean he wanted my ticket.

I gave him the ticket and said, "I need to get off at Heidelberg. Will you tell me when we get there?"

"Ja, Ja, I tell you," he said, as he punched my ticket and gave it back to me.

I watched the conductor waddle on down the isle and check the rest of the passengers' tickets. The trip to Heidelberg didn't take much more than an hour it seemed.

As we started getting into a more populated area the conductor came through the far door of the rail car and when he got beside me he pointed out the window and said, "Heidelberg."

I thanked him and began to wonder what I was supposed to do when I got off. Was I supposed to take a cab to wherever the 529th MP Company was located? Was there someone I could call?

The train came to a complete stop, and I hopped off the last door of the train farthest from the front of the Bahnhof and proceeded down the walkway.

Before I had taken a dozen steps this corporal stepped in front of me and said, "Private Shepard, I'm Corporal Warden, the company commander's driver. I've come to pick you up."

"I'm glad to see you. I had no idea what I was supposed to do. How did you know when to come pick me up?" I asked.

"The guy in Personnel at Frankfurt called and told us what train you would be on. We have a pretty good working relationship with those guys."

Warden picked up my small suitcase and we started for whatever transportation he had waiting.

I couldn't help but notice that this Corporal Warden looked like he just stepped out of a recruiting poster. In the limited time I had been in the military I had never seen anyone in uniform that looked like this guy. His uniform was tailored to perfection. His brass was shined enough to blind you when the light bounced off of it and you could see yourself in his low quarters (shoes) and his hat bill. If nothing else along the way from Frankfurt to Heidelberg impressed me, he did. Well, he and the lady in the Frankfurt Bahnhof.

We didn't say a lot on the drive to the Company. I just kind of took in the sights of Heidelberg and tired to keep from squeezing the arm rest off the door from the German driving. We finally pulled in to a gate manned by MPs and the sign over the gate read Patton Barracks. We took a quick right then drove straight down the street as far as we could there were buildings on our left and a little park area with a fountain in the center of it on our right. Warden turned to the right at the end of the street and we drove to the far end of the street.

Warden parked the sedan right in front of the double doors of the building on our left; we got out and went around and got my bags out of the trunk of the car. There were several guys sitting around the outside of the door smoking cigarettes and obviously giving me the once over.

"Hey, Warden, what have you got there? A new 'cruit (slang for recruit)?" one of the voices asked.

"He is one skinny dude. Looks like a bag of bones. Is he going to the Honor Guard or the Snake Pit first?" still another voice asked.

Warden told me to ignore those clowns and follow him to the Orderly Room. We walked down the stairs to the basement and into the first door we came to. Warden introduced me to the Company clerk whose name I can't remember. The clerk asked for my paper work and I gave it to him. While I was waiting the first sergeant came out and introduced himself and shook my hand. First Sergeant E J. Willis from Boston, that's one man I'll never forget.

After the Company Clerk finished my paperwork he took me upstairs to the second floor and down to the first room on the left. The room was a large room with about eight bunks in it. The clerk told me to pick one that wasn't occupied and drop my bags; this would be home for a few days anyway. One of the guys in the room was one of the ones that were downstairs. He came over and introduced himself as Private Oakley. Oakley was a tall, kind of husky kid that had been down stairs calling me skinny and a bag of bones. Humph, I thought this from a guy that looked like he had been hit with an ugly stick. Oakley seemed friendly enough and we shook hands and struck up a general conversation, the usual banter, where you from? How long have you been in? Where did you take basic and so on?

Other guys that slept in the "Snake Pit" (which I learned was what this particular room was called) began to wander in. A couple was just getting off duty, and a couple had just been out for the day. They all came over and introduced themselves. The Snake Pit, I was told, was like a holding area until a bunk came open in a regular, smaller room that usually had no more than four people in it or until you got sent down to the Honor Guard.

There were a couple of other guys sleeping in the Pit, besides Oakley, and a self-proclaimed Greek god named Rizzo stood out in my mind. Rizzo had the dark complexion and dark hair, great smile, and was a well-built fellow, but most of the guys there were well built to one extent or another. But Rizzo was a trip. As I soon learned, his favorite expression was, "Hey, what do say, lover?" You didn't have to see him to know it was him if you heard that. His other outstanding characteristic was he never had a cigarette of his own. He was the biggest bum in the company.

I found out that when you were a 'cruit everybody and his brother had to come by and check you out. I think I met the whole company that evening and never left my bunk except to go to chow. Things settled down as the evening wore on and guys started drifting off to sleep or were working on their gear. Working on your gear seemed to be a priority.

There was a curfew in Germany at that time you had to be in your quarters, rented accommodations or some other facility by midnight. You could not be on the streets in town. And if you didn't have an over night pass you had to be in your bunk. The CQ came around and took head count and then it was lights out.

I lay there in my bunk smoking my last cigarette of the day. My mind again wandered over the past couple of days. I had flown from one country to another I had traveled from one German city to another without knowing the language. Met an attractive German girl but failed to get her name, even if she didn't live in Heidelberg I still should have gotten her name. And now I find myself sleeping a room called the Snake Pit with some guys I really don't know except one is named Oakley and another one that thinks he is a Greek god and never has a cigarette of his own. It should be an interesting next couple of years.

GERMANY
Chapter 33

Not counting basic training, this was the only place I had been where they actually had reveille. That bugle went off at 0530 in the morning; blaring out in all direction from speakers mounted atop a pole in the middle of the little park that was right across the street from our building. It scared the shit out of me.

Everyone rolled out of bed and began getting dressed. Fatigues were the uniform of the day unless you were going to work but you still slipped into fatigues for reveille. The troops fell out in the company street facing the front of the building. Squad leaders took a head count and reported to the platoon sergeants who in turn reported to First Sergeant Willis who gave out any information that needed to be given out to the group as a whole or to a specific individual. Some mornings he didn't have anything to put out so as soon as the platoon sergeants reported the status of his platoon we were dismissed and most guys headed to the mess hall which was just down the road and to the left. It was a short walk.

I guess I should mention here there was one other member of the unit that always went to the mess hall with us. His name was Trooper and he was one big Saint Bernard dog. He was the company mascot. Going to the mess hall in the morning was about the only exercise Trooper got; he spent the rest of the day lying around by the front door to the barracks. I learned later on that Trooper actually had a Personnel File. He got promoted to sergeant at one point but then got busted when he went AWOL chasing some sexy little French Poodle off the Caserne. Getting busted didn't seem to bother Trooper too much; he still got fed and lay around the barracks all day.

This was an MP mess hall; we were the only ones that ate there. As I found out later the only meal we didn't eat there was midnight chow which the midnight shift ate at the consolidated mess hall at the end of the company street prior to going on duty at midnight.

There was a mandatory work call formation at 0700. So unless you were on duty, getting ready to go on duty or on leave or break you had to make the work call formation. Normally the biggest thing that happened at work call was you performed police call. Remember police call? That's where you line up and walk up and down the company area and pick up cigarette butts and any other trash you found laying around.

After police call, you were pretty much on your own unless your platoon sergeant had some special detail for you; or you had some type of appointment to keep. You were expected to stick around the company area and straighten up your room; which included buffing the floor when you could get your hands on the buffer. There was only one buffer per floor and you had to grab it when you could. I thought the floors in the barracks at Fort Huachuca were highly buffed. They were nowhere near the shine they put on these floors in their rooms here.

As the newest 'cruit, I got the honor of buffing the floor in the Snake Pit. I also got plenty of instruction from other members of the room, especially Oakley. After you buffed the floor once, then they had a piece of an old wool army blanket they put under the buffer and you buffed the whole floor again. While I was buffing, everyone there were making their bunks or working on their gear.

There were several things about this unit that you noticed immediately. Everyone wore very tailored fatigues and highly shined boots even if they weren't working. Most of the guys that weren't on duty were in their rooms. Those that had just got off the midnight shift were most likely asleep. Those that were getting ready for work were putting the final touches on their uniform. Those that were off were working on their gear.

I was called down to the Orderly Room, given some paper work and told to report to Personnel and Finance to process in. I should have known, you don't go anywhere in the Army without processing in or out. This was obviously a small compound commonly referred to as a caserne. I didn't have any problems following the directions the clerk gave me to Personnel and Finance. I was in and out of there in less than an hour and reported back to the company clerk.

After filing my paperwork wherever it was it needed to be filed, the clerk told me to follow him and we walked outside the Orderly Room and he turned to the right with me right on his heels. At the end of a short hall way was a Dutch door, with only the top half open. Inside the room was a full blown press shop. You could see uniforms hanging all over the place.

"This is where you get all your uniforms cleaned and pressed unless you don't want to pay a small monthly fee like the other guys. Then you can use the post cleaners, but this is a lot cheaper in the long run, and you can come down and get your clothes any time or turn them in any time. All the guys use this place."

"How much is the fee?" I asked.

"Five bucks a month."

"Sounds like a deal to me."

"Helga, kommen Sie hier, bitte?" the clerk said, and this rather stout German lady walked over to the door.

"Helga, this is Private Shepard. He is a new guy and will be using the cleaners."

"Willkommen, we will take very good care of you here," Helga said.

I thanked Helga and we moved on to the next place which was back down the other end of the hall and just at the bottom of the stairs. This was the supply room. The company clerk turned me over to the supply sergeant and disappeared.

The supply sergeant gave me my military police gear, including white gloves and white hat cover to put over your saucer hat. Then came the rest of the gear: first a holster with a suicide strap. That's what we called this strap that ran across your chest through the epaulet on your left shoulder back across your back and reattached to the back of the holster on your right side. None of the guys liked wearing it, but it was part of our uniform. You also got a first aid pouch, an ammo pouch and a night stick holder; although they didn't issue night sticks. They gave us one other little piece of equipment to go along with all that; it's called a lanyard. The lanyard was looped through and under the epaulet on your right shoulder and the other end was attached to a small round metal loop on the bottom of the handle of your .45 pistol. This was supposed to keep you from dropping your weapon and/or help prevent someone from taking your weapon away from you. The leather gear, i.e. holster, belt, and pouches, looked like it had been run through a gravel machine.

I guess the look on my face said it all because the supply sergeant said, "Don't worry; it all looks that way when I issue it out." I couldn't believe it from what I saw the other MPs on duty wearing. Their stuff was so highly shined, spit shined if you will, you could see yourself in it.

"How am I supposed to get this shit to look like what the other guys are wearing?" I asked.

"Don't worry, you'll figure it out," the supply sergeant said with a wicked little grin on his face.

After he gave me all this gear, he then handed me some more paper work and told me to go around to the Central Issue Point and they would give me my field gear. The CPI was located down the street and around the corner to the right. I took all my gear back up to the Snake Pit and threw it on the bunk. Oakley was on the bunk next to me shining his boots. Rizzo was doing the same thing. There was a guy named Truman that was next in line for a more private room asleep on his bunk and another guy I hadn't met yet asleep in his bunk.

"I see you found the supply sergeant," Oakley stated.

Rizzo looked up from his boots and said, "Hey, what do you say, lover? Got a cigarette?"

I threw a cigarette at Rizzo and sat down on my bunk and lit one up. All I could think about was, *How the hell am I supposed to get this gear looking like everyone else's?*

As if he were reading my thoughts, Oakley said, "You have to learn how to spit shine, just like the rest of us had to do. I'd suggest you go over to the little PX and get a couple of cans of black polish and a bottle of rubbing alcohol and some cotton balls. And pick out your worst T-shirt; you're going to need that too."

"Okay, what else?" I asked.

"You got any money?" Oakley asked.

"I got my travel pay."

"After chow, I'll take you across the street to the shoe shop. Bring your boots; you'll need to get them fixed."

"Fixed? What the hell is wrong with my boots?" I asked.

"You need to get 'em double heeled, double soled, and taps put on 'em," Rizzo chimed in, "See? Like this," he said, as he held up one of his boots.

"Is there anything else?" I asked again.

"You need to get a couple extra pairs of fatigues if you don't have extra already, and then take them around to the tailor shop by the motor pool and get them tailored. After chow today ask the cook for a couple of number-10-size cans," Rizzo said.

"What the hell am I going to do with a couple of number 10 size cans?" I inquired.

Rizzo stood up and said, "Look at the bottom of my fatigues."

I looked, and the bottom of his fatigues were perfectly round and if you looked close enough you could see the out line of what appeared to be a can. The can kept the bottom of your pants nice and neat and hung down over the blousing rubber that you used like a garter to hold your pants legs tight around your legs; so that all anyone saw was a nice smooth, round pant leg hanging just over the top of the boots.

"Is there any fuckin' thing else?" I growled.

They both laughed. Rizzo said, "That will get you started. We'll tell ya about your field gear later. Got a cigarette, lover?"

"Fuck you, Rizzo. Go buy some."

"Oh, the 'cruit is getting testy already."

Oakley looked at his watch. "Let's go to chow, he said, and got up and grabbed his blouse and hat and headed for the door. It was obvious that Oakley didn't miss many meals. I didn't have anything else to do until after chow so I grabbed my hat, and Rizzo and I followed him out the door.

After chow I went to the CPI and picked up my field gear and returned to the barracks and dumped it all on my bunk with the rest of the stuff. Now I gotta figure out where all this shit goes I thought.

GERMANY
Chapter 34

I spent the next four days trying to get all this stuff done that Oakley and Rizzo had told me I needed to do. I got some fatigues over to the tailor's to get fitted; the pants legs were tapered to 17." From the cook in the mess hall I got two number 10 cans, which is about a gallon-size can. Oakley had taken me out to the shoe shop, and I left one pair of my boots to get double soled, double heeled, and horseshoe taps put on the heels with small taps on the toe and double click taps put on the inside of the heels. Nobody told me that those number 10 size cans just didn't fit inside your tapered pants. You had to cut the cans and then warp them around until they fit very snuggly into a size-17 tapered pant leg, and then you wrapped them in duct tape to hold them together.

While all this was going on I was spending my spare time trying to shine all that leather gear to look like what everyone else was wearing. I couldn't get anything to shine for shit. It all looked like I was shining them with a Hershey bar.

By Saturday night I was done. I was so frustrated and tired of trying to get that crap to shine I threw it all down on my bunk and went to the Enlisted Club with Oakley and Rizzo, which was located just adjacent from our barracks. There was a live band in the club that Saturday night and we all sat and had a few drinks and watched those that had dates with either a WAC (Women's Army Corp) or a German girl dance.

About 2200 hours, I had enough of the club and headed back towards the barracks. When I got back to my room I found all my MP gear laid out on my bunk. Half my first aide pouch was shined, half my ammo pouch was shined, and half my holster and leather belt was shined. Someone was sending me a message, like, "Get with the program, 'cruit. We did half of it for you; now you get the rest of it done." *Okay,* I thought, *I guess I better get with the program if I expected to be accepted around here.*

I opened my can of polish, took the top of the can down and filled it with cold tap water and went back to my bunk. I sat down and wrapped the T-shirt around my right index finger until it was taunt and smooth. I dipped the T-shirt in the polish just to get enough on it to make it black and then dipped that into the lid of tap water and began to make little circles over the first aide pouch. To my surprise it didn't take long before I started to see some results. I was elated I was actually spit shining something. The more I worked the better I got and the better my gear started to look.

By the time Oakley and Rizzo came back from the club I had a little shine on all my gear.

"Hey, lover, you figured it out, huh?" asked Rizzo.

"I had some help; while we were at the club someone came in and shined half of each piece of my gear," I replied.

Oakley looked at Rizzo and almost together they said, "Corporal Mapes."

"Who the hell is Corporal Mapes?" I asked.

"He is really Corporal Mapes who wants to be Sgt. Mapes," said Rizzo.

"He does this kind of shit all the time with 'cruits. He did it to me too," said Oakley

"Why does he do it?" I asked.

"Who the fuck knows? He is one strange dude. He has his own little room down at the end of the hall. He doesn't come out much unless he is going to work. He ain't a bad guy to work for," said Rizzo.

"He may think he is helping you or he may think he is putting pressure on you to get your act together," said Oakley.

"Well, I guess he accomplished both with me," I said.

The following week I got my boots back from the shoe shop with all the goodies on them. My fatigues were back from the tailor shop and I got my cans cut and taped. I was getting the hang of spit shining which was a good thing because I had a bunch of stuff to shine.

I found out that the whole company was wearing leather right now because the commander was not satisfied with our overall appearance and he had put the whole company in leather about a month ago. Normally you could wear patent leather gear on duty. Being put in leather was considered a punishment and could be applied to an individual or as in this case a whole company punishment. This was the reason everyone was working on their leather so much. Normally once you got it shined it just hung on your wall locker door as part of your locker display. If you had to wear it every day, it would get scuffed and scratched and you had to shine it before you went to work again.

Oakley told me I could pick up some patent leather gear over at the main PX. He said he would take me over there on payday. That sounded good to me, this past week I had spent a ton of money on fatigues and boots.

I still had one more thing to learn to do. Remember I said they gave you a white cover to put over you saucer cap so you would have a white MP Cap? Well, that was okay except when you did that you didn't have a green saucer cap to wear when you needed it. The trick it seemed was to get another green saucer cap and if you really wanted to have a good MP hat you cut the green cover off at the rim around the green cap, took the grommet (the thick rubber band that runs around the top of the hat to give it its round shape) out of the cover you just cut off and stretched the rubber grommet until you could put it inside the white cover and stretch it out until you had a nice saddle in your hat. (Remember we did the saddle thing with the hats back at Fort Huachuca).

One thing about this company, they gave you a chance to get your act together before they sent you out to face the public. I had been there two weeks and other than making reveille and police call they had left me alone to get all my stuff ready. The boots got to be the big thing. They were hard toed airborne boots, or so they were called and you could shine those toes and heels on those boots until they looked like a mirror. But you didn't stop with just toes and heels. They wanted the instep and the soles shined too. (Now I knew why I got double soles and heels) and don't forget the sides. Basically they wanted the whole boot spit shined. They would accept less on the instep and sides but you weren't going to make many points with anyone if you didn't at least make a good effort to meet the highest standards. Some people just were not good at spit shining as others. And there were a few tricks to shining that some used and some didn't.

One trick was to wear your boots until they were well broken in and the instep was particularly well broken in. Once that was done then you took Duco Cement Glue and spread it around inside the instep of the boot until it dried and was hard enough to shine just like the toe. And while you were at it you could do the same thing with the sides of the boots. The other trick was to cut out very thin pieces of cardboard like a shoe box and cut pieces to fit the sides of the boot; but that wasn't as successful as just using the glue.

There were tricks to spit shining too. You could use a floor wax to as a base on the boots. The best way to get the most shine you could on your boots was to fill in all the pours of the boot. So you could smear the floor wax all over the boot and then take one of those small hand held blow torches or a cigarette lighter and melt the wax into the boot. Of course you didn't want to melt it until it rolled off the boot so when it was just right; you rubbed it in with your T-shirt and let it sit until it hardened.

This was not just one pair of boots we are talking about here. Everyone had at least two pair of boots and some people had three or more and then there were your low quarters; they got the same attention as the boots. Your hat bill got a great deal of attention. It was the first thing people saw when they looked at you.

Now you have all your footgear shined, and your uniforms all tailored and your cans ready to go; you still had your brass to shine. Most of the guys spin-shined their brass. That meant cleaning it up with Brasso, then taking a tent peg and putting it through the hole in the back ground of your brass and spinning the brass on a soft towel to give it that spin look and then cleaning it again with a jeweler's cloth.

Once you got your uniform ready to go, the last thing you did before you were ready to go to work was take your boots, hat, and leather if you were wearing leather to the latrine where they had a big sink. You would turn on the cold water and take each piece of leather and put it under the water and with a wad of cotton balls you would wash out all the little circles you left when you were shining your leather. Once you got all those circles out of your leather; you were ready to go. All you had to do now was pass Guard Mount. Remember Guard Mount?

GERMANY
Chapter 35

Another week passed during which I got my other uniforms in the tailor shop fitted and tapered. While I was waiting on those I continued to work on my MP gear. Oakley and I went to the main PX and I got some patent leather gear. That turned out to be a good move since the commander decided the company had been punished enough and allowed us to start wearing the patent leather again.

When I took a break from shining my gear, I was learning some other things about the company and its operations. One of the first things I checked out was the duty roster. This was run totally by First Sergeant Willis. At the time I didn't really realize how unique this roster was. It was a master roster with every man that pulled duty on the roster. The Honor Guard Platoon worked the swing shift only; 1700 to 0100. This gave the Honor Guard time to practice in the mornings and in most cases perform any ceremonies they were called upon to do before having to go on duty. The Duty Platoon worked the day shift, 0900 to 1700 and the midnight shift, 0100 to 0900.

The unique element of this roster was the way First Sergeant Willis scheduled the personnel. If you went to work on the day shift your first break would be 16 hours, you went back to work on the day shift the following day. After the second day you got a 32 hour break which meant you went to work on the midnight shift. The next break was 48 hours; followed by 54 hour break and then 72 hour break. These hours were subject to change of course depending on scheduled leaves or unscheduled absences such as hospital admissions or other emergencies. But basically if all went well you were sure to get a 72 hour break, three days off about every 10 days or so. And there were variations to the schedule: as an example a man could volunteer to work a straight five-day week and have every weekend off. Or if for some strange reason you preferred a different two days off, First Sergeant Willis could work that out for you too.

As I began to grasp all the possibilities and unpredictability's I was amazed and totally impressed with Sergeant Willis's ability to keep up with it all; plus keep up with his normal first sergeant duties. Usually you had and operations sergeant that ran the duty roster.

You rarely heard anyone bitch or complain about the duty schedule and if you had a complaint all you had to do was talk to the first sergeant about it and if he had screwed up he would make it up to you and if you needed something special he would help you out. But he also would ask you to miss a break every now and then if he needed an extra body for something.

Of all the first sergeants I ever worked for or knew Sergeant E.J. Willis was the best of the best. I never went to another unit after that; that I didn't miss Sergeant Willis.

While Sergeant Willis was the best first sergeant I ever had, Staff Sergeant Altman, my platoon sergeant was probably the worst sergeant I ever worked for. Pappy Altman, as we called him, wasn't a bad or mean guy; he just wasn't much of a leader. There were a lot of stories going around about Pappy, one was he was a drunk, but I never got that impression. Another was he had been a prisoner of war in the Korean War. Whatever his background it was obvious that Pappy just wanted to get his time in and then retire. Pappy had a couple of sergeants that pretty much took care of the platoon for him and they could pretty well run the platoon and get Pappy's backing on any decisions they made. Fortunately they were good soldiers and usually made the right decisions.

Sgt. Faxson, the platoon sergeant, on the other hand, was a very sharp NCO, and he ran the Honor Guard. My impression was that he was tough but fair and kept the appearance and the proficiency of the Honor Guard at its peak.

I finally got a chance to watch the Honor Guard drill one morning. They started with a formation in front of the company. They all had on very tailored fatigues, with cans, and highly shined silver helmet liners. They wore a white scarf around their neck, tucked neatly inside their fatigue blouses with a blue USAEUR (United States Army Europe) patch sewed on the front of the scarf. Their pistol belts were white and the only item on the pistol belt was a silver sheath with silver handled bayonet. The boots were obviously highly spit shined and had white laces affixed in a ladder lace configuration.

It would be impossible to describe with any clarity how to form a ladder lace just try to picture in your mind's eye if you can a rope or rawhide ladder running from the bottom to the top of the boot. You might picture it as a rope bridge you see sometimes in jungle movies or the rope ladders they use to lower troops from a troop ship to waiting smaller boats below.

Sergeant Shire was the Honor Guard Drill Team leader. He was a little shorter than the average member of the Honor Guard, but he was good. When he called the formation to attention you could hear the boots click in unison. Every command given was done in unison and exaggerated so you could hear every movement; kind of like Do Re Mi only more so.

When Sergeant Shire gave the command forward march you heard the horseshoe taps on the heels of their boots slide across the cobblestone streets and they echoed all over the caserne. Everybody knew the Honor Guard was on the move. If you can recall some war time movie with troops marching and imagine that sound in your mind it will give you some idea of what the Honor Guard sounded like.

As they marched they went through what I learned was called a sixteen count manual of arms movement. It's hard to describe to those that have never done or been exposed to a normal manual of arms in the military. It includes every position you can move your rifle into while standing in formation or marching, i.e. right shoulder arms, left shoulder arms, port arms, etc. The sixteen count manual included all of those and a few others that really aren't in the manual.

I watched the Honor Guard from the sidelines as they practiced and went through their paces on the soccer/football field. There is nothing I enjoy more or impresses me more than a well trained unit moving in unison and executing precise movements without ever missing a beat. I watched them twirl their rifles as they marched and toss their rifles in the air to the person behind them while continuing to march or form a circle and toss their weapons across the circle to one another. I was really impressed when they formed two columns facing each other and tossed their weapons in a twirling manner, with fixed bayonets to the man across from them as Sergeant Shire walked in between the two columns. Each rifle was tossed just in front of Sergeant Shire and had to be tossed at precisely the correct time or Sergeant Shire took the risk of being seriously cut or severely injured by one of those bayonets. It was said that Sergeant Shire sustained a cut on his face as a result of someone failing to toss his weapon at the exact time. Shire had been with the 529th probably longer than anyone, I assumed he re-enlisted for his own vacancy and no one else had been in the Honor Guard and longer than Sergeant Shire.

After they finished their drills and returned back to the barracks I followed them back and felt I had just watched one of the most impressive performances of precise and unique skills I had ever seen. And this was just a practice session.

I realized I hadn't been in the Army very long and hadn't seen all there was to see, but I honestly believed I would never see anything any better than what I had just seen. I was very proud just to be a member of that organization if I was in the Honor Guard or not.

To my knowledge the only other Army Honor Guard unit still in existence is the Presidential Honor Guard at Fort Myers, VA.

GERMANY
Chapter 36

After being in the company for approximately three weeks I was getting to know most of the other guys in the unit. I had met Truman, the other guy in the Snake Pit. Truman was kind of strange and a loner. I remember one night, Oakley, Rizzo, Truman, and I were all sitting around shining boots and talking about women. Everybody had something to say but Truman.

Rizzo was pretty much leading the discussion; he seemed to think he was the most experienced of the group. Who was I to argue with a Greek god? Finally Rizzo turned to Truman with some questions; actually it was only two questions.

"Hey, Truman, you got a cigarette?" Rizzo asked.

Truman pitched Rizzo a cigarette and lit up. "So what do say, lover, what do you think about women and sex?

Truman just kept shining his boots.

"Hey, lover, Truman, I'm talking to you, what do you think of sex?"

Truman kept on shining his boots, but muttered something under his breath.

"Speak up, son; we can't hear you," Oakley said.

Finally Truman stopped shining his boots and looked at us and said, "I think sex is a passing fad."

The room went dead silent for a minute and Oakley, Rizzo and I all looked at each other not sure what we had just heard. Then we all just burst out laughing. I think Rizzo swallowed his cigarette, Oakley rolled off his bunk. I spit out a coke I was drinking. Truman got pissed, threw his shine rag at Rizzo; shot us the finger and stormed out the door. We probably wouldn't have gotten so excited about it but Truman didn't sound like he was joking.

A couple of nights later, a Saturday night as I recall, I was sitting on my bunk smoking a cigarette when a couple of the guys I had been getting pretty friendly with, C.M. Lane and Alan Johnson (we called him Roach, but more about that later) came in with Rizzo and had a question.

"Hey, Bones, you been down town on the Strasse (street) yet?" Chuck asked.

Bones was my new nickname Oakley had given me because he thought I was skinny, and it caught on.

"I ain't been anywhere off this post except across the street to the shoe shop," I replied.

"Come on, we are gonna take you downtown and get you laid," Roach said.

"I don't know any girls, and I don't have any money."

"Hey, lover, we know the girls, and you won't need any money. The first one is on us."

"I can imagine the kind of girls you know, Rizzo," I said.

"Come on, Bones; everybody has to go at least once. It's a company tradition," said Chuck.

"I don't have a pass."

"Your pass is down in the box unless Pappy pulled it. You haven't done anything to get in trouble have you?" Roach inquired.

"Not that I'm aware of."

"Okay, let's go then, lover. You can pick up your pass and sign out downstairs by the Orderly Room. Got a cigarette?"

Who was I to break company tradition? I got up and slipped on my shoes, stopped by the Orderly Room, found my pass in the pass box, signed out and off we went in Chuck's 1954 Mercedes.

I have no idea how we got to our final destination which was in a small parking area just off a street I later learned was called Rohrbach

Strasse. Chuck turned off the engine to the car, and everybody rolled down the windows, and we just sat. It wasn't long before I began to notice "ladies," starting to pass by the car. Occasionally one would say something in German and then move on down the street, only to return a few minutes later.

Finally Rizzo called one of the "ladies" over to the car. I couldn't hear or understand everything that was said between the two of them; but after a brief discussion Rizzo climbed out of the car and motioned for me to get out, too. I got out of the car and stood next to Rizzo.

"Here ya go, lover; she is all yours," Rizzo said.

"But what if I don't want her?"

"It's too late now; she is already paid for, and there are no refunds."

"Go on, Bones," Roach shouted from inside the car.

Before I had a chance to protest any more the "lady" took me by the hand and started leading me off across a small park until we came to a set of very long steps leading up to…something or somewhere. We walked up the steps until we were more than half way. Along the way I saw other couples along the railing of the stairway and it was pretty obvious what they were doing.

Finally the "lady" stopped. She climbed up on the top rail of the steps and spread her legs.

"You want sex or blowjob?" she asked in a rather heavy German accent.

I guess I took too long to answer. Suddenly the "lady" grabbed me and pulled me between her legs and was unzipping my pants.

Before she could get that done a man walked by and said something to the effect, "So he is your husband for the night, Fraulein?"

That did it. I couldn't do this. I backed away from the "lady" and zipped my pants back up and started walking down the steps.

"Where you go, GI?" she asked.

"I'm going back to my friends," I replied.

"You don't get money back," she yelled as I got further down the steps.

I walked back down the step and back to the car where all the guys had gotten out and were talking to other "ladies" that were on the street. I walked over to the side of the car.

Rizzo was the first to notice that I was back. “Hey, lover, that was quick. Been a while or was she just that good?”

“Yeah, she was great,” I lied. Thanks, guys. Can we go get a beer somewhere?” I asked. Actually I just wanted to get out of there before that gal got back down there.

We all piled back in the car and went to a place called the Whackelburg Club, a popular hangout for the guys from the MP Company. There were several of the guys from the company already there when we walked in. We pulled a couple of tables together and joined the rest of them.

“We just got back from Rouherbach. Got Bones German cherry popped,” Oakley announced.

A big cheer went up from the group and some suggested I buy the next round. If I would have known I was going to have to do that I would have made better use of Rizzo’s money. I bought the next round. I drank a coke. We stayed for one more round and then decided to go back to the barracks. Some of the guys wanted to go to the Enlisted Club to see if they could find a WAC that wasn’t busy.

We got back to the caserne, Chuck let us out in front of the building then went on to park his car. Some of the guys took off for the club right across the street.

Roach and I headed back to the barracks. We went up to the 2d floor and he came into the Snake Pit with me.

All the rooms had huge windows, almost floor to ceiling. We opened the window next to my bunk and sat up on the window sill and smoked a cigarette and drank a coke.

“You didn’t get laid tonight, did you?” Roach asked.

“Naw, just not my style, know what I mean?”

“Yeah, I know, I didn’t either when they took me up there. I just smoked a cigarette and shot the shit with the gal.”

“There has gotta be something better than that around here,” I said.

“Oh, yeah, there is. Wait until you get to work; you’ll meet a lot of nice-looking girls. Just be sure they shave their legs, unless you like hairy legs,” Roach said.

“You mean they don’t shave their legs over here?” I asked in surprise.

"Not all of them, they can be pretty as hell 'til you look at their legs. And if they don't shave their legs there is a good chance they don't shave under their arms either."

"Now you're making me sick," I said, "How did you get a name like Roach?"

"I'm a night runner; I have a problem sleeping at night, always have. Someone said I reminded him of a cockroach running around the hallways all hours of the night. So the name stuck. Like you being named Bones."

We didn't talk much more, just sat and watched the people coming and going from the club. Finally Roach said he was going back to his room and read a book. I lit another cigarette and continued to watch the traffic in and out of the club. When I saw the midnight shift come out of the building and head for the mess hall I figured it was time for me to go to bed. I got up, got undressed and crawled in bed. By the time Rizzo and Oakley got back to the room I was almost asleep so I pretended I was. I wasn't in any mood to talk to them right at the moment.

I was starting to get comfortable around this place; my boots and general appearance were starting to get good comments from the other guys so I was feeling like I was part of the gang now. I was looking forward to my first tour of duty.

GERMANY
Chapter 37

The Monday morning after my first trip to town the first sergeant sent for me. My first thought was that I was in trouble for something. But I had no idea what for. I reached the Orderly Room and went inside. The clerk said to go on in and motioned towards the 1st Sgt's office.

I walked up to the door knocked, stuck my head in and asked, "You wanted to see me, Top?" (Top was what you called a first sergeant because he was the top sergeant in any unit.)

The first sergeant looked up, and with his Boston accent said, "Yes, Sammy, come on in."

He always called me Sammy. I walked in and stood in front of his desk.

"I was looking at your records this morning, and I noticed you were supposed to make PFC last month. Is there any reason why you didn't?"

"Not that I'm aware of, First Sergeant. First Sergeant Passino, at my previous unit told me and some other guys that he would get us promoted after the IG Inspection, but I got orders right after the inspection and was in transit until I got here."

"Well, you should have been promoted after eight months of service and you're about a month overdue. I'll have your orders for PFC cut this week. You can start getting the stripes sewed on your uniforms."

"Thanks, Top, I appreciate it," I said.

Top put his glasses on and looked back down at his desk which was covered with the duty roster. I assumed we were through and started to leave.

"I have one more thing, Sammy."

I stopped in my tracks and turned back around, "Yes, Top?"

"How would you like to be in the Honor Guard? I don't have any space for you down there now; the company is way over strength, but when the time comes, I'll move you down if you would like that."

"Yes, sir, I would like that," I was about to jump out of my skin. Just being considered for the Honor Guard was something special to me. "Thanks again, Top," I said as I turned and walked out of his office.

I went back to the Snake Pit taking the stairs two at a time. I burst into the Pit and jumped up and clicked my heels.

Rizzo was just making his bunk, Oakley was buffing the floor, and Truman was just getting ready to get in bed after getting off the midnight shift. "Hey, Lover, what's up and got you so excited, and what did the first sergeant want?"

"Two things, I'm gonna make PFC and Top asked me if I wanted to go to the Honor Guard," I said.

"You dog! How are you getting promoted already? I got here a month before you did," Rizzo said.

"I was supposed to get promoted last month when I hit the eighth-month mark, but I was in transit. So actually I'm getting promoted a month late."

"How did a skinny-ass like you get selected for the Honor Guard, is what I wanna know?" Oakley asked.

"That's exactly why I got selected Oakley, because I got a skinny ass and not a fat ass like you."

"Humph, I didn't wanna go to the Honor Guard anyway; too much work." Oakley snorted.

Truman joined in the conversation and asked, "When are you moving out of the room?"

"I won't be moving right away. They don't have any openings down there yet, so I'm staying here until something opens up. Top says the company is way over strength right now so nobody is moving until someone leaves."

Truman rolled over in his bunk to go to sleep but I heard him mutter, "You won't like the Honor Guard."

I went back downstairs to the pool room and found Roach and Chuck shooting pool, I had to tell them what the first sergeant had said.

GERMANY
Chapter 38

For the next four months, I watched the drill team practice every chance I got or watched a ceremony when they preformed. When I got a chance and could borrow one of the guy's rifles I would practice and they would give me some pointers on what to do or mostly on what I was doing wrong.

I spent a lot of hours learning to twirl that rifle and how to do the 16 count manual of arms and how to do the Queen Ann Salute. When Sergeant Shire would catch me he always told me if I dropped that weapon I had to drop and give him twenty pushups. I tried to be sure he wasn't around when I would practice.

There was this one little buck sergeant named Rickman, who was the second in charge of the drill team. I had to wonder how these little short guys got to be in charge since everyone else in the Honor Guard was about six feet two or taller. I have to give Rickman credit for being a sharp-looking soldier. He even went so far as to pin the back of his T-shirt with a safety pin so it would stay tight around his neck and not sag. He walked with his arms straight down by his side so as not to get a crease in the sleeve of his blouse.

I worked the day shift and the midnight shift at either Campbell or Patton Barracks. The Honor Guard Platoon worked the evening shift. My evenings were spent either working on my gear or running the clubs with whoever else was off, Roach, Chuck, or Rizzo We spent most of our time in a place called the Rendezvous Club down near the old Heidelberg Bridge.

Until I worked Campbell Barracks I didn't understand that Patton Barracks was basically the housing area for the troops. The MP Company and a Transportation unit were the two biggest units that lived on Patton Barracks. There was a small medical detachment that handled sick call and some emergencies; and there was a small administrative detachment that handled personnel actions and finance. The Medical Personnel, Finance, and Personnel people were actually assigned to Headquarters Company that also housed the cooks and other mess hall personnel and some motor pool people such as mechanics for repair on various vehicles in the motor pool that weren't assigned to the transportation unit.

Campbell Barracks was the hub of the work force for Headquarters, USAEUR. It had seven gates, including one pedestrian gate. All the gates were open and manned by MPs during normal duty hours; except the pedestrian gate which was only opened during the morning when people were coming to work, at lunch and again in the evenings when people were going home. Campbell Barracks was surrounded by Government housing area hence the pedestrian gate. It allowed people that lived on that side of the caserne to walk to and from their quarters and to go home for lunch if they desired to do so.

Campbell Barracks was larger than Patton Barracks. Campbell was actually a quadrangle. In the middle of the quadrangle was a huge parade field. This was where the Honor Guard performed when called upon; usually when the CINC was entertaining a visiting dignitary. The main gate, logically designated Gate #1, into Campbell Barracks was located in the middle of one side of the quadrangle. Just outside the quadrangle was a small building designated as the Information Center. Actually it was manned by the MP desk sergeant for Campbell barracks and during normal duty hours, Monday through Friday we had a German interpreter that worked inside the Information Center with us. His name was Hans.

Just as at the other gates there was both vehicular and pedestrian traffic going in and out of Gate #1. The only difference between Gate #1 and the other gates was that to get inside the quadrangle you had to pass under one of the buildings that was actually occupied. It was like a small, short tunnel with offices overhead, watching the traffic come in and out and waving at the MP standing in the middle of the street.

The day shift required eight men to man the posts during the day time. The swing shift only needed five since the gates with the exception of Gate #1 were all closed. It was the same procedure as used at Patton Barracks, one MP checking cars and one checking pedestrians; two on foot patrol around the caserne. The foot patrol was supposed to relieve the gate guys every hour, but that didn't always happen. Usually after things really slowed down we only used one guy on the gate to handle both pedestrian and vehicle traffic and the foot patrol came back to the Information Center and chilled and we basically had a four man rotation on the gate. That was okay unless you had the wrong desk sergeant and or patrol supervisor working.

It was summer time now and hot. We had gone to the summer khaki uniform with long sleeve shirts, and we still had to wear a cravat around our neck so it wasn't the most comfortable summer uniform ever worn. I was happy to work a midnight shift during the summer because it was cooler and the sun didn't melt the polish on your boots. I was still living in the Pit with Oakley, Rizzo. Truman had finally been assigned to a smaller room. Oakley and Rizzo and I all bitched about the sun melting the polish on our boots and having to re-shine them again after work.

Two new guys had moved into the Pit. Both were from Alabama: Galbreath and Hobbs. I don't know if they came in on the buddy plan or if it was just coincidence they were both from Alabama. I think it must have been coincidence, because while they seemed to be friends, they just didn't fit together. Galbreath was cool, but Hobbs, while a really nice guy, was just a little bit too much hillbilly. But more about them later.

While I was stuck working the gates and walking patrol at Campbell and Patton Barracks the Honor Guard was working at the CINC's office and his quarters. The office was right next to Campbell Barracks, just a short walk from Gate #2 and just a bit further to gate #1. His quarters were located in an entirely different part of the city. I think I was only there once and can't remember how we even got there; I only remember driving down the Hauptstrasse (Main Street) of Heidelberg until it split into two streets. I'm not sure which way we went from there.

While the little time I got to practice with the rifle had improved my skills. There still had been no openings come up in the Honor Guard Platoon. There was one particular incident I that made me wonder if I really wanted to actually become a member of the Honor Guard or not.

Specialist Four Barker was one of the gun bearers on a ceremonial detail in the garden behind the CINC's office. It was an awards ceremony of some sort and all you had to do was stand there at attention. It seems that during the ceremony one of the keepers on Barker's white gun sling came loose and the sling just went limp. I guess nothing like that had ever happened before. Barker reached down and readjusted his sling and pushed the keeper back down in place as tight as he could and reassumed the position of attention.

I don't think anyone thought it would be much of a big deal, But Barker no more than got back to the Company area and the company commander wanted to see Barker. Barker walked in the commander's office a SP4 and walked out a PFC. The commander busted him for failure to repair or some shit like that. Sgt. Shire checked out Barker's weapon and sling and found out the damn keeper was broken and would mal-function at times. Everybody went to bat for Barker, but apparently there was no changing the commander's mind. Even the first sergeant who carries a lot of weight in situations like this couldn't get the "old man" to change his mind.

You can believe everyone else checked and double checked their keepers; in fact Sgt. Shire and Sgt. Faxson had new keepers in a couple of weeks. It was apparent to everyone that this was just an unavoidable accident and couldn't figure out the reason for the commander's actions. Some thought he had it in for Barker since Barker had filed an IG (Inspector General) complaint sometime back about something he couldn't seem to resolve on his own to his satisfaction. Barker was leaving in a couple of months and getting out of the army so he really didn't get too upset over the whole thing.

In my four or so months in the company that was the only time I knew of any such punishment like that being taken. A couple of guys had their passes pulled for a couple of days for missing bed check or not keeping their area squared away in the barracks, but nothing like this and for something so....stupid.

Despite the incident with Barker I was still looking forward to joining the Drill Team looking forward to the prospect of being able to participate in first full fledged ceremony.

Little did I know how much my life was going to change in the next month and my chances to really become a member of the drill team were never going to happen.

GERMANY
Chapter 39

Sometime in late August, the Company had to be split up so everybody could go to the gun range in order to qualify with the .45 pistol. I ended up working the main gate at Patton Barracks.

Since Patton was such a small caserne it didn't take long to get to know a lot of people, most you saw almost on a daily basis somewhere around the post. About 1600, this guy named Barry came driving a deuce and a half through the gate. I knew Barry from just seeing him around but had never really been involved in any activity with him.

He stopped at the gate and said, "Hey, Bones, I just came through town, and there are a shit load of tourist buses down there. Want to go down and check it out this evening?"

"I dunno, still a long time to payday, and I'm a little short on money," I said.

"Come on. It won't cost us much to at least go look."

I really didn't have anything else to do, and I hadn't been to town in a long time, so I agreed to go.

"All right, come by the barracks and get me. I should be ready about 1900 or so," I said.

Barry gave me thumbs up and drove off.

Heidelberg was a tourist town back in those days. A lot of tourist from all over Europe, Scandinavia and the U.S. came over and visited.

Some of the attractions were the Heidelberg Castle; I think a movie called *The Student Prince* was filmed there. And there was a little German Pub called the Roter Ochse or Red Ox I believe also played a part in the movie, and there were a couple of other Pubs the names of which I can't recall.

It was a custom of the GIs at Patton Barracks, at least the MPs and apparently the truck drivers too; to go downtown when the tourist were in and see if you couldn't pick up one or more of the ladies from another country. Apparently someone figured out that the tourist really wanted to see some of the spots in town that the tourist guide didn't care to take them too. So we were more than happy to oblige them.

Barry showed up right at 1900, I went down and got my pass out of the pass box, signed out and we were off. We took a taxi from the main gate down to a spot on the Hauptstrasse not far from where the tourist busses parked. Barry paid the taxi driver and we started walking. Usually you can tell if there are a lot of tourists in town because they will be shopping the little stores near the Bus Park Platz (place)

We walked all the way up to the Park Platz and saw no tourist and no busses. What a revolting development this turned out to be.

"I thought you said there were tons of busses up here?" I asked.

"There were when I came through here this afternoon, Bones, I swear," Barry replied. "I don't know what happened to them all."

"Obviously they left," I snorted.

"I guess so," Barry shrugged.

We walked on up the street to the next intersection then turned right and walked on down to the adjacent street to the Hauptstrasse. There were a couple of lively little pubs over there; we figured we might as well check them out as long as we were there.

We went in and sat down at a table. There was an oompa band playing but no tourists only locals. An oompa band, for those of you that might want to know, is what we called the little German band that had drummer and maybe some guy playing a piano but no matter what else they may have they always had a tuba player and it was always oompa, oompa, oompa. that was our interpretation of the sound coming out of the tuba.

All these places were the same. The guys in the band all wore short lederhosen (leather pants) with suspenders a white shirt and a little fedora hat with a feather in it; and the tuba player was always fat. The Fraulein's, in the band and waiting tables all wore an off the shoulder white top with a flowery colored dress and lots of petticoats on under it. If you had seen one you had seen them all. But that's what the tourists wanted to see at least that's what everyone thought.

Barry and I sat there and drank a beer; he drank a beer I had a coke, smoked a couple of cigarettes, and pondered our options. We decided to check out a couple more places and see if they were anymore lively than this place was. We paid for our drinks and headed down the same street to another little place. We just stuck our head in the door and didn't even bother to go in. We walked back over to Hauptstrasse and headed back up towards the Park Platz; just past the Park Platz was the famous Red Ox Pub.

We walked in; this was one of the few places that had high backed booths around the walls so you couldn't see the whole seating area by just looking in the door. We walked around the hall checking out the booths. We passed one booth with two girls sitting in it, but we passed it by and kept on walking. We made our way back around to the front door and left.

About halfway back down to the Park Platz, I looked at my watch and it was almost 2100 hours already. I stopped in the middle of the sidewalk; pulled out a cigarette and lit up and gave one to Barry.

"You know it's almost 2100 already, and we have to be back at midnight; if we are gonna see any action tonight we better go back and talk to those two in the Red Ox."

Barry agreed, and we headed back up the street to the Red Ox Pub. If I had only known then what I know now.

GERMANY
Chapter 40

Barry and I returned to the Red Ox went in and started making our way around the tables again only this time coming from the other direction. Barry figured if we went the other way the girls might think we had been sitting somewhere else in the pub that they couldn't see.

We got back to the table the girls were sitting at and stopped and asked them if they were American. They said yes. We went through the usual conversation you go through when you meet someone from the same place you are. You know, where you from in the States? I've been there, or I've never been there; and so on and so on and so on.

We asked if could buy them a drink and would they mind if we sat with them. They accepted our offer so Barry and I sat down. There was no picking or choosing or any pre arranged plan; we just sat by the girl we were closest to.

"My name is Rick," I said.

"I'm Sara."

Barry introduced himself and the girl he was sitting next to was Mary Ann. Sara was from a small township in Pennsylvania somewhere around Philadelphia and Mary Ann was from a place near Baltimore. I think Barry was from Tennessee. The conversation was going well; we told the girls what we did in Germany and the Army. We learned they were both school teachers that had just arrived in Germany to start teaching in the American Military Dependent School System. Both were going to teach in Kaiserslutern, Germany.

They had taken a train to Heidelberg to do some sight seeing since they had sometime to kill before school started. They had just come down from the castle and stopped in the Red Ox to have a beer. They had already found hotel accommodations for their stay. They planned to be here in Heidelberg until Sunday afternoon.

It was getting close to curfew for Barry and me. I motioned to him with my head and pointed at my watch. He got the idea.

"Sara, would you and Mary Ann like to go for walk down by the river? It's a pretty night out," I asked.

"I think that would be nice. What do you think, Mary Ann?"

"It sounds good to me," Mary Ann said.

We all got up and the girls grabbed their purses and a couple of little packages they had and we paid for our drinks, left the Red Ox and headed down towards the Neckar River. It was actually part of the Rhein River and officially called the Rhein-Neckar River but we just called it the Neckar.

Sara and I walked down to the river hand in hand; Barry and Mary Ann were right behind us. Once we got to the river we found a nice grassy area and sat down to smoke a cigarette. Sara smoked Salems, I think. I had long ago got away from Salems; I just couldn't handle the menthol. I was smoking Winstons. Barry and Mary Ann quietly slipped off to another area further down the banks of the river.

"How long have you been in Germany?" Sara asked.

"About six months," I replied.

"Do you like it?"

"Yeah, so far I haven't had a chance to get downtown much or see any of the rest of the country yet. Work has been keeping me pretty busy," I said.

"Exactly what is it you do again? I know you said you were in the Military Police something or other?" Sara inquired.

"I'm in the Military Police Honor Guard. We are assigned to provide security for the Commander in Chief of United States Army in Europe and provide honor guard ceremonies when required," I explained. I tried to make it sound as important as I could.

"That sounds interesting," Sara replied.

"How long have you been teaching school?" I asked.

"I taught one year at home before I came over here. My contract with the government is for two years," she said.

"You think you'll like it here?" I asked.

"Yes, I think I will. I want to travel during my time off and see more of Europe."

I didn't know what time it was, but I knew time wasn't on my side. If I was going to make any headway in the romance department I knew I had to do something quickly. I had inched in closer to Sara as we sat and talked and had been sitting there beside her with my arm around her shoulders and rubbing my hand up and down her arm. I leaned over and gave her a kiss on the cheek. She didn't resist and turned, faced me, and we fell into a full fledged lip lock. I gently pushed her back on the grassy knoll. We lay there making out, but she was good at fighting off my attempts to gain any ground.

Suddenly there was a bright light shining on us. We sat up and turned around, and there stood a German policeman. I glanced at my watch; it was 0200. *Holy shit!* I thought, *I'm in big trouble now; I missed curfew, bed check, and I didn't have an over- night pass.*

The German Policeman said something in German, and I didn't have a clue as to what he said. But to my surprise Sara spoke German right back to him. I sat there for the next few minutes while Sara and the German cop carried on a conversation. Whatever she said must have worked; the cop never asked us for any identification and just walked off.

"Asking if you speak German would be kind of stupid, I guess, huh?"

She laughed and said, "I speak some but not as well as I would like to. That's another reason I wanted this job; I have relatives over here, and I would like to practice my German before I go visit them."

Barry and Mary Ann came walking up. Sara asked, "Did the Policeman find you too?"

"I told him we had a couple of friends down there somewhere when he came by here," Sara said.

Barry and Mary Ann sat down, and we all smoked a cigarette. I explained to the girls that Barry and I had a problem. I told them we were out past curfew and our only chance of getting through this was to stay out until around 0800 in the morning and then walk through the gate as though we just went out. Since I was an MP they probably wouldn't check my pass, and since Barry was with me they probably wouldn't check his either.

"The problem is we don't have any place to stay until then," I said.

"You can stay with us at our hotel. We have two rooms. You guys can use one, and Sara and I can use the other," Mary Ann suggested.

Nobody objected so we got up and actually found a taxi, and Sara told him where to go. As it turned out they were staying at a small hotel not far from Patton Barracks and near the Bahnhof.

When we arrived at the little hotel Sara had to ring the bell to wake up the clerk or whoever it was that was on duty. Sara spoke to the lady in German and she let us in. We went right up to the rooms. Sara grabbed some stuff out her room and took them into Mary Ann' room. We all had one more cigarette, made some plans to get together later, around noon, and go to the Heidelberg Zoo.

About 0330, the girls said good night after giving us an alarm clock we could set.

"Well, shit, I didn't exactly have spending the night with *you* in mind when we left this evening," Barry said.

"Hey, you weren't exactly my first choice either, ya know?"

"You can sleep on the bed; I'll take this sofa. Just give me a pillow," I said.

Barry tossed me a pillow; I grabbed a light blanket off the foot of the bed and fell asleep on the sofa in a couple of minutes.

GERMANY
Chapter 41

Barry and I were up and running as soon as the alarm went off. We didn't bother to disturb the girls we just left the hotel hailed a taxi and headed for Patton Barracks. We asked the taxi driver to drop us off in front of the Last Chance Saloon, which was located just outside the gate but out of sight of the MPs view. We wanted to walk up to the gate like we hadn't been far away and it gave us a chance to see who was working the gate.

Luck was on our side, Roach was on the gate, I knew he wouldn't be checking our passes. He was busy with a vehicle wanting to come in the caserne and just turned toward us for a second and waved us on in.

Barry said, "see you about 1130," And went inside his building.

I waved at him to signal I heard him and walked on back to my barracks.

As soon as I hit the Pit, I stripped and headed for the shower. I really needed a good long hot shower. I just stood under the hot water for about ten minutes letting it beat down on the back of my neck, shoulders and back. While the water was pouring over me, I thought about last night. Sara was an attractive girl, and she was tall, about five feet seven or eight, brown hair, pretty brown eyes, a nice smile. The best I could tell from what she was wearing that night everything else seemed to be proportioned appropriately. She was fun and had a nice laugh and seemed very out going.

I stepped out of the shower and moved over to the sink, got the hot water going again and shaved, changed to cold water and brushed my teeth. I grabbed my shaving gear and with the towel wrapped around my waist headed back to the Snake Pit. I grabbed a clean T-shirt and shorts out of my foot locker and put them on. I sat back on my bunk, found my cigarettes, fired one up and looked at my watch it was only 0930. I finished my cigarette and lay back on my bunk.

Rizzo came in after just getting off the midnight shift. "Hey, what do say, lover? You just coming in or going out?"

"Both," I said, "How about doing me a favor and waking me up about 1130 or before you go to bed, okay?"

"No problem, lover. Can I have a cigarette?"

"Yeah, help yourself," I said pointing to the cigarettes on my foot locker. I couldn't help but laugh to myself. Rizzo never failed to worm a cigarette out of you when he got the chance.

That was the last thought I remember having until Rizzo shook my shoulder and told me it was time to get up. I jumped up and looked at my watch it was 1125. I got up, grabbed some clean clothes out of my wall locker got dressed; and was out the door by 1130.

I saw Barry heading for my barracks as I was heading for his. We met about halfway and then started for the gate. We exited the gate, grabbed a Taxi, and told him to take us to the Bahnhof. Neither of us remembered the name of the hotel the girls were at but knew we could find it from the Bahnhof.

We found the hotel, and the girls were waiting for us in the small lobby. I think they looked a little surprised to see us. I was actually a little surprised that they were still there. I walked over to Sara, gave her a kiss on the cheek and said, "Good morning."

"Good morning, did you get any sleep?" she asked.

"Yeah, I got a little here and there. How about you?" I replied.

"I was out the minute my head hit the pillow." Sara laughed.

"Anyone hungry?" Barry asked.

"We have only had coffee. I could eat something," Mary Ann said.

"I could eat some breakfast."

Sara nodded in agreement. The only question was where we could find a place we could still get breakfast this time of day. We unofficially appointed Sara as the group official spokesperson. She asked the lady at the hotel and apparently got directions to a nearby café that still served breakfast.

"Danke," Sara replied to the woman.

"Bitte," the woman replied.

We all left the hotel, and Sara and I took the lead. Okay, she took the lead. I just tagged along, with Barry and Mary Ann right behind us. The more we walked the more it looked like we were headed for the Bahnhof.

I leaned over and whispered in Sara's ear, "Are we going to have to catch a train to go eat?"

She laughed. "The Bahnhof has a very good restaurant that severs breakfast all day long."

"Well, that's good to know," I said.

We entered the Bahnhof and Sara led us right to the restaurant. We found a table near the windows so we could look out towards the front of the station. We didn't wait long for a waiter. Again Sara spoke for the group since she spoke German. We all ordered eggs. I asked for ham with mine, Barry wanted bacon and Sara and Mary Ann both decided on sausage. All ordered coffee but me. I never have liked coffee. I really wanted some milk but I had seen some milk on another table and it kind of looked like dish water so I asked for some orange juice. After Sara had given the waiter all our orders we all lit up a cigarette while we waited.

Breakfast was served promptly and devoured in a hurry. Apparently we were all hungrier than we actually realized. During the after breakfast cigarette we decided the Zoo was definitely the place we wanted to go. Sara found out where the Zoo was located and off we went to grab a taxi.

The Zoo was located on Tiergarten Strasse. We paid the fee to get in and began our tour through the area. It was a pretty place, but let's face it. A zoo, is a zoo, is a zoo. Barry and I never talked about it, but I think we both realized we were only on this safari because the girls wanted to go. There were several places to stop and relax and drink a beer and just relax. We made the most of these places. I think we hit 'em all.

Barry and I made fun of the animals and did our own personal imitation of some in our feeble attempts to amuse the girls and make them laugh. They laughed and took some pictures as we made our way around the zoo. After three hours we decided it was time to get back to town. The girls' train back to Kaiserslutern was leaving at 1700 and they had to go back to the hotel and get their bags and check out.

We grabbed a taxi and back to the hotel we went. Barry and I went in and helped Sara and Mary Ann with their baggage. They paid their bill and we all carried baggage on the short walk to the Bahnhof. We had about and hour to kill when we got there; the girls already had their tickets, so we sat at the bar in the Bahnhof and had a drink.

"Have you got an address or phone number in Kaiserslautern yet?" I asked.

"I have an address but no phone number yet," Sara replied.

"Wanna exchange addresses and maybe keep in touch?"

"Sure." Sara pulled out some paper and a pen and wrote down her address and passed it to me.

"Loan me your paper and pen for a minute."

Sara slid the paper and pen towards me, and I wrote down my address and the company phone number and gave it back to Sara.

It was time to get down to the train platform. We all walked down to the loading area. I gave Sara a kiss and thanked her for a nice weekend. She said she enjoyed it too and boarded the train with Mary Ann following her aboard. Barry and I stood on the platform and saw the girls find a seat on our side of the train and we waved at them as the train began to move and they were out of sight.

Barry and I left the Bahnhof and grabbed a taxi back to the barracks. Neither of us said much and when we got to the caserne Barry went to his barracks and I went to the mess hall, I was hungry and tired. The mess hall wasn't crowded I sat down at a table by myself and began to eat. The guys from the day shift started to drift in. Galbreath and Hobbs came over and sat down. They asked where I had been all weekend. I just told them I'd been out.

"Where is out?" Galbreath asked.

"Yeah, where is out?" Hobbs mimicked.

"I went to the Zoo if you must know," I said.

"Yeah, right," Galbreath said.

"Went down to make faces at the monkeys?" Hobbs chuckled.

"Only if they made faces at me first," I replied.

I think they got the idea I wasn't really going to tell them anything exciting so they kind of backed off, and we all just finished our meal. We smoked a cigarette and walked back to the barracks together.

I had day shift Monday morning, so I got out my duty boots and checked them out. They didn't look bad so I just took them down to the latrine and washed them off in the big sink. I returned to the room, set the boots under my bunk, and headed down to the cleaners to pick up a fresh pressed uniform. I stopped to pick up the keys to the cleaners from the C.Q and was told it was open already.

As I approached the door Shep Williams was just coming out with his uniform. Shep was a really nice guy and the only black assigned to the unit.

"Hold the door, Shep," I hollered at him.

"Hey, Bones, you working tomorrow?" Shep asked.

"You got it," I replied.

Shep handed me the keys to the cleaners and headed on back towards the stairs. I found my uniform and closed the cleaners, locked the door, returned the keys to the CQ and headed back to my room. I checked to make sure I had all my gear ready for tomorrow; hung my uniform and pistol belt on the outside of my wall locker.

I finally felt the tiredness settle in all over my body. I sat back on my bunk, lit a cigarette and found myself wondering if I would hear from Sara again. It was early, but I was tired. I put out my cigarette, got undressed and climbed in bed and was asleep in a matter of minutes. I didn't hear anything else until reveille the next morning.

The first part of the week was pretty routine; then about Thursday I got a card from Sara, thanking me for showing her around Heidelberg and saying that she really enjoyed the time we spent together. Her phone had been installed and she gave me her phone number. I was kind of surprised to actually hear from her but was excited that I had. I was off on Friday so I thought I would call her then.

It took me forever to get my turn at the phone by the Orderly Room Friday night, I was afraid it was going to be to late to call but I finally got to place my call. Sara answered after the first ring.

"Hi, this is Rick in Heidelberg. I got your card with your number enclosed so I thought I would call."

"Hi, I'm glad you called. Thank you. Are you off duty tonight?" she asked.

"Yes, I got your card yesterday but had to work. I go back on shift tomorrow night and won't be off for another couple of nights."

We talked for a while she asked if I ever got a weekend off. I told her it was rare when my schedule worked out so I would get a full weekend off but sometimes it worked out that way. I tried to explain the 1st Sgt's master duty roster to her but it was rather difficult to explain. I told her I might be able to swap duties with someone one night if I could get the first sergeant to approve it. I asked if she would be interested in me coming up to K-town to visit if I could work out a swap some weekend and she said she would.

By this time there were other guys getting impatient to use the phone, so we said goodbye with the idea that I would see if I could get a weekend off. Maybe next weekend if she didn't have any plans. She said she didn't have any plans.

Monday morning I went in to see the first sergeant and asked him if he would approve a swap next Friday night if I could find someone to swap with me. He said sure but I had to bring the guy I got down there and tell him in person that he was willing to swap with me. It took me a couple of days but I finally got SP4 King to swap with me and go down and tell the first sergeant he in fact would swap a day with me.

I called Sara and told her I had found someone to swap with me and I was off Friday, Saturday but had to be back by Sunday afternoon. She said that was great and she would look forward to seeing me Friday evening. She said there was no sense in me getting there too early because she usually didn't get home until around 1700.I said that was fine with me.

The week seemed to drag but Friday finally arrived. Sara and I had talked a couple of times when I could get to the phone. I asked Hans the translator at Campbell one evening before he left how long it would take to get to K-Town by train. He said it was a short trip maybe only two hours at most. I figured if I caught a train about 1400 hours that should put me in K-Town about 1600 and give me an hour to find a taxi and get to Sara's BOQ (Bachelors Officers Quarters). I had no idea how far it was from the Bahnhof to her place.

I got a ticket for the train leaving at1415 hours. I figured that should give me plenty of time. The train left on time and arrived on time, just like all German trains did. I found my way to the front of the Bahnhof and had no problem finding a taxi. I had written down Sara's address and told the taxi driver where I needed to go and he didn't bat and eye so I figured he knew where to go. Getting to the housing area was only about a ten minute drive but it took another ten minutes to find Sara's building number. It was only about 1640. I was early; I didn't know if I should go on up, she was on the 3rd floor or just wait down here.

It was a little bit chilly outside standing on top of that hill so I decided what the hell I can go up knock on the door, and if she isn't there I can wait out in the hallway. I went in, made my way to the third floor and found her room; it was the first unit at the top of the steps after you entered the door from the stairwell. I took a deep breath and knocked on the door. Within seconds Sara answered the door. She said hello smiled, stepped aside and motioned me to come in. I stepped inside leaned over and gave her a kiss on the cheek and said hello.

Sara shared a unit with Mary Ann. The unit was like a duplex. The outside door opened into the middle of small hallway with the bathroom immediately in front of you when you walked in which the girls shared. To the left was Mary Ann's room, Sara's was to the right. Of course each room had a door for privacy. Mary Ann was there, and she stuck her head out of her room and said hello.

"Would you like some coffee?" Sara asked.

"No thanks, I don't drink coffee," I replied.

"Oh, that's right, you told me that. How about a coke?"

"Coke sounds good, thanks."

Sara's room had a small day bed, a desk with a chair, a small refrigerator and she had purchased a radio/record player that was near the bed. I sat on the bed and Sara sat on the chair at the desk. The BOQ was located at the top of a hill along with several other BOQs; from the windows in her room you could look down over a wooded area and into the main shopping area and the high school where Sara worked.

Mary Ann came over and joined us for a drink and a cigarette and we all just sat around talked about anything that came up. The girls were excited about their new jobs and had some comments about some of the people they had met already. Occasionally they would ask me something about my home town, schools I attended, which was one; and sometimes they would ask more about my job.

"Is anyone hungry?" Sara asked

"I could eat a little something," I said.

Mary Ann agreed. We talked about what we wanted to eat. Nobody wanted to go out; it was getting late. Both girls checked their fridges and came up with some eggs, bread and some ham. We all agreed that breakfast sounded great.

Sara fired up her little hot plate and scrambled a bunch of eggs, cooked the ham, and made some toast in her new toaster. She had some milk she had picked up at the local commissary, so I had milk; they had coffee.

After we ate the girls had a drink. I sipped on a coke, and we all smoked a cigarette and sat around and talked some more. Mary Ann excused herself and said goodnight. I looked at my watch, and it was almost 2300 hours.

Sara and I had never discussed any sleeping arrangements, and I wasn't going to bring it up. Sara seemed to be reading my mind and she said she had made a reservation for me at the Guest House just down the road, and if I felt like it was time for bed she would drive me down there in Mary Ann's car.

"I am kind of tired, and I'm sure you had a long day, so maybe I should go on down to the Guest House."

Sara said, "Okay."

She got up, slipped her shoes and coat on, then we walked out the door to Mary Ann's car. Sara backed the car out and we drove back the way the taxi had brought me in but made a right turn near the bottom of the hill.

Sara stopped at the second building on the right and said, "This is the Guest House. I made the reservation in your name so they should have a room ready for you."

"Thanks, you want me to call you in the morning or you wanna call me when you're ready?" I asked.

"Do you have an alarm clock?" Sara asked.

"No, I didn't think to bring one."

"Then how about I give you a wake up call when I get up, then we will both have some time to shower and get dressed. Then I'll come down and pick you up."

"Sounds like a plan to me," I said.

I leaned over and gave Sara a kiss said good night, got out of the car and headed for the entrance to the Guest House. Sara turned the car around and headed back up the hill.

I walked in the Guest House, walked up to the sign in desk and gave the clerk my name. He checked his register and then had me sign in while he found my key.

"Your room is right down the hall on the left," he said.

"Thanks," I replied.

I grabbed my little over night bag and headed for my room. Fortunately the heat was already on low so the room was warm. I slipped out of my coat and shoes and lay back on the bed and lit up a cigarette.

I don't know what I had expected, but I was a little surprised to find myself in the Guest House. I had enjoyed the evening with Sara but with the exception of the few hours we had on the river bank we really hadn't been alone yet. *Oh, well,* I thought, *what's the rush? We just met.* And there was always tomorrow.

GERMANY
Chapter 42

I woke up to a ringing phone about 0800. I answered with a sleepy hello.

"Good morning," came a cheery reply from Sara. "Did I wake you up?"

"No, I had to get up to answer the phone anyway," I replied.

Sara laughed and said she was going to start getting ready and should be down to pick me up in about an hour. I said that would work for me.

I rolled out of bed and lit a cigarette. I was curious to find out what today would bring. I finished my cigarette and headed for the shower. The hot water felt good and I soon began to feel like I was alive again. I finished my shower, shaved, brushed my teeth and got dressed. I was done in about 20 minutes; so I had about 30 minutes before Sara would show up. I sat back down on the bed and smoked another cigarette.

I finished the cigarette and walked out of the Guest House just as Sara was pulling up out front. Good timing I thought. I slid in the car and gave her a kiss and we started back to the BOQ.

We got back to her room; I said good morning to Mary Ann who was moving about in her room. She shouted a good morning back. Sara poured herself a cup of coffee and asked if I would like anything. She said she had some hot chocolate. I said that sounded good. I hadn't had hot chocolate in ages.

"Mary Ann and I both need to go to the commissary and the PX today; we thought we would do that this morning. Would you like to come with us or just wait here?"

"I'll go. I'd like to see what the commissary is like. I've never been in one," I replied.

We finished our coffee and chocolate, left and drove to the commissary. The commissary was like a big grocery store. They had everything you could want as far as I could tell. I pushed a cart around and Sara filled it up. She asked me what I liked and I mentioned some stuff that I liked to eat or snack on. Sara stocked up on eggs, bread, ham, some cookies, some cheese, crackers and some cokes. That little fridge didn't hold a whole lot of stuff.

We left the commissary and went by the PX. I didn't need anything from the PX but some cigarettes. I got a carton of Winstons for me, and Sara said she could use some Salems. While I got the cigarettes, she and Mary Ann got some girls stuff, make up and the like. We left there, went back to the BOQ and unloaded the car.

After we got the car unloaded and the groceries put away we all gathered in Sara's room and had coffee and cokes. I found out that both girls were pinochle players. Pinochle was a popular game back at the barracks so that worked out well. We sat around and played cut throat pinochle most of the afternoon. Sara had some German albums she had purchased and we listened to that. I didn't understand much. Okay, I didn't understand a damn thing, but I liked some of the music. I could do without the oompa stuff though.

About 1800 we were getting hungry, at least I was. I asked if anyone else was.

"I'm getting that way," Sara said.

"I'm not hungry now but ya'll go ahead and eat if you want to," Mary Ann replied.

"Rick, what are you in the mood for?" Sara asked.

"I dunno; I could eat a sandwich or not," I said.

"I'm in the mood for a steak and baked potato," Sara said.

"That really sounds good. I haven't had something like that since I left the States."

Mary Ann said, "Why don't ya'll take my car and go to the club and eat there; I'm not really hungry, and I have some letter writing to do.

Sara and I thought that would be a great idea, so we got dressed and headed for the club. Since Sara had a GS rating she was authorized to go the Officer's Club at Ramstein AFB, which is located in the K-Town/Landstuhl area. I had some reservations about going to an Officer's Club as a PFC but she said I was her guest and she didn't see anything wrong with it. So off we went.

It was a nice club with a very nice dining room. The dinning room wasn't busy but somewhere in the building you could hear a band and people talking and laughing so apparently there was a bar somewhere near by. We picked a table and a waitress came over, brought us some water and menus then disappeared as waitresses do. We looked over the menus but knew what we wanted already we just had to find it.

When the waitress came back again we ordered a New York Strip sirloin steak with baked potatoes and a green salad with Blue Cheese Dressing. Sara ordered a glass of wine and I had ice tea.

While we waited on our supper, we made some small talk. Sara said she and Mary Ann came out here for dinner a couple of times a week. It got old eating in the room all the time. I said I usually ate in the mess hall or went to the little snack bar on Patton Barracks if I just wanted a hamburger and fries.

Our salads arrived quickly and we ate pretty much in silence. The steaks were not far behind the salads which I liked. I always hated waiting for a long time between salad and main course. We made a little small talk during the meal but mostly just ate in silence. When we finished we had a cigarette, Sara had another glass of wine and I got a refill on the ice tea. When we left she paid for supper and I left a tip for the waitress. I liked that arrangement since I was going to be cutting it pretty close if I had to pay for the meal too.

It was a little after 2200 before we left the Club. I told Sara on the way back that she might as well drop me off at the Guest House on the way rather than getting back out again in a couple of hours. She seemed kind of surprised but said okay.

We pulled up in front of the Guest House. I leaned over to give her a kiss. There was something different about this kiss; it was the first time I really felt like she kissed me back. Now I was wondering if I had made the right call in coming right back to the Guest House. We lingered just a little bit in the car then I decided I better get out now so I gave her one more kiss got out, told her to call me in the morning. She said okay and drove off toward the BOQ.

I got back to my room undressed and got under the covers, propped my pillow up and lit a cigarette. I was starting to really like being around Sara, and tonight I got the feeling that she was starting to feel a little more comfortable with me. I put out the cigarette and went to sleep.

Sunday morning Sara called about the same time. I was already awake just smoking a cigarette waiting for her to call. I told her I'd be ready by the time she got here, hung up and headed for the shower. I took a little bit more time in the shower this morning. I do enjoy a hot shower.

When Sara pulled up out front I was waiting for her. I got in the car, said good morning and gave her a kiss. We turned around and headed for the BOQ. As we entered the unit Mary Ann was putting on her coat, she was going to go check out the church service at the base chapel on Ramstein. Sara reminded her that I was leaving this afternoon and she wanted to give me a ride back to the Bahnhof. Mary Ann said she would be back right after the service.

"Would you like some breakfast?" Sara asked.

"I think I could just eat some buttered toast and have a glass of milk," I replied.

"How many pieces of toast do you want?" she asked, as she got the bread out of the fridge.

"About four," I said.

"You always eat that much bread?"

"I'm a pretty big bread eater," I said.

Sara toasted the bread buttered it and poured me a large glass of milk. She fixed herself a couple of pieces of toast and had a cup of coffee. She put on some albums after she finished her toast and coffee and curled up next to me on the day bed as I leaned back after finishing my toast and milk and lit up a cigarette. This was the first time we had been totally alone since the river bank. I put my arm around her and pulled her closer to me. We sat there and listened to the music and did a little light petting which led to a little heavier petting but before anything got too far; Mary Ann came walking back in. Unfortunately we had not bothered to close the door to Sara's room.

It was just as well, it was almost time for me to go catch a train. I had to go to the barracks. Sara and I got off the bed and began to put on shoes and coats. I had already checked out of the Guest House so I had my little bag with me. Sara got the keys to the car from Mary Ann. I told Mary Ann goodbye and we headed out the door.

Sara didn't have any problems dealing with the German drivers. We got to the Bahnhof; she parked the car and came in with me. She checked my ticket and walked down to the right track with me. The train was already there.

"I really enjoyed this weekend," I said.

"So did I; I'm glad you came down."

I put my arms around her gave her a kiss, and again I felt like she actually kissed me back. This was getting interesting.

"I don't know when I'll get another weekend off. I may get one day off the weekend and a Friday or a Monday sometime," I said.

"Let me know what your schedule is, and maybe you can come down and wait for me at the BOQ sometime. I have a spare key or can have one made."

"I'll call you and let you know," I said.

The conductor said something and Sara said I had to go. I gave her a kiss real quick and climbed aboard the train. I found a seat on her side of the boarding platform and waved to her as the train pulled out.

I spent the whole trip back to Heidelberg thinking about the past weekend. It was different than what I was used to spending with a girl. Maybe that was the difference, Sara wasn't a girl. She handled herself differently from all the other girls I had ever been with, and that was earning my respect. I was experiencing some new feelings now, and I wasn't exactly sure what they were.

GERMANY
Chapter 43

From that weekend in September, Sara and I spent every minute we could squeeze out of our schedules to be together. By Thanksgiving I was pretty sure I was in love with her and felt she might feel the same way too.

I managed to get a couple of days over Thanksgiving off. Sara had bought a little blue Renault with a sun roof she named Blue Bird. I preferred Blue Bitch, but more about that later. She drove down and picked me up at the barracks and then we headed right back to K-Town. I asked Sara on the way up if she had made reservations at the Guest House already and she said no.

"Are you going to stop on the way up to the BOQ?" I asked

"Mary Ann is going to be out of town the whole weekend; I thought you could use her room," Sara replied.

"Sounds good to me."

Before we went back to the BOQ we stopped and picked up some pizza down at this little pizza place next to the PX. I think that was the first pizza I had since I left the states. We went back to the BOQ and ate the pizza; Sara had a beer and I had a coke with my pizza. Sara had some new records; she put them on while we ate. We had a cigarette after we finished the pizza and continued to listen to the records.

We snuggled for a while on the day bed and continued to listen to the music. Before I knew it Sara was asleep on my shoulder. I just let her lie there for a while, and I continued to listen to the music until the last record played. I tried to get my arm out from under Sara's head so I could reach my cigarettes but she woke up. I asked her if she was ready to go to bed.

She said, "I guess I'm tired I fell asleep here."

I said, "Okay."

I got up grabbed my cigarettes and headed for Mary Ann's room. I got undressed, climbed in bed, and was lying there in the dark, smoking. I could hear Sara moving around on her side and going into the bathroom. When she came out of the bathroom, she stuck her head in Mary Ann's door, stood there for a couple of minutes, and then said, "Good night."

"Good night," I said.

Sara turned around and walked back to her room. I lay there and finished my cigarette and just as I put it out I heard Sara. "Rick?"

I got up walked over to her room, climbed over her and crawled under the covers next to her. She rolled over in my arms and kissed my neck. That was the first night we spent together.

Now I had a dilemma on my hands. That night pretty much sealed the deal for me but I wanted more time to spend with Sara. As much as I wanted to be in the Honor Guard, I knew I was going to have to give it up.

I went down to the Orderly Room the Monday after Thanksgiving and talked to Sgt. Willis and explained my situation to him. I asked him if I could work his straight 9-5 week day schedule so I could have the weekends off to spend more time with my Fiancée. (I figured Fiancée would carry more weight than girlfriend.)

"You think this is the one, Sammy?" Sgt. Willis asked.

"Looks like it could be Top," I replied.

"Well, I think we can help you out, at least for now, but we may have to call upon you to fill in sometimes if things go south on us. We do have a lot of projected losses coming up this year."

"I appreciate it Top, if you need me to fill in just let me know, that won't be a problem," I said.

I had left the Snake Pit in October and moved down to the 1st room to the right of the stairway as you entered the second floor. I was in a four man room with the "Greek god" Rizzo, a guy named Barger and Harry "Horse Face" Stellers. Of course I new Rizzo pretty well already; Barger and Harry weren't new but I just never had much to do with them so far. Harry had actually got to the Company a couple of weeks before I did. Barger was pretty quiet, and I didn't know much about him but I did know he was a short timer. A short timer is a person that only has a few days, weeks or a couple of months before he goes home. There is usually a short timer's party for the person leaving. Some parties are big deals, and everyone attends, or sometimes it's some of the short timer's friends who take him out and everybody gets drunk.

I sat on my bunk and smoked a cigarette and as I sat there thinking I made a decision right then that I was going to give Sara a ring and ask her to marry me. When I had sometime off during the week I went out looking for rings. I found one in some really off the wall jewelry store over near Campbell Barracks. It was a cheap little thing but it was the best I could do on a PFC's pay.

In mid December Sara and I had sometime to ourselves one evening when Mary Ann was out. I decided this was as good a time as any to ask her. I didn't know any other way but to just ask her so while we were sitting on the day bed, she was having a glass of wine and listening to some music I got up and walked over to my little tote bag and got the ring. I returned to the day bed, sat down by Sara, and took a deep breath. "I got something to ask you," I said, she looked at me as if to say "well?"

I opened the box and just said, "Will you marry me?"

She took the last sip of wine out of her glass, set it down on top of the record player, turned around, put her arms around my neck and said "Yes."

She gave me a kiss and I slipped the ring on her finger. I was certainly glad that was over with because I was scared shitless.

When word got around the company that I was dating a twenty-five year old school teacher my status among some of my peers seemed to go up considerably. They all wanted to know if she had a friend. Naturally she did, but by this time Mary Ann had found a guy named Harold that she had dated during college.

Over the Christmas holidays; Mary Ann, Harold, Sara and I took a trip in Blue Bird to the Garmisch/Berchtesgaden area located in the southern Bavarian area of Germany not far from the border of Austria. Since we were in the general vicinity we stopped in Regensburg and visited with some of Sara's relatives, Albreck and Helga. I remember we stayed in a Hotel in Regensburg and Albreck came down to the hotel unexpectedly and rousted us out of bed early the morning after we arrived. That kinda caught us all off guard, since Sara and I were sleeping in one room and Mary Ann and Harold in another. After visiting with Albreck and Helga we continued on our journey.

While in Garmisch/Berchtesgaden area we stayed at The General Walker Resort Hotel operated by the U.S. Army. It was a nice place; I thought it was pretty fancy for a SP4 to be staying in. I understand the General Walker Hotel has since been demolished. Points of interest in the Berchtesgaden area were the Berchtesgadener Hof Hotel where famous visitors stayed, such as Eva Braun, Erwin Rommel, Josef Goebels, Heinrich Himmler, and Neville Chamberliain. There was the Kehlsteinhaus (Eagle's Nest), which was built as a present for Hitler's 50th birthday in1939.

In Garmisch we went ice skating in the Olympic skating rink built by Hitler for the 1936 Olympics; where the famous Norwegian skater Sonja Henie won her 3rd Gold Medal for figure skating. Ice skating wasn't one of my strong suits, but I managed to stay on my feet.

The mountains in and around that area are spectacular to say the least, especially in wintertime with all the snow caps on the tops of the mountains. The drive is something else or was back in those days. The roads weren't all that wide and it was all Blue Bird could do to make the climb up those mountains loaded with four people plus luggage. And German drivers don't make things anymore relaxing for you. They aren't known for their slow drivers, especially on the Autobahn. Going back down was even more scary.

This was without a doubt the most exciting trip Sara and I had made so far. It would be safe to say a good time was had by all.

GERMANY
Chapter 44

Sara had spring break coming up in March 1961and I still had some leave time. She wanted to do some traveling so after checking out our options we decided on Munich and then on to Vienna, Austria.

The first thing I did Monday morning was stop by the Orderly Room and drop off my request for leave. The leave was approved and I was excited about getting away. The Friday before my leave actually started I asked Roach to sign me out on Monday morning and I took off for K-Town. It would have been easier for Sara to stop by and pick me up since we had to drive through Heidelberg to get to Munich but I figured it would be easier to pack the car all at once instead of having to do it again when she picked me up.

We spent Friday evening checking and double checking out packing to be sure we had everything we needed, consolidating where we could so we wouldn't have so many bags to carry. I was beginning to learn that there is no way a woman can go anywhere with just one or two bags. I had two bags and both were relatively small. Sara had two and hadn't packed her clothes yet. She worked until almost midnight getting everything just the way she wanted it. I lay on the bed and watched. Every time I made a suggestion she had a reason why it wouldn't work so I stopped suggesting.

Finally when she was satisfied she sat down at the desk with a glass of wine and lit a cigarette. I could tell she was still going over it in her mind. I wouldn't have been surprised if she had started over again.

"You want to take a shower first?" I asked.

"You go ahead; I think I'll just sit here and relax for a few minutes."

I got up off the bed, undressed, and headed for the bathroom. I turned the water on and let it run; it took awhile for the hot water to get to you. While I was waiting I brushed my teeth, by the time I was finished the hot water was pouring out of the shower head. I stepped in and worked my way into the hot water slowly. I didn't linger in the shower; the hot water didn't last long so I hurried so Sara would have some hot water when she got in.

I got out of the shower and toweled off, wrapped the towel around my waist and walked back to the room. "It's all yours," I said.

Sara had already undressed and had her robe on and headed straight for the bathroom. I turned the records over on the record player, threw the towel across the chair and climbed into bed. I lit a cigarette and just lay there and listened to the music. Sara seemed to be taking her time in the shower.

Finally she came out of the bathroom wearing her robe and a towel around her head. She sat down in the desk chair, the robe falling away from her legs as she lit a cigarette.

"I needed that hot shower," she said.

"I guess you think you're just going to come to bed and fall right to sleep now, huh?" I asked.

She looked over at me and said, "I can see you have other ideas."

"Maybe," I shrugged.

She put out her cigarette, turned out the overhead light, walked over to the bed took the towel off her head, dropped her robe and climbed into bed.

We were up and moving by 0700 Saturday morning we wanted to get an early start. Sara had to have her morning coffee. I grabbed some bags and started carrying them down to the car. By the time I got the ones I had packed in the car; Sara came out with what was left. We moved and adjusted until we had the bags arranged the way we wanted them. Sara went back up to the apartment to look around one more time to make sure everything was as it should be and all the electrical stuff was turned off.

Sara came back down we hopped in Blue Bird and we were off. A quick check of the map showed we had quite a trip ahead of us. Sara was a good traveler, at least from a man's point of view; she didn't seem to have one of those little tiny bladders most women seem to have and need to stop every 50-100 miles. She had packed some sandwiches and snacks put some cokes in a little cooler and iced it down so we didn't have to stop for anything except gas.

One thing I discovered about myself while I was in Germany, I had developed road hypnosis from driving or riding in those little tiny cars like the Renault. I was good for about 100 miles then I would start to feel like I was going to fall asleep and have to turn the driving over to Sara.

The weather was great and the scenery was awesome the further south we got. There wasn't a lot of traffic on the road and we had Blue Bird cranked up to the max; so we made pretty good time.

We exited the Autobahn around Munich. Sara followed some signs that led us to a nice-looking little hotel/inn. We got out, stretched for a couple of minutes, then went inside. Sara asked the lady if they had a room and what was the rate. When she was satisfied it was a good place to spend the night we registered and the lady took us to our room. She and Sara were yakking away; I just tagged along so I would know where our room was; then we went back to the car and got the luggage and carried it back to our room.

"The lady told me there was a nice little restaurant we could walk to just around the corner if you're hungry," Sara said.

"I could eat something," I replied

"You want to go now or wait a while?"

"Let's go eat and get that out of the way. I think I'm going to sleep very well tonight."

"You slept in the car most of the trip."

"That doesn't count; it's not like real sleep; besides, I only pretend to be asleep so I don't have to watch you drive."

"Are you saying I'm a bad driver?" Sara asked

"Oh, no, I wouldn't dare say that, especially when you have that curling iron in your hand," I replied.

"Okay, I'll let you off the hook for now. Let's go eat."

We left the hotel and found this typically quaint German-looking restaurant and were seated at a small table in the corner; the waitress left the menus and then left. I didn't need to look at it; I was sticking with my usual, Wiener Schnitzel mit Pomme Frites. Sara ordered some Bratwurst with Sauerkraut. She had her usual glass of wine and I had my usual ice tea.

"What are we going to do tomorrow?" I asked as we waited on our meal.

"We can see the sights we want to see in Munich, or we can go to Vienna and stop in Munich on the way back."

"If you're giving me a choice, I'd rather drive on to Vienna and see how much time we want to spend there then come back to Munich," I said.

"Actually that was what I was thinking."

"Okay, that sounds like a plan to me," I replied as the waitress brought us our dinner.

"How is your Wiener Schnitzel?"

"It's good; tastes like all the other Wiener Schnitzel in Germany. How's your whatever it is over there?

"It's Bratwurst with Sauerkraut. Want a bite?"

"Is that a threat?" I grinned.

"Try it. You might like it," Sara said.

"Okay, give me a bite, a small bite."

Sara cut off a little piece of the Bratwurst put some Sauerkraut on the fork and stretched her arm across the table. I leaned forward took the bite off her fork and immediately sat back. I swallowed it in a hurry and drank some tea.

"You didn't like it?" Sara asked.

"The bratwurst was okay, but you can keep that other shit. Yuck!"

I had been in Germany almost a year now and hadn't really been able to find anything in the food department that I really liked besides my Wiener Schnitzel and Pomme Frites. Even the desserts I had tried seem to be dry and gritty; except for the strudel they weren't bad.

We finished out dinner, paid the bill and returned to the hotel. Once we got back to the room we kicked off our shoes, sat back on the comfortable sofa and lit a cigarette. It was still early but Sara and I were both tired. When we finished our cigarette, we got undressed and went to bed. I think we were both sound asleep by the time our heads hit the pillow.

We hadn't bothered to set an alarm, but we really didn't need one since we were on vacation and had no set schedule but I woke up; checked my watch and it was only 0530. I got out of bed, walked over to the sofa and lit a cigarette, Sara was still sound asleep. Before I finished my cigarette; Sara sat up, stretched and asked what time it was.

"It's almost 0600," I said.

Sara climbed out of bed went over to one of her little bags found her little jar of instant coffee and turned on the water in the bathroom sink. Unlike her apartment the water got hot in a hurry so she had her coffee in a matter of minutes. She came over, sat beside me on the sofa, and lit a cigarette.

I finished my cigarette, got up and headed for the shower. The water was good and hot. I was facing the wall just letting the water cascade down over my head. It felt good. To me a good hot shower was one of my favorite things. It always made me feel alive. But I think I said that already. I finished my shower got out, shaved and stepped out into the bedroom. I walked over found some clean shorts in one of my bags and put them on. Sara had already disappeared in to the bathroom.

By 0730 we were dressed packed and had the bags in the car. Sara went into pay the hotel bill and came back out.

"The restaurant is open for breakfast if you're hungry," she said.

"I could eat something. How about you?"

"Yes, I want some more coffee and maybe a strudel," Sara replied.

We made sure the car was locked and walked around to the restaurant. The same lady that waited on us last night was there this morning. I suspected she was the owner or the owner's wife.

"Guten Morgen," the lady said, smiling broadly. "Schliefen Sie gut?"

"Guten Morgen. Ja, danke," Sara replied.

We picked the same table we sat at for dinner and the waitress brought us both a cup of coffee. Before I could tell the lady I didn't drink coffee, Sara said to just take it. She would drink it.

"You're gonna be peeing all the way from here to Vienna. We'll be stopping at every gas station we pass," I said.

"I can't drive without my coffee," Sara replied.

Sara ordered each of us an apple strudel and a glass of orange juice for me. We ate quickly, paid the bill and headed for the car.

Before we got in the car Sara said, "I'll be right there. I need to go use the bathroom."

"See, it's startin' already!" I yelled at her. Laughing, I got in the car and waited for her to come back.

I started out driving. Sara played navigator and guided me back out on the right road to get us back on the Autobahn. I lasted for a little over 100 miles and my hypnosis started to set in. I pulled over at the next park platz, and Sara took over the driving chores. We hardly got 10 miles down the road, and I was asleep.

We crossed the border into Austria at Salzburg, stopped for gas, and from there we went to Linz and finally entered the city of Vienna (Wein). Sara had the name of a hotel that had been recommended to her and with the help of a couple of friendly citizens we found our way to the hotel. It was an older hotel not far from the Danube. We pulled in front of the hotel, checked in and had the bags brought up to the room. Again we found ourselves worn out from the trip and ate in the hotel restaurant. I thought I would try something different and ordered some kind of fish. Sara thought that sounded good and ordered the same.

I smoked a cigarette while we waited on our meal. Sara had her nose stuck in a book of things to do, places to go, and things to see in Vienna.

She earmarked a few pages and passed the book across to me. The first thing that caught my eye was the Riesenrad (giant wheel). They had a Ferris wheel at the entrance to the Prater Amusement Park. It was one of the earliest Ferris wheels, built in 1897.

The Tiergarten Schonbrunn is a zoo located in the grounds of the Schonbrunn Palace. That Palace is huge, and the zoo is the oldest in the world. The first elephant in captivity gave birth on July 14th, 1906 in this zoo.

Those were a couple of tourist attractions; the book also mentioned that there were more than 100 art museums in Vienna and mentioned sites associated with the many composers who lived in Vienna such as Beethoven and Mozart. Another famous guy that lived in Vienna for a few years was Adolph Hitler.

The waiter brought our supper and I gave the book back to Sara. I wasn't sure but I think they just caught that fish and threw it on my plate. I swear I saw the tail move. It looked totally raw to me. I took a couple of bites, and it kinda sent shivers down my back. There was some kind of sauce they brought with it, so I tried dipping it in the sauce; that didn't help a lot. Sara was having more luck with her fish than I was. That was not surprising. I was learning that Sara would or could eat about anything.

I leaned across the table and whispered. "Are you really gonna eat that shit?"

"It's not all that bad once you smother it with the sauce and add a lot of salt and pepper."

"Well, you can have mine when you finish yours if you really like it," I said as I pushed my plate to the side. That's what I get for drifting from my usual I thought.

We didn't sit around after supper, instead we went right back to our room, kicked off our shoes and relaxed. It had been a long trip. I think it was longer than either of us thought it would be. I popped a coke from the cooler and lit up a cigarette.

"So what struck your fancy in that guidebook?" I asked.

"I would like to go ride the Ferris wheel; maybe we could get some pictures from the top of the Farris wheel, and I would like to visit the zoo and tour that palace while we are there. Maybe we could visit a couple of the museums. Anything particular you would like to do?" Sara asked.

"I like the Farris wheel, and the zoo is okay. I didn't see anything in that book about the Danube River. I thought that was a big attraction."

Sara got out the book and thumbed through it for a minute and then began to read. A couple of minutes she said, "It says here you can take tours of the river, anything from a day trip to a 12-day cruise."

"A day trip might be fun, but I'll pass on the 12-day cruise."

We got undressed and climbed in bed. Sara found some acceptable music on a radio by the bed. We listened to the music and smoked a cigarette. We finished our cigarettes about the same time, Sara turned off the radio; I gave her a kiss goodnight and was asleep in a manner or seconds.

We woke up early the next morning but we were in no rush this morning. Sara went in for her shower first and spent a good hour in the bathroom. I drank a coke and smoked a couple of cigarettes while I was waiting on her. Finally she came out in her robe with her hair all wrapped up in a towel and a cup of coffee in her hand.

"Did you leave me any hot water?" I asked.

"There should be plenty," Sara said.

I got up, went to the bathroom and turned on the water. It was hot so I grabbed the soap and shampoo from the sink and hopped in the shower.

After we dressed we went down to the restaurant and ordered breakfast. I was hoping they cooked their eggs more than they cooked their fish. I told Sara to make sure she told the waitress I wanted some well done eggs.

Breakfast came quickly, the eggs were well done and so was the toast. Sara had more coffee and I had orange juice. Since I hadn't eaten supper I was hungry and made short work of the eggs and toast.

We got out the map and found the Schonbrunn Palace. We toured the palace and the zoo. It occurred to me while we were at the zoo; this was the second time Sara had wanted to go to a Zoo. That was the place we went in Heidelberg when we first met. I wonder what the big attraction of zoos was for her. We spent a good portion of the day at the zoo and Palace. We found a small sidewalk café down the street; stopped and grabbed a bite to eat. Sara stuck her nose in that tourist guide book. I smoked a cigarette and watched all the tourist walk by.

We found our way back to the hotel. Sara noticed there was a nice looking restaurant just down the street from our hotel and suggested we go out for supper tonight. I didn't have a problem with that. I knew what I was going to eat no matter where we went. We decided we had time to take a short nap since nobody but Americans really ate supper early in Europe. A nap worked for me; I guess I was used to sleeping in the car.

I must have slept for a couple of hours. When I woke up I could hear Sara in the shower. I walked into the bathroom and peeked around the curtain. Sara was standing with her back to me. The thought occurred to me it was not a good idea to waste so much water so I slipped off my shorts and stepped in behind her. I slipped my arms around her waist and she jumped and squealed. She turned around and said, "You're not supposed to be in here, cowboy."

I gave her a kiss and said, "I'll wash your back if you'll wash mine."

"Your back?" she quipped.

"I'll leave anything else to your discretion," I took the bar of soap and washcloth from Sara's hand turned her around and began to wash her back. She turned back around put her arms around me and gave me a kiss. The shower took longer than it should have, but we both stepped out feeling much more refreshed.

We dressed slowly and finally left the hotel. We walked down the street to the restaurant Sara had noticed earlier. It was a pretty swanky place. Heavy carpet on the floor, chandeliers hanging from the ceiling turned down low and candles on the table. A head waiter met us at the door directed us to a small booth near the back of the main dining room. Another waiter was there almost before we sat down with menus and a wine list. I almost didn't bother to look at the menu but decided to at least peruse it. As I looked down at the menu I noticed there were some things written in English. One of the entries I read said New York Strip Sirloin Steak.

"Do you see what I see on this menu?" I whispered to Sara.

"Yes, I do," she said.

"Ask the waiter when he comes back if that's real steak." Before I could get the sentence out of my mouth the waiter was there.

"Have you selected a wine or other drink," he asked. My head snapped back. He was speaking English.

"No, we haven't yet, but I have a question," I said.

"Yes, sir, how may I help you?"

"Is this a real New York Strip Sirloin you have on the menu?"

"Yes, they are, sir."

"I'll have one, medium rare. Do you serve baked potatoes or French fries?"

"We have either one you want, sir."

"I'll have French fries with my steak," I said.

Sara said, "I'll have the same thing, but I want a baked potato."

"Yes, madam; and to drink, sir?" the waiter asked.

"What do you suggest?" I asked.

He rattled off something I didn't understand, but I wasn't going to let him know that. "That sounds fine. Bring us a Carafe, please."

The waiter was right back with our wine almost immediately; he poured some in my glass to taste. I tasted it; waited a second like I had seen them do in the movies and then nodded my head. The waiter nodded back and poured a half glass of wine in each of our glasses.

Sara was looking at me with a rather amused and surprised look on her face.

"What?"

"You handled that very well." She smiled.

"Well, just because I'm from Texas doesn't mean I'm a cowboy all the time, ya know."

We lit a cigarette while we waited for our steak. We barely finished our cigarettes before out steaks arrived. They smelled delicious. The waiter refilled our wine, while the head waiter quietly slipped one of those little folders with our bill in it on the edge of the table. After the waiters left I peeked at the bill and then shut it real quick.

"How much is it?" Sara whispered.

I slid the folder over to her so she could see for herself. She opened it up and looked at it and then closed it real quickly. "Oh, my!" she said.

"It's gonna take a hundred bucks to get us outta here after you include a tip," I said.

"Can you pay for it?" Sara asked.

"Yeah, I got the money, but I won't be eating for the rest of the week," I said.

I pulled five twenty dollar bills out of my wallet and slid them in the folder. We got up and headed for the door. The waiter passed us on the way and told us to have a good evening. We nodded and kept on moving.

"That was a very nice supper and the food was great, but I don think I'll be eating there again anytime soon," I said.

Sara laughed and agreed. We decided to walk around a little bit to walk off a little of that expensive supper, so arm and arm we strolled down the Strasse past our hotel. There weren't a lot of people on the streets we pretty much had the street to ourselves.

A couple of blocks past our hotel we could see the Danube River through some trees just beyond a park like area. We crossed the street, walked over to the park and found a trail winding down towards the river. There were a few benches along the path; a few were occupied by other couples. We came to the end of the path when it ran into a paved walk way running parallel to the river. We turned to the right where more lights of the city could be seen. As we walked along I kept thinking of the Blue Danube Waltz.

I stopped and turned Sara around and took her in my arms and began to waltz. Okay, so it was more like a Texas Two Step or something in between.

"What are you doing?" Sara asked.

"We are on the Danube River in Vienna Austria; I'm doing the Blue Danube Waltz."

"Don't you think you should actually learn to waltz first?"

"Shut up and dance, woman, I'm trying to be romantic here."

She laughed and did the best she could to follow my lead. She didn't lose too many toes in the deal. We danced our way down to the next path that led back to the street where we stopped and caught our breath. There was a bench on the walkway so we sat down and smoked a cigarette.

"How did you know about the Blue Danube Waltz?" Sara asked

"Ah, you would be surprised what I know about music," I bragged. "Actually I used to date the daughter of a dance instructor. When I drove over to pick her up after her dance class, sometimes I would get there early, and I'd sit and watch the girls dance. They were working on a dance to the Blue Danube Waltz. I also know that isn't the real name of the music, but that's the American name for it."

"An der schönen blauen Donau," Sara said.

"That sounds right. How did you know that?"

"I'm German, and I play the piano, remember?"

"Oh, yeah, I forgot about that."

We put out our cigarettes and headed back for the hotel. The little excursion along the river had tired us both out and we both fell asleep quickly.

The next morning we went down to the hotel restaurant for breakfast. Sara looked at the tour guide book; got the name of the street the Ferris wheel was on and asked the waitress if she could give us some directions.

Sara followed the directions and we found the Ferris wheel located just inside the Prater amusement park. The Ferris wheel is the best known attraction of the park. The park also had bumper cars, carousels and more. The one thing I liked about the park is there was no admission fee. Each attraction charged its own fee. I think the park used to be a hunting preserve for somebody and the park is built in, around and among the trees and Forrest like area.

Sara and I wandered around the whole park, stopping a couple of times at the various food and drink booths that are located inside the park area. After wandering around for a couple of hours it seems; we finally decided it was time to go for a ride on the Ferris wheel. We made our way back to the big wheel, paid our fee and away we went. The views from the top of the wheel were beautiful. You could see for miles. Sara snapped a couple of pictures from the top each time we came around. We finished our ride, found a place to sit and get something to drink. Sara opted for a beer; I stayed with my coke. We smoked a cigarette, drank our drinks then left the park. It had been an interesting but exhausting day. By the time we got back to the hotel we both decided that a little nap was in order before supper.

When I awoke Sara was sitting on the sofa looking through the guide book. I sat up and lit a cigarette. "Find anything interesting in there?" I asked.

"No, not really," she replied. "Well, that's not exactly true," she corrected herself. "There are a lot of interesting things, but we don't have time to see them all. I think I have seen enough of Vienna for one trip; how about you?"

"Oh, yeah, I've seen plenty," I said.

We decided we would leave Vienna tomorrow and go to Munich. We went to the hotel restaurant for supper again. I stuck with my usual and Sara had the Bratwurst with Sauerkraut. After supper we walked around the block then returned to our hotel room.

Since we were leaving in the morning we started re-packing our luggage; leaving out only what we would need in the bathroom in the morning. After getting the luggage ready to go we sat on the sofa together had a cigarette then went to bed.

Up early the next morning, we showered, dressed, finished packing our bags and toted them down to the desk. Sara dealt with the desk clerk while I took the bags to the car. When I came back in, we went to the restaurant and had a light breakfast. Apple strudel with coffee and milk. We didn't linger long over breakfast we were anxious to get on the road, we paid our bill and left.

We retraced our steps to Salzburg, stopped again and gassed up the car. It was a pretty drive the trees and mountains were like looking at a picture post card. I checked our snack sack we had some cheese left so I broke them out.

"Oh, I forgot we had those. Fix me one," Sara said.

I fixed cheese and crackers for us both while Sara drove. One for her, two for me. She sipped on my coke. We ate all the crackers and finished the coke. I wrapped what was left of the cheese and put it back in the sack.

We arrived in Munich but before we got into town Sara pulled over at a park platz and got out the map and the tour guide book. She didn't trust me to read it I guess. Munich had a lot of attractions but the one we wanted to see most was the Hofbrauhaus am Platzl, normally just referred to as the Hofbrauhaus.

The Hofbrauhaus is a world famous beer hall in the city center of Munich. During WWII everything but the main inn in the Platzl was destroyed and was not completely rebuilt until 1958.

Sara got her directions straight and we drove on into the city. She got us downtown and found a hotel near the Hofbrauhaus. We checked in and unloaded the car. We slept for a couple of hours; it was dark out by the time we woke up. We jumped in the shower real quick, changed clothes and walked down to the lobby of the hotel and got directions to the Hofbrauhaus. We were well within walking distance.

The place was jumping. The beer hall was crowded and there were no strangers. You just found a place to squeeze in and sat yourself down. The oompa bands were blaring away. The waitresses were carrying mugs of beer on their heads and anywhere else they would fit. You can't go to Germany and spend any time there at all without learning at least part of the Hofbrauhaus song. It goes "In München steht ein Hofbrauhaus, eins, zwei, g'suffa!" (There's a Hofbrauhaus in Munich—one, two, drink!) There is more to the song, but you have to know at least that much because the oompa band is going to play it, and everyone in the place holds their beer mugs up high and sings along, clinks their mugs together, and drinks away.

Sara and I squeezed in at a table with other couples and were promptly welcomed to the table with a toast. Sara was all grins; she loved this stuff and was having a ball speaking German with all the others at the table. Every once in a while I got a word or two tossed my way. Surprisingly the more beer I drank the better my German got. I was definitely not a beer drinker. We managed to get some Bratwurst and bread to the table and that was supper. We found our way back to the Hotel about midnight. I think we were both a little tipsy.

We slept late Saturday morning, Sara hit the shower first. I smoked a cigarette and told myself I wasn't ever going to drink beer again. I really didn't even like the stuff. Sara was out of the shower quickly and I hopped right in; I needed to feel that hot water beating on my head neck and back. I tried not to stay too long but it was hard to get out of the shower.

We got out, packed the bags, headed for the desk; Sara paid the hotel bill, I got the car and began to load the baggage. Sara came out and was helping arrange the bags in the car. She raised her head up and asked me if I had opened the sun roof this morning. I said no.

"Well, it's not closed completely and not locked."

I walked around, sat down in the driver's seat, and looked. She was right. I pulled the sun roof forwarded and managed to get it to lock. I looked around in the car.

"Where is your camera?" I asked.

"I left it on the floorboard in the backseat," she said.

We both looked but couldn't find the camera. There were a couple of other things missing. I cussed, she cussed, the camera was expensive and there was still a roll of film in it with pictures on it. Sara saw a German Policeman up the street and she walked down to tell him the car had been broken into. She came back a few minutes later and I could tell she wasn't happy.

"What did he say?" I asked.

"He said we could go to the station and report it, but not to expect any results, especially since I didn't have any serial numbers or other type of identification on the camera besides the brand name and model."

I kinda figured that was the response she was going to get. "What do you want to do?" I asked.

"Let's just go. I'll get another camera when I get home"

We got back in the car and back on the road to Heidelberg. It was a pretty quiet drive for many miles. I felt sorry for Sara she had her expensive camera stolen. What had started out as a great little vacation was ending on a less than happy note. There was one other thing that was bothering me; I was going back to Heidelberg and she was going to be in K-Town. I kinda got used to waking up with her every morning.

Things lightened up some the closer to home we got. We were pushing hard to get as close to Heidelberg as we could before we had to stop.

"We are going to have some options here. We can make it to Heidelberg, and you can spend the night there, or you can just drop me off and drive on to K-Town. Or I can drive on to K-Town with you and take a train back to Heidelberg on Sunday."

"What would be easier for you?" Sara asked.

"That's not the question here. The question is what is easier for you?"

"I don't know what to say."

"Humph, Since when?" I laughed.

"What do you want to do?" Sara asked.

"I think we should get into Heidelberg, find a hotel, and spend the night there. We can sleep in tomorrow. You can relax and unwind. We'll have some time to spend together; then you can drop me off later on in the evening and drive on back to K-Town. I think that's the best way to go."

She agreed, and we continued to push to get to Heidelberg as early as we could. We got in about 2200 hours. We went to that little hotel Sara and Mary Ann had stayed in near the Bahnhof. The lady remembered Sara, was glad to see her and just chatted up a storm as Sara registered.

We got the bags and took them inside but first made sure there was nothing left in the car anyone could steal. Once in the room we sat back, relaxed, and smoked a cigarette. Both of us were too tired to even take a shower. We put out our cigarettes, got undressed and fell asleep in minutes.

I woke up about 0900, Sara was still asleep. I grabbed my cigarettes and moved over to the sofa and lit one up. I had to sign in by midnight tonight. Actually I could use a day of grace and not sign in until Monday but I suspected the first sergeant was expecting me to work on Monday morning. I had really enjoyed traveling around with Sara, just the two of us. I put my cigarette out and headed for the shower. I took a long shower by the time I got out Sara was awake and fixing herself some instant coffee.

“Morning,” I said from the bathroom.

“Morning,” she said as she walked in the bathroom and gave me a kiss. “How long have you been awake?”

“I got up about 0900. What time is it now?”

She walked out and looked at my watch, came back, and said, “It’s 0945. Did you use all the hot water?” she asked.

“It was still hot when I got out.”

I finished shaving and moved out of the bathroom to give Sara her time. I walked over and got a fresh pair of shorts and slipped them on. I went over and looked out the window of our room. It looked like another pretty day out. I moved back over to the bed lit a cigarette, propped the pillows up behind me and lay there smoking and wishing I didn’t have to go back to work.

Sara came out of the shower she just had a towel wrapped around her and one on her head. She lit a cigarette and pulled the towel off her head, sat down on the sofa and began to brush her hair. She continued to brush her hair for a few minutes after she put out her cigarette. She walked over to her overnight bag and got some stuff out of there and rubbed something on her hands, wrist, up her arms and then rubbed her hands along her neck. She came over and stood by me. I looked up at her; she was looking down at me. I reached up and pulled her towel off and pulled her down on to the bed.

It was noon before we got out of the room. We were both hungry so we walked over to the Bahnhof and ate breakfast in the restaurant. While we were in the restaurant we overheard some GIs talking and heard them say Elvis’ new movie, *Blue Hawaii,* was playing at the theater on Patton Barracks. I knew there was a movie at 1400; I asked Sara if she wanted to go. She said sure, so off we went.

I drove through the gate at Patton the guard waved me through and waved to Sara and me. I drove down the company street and parked on the side of the building. We got out, locked the car and headed for the movie house. Harry and Rizzo saw us from the windows of our room and hollered at us. We waved back.

Sara and I went around to the movie entrance and bought our tickets. We grabbed some popcorn and a coke. We found a seat on the side row about half way down. I liked to sit on the inside next to the wall. I hated people crawling all over me getting in and out of a row.

The movie started, the first thing was the National Anthem, everybody stood up and waited for it to be over so we could get on with the movie. They showed a couple of previews of coming attractions and finally the movie began.

We got out of the movie about 1600 hours. We walked over to the Club and got a drink. It was early for the club crowd so there were few people in the club. We sat at table for two and had a coke.

"I really enjoyed this trip," I said.

"Me too. It was great, except for my camera getting stolen."

"I know that sucked, but at least you can get a new one at the PX, and probably cheaper than what that one cost you new."

"I know. I'll probably do that this week sometime."

"Are you going to be home next weekend?"

"Where else would I be?" she quipped.

"How do I know?" I shrugged.

I looked at my watch, it was almost 1800. I didn't want her out on the Autobahn too late and after dark.

"I hate to say this, but I think you should hit the road. I don't want you out there too late."

"I'm a big girl. I can take care of myself."

"Yeah, yeah, I know; just humor me a little here, okay?"

We got up and walked out of the club and down the street to her car. I opened the door, handed her the keys. I put my arms around her and gave her a kiss, which she returned with some energy.

"I love you, Sara."

"I love you, too, Rick."

She got in and started the engine. "I'll see you next week?" she asked.

"I'll be there. I'll call you one night during the week."

She waved, backed the car out and headed for the gate. I stood and watched her until she was out of sight. It wasn't until I started up the stairs to my room that I realized that all my bags were still in her car. Shit! This week is already starting off wrong.

GERMANY
Chapter 45

In April I got a three day pass which gave me Friday, Saturday and Sunday off. And just like a leave I took off on Thursday night and got one of the guys to sign me out at 0001 Friday morning. That's one minute after midnight on Thursday night. Sara took Friday off, too, and we took a quick trip to Hamburg to visit some of her relatives. Karl and Helga, I believe, were their names, and their two kids; I can't remember their names. But they were nice people and we spent a couple of nights with them. Karl spoke a little English and we could at least communicate on very basic level.

Hamburg is the second largest city in Germany and is the second largest port city in Europe. Despite its blue-collar appearance; it has a diverse culture and many state owned theaters, one of the oldest in Germany is the Thalia Theater, founded in 1843. Sara would have loved to have gone to a play but that wouldn't have been one of my favorite things to do. I was uncomfortable just sitting there listening to everyone else talk in a language I only new a few words of. I could just imagine how bored I would have been sitting through a whole play.

On the other side of town is a place called the Reeperbahn or "die sundige Meile," (The sinful mile) a street in Hamburg's St Pauli district, the centre of Hamburg's nightlife and also the city's red-light district. The street is lined with many restaurants, discos and hundreds of bars. There are also strip clubs, sex shops, brothels, and a sex museum. Street prostitution is legal during certain times of the day on Davidstrasse. The Herbertstrasse is a short side street that has prostitutes behind windows waiting for customers. Unlike De Wallen, the red-light district in Amsterdam, it is closed off, with a large gate, and juveniles and female visitors are not allowed in. How do I know all this, you may ask? Well, I'll tell you later, but I'll give you a hint. Sara's cousin Karl had a hand in it. I liked Karl. We said goodbye to Sara's relatives on Sunday afternoon and headed back to Heidelberg where Sara dropped me off and then went on to K-Town.

In the mean time back at the company, Barger had left and in his place PFC Dietz, the crazy Pollack had moved in. Dietz was definitely a trip. I think he and Roach had a contest going to see who could make PFC the most times. Other than being a little bit left of center Dietz fit in great or maybe because he was a little left of center is why he fit in.

Roach and Bobbie Jo were fighting again they always seem to be going at each other for something. I think they liked fighting; they never seemed to be happier than after a big fight. Chuck and Marta his little peaches and cream girlfriend were still together. Somewhere along the way Rizzo had bought a car and picked up a girlfriend. He tried to pass her off as Greek but she was really Italian; nice looking girl no matter what country she came from.

The one thing I liked about this company more than anything else, it was tight. There were no real cliques that couldn't be penetrated or little groups of prima donnas. Everyone assigned to the MP Company was a member of the company and Lord help anyone that tried to take advantage of any member of the company because he would bring down the wrath of the whole company on himself. There were some members like Dietz and Truman and Charlie Waters and even Sgt. Rickman that were a little different in some way but they were still one of us. I liked that.

Back to Dietz for a minute, it was hard to tell sometimes if he was drunk or just crazy. I remember one morning we were standing Guard Mount. Dietz and I were standing next to each other. He was to my left which meant when Lt. Samuels came around to inspect us I would be inspected first then he would inspect Dietz. Dietz was not one of the sharpest looking guys in the company, he passed inspection but didn't really put a lot more than just enough effort to get buy.

Samuels didn't really like Dietz. He could never really nail Dietz on anything appearance wise; so he always tried to catch Dietz with some off-the-wall question. When the inspecting officer stepped in front of you were supposed to say your name and what post you had been assigned for the day. Dietz had Gate #7, the pedestrian gate.

When Samuels stepped in front of Dietz; Dietz did just like he was supposed to.

"Sir, PFC Dietz, Gate #7."

"Morning, PFC Dietz," Samuels said as he inspected Dietz's uniform. Samuels made notes of a couple of minor things like a "rope" hanging off the pocket of Dietz's uniform, and his brass had a fingerprint on it.

"PFC Dietz, suppose while you're standing on your post today, the pedestrian gate, you look out the gate and see a Russian submarine coming toward you. What do you do, PFC Dietz?"

Without even hesitating Dietz said, "Sir, I would reach inside the guard shack, pull out my bazooka and shoot the submarine, sir."

"PFC Dietz, just where the hell did you get that bazooka?"

Without cracking a smile Dietz replied. "The same damn place you got that submarine, sir."

That was it…the whole Guard Mount and anyone else standing in ear shot just cracked up. We fell on the ground laughing so hard. No matter how mad he might have been, even Lt. Samuels had to laugh.

I think that was the last time he ever asked Dietz a question.

GERMANY
Chapter 46

In May of 1961 Sara gave me some news I was just totally not prepared for. Her mother and father were coming to visit. They would be here for about a month when school was out for the summer.

I didn't have to wait until they got here to know I wasn't ready to meet future in-laws. I guess this just scared the hell out of me. I already felt like I had expectations to live up to and they weren't even here yet.

From what Sara had told me I knew that her father had been born in Germany and escaped from the East Zone many years ago. I also knew that her mother's parents had been born in Europe. That explained all the relatives scattered about the country.

"So you're going to be traveling around with them when they get here?" I asked.

"Yes, I suppose I will, at least some of the time. I know they want to go to the East Zone to visit relatives they have over there if they can get in; but I know I won't be able to go in with them."

"Your not expecting me to go with you, are you?" I inquired.

"Well, I don't expect you to go everywhere, but it would be nice if you could get some time to at least meet my parents and maybe go a couple of places with us," Sara replied.

For the most part Sara and I had few disagreements or arguments; I didn't realize then what other men, older and wiser men, mostly married I would suspect, already knew. Women don't always tell you when they are mad or upset. You're just supposed to know. And you're supposed to know why. I'm sure Sara got the idea that I wasn't too happy about her parents coming to visit. If Sara was upset about my attitude about meeting her parents I didn't sense it.

I knew I was going to have to meet them sooner or later but I just would have preferred it been later. Sara and I had already decided we weren't going to get married until we both got back to the States; and I would be back a couple of months ahead of her since her contract ran through June of 1962 and I was scheduled to come home in March of '62. So in my mind there would have been time to meet the in-laws then.

It was almost the end of May now; Sara was busy getting ready for final tests before school was out. The company had not been receiving replacements as fast as guys were leaving so things were getting tight on the duty roster. First Sergeant Willis constantly had to adjust the duty roster but fortunately he left me alone for the most part.

With summer fast approaching it wasn't unusual to see more tourists around Heidelberg. Occasionally some of them found their way to the Information Center seeking information about everything and anything.

One afternoon there had been a late Honor Guard ceremony at Campbell Barracks. The gates had all been closed already except for the main gate just outside the Information Center. All eight guys from the day shift were sitting around the Information Center waiting for the Honor Guard to get back from the ceremony and assume duties at Campbell Barracks. Except Roach who was working the main gate.

A van pulled up outside and parked in the parking lot and about six young ladies piled out and headed for the Information Center. Roach didn't want to be left out so he moved over to the sidewalk just outside one of the open doors that led to the inside of the Information Center, there he could still control the traffic and hear what was going on inside the center. Cpl. Mapes was sitting behind the desk where the sign read, "Desk Sergeant." Charlie Waters was sitting behind the desk and the sign that said, "Interpreter."

Now Charlie was a really nice guy from the hills of Tennessee. His one very distinguishable characteristic besides his accent was his nose. Somehow his nose was very flat and crooked; at the right angle it looked like the tip of his nose was under his right eye. Okay, maybe that's a little exaggerated but his nose was way out of line.

The girls, all from Australia came in and were asking for some information about jobs and directions and such. Naturally all the guys were gathered around checking them all out. Charlie was just sitting there and never opened his mouth; when one of the girls noticed the Interpreter sign Charlie was sitting behind.

She looked at Charlie and asked, "Are you really an interpreter?"

Before Charlie could say anything Roach from the doorway said, "Sure he is; he is a great interpreter."

The girl looked at Charlie a little skeptically and asked, "How many languages can you speak?"

Again Roach jumped in and said, "He can speak five languages: English, German, French, Italian, and Greek."

The girl looked at Roach and said, "I don't believe you." Then she turned to Charlie and said, "Say something in Greek."

Charlie looked at the girl for a few seconds and then said, "Hey, what do say, lover?"

Mapes, who had been leaning back in his chair, fell down. Roach draped his arms around my neck and almost dragged me down, laughing, and everybody else was howling so hard you could almost see the plate glass windows in the front of the Information Center shaking. Of course the girls just stood there with this strange look on their face not having a clue as to what just happened and didn't understand why we were all laughing so hard but they had to laugh with us just because we were all laughing so hard.

If the girl had picked any other language it would have just been a funny little incident. But when she picked Greek and Charlie came up with Rizzo's traditional greeting…well….it was just funny as hell. But maybe you had to be there to really appreciate it. I don't think Charlie realized what he had done until we all broke out laughing. I'm still not sure to this day if he knows.

If nothing else that broke some ice and before the swing shift arrived there were some addresses and phone numbers exchanged and the girls were just driving off as the truck driver was showing up with our relief. We were still laughing trying to explain it to the guys from the swing shift.

GERMANY
Chapter 47

June was upon us before I knew it. School was out and Sara's parents were in country. The first weekend in June I took the train up to K-town, Sara picked me up at the Bahnhof and drove me back to the Guest House where her parents and I were staying. Already I was unhappy.

I met her parents for a few minutes in the lobby of the Guest House then we all went our separate ways to get ready for dinner at the club at Ramstein. Her parents seemed to be nice people; perhaps a little older than I expected. About 1900 hours, Sara came down and picked us up. We all piled into Blue Bird and headed for the Officer's Club at Ramstein.

Dinner was kind of awkward, not only for me but for her parents also. I could tell they were a little....uptight. Sara did the best she could to keep the conversation going but it seemed like most of it was about how things were back home. For the most part I just sat there and kept my mouth shut and spoke when I was spoken to. When I think about it now most of the conversation was between Sara and her mother. Her father was like me, he sat there and kept his mouth shut for the most part and just ate. There must have been a message for me in there somewhere, but if there was I didn't get it.

After dinner we drove back to the Guest House and Sara came in for a few minutes. We chatted in the lobby and then said our good nights.

Mom and Dad went to their rooms and Sara walked me on down to mine.

"I don't suppose you're planning on staying here, are you?" I asked.

Sara laughed and replied with a very emphatic, "No."

We reached my room, and I unlocked the door, and was about to walk in, Sara tugged on my arm. "Don't I even get a kiss good night?" she asked.

"I didn't know if that was allowed or not," I said.

Sara stepped just inside the door but left it open, put her arms around my neck, and gave me a kiss. "I'll see you in the morning. They wanted to get an early start and drive up to Frankfort and visit my cousin and then drive on to Hamburg on Sunday."

"What am I doing?" I asked.

"I thought you could ride back with us, and we would make that little detour over to Heidelberg and drop you off," she said.

"Sounds like a plan," I said, but I was thinking I would rather take the train.

Sara gave me another kiss and said, "Goodnight, I love you; see you in the morning."

"Goodnight, love you too."

I got undressed and sat down on the bed and lit a cigarette. Sara's folks seemed like really nice but uptight people. Maybe the uptightness came from them meeting me for the first time. I knew I was uptight meeting them and felt like I was being inspected. I really would have preferred to ride the train back to Heidelberg but I knew that would piss Sara off so I would just suck it up and ride with them and make the best I could out of it.

Back in those days they didn't have TV's in every room. They didn't have TVs in any rooms; but they did have a radio. I turned it on and finally found the Armed Forces Radio Network and listened to some music and news. I smoked another cigarette, turned the radio off and finally fell asleep.

The next morning everyone put on their best faces, said good morning and talked about how they slept....or didn't sleep. Sara was there promptly at 0800 when she said she would be. Must be the

German in her I thought. We piled in Blue Bird and went down to the main cafeteria and ate breakfast.

"Are you off today, Rick?" Sara's mother asked.

"Yes, I'm off every weekend. I got my schedule arranged so that I would be off when Sara was so we could spend more time together."

"Well, that was a nice thing to do," she replied.

Maybe it was just me but I thought I detected a little sarcasm in that reply.

We ate quickly and got on the road. Sara asked me if I wanted to drive, but I declined. It wasn't that I didn't want to drive; I just didn't want to expose my road hypnosis to her parents. I already was feeling inferior around them anyway, and I didn't want to show any more weaknesses in their presence.

So Sara drove, and she and her mother talked, and her father and I sat quietly. I fell asleep in the front seat. Maybe he fell asleep in the back, too; I don't know. Between the road hypnosis and the chatter of Sara and her mother it didn't take long for me to be asleep.

Sara reached over and nudged me as we entered the outskirts of Heidelberg. All the fog had gone and it was a pretty morning. It was probably going to be a little on the hot side today, I thought. A good day to be outside. The trouble was I really didn't know what to do on a Saturday by myself anymore. Sara and I had spent almost every Saturday together now for about the last nine months. I guess this would be a good time to find out what the other guys did on their days off.

I asked Sara to just drop me off at the gate at Patton. I told her I needed to stop by and check the schedule at the desk. That really wasn't true but I just didn't see any point in her driving me all the way back to the barracks and just turn around and come out again. She pulled up by the sidewalk leading to the pedestrian entrance to the gate.

I half turned in my seat and told Sara's folks, "It was nice to meet you; have a safe trip to Hamburg, and I'll see you when you get back down this way. Goodbye now."

"It was nice meeting you too, Rick," they both said together

I leaned over and gave Sara a kiss and said, "Call me if you get a chance."

"I will. Love you."

"Love you too," I said as I got out of the car and headed for the gate.

I turned just in time to see Sara make a U-turn and head back down the road. I was hating this weekend more and more already and looking forward to work on Monday.

GERMANY
Chapter 48

I walked back to the barracks wondering what I was gonna do this weekend. When I reached the barracks I went up to Roach's room he shared with Chuck and Galbreath and Truman.

Truman was shining his boots, he was working the midnight shift, but he didn't know where anyone else was. I walked back to my room. Harry the horse was the only one there, he was lying on his bunk in his shorts and T-shirt reading a book.

Harry looked up as I walked in. "Hey, Bones, what are you doing here on a Saturday? Figured you would be in K-Town," he said.

"Sara's parents came over from the states to see their little girl," I said sarcastically.

I sat on my bunk and lit a cigarette, kicked my shoes off and leaned over on one elbow.

"So did you meet your future in-laws?"

"Oh, yeah, met 'em last night; we all went out for supper," I said

"How did that go over?"

"Like a lead balloon. I don't think they like me, and I was uncomfortable as hell all evening."

"How long are they gonna be here?" Harry asked.

"Beats the shit outta me; they have relatives all over the place. They are on their way to Frankfurt today and then going to Hamburg tomorrow, I think. I dunno what the schedule is after that."

"Well, good luck; maybe they will leave soon," Harry said.

I put my cigarette out and lay back on the bunk. It didn't take long, and I was sound asleep.

"Bones! What the hell you doin' here on a Saturday?"

The sound of Roach's voice woke me up. I sat up on the bed and swung my legs over the edge.

"Long story," I said.

"You and Sara have a fight?"

"No, her parents are here in Germany. They came to visit," I said. I looked at my watch; it was 1200 hours.

"So you're a bachelor this weekend?" Chuck asked.

"I may be a bachelor for the whole summer," I said.

"Well, join the club," Roach said as he lit a cigarette, "Barbara and I had a knock-down, drag-out fight last night. I'm through with that little shit."

We all laughed. "Sure you are, buddy. That's what you said last weekend," Chuck said.

"No, this time I'm serious; she really pissed me off this time."

"Okay, that's two of us. What about you, Chuck?" I inquired.

"Marta is out of town with her parents visiting somebody."

"Hey, hey, hey," Harry said, "the three lover boys are all by themselves this weekend."

"Okay, I got it. Let's all go to town and get drunk," Roach said.

"You wanna go, Harry?" Chuck asked.

"Sure. I'm in."

"Is Galbreath around?" I asked

"He works mid-shift tonight; I think he said he was just going to the early movie and then chill," Roach said.

"What time do you plan on going to town?" I asked.

"Right now let's go to the mess hall and get something to eat. I'm starved," Chuck said.

"What are they having?" Roach asked.

"It's something that you won't like probably," Harry said.

"I have an idea. Let's all go to the snack bar and just grab a burger and fries," I suggested.

Everybody looked at each other and all nodded in agreement; so off we went to the snack bar.

"Harry," Roach asked, "You gonna put on the feed bag or just eat off a plate like the rest of us this time?"

"Fuck you." Harry grinned as he pulled up his jeans and slipped into a pair of shoes.

We all got our burgers and fries with a coke and took over a table in the corner of the snack bar. We pretty much gulped down the burgers and didn't do a lot of talking. One by one we finished and lit up a cigarette.

"So what time does everybody want to go to town?" Harry asked.

"I think we should get down there early; this is a Saturday night, and you know the places are gonna be packed, especially when those guys from Mannheim start coming over here," Roach said.

"So what's early?" I asked.

"About 1800-1830, some time around then," Roach offered.

"It works for me," I said. "It gives me time to take a shower and clean up and just chill for a few hours before we take off."

"Okay, we'll meet in my room about 1800," Chuck said.

"Why does it have to be your room?" Roach asked. "I sleep there too, ya know?"

"Shut the fuck up and let's go," Chuck said as he pushed Roach out of his chair.

We walked back over to the barracks and we each went our own way; we had about 4 hours to kill before we headed downtown. I went to my room, stripped and headed for the showers. Harry was right behind me. I finished my shower, shaved and headed back to the room; slipped into some clean shorts and T-shirt, lit a cigarette then, lay down on the bunk. A few minutes later Harry came in buck ass naked.

"Man, put some clothes on," I said. "Now you really look like a horse."

Harry ignored me, other than to shoot me the finger, and went over to his locker. If you'll remember I said that all the rooms on the second floor had almost floor to ceiling windows. Harry's locker was right next to one of those windows that were wide open. Harry was standing there in front of his locker naked as a jaybird, putting on after-shave and deodorant. Anybody coming or going out of the club could have seen him if they happened to look up.

Harry must have had a little bit of exhibitionist in him I guess.

GERMANY
Chapter 49

Exactly at 1830, we rolled out the gate in Chuck's old Mercedes. We went to the Westhof Club; Chuck dropped us off while he found a place to park. We waited until he joined up before we went inside. Naturally it was dark in the club and you had to wait for your eyes to adjust before you could really see what was going on.

We found a table over near the bar but away from the band area. We didn't want to be trying to talk over the band when they started. The waitress came over and took our orders, three beers and a coke. I was the coke drinker naturally. I intended to add some rum to it later on but didn't want to get started to early otherwise I'd be sleeping it off in the backseat of Chuck's car.

The club wasn't crowded yet, but there were a few people around. A couple of tables of guys, one or two couples and some single women sitting at the bar. You had to figure that the women at the bar were getting some liquid courage before they hit the street down on Rohrbach Strasse or maybe hoping to get lucky in the bar so they wouldn't have to hit the streets. The jukebox was playing some rock and roll, a little Elvis, Dion and the Belmonts, Chuck Berry, Fats Domino, and such. One of the most popular songs over there about that time was "Der Loewn Schlaeft Heute Nacht" (The Lion Sleeps Tonight). Probably the most popular one was Chubby Checker's, "The Twist."

We sat, drank our drinks, and listened to the jukebox. About 2030 the place was almost full and the band was starting to warm up. Chuck had eyed a gal he thought he knew and went over to find out. He spent a little time talking to her then came back and sat down. It seems he had met her one night when he was out with Marta so that was a no-no. He couldn't be messing around with any of Marta's friends.

By 2100 hours the band was playing and the dance floor was beginning to fill up. Roach was already starting to feel good and decided he found a girl he wanted to dance with. This is how you knew Roach was getting drunk; he never danced when he was sober. Harry just sat back and watched, and I kept my butt in the seat too. Chuck was really the Cool Hand Luke of the group. He decided he could at least be polite and ask Marta's friend to dance; so he did that. We didn't see him again for about an hour.

Roach came back to the table, grabbed his beer, and chugged it down; slammed the bottle down on the table and said, "I'm gonna kill that son of a bitch!"

I thought, *Oh, shit, here we go.* "What's wrong now?" I asked.

"That asshole over there is messing with my girl."

"Your girl is probably home waiting for you to call her," I said.

"I'm not talking about that girl. I'm talking about the one that is right over there," Roach said, pointing off in the general direction of the band.

"Why don't you just sit down and have another beer?" Harry offered.

"I have to go kick his ass."

"You're not pissed at him; you're pissed at yourself because you're not with Bobbie Jo right now," I said.

"Oh, Dr. Bones has it all figured out, huh?"

"Tell me I'm wrong," I said.

"I still need to go kick his ass," Roach said.

Roach was starting to settle down some, Harry helped him find his chair again, and he sat down. Chuck finally showed back up with a smile on his face. Nobody asked him why he was smiling. I leaned over and told him we needed to get Roach back to the barracks before he got himself in trouble. Chuck nodded he understood and slid over next to Roach.

"Hey, we need to get back to the barracks. It's getting late, and I have to work in the morning, and I think you do, too, right?" Chuck asked.

"I don't remember," Roach said.

"All the more reason to get back, then; don't want you getting screwed up tonight and not being able to make Guard Mount in the morning."

Harry and I helped Roach get to his feet, not that he couldn't do it on his own we just wanted to be sure he walked out with the rest of us. Chuck went ahead and got the car and brought it around to the front of the club. We got Roach in the car and headed back to the barracks.

We drove back to the barracks with all the windows down in the car and by the time we got back the fresh air had kinda sobered Roach up.

As we pulled into the company parking lot Roach said, "You guys just ain't gonna let me get in trouble, are you?"

"Somebody has to watch you when Bobbie Jo isn't around to do it," I said.

"Screw you, Bones; I hate it when you're right."

"I know; it's a curse, but someone has to bear the burden," I said.

I thought it was funny how I could seem to say the right things to Roach when I had no idea sometimes how to respond to situations in my own life. On the other hand, Roach and I responded to things differently in situations so maybe that had something to do with it. I was really too tired to try to figure it out tonight. I had all day tomorrow to think about stuff like that. I smoked my last cigarette, put out the butt, and went to bed.

GERMANY
Chapter 50

I was glad to see Monday get here; it had been a long weekend. I'd spent Sunday hanging round the barracks. I worked on my gear, I did go to an early movie at the little post theater, and stopped by the day room and whipped Tom's butt in some ping pong. Then we played some pool. We always played nine ball; he was a better pool shooter than I was, but every now and then I would get lucky.

For those of you that never played nine ball, it's a money game using only the balls numbered one through nine. The nine ball and sometimes the five ball are called the money balls. You take turns shooting at the balls in sequential order starting with the one ball and whoever sinks the five and/or nine ball first wins the game. You can use a combination of balls to sink one or both of the money balls if you get the chance or think you can make a combination shot. Whatever money I won from Tom playing ping pong he won back at pool.

I had the main gate on Monday at Campbell Barracks so I stayed busy naturally that was the busiest gate during the week, especially on a Monday. The day went by fast and I was a little surprised to see the duty driver show up with the swing shift when they did. The change of shift was fast and we were back at Patton Barracks and on the way to the Mess hall. Hobbs, Truman and I had all worked the day shift and we fell in with Chuck and Roach who had been off but were also headed for the mess hall.

We all found a table and sat down. Roach was sitting on my left, and Hobbs was on my right. They were serving hamburger steak and you had a choice of mashed potatoes or fries and whatever other vegetable you wanted. I picked the fries and no other veggie. Roach had picked the mashed potatoes but decided he didn't like them so he just ate the hamburger patty and pushed his tray aside.

The rest of us were still eating and talking; when Roach reached over and took one of my fries off my tray. I just kinda looked at him and didn't say anything. A couple of seconds later he took another one.

"If you want some fries, why don't you go get some?" I asked.

"I like yours," he said as he reached over and took another one.

"Do that again and you'll pull back a nub," I said.

Roach's eyes got small as he squinted at me; I knew he was gonna challenge me to see if I meant what I said and everybody else at the table knew it too. It was a stare down.

Suddenly Roach made his move and tried to snatch another fry but I was quicker than he was and jabbed my fork in the back of his hand.

Roach jumped up from the table, holding his hand.

"Holy Shit, Bones! Damn, that hurts!" he shouted as he danced around the table.

The guys at the table were laughing; everyone else in the mess hall was looking at Roach hop around the table, trying to figure out what they had missed.

"What the fuck is the matter with you, Bones?" Roach asked. He sat back down, wrapped some ice in a napkin, and put it on the back of his hand.

"I told you not to mess with my fries anymore, but you just had to test me, didn't you?"

"You coulda just smacked my hand with the fork, you shit head. You didn't have to puncture me with the fuckin' thing."

"Next time don't push me," I said.

I pushed my tray away got up and walked out of the mess hall. I went straight back to my room and got out of my boots and uniform; slipped into a civilian T-shirt, some jeans and sat on the edge of the bed and lit a cigarette.

Before I finished the cigarette Roach walked in. I looked at him and knew he wasn't there to start or try to finish anything. He still had his hand wrapped in a napkin with ice in it.

He sat down on Rizzo's bunk across from mine and asked. "What's the matter with you? That's not the Bones I know; it's not like we haven't played those games before."

"I know. I'm sorry I jammed my fork in your hand; you okay?"

"Yeah, it'll be okay; I'll keep some ice on it for a while. It will probably swell some, but it will be okay."

I lit us both a cigarette and handed one to Roach.

"You still didn't answer my question."

"What question was that?" I asked.

"I asked you what's wrong; you must have something bothering you. You didn't drink with us Saturday night; that's not like you. You usually have a couple of rum and cokes, anyway."

"I'm surprised you noticed. You seem to be too occupied with whipping some guy's ass."

"Well, you and the guys kept me from making an ass of myself, again. Thanks."

"Well, that's what friends do; keep the other out of trouble. And stick a fork in their hand when one fucks with the other one's food."

We both laughed and shook hands; Roach had to use his left hand. I got up and walked over and opened the window by Harry's bed and sat on the window ledge and looked out over the little park; watched the people going to the club and the theater. Roach came over and started to help himself to a cigarette out of my pocket.

I looked at him and said, "Damn, you don't ever learn, do you? Why don't you try asking?"

"You don't still have that fork in your other hand, do you?"

"No, lucky for you; here, have a cigarette." I took the pack out of my shirt pocket and handed it to him.

I lit up another cigarette and we both just watched the people coming and going for a few minutes. I thought about what Roach had asked me. I really didn't know what was bothering me but I seemed to be out of sorts.

"I don't know what's bothering me, but I don't feel right about things right now," I said.

"Is it because Sara's folks are here taking up your space and time with Sara?"

"That's a possibility," I said, "but there ain't anything I can do about it. I know Sara knows I'm not thrilled about all this, but there is nothing she can do about it either. I guess I'm just gonna have to suck it up and live through this."

"How long are they going to be here?"

"I have no idea, but I'm betting it's going to be at least a month."

"Well, look at it this way. It gives you a chance to be alone and think while Sara is out traveling with them."

"Now who is playing doctor?" I laughed.

"Sorry. Didn't mean to cross over into your area," Roach said.

"So what's up with you and Bobbie Jo?" I asked

"I don't know; she can just do some dumb shit that just really pisses me off. I don't even know what we are fighting about this time."

"Why don't you go call her. Maybe she remembers," I suggested.

"You know what? That sounds like good fuckin' idea. Are we okay?" Roach asked.

"I'm okay if you're okay."

"I think I'll go make a phone call. Talk to you later, Bones." Roach turned, walked out the door, and I went back over to my bunk and lay down.

Chuck stopped by; Galbreath came over to see if things were okay with Roach and I. I told them we were good. Harry came back to the room and shortly behind him came Dietz followed by Rizzo.

"Hey, whacha say, lover? I hear you forked Roach in the mess hall," Rizzo cracked up at his own little play on words.

"Cute, Rizzo," I said.

"I thought you guys were friends?" Dietz asked.

"We are friends; shit happens sometimes. He was just here. We talked it out. Everything is cool," I said. I was beginning to get tired of talking about this. I looked at my watch it was only about 1930, too early to go to sleep so I got up and slipped on some shoes and went down to the day room and played some ping pong with Charlie Morrison, Charlie was the oldest PFC in the company, not in age but with time in grade. He should have been promoted to SP4 a long time ago. Even Sgt. Willis didn't understand why he couldn't get him promoted. He wasn't a problem child. He was pretty quiet and just did his job.

I was beginning to wonder if Roach and I were going to be in trouble. Mostly I was wondering if I was going to get in trouble. I knew the first sergeant was gonna hear about the mess hall forking. Nothing got past the first sergeant. I had to laugh at myself. Mess hall forking? I knew that was gonna be what it would be referred to from now on. Everybody would be trying to figure out who was the Forker and who was the Forkee.

GERMANY
Chapter 51

Tuesday morning I was standing in line waiting to draw my .45 pistol from the Arms Room; when the first sergeant came down the steps. He stopped right beside me and put his hand on my arm.

"Sammy, I hear you forked the Roach in the mess hall," he said.

"Damn, Top, you just got here, and you heard about that already?"

"I have spies everywhere, you know. I knew about it last night. Have you and Roach worked it out, or is there a problem I should know about?" he asked.

"No problem, Top. We worked it out: just something that happened. We're good."

"Good man, Sammy; remind me never to take one of your French fries, will ya?"

The first sergeant grinned patted me on the shoulder and walked away.

At least I knew I wasn't in trouble with the first sergeant I went on to work. I had Gate #6 today, the slowest gate there is. It was a back gate used by oversized vehicles bringing or taking supplies or whatever to and from the caserne. A few pedestrians came through every now and then since there was a housing area just across the street. The one good thing about Gate #6, it was kinda tucked away between buildings and you could sneak a smoke every now and then.

Unlike Monday I was pretty much left to myself and my thoughts. Gate #6 was never really busy. I wondered what Sara and her folks were doing and where they were. Were they still in Hamburg? Had they gone some place else? All I could do was wait to hear from Sara.

I realized that I was really uncomfortable with Sara's folks around. I didn't know them very well obviously but I just got the initial impression that they weren't too impressed with me. I didn't know if it was that thing you always hear about "no man being good enough for my little girl," or if they just didn't like me. I didn't sense that as much from Sara's father as I did her mother. He didn't seem to have a lot to say, so we had something in common in that respect.

I felt like I was caught between a rock and a hard place. I couldn't avoid them without pissing Sara off, and I had to try to make nice when I was round them, or I'd piss her off. I'm sure it would not make a very good impression on them either. On the other hand I really didn't want to pretend to be somebody I wasn't. But who was I really?

I already knew I was a different person around Sara than I was when I wasn't with her. When I was with Sara and her friends, even just Mary Ann and Harold, I was the youngest and least educated of the group. I think I felt a little inferior when I was with or around them. I can't say it was anything they did; they were just ahead of me in life. I guess basically I needed to grow up and mature, although there were times I felt they were more like kids than the guys I hung out with.

I guess I tossed those thoughts around most of the day until I got relieved. I went on back to the company, changed clothes and went back to the mess hall. I got all sorts of comments and reactions when I walked in. Guys would back off and get out of my way and bow and shit like that.

"Welcome, oh King of the Fork," someone said.

"Hey, the Forker is here; everybody keep their hands in their pockets," another yelled.

I shot 'em all the finger and waved a fork at 'em, made my way through the chow line, and found a table. Oakley came over and stood beside the table with his tray in his hands.

"You won't fork me if I sit down will ya?" he asked.

"I may fork you in the balls if you keep standing there. Sit the fuck down," I replied.

He pulled a chair out and sat down. Tom and Harry came over and joined us. They didn't have anything to say about the forking incident. And it wasn't mentioned anymore that evening.

The rest of my week was just more of the same old stuff. Nothing but work the gates, eat and work on my gear. Friday at mail call I got a card from Sara. She mailed it through Die Bundespost (German Federal mail) which took it a little longer to get to me I think.

They had left Hamburg on Monday and they were on their way to someplace near Berlin where they had relatives and were going to try to get into East Berlin to see if they could visit some other relatives. Sara had already said she wasn't going to be able to go in; she didn't say but I assumed that meant she would just stay with relatives in the west zone. She said she would write again as soon as she knew more. It didn't look like I was going to see her this weekend.

Roach and Chuck were working midnight shift which meant they would be sleeping during the day. Roach and Bobbie Jo had made up, again. Marta was back in town after visiting relatives so even when they were off Roach and Chuck would most likely be spending time with them. Rizzo wasn't around as much since he met that little Italian girl. Can't say as I blame him, if I had a choice I'd pick her to over a bunch of guys.

Harry, Dietz, Tom, Hobbs and I all went to the club Saturday night. They had a live band; not that it meant much to any of us because none of us were real dancers. But we enjoyed watching some of the other folks dance. You never knew who was going to get falling down drunk on that dance floor. Or when a fight might break out. Actually there was very little trouble in that club. I don't know if it was because of a heavy MP presence or if it was just a well run club. I suspect it was a little bit of both. We closed the club down that night. Harry was totally smashed, Dietz wasn't far behind. Tom and Hobbs could still speak English, and even I had a little buzz on. Somehow we all made it back to the barracks, which luckily was just across the corner of the little park.

Sunday I slept in late, as did everyone else I think. I didn't even get up in time for lunch. When I did get up Harry and Dietz were still in bed and Rizzo was gone already or never came in. His bunk was made, so I dunno if he got up and made it already or just never slept in it. I don't remember if he was there or not when we all came in.

I got up and headed for the showers. The usual steaming hot water beating down on my neck and back eventually brought me back to feeling human again. It was Sunday I didn't bother to shave, just brushed my teeth and headed back for the room. I slipped on a pair of jeans and a shirt and headed for the snack bar. I was hungry and couldn't remember if I had eaten supper the night before or not. I was tired of hamburgers and fries so I ordered a couple of grill cheese sandwiches with onion rings and a coke.

I ate by myself, smoked a cigarette when I was finished walked back to the barracks to my room. I sat down on the bunk, kicked my shoes off, and lay back on the bed. Life sure seemed boring lately. Something was missing.

GERMANY
Chapter 52

The following week I got another card from Sara. Her folks had gotten into the East Zone and were back out; now they were planning on going to Regensburg to visit the other relatives. Sara thought they would be back in K-Town on Friday or Saturday. She said she would call when they got in.

I was glad they were going to be back in K-Town but it didn't sound like we would be spending anytime this coming weekend together. All I could do was wait for her to call and see what kind of plans they had. I was really getting frustrated with this whole situation.

About 0800 Saturday morning the CQ woke me up and said I had a phone call. I jumped up and got some clothes on and hustled down to the phone.

"Hello," I said, half awake.

"Good morning. Did I wake you up?" Sara asked.

"Yeah, well I usually sleep in on the weekends these days," I said. I'm sure there was a little sarcasm in my tone.

"I'm sorry, but I wanted to try to get in touch with you before you got too far away from the phone."

"That was a good idea. Are you home?" I asked

"Yes, we got in last night about eight p.m. We were all dead tired. I dropped Mom and Dad off at the Guest House, came back to my place, and went straight to bed. It's always so good to sleep in your own bed," Sara said.

"I dunno, I don't think I've slept in my bed in the past three weeks," I said.

"Oh, where have you been sleeping?" she inquired.

"You know what I mean," I replied.

"Well, it won't be much longer," she promised.

"What are the plans now?" I asked.

"We don't have any traveling plans for this weekend. I thought it would be best if we just came back here; washed clothes, and unwound and relaxed for a day or so and figured out what to do next.

"Figured out anything yet, or is it too early to ask?"

"I don't think we have to go visit any more relatives, so it's really just whatever they want to do from here on, I think. Maybe just some day trips," Sara said.

"Do you know when they are leaving yet?"

"I think sometime week after next."

"You mean like after next weekend they will be gone?" I had to have some clarity here.

"Yes. I think they will be here this week and the following weekend, and then leave the week after that," she said.

Things were looking better I thought. Maybe then we could get back to things being like they had been.

"Would you like to come up next weekend and spend some time with us?"

Now I was caught between a rock and a hard place again. I didn't really care about spending anymore time with her parents but would like to spend sometime with her. On the other hand how could I say no?

"Sure, just let me know when I should show up," I replied.

"Okay, I'll call you as soon as I have some idea of what we are going to do. I missed you."

"I missed you too."

"Okay, I'm going to run jump in the shower. I have to go pick them up so we can go eat. I'll call you soon. I love you."

"I love you too. Talk to you later. Bye, now."

I hung up the phone and felt better; at least she was back in the area and I could finally see a light at the end of the tunnel. Things were definitely looking up. I walked back up to my room, lit a cigarette and sat back on the bunk.

I had missed early chow but I thought maybe I could sneak in with the off coming shift and get something to eat. They always had a late breakfast for the guys working the midnight shift since they didn't get relieved until 0900. Everybody else in my room was on the midnight shift and should be coming in any minute now. I'd wait and walk over with them. I should be able to slide in the line. The cooks usually didn't care as long as the whole company didn't wait to eat late chow. They only needed one cook to work the grill and fix eggs if anyone wanted 'em; but they did have to get ready for the noon meal so they didn't want to tie that one cook up all morning.

I didn't have any problems getting fed. I got some scrambled eggs, toast with some sausage and a glass of milk. I finished my meal, smoked a cigarette and walked back to the barracks with Rizzo and Harry.

Dietz was already asleep when we got back to the room; he didn't bother to go to breakfast.

I lay back on my bunk and thought about the week and weekend to come. I knew I could get past the work week now if I could just make it through the next weekend with Sara's parents without screwing it up; I would be a happy man.

GERMANY
Chapter 53

The week seemed to fly bye at times and other times it seemed to drag but finally it was over. Sara called early Friday evening. She said they planned a day trip to Speyer on Saturday, which was located about 25 km (kilometers) a little more than 15 miles south of Ludwigshafen and Mannheim. That wasn't far from Heidelberg, so Sara figured if I wanted to go along they would come pick me up, and then we could drive to Speyer from Heidelberg. I thought that sounded like a plan to me and they didn't have to wait on me to catch a train to K-Town just to turn around and drive back the same way.

Sara said they should be there between 1130 and 1200 hours. I told her I would meet them at the gate so they wouldn't have to drive on post. Sara said okay. We didn't talk long since Sara's folks were there and waiting on her to go eat.

About 1145 Saturday morning, Sara and her folks pulled up just outside the gate in Blue Bird. I got in the front seat, leaned over gave Sara a kiss, shook hands with her father and said hello to her mother; and we were off.

I tried to make conversation with the parents as we drove. I asked how their visits had been and if they got to see everyone they wanted to see. I found out that it was his relatives that were still in the East Zone and while they had done everything they were supposed to do, and their paper work was all in order; the border guards still gave them a hard time but finally allowed them in to visit for two days.

Apparently they had to catch a train after they got in the East Zone and from previous experience when they had visited several years ago, they took little or no luggage with them. It had a tendency to get lost or misplaced so they didn't put anything of value in their luggage.

It seems the attraction at Speyer, besides the wine fest they were having, was the Speyer Cathedral most often called the Kaiserdom zu Speyer (Imperial Cathedral of Speyer). It is very large and the city's most famous landmark, visible for miles around and also the burial site of seven or more German emperors and kings and some of their wives. I didn't know if that meant that some of those emperors and kings had more than one wife or not but I really didn't care. It really was a very large and imposing basilica of red sandstone.

I may have mentioned it once before but I was finding out something about myself. These sorts of attractions were just not my cup of tea at this particular time in my life. I just couldn't get interested and to be honest I really resented having to pay a friggin' admission fee to walk through a church. I know that's how they pay for the upkeep of the place but somehow it just didn't seem right to me. In fact, thinking back on this time of my life, I really wasn't much of a tourist; I liked going to these places but mostly so I could just say I had been there. I think I would be more appreciative of things today.

We took the tour of the church and walked around the little shops of the town, taking a break every now and then to have a glass of wine and enjoy some of the festivities going on with the wine fest. I really wasn't a wine drinker, but I had a couple of glasses.

We found a little restaurant and decided to have supper. I had my usual Wiener Schnitzel mit Pomme Frites (loosely translated that's a breaded veal cutlet with French fries) and a glass of ice tea. I'm not sure what everyone else had. We lingered in the little restaurant while Sara and her mother had another glass of wine. I put it off as long as I could but I finally lit a cigarette. It wasn't like they didn't know I smoked. I don't know if Sara's parents knew she smoked or not but she didn't ever smoke in their presence while I was around.

We continued to walk around the town for a while after we ate; walking off some of our supper I suppose. Sara leaned over while we were walking behind her mother and father and whispered in my ear, "I got you a room at the Guest House if you want to come back to K-Town with us tonight."

"Do you have plans for tomorrow?" I asked

"Not yet; they haven't mentioned anything they want to do," she said.

"I have to be back in Heidelberg tomorrow night. That means you have to bring me back, or I have to take a train. And I didn't bring any change of clothes along."

"You have some at the BOQ you could use," Sara reminded me.

"How am I getting back to Heidelberg?" I asked.

"We'll figure something out."

"Okay, I'll go back to K-Town."

Sara squeezed my hand and we kept walking behind her parents. We finally made our way back to the car, climbed in and off we went back to K-Town. Sara drove and I dozed. I faintly remember hearing her and her mother chatting but I have no idea what they were talking about.

When we got back to K-Town Sara pulled up in front of the Guest House and said, "Mom, I'm going to drop you and Dad off now; Rick has some things he needs to pick up at the BOQ, and I'll probably just let him drive the car back down here, and you can come pick me up in the morning."

They said that was fine with them, and they would see us in the morning. I was getting the feeling there was more to this than met the eye. Sara backed out and started up the hill to the BOQ.

We got out of the car and made our way up the stairs to the apartment. Sara got out her keys and opened the door. I automatically hollered out, "Hello, Mary Ann," but there was no answer.

"She is gone for the weekend," Sara said.

"Oh, where did she go?" I asked. This was getting more suspicious all the time.

"I'm not sure; she and Harold went somewhere."

"I lit up a cigarette, and Sara asked if I would light her one. She said she hadn't had a cigarette since her parents had been here. I lit her one and handed it to her. She said thanks and leaned over and gave me a kiss.

We sat on the day bed and smoked our cigarettes. There wasn't a lot of talk but there was a lot of heat; more than the cigarettes were putting out. I finished my cigarette and put it out in the ash tray.

"Where are my things I need?" I asked.

"They are in your drawer in the dresser," she said.

"I didn't know I had a drawer in the dresser."

"You do now." she said.

I got up to walk over to the dresser and she grabbed my arm. "You in a hurry?" she asked.

I decided I wasn't in that big a hurry and sat back down on the bed. It had been a real long time.

GERMANY
Chapter 54

I was waiting in the lobby the next morning for Sara's mother and father to come out. My biggest fear was they would ask me what time I got back to the Guest House last night or they had been waiting up for me to come in.

They finally came out of their room and walked down to the lobby.

"Good morning," they said together.

"Good morning."

"Did you sleep well?" Sara's mother asked

"Yes, I did, thank you, and you?"

"Very well, thank you. We didn't even hear you come in. We must have been really tired. Mom was pumping me I thought.

"Well, I tried to be quiet; didn't want to disturb you," I replied.

"I called Sara and told her we would be on our way shortly. She said she would be ready and waiting. I was definitely changing the subject.

We walked out, got in the car, and I drove up to the BOQ. Sara was waiting outside and hopped right in the passenger side.

"Good morning," she said and leaned over and gave me a kiss.

Sara turned to her mother and father in the back. "Guten Morgen, Schliefen Sie gut?" (Good Morning, Did you sleep well) she asked

"Ja, danke, und Sie?" (Yes, thank you and you?) her mother responded.

"Sehr gut, danke. Haben Sie hunger?" (Very well thanks. Are you hungry?) Sara said.

"Ich möchte Kaffee" (I would like coffee), Sara's father chimed in. That was the most I had heard him say the whole time I had been around him.

My German was improving; I understood that whole little exchange there. Sara turned to me and told me to just drive down to the cafeteria in the shopping center, and we could eat breakfast there.

"Ja wohl, Fraulein" (Yes, ma'am, more or less), I stated and backed the car out of the parking place and headed for the cafeteria.

We got to the cafeteria, it seemed to be crowded, but I found a parking place near the front door, parked and we went in. Sunday morning breakfast was strictly buffet style. They had about everything you could want for breakfast, and you just helped yourself. I went for the scrambled eggs, biscuits and gravy with hash browns, some ham and a glass of milk.

One thing about the Germans, they enjoy their food and take their time eating. Sara and her parents were no different. I, on the other hand, had been in the Army and was taught to gobble it down and move out. I was finished before they were half way through. Of course I may have really been hungry after last night. That thought must have brought a smile to my face; when I looked up everyone was looking and smiling back at me.

"You have a good appetite, this morning Rick," Sara's mother said.

"I don't usually have a breakfast this good. I just like to take advantage of the opportunity when it comes along," I said. That was the best answer I could come up with on the spur of the moment. I didn't think I should tell her what I had been thinking.

I had a cigarette while everyone else finished off their second and third cups of coffee. While they finished their coffee and I smoked my cigarette, they discussed what they were going to do for the day. There weren't a lot of things that seemed to grab their interest.

Finally Sara's father said, "How about we just stick around the Guest House and maybe go for a walk later in the woods around here?"

Wow! I thought *he speaks.* Somehow I got the feeling that was more than a suggestion; nobody disagreed with it.

"I could use the time to get caught up on my laundry. I never got it all done the other night," Sara said.

"I could write some cards," Mom said.

I guess the rest of the day was planned. We left the cafeteria and drove back to the Guest House; dropped off Sara's parents before she and I went back to the BOQ. We got out of the car and before going up to the apartment Sara checked the wash room which was in the basement. It was empty so we hurried upstairs and she put together a load of wash and took it back downstairs. I put on some of her German music that I was beginning to like and lay down on the bed. I lit a cigarette.

Sara came back a few minutes later, made me scoot over to my side of the bed, as she called it, lay down beside me, and lit up a cigarette. We just listened to the music for a few minutes and finished our cigarettes. I sat up and leaned back against the wall. "What are you going to do this evening? What do you want me to do?" I asked.

"What do you want to do?" she asked.

"I can do whatever is best for you. I can take a train back if that would make it easier for you. You're going to have to take your parents out to eat at some point in time. You can take me back to Heidelberg early and then come back and go eat with them. I can stay and eat with you; and then you can take me back; but that puts you out on the road by yourself pretty late. Maybe it's better if I just take a train back, and you can take care of your parents."

"That would probably work out better, but what time will you leave?" she asked.

"If I leave early you can go walking with your parents this afternoon. I'm really not interested in a walk through the woods. So you can take me to the Bahnhof before they go for their walk and then take them to supper. Did they mention what time they intended to take this walk through the woods?"

"No, but if I know my parents, they won't go until around three or four this afternoon," Sara replied.

"Then you can take me to the Bahnhof around 1400; I think there is a train around 1430, and then get back here in time to walk with them. I think that would work out best for everyone."

"Okay, let me go get the wash into the dryer, and then we will have some time to ourselves," Sara said as she got up off the bed and headed back to the washroom downstairs. She didn't explain what she meant by having some time to ourselves. I could only hope, I guess.

She came back to the room a few minutes later, locked the door to the hallway and shut the door to her room and locked it. I watched her as she took off her blouse and slacks; and walked over to the bed and pushed me down. I guess I knew what she meant by time to ourselves now.

About 1330, Sara called her parents and told them she was taking me to the Bahnhof so I could catch a train back to Heidelberg and she would be back to go walking with them. She listened for a few minutes to her mother, I presumed, and then she said, "Okay," and hung up.

We left the BOQ and drove to the Bahnhof in relative silence and smoked a cigarette. When we pulled up in front of the station she turned the car off and turned to face me.

"My parents are leaving next Thursday. They told me to tell you it was nice to meet you and they thought you were a very nice man."

I had to admit that took me by surprise. I'm not sure that's all they said but for now I'll take that and be happy. Sara leaned over and gave me a kiss and thanked me for being patient. She said that she would see me next week, and we would have the whole weekend to ourselves. I kissed her back and said I would be down next Friday evening and I'd call her before I leave so she could pick me up if she wasn't busy.

I got out of the car and headed for the station and turned to wave to Sara as she drove off. I just made it to my train; there was a line at the ticket station. I got on and barely got seated before the train was moving.

I lit a cigarette and thought about these past couple of days. Sara certainly surprised me. I really wasn't expecting anything to happen between us until after her parents had left the country. Not that I'm complaining. I just thought that was a little out of character for her.

Maybe she had had enough of her parents too and was just being a little rebellious.

Whatever it was that fired her up I was happy with the results. This next week was going to be much easier to get through. Stress relief can work wonders sometimes.

GERMANY
Chapter 55

The next week flew by; it was Friday before I knew it. Nothing new or exciting had happened in the company.

Friday night I was back in K-Town. Sara had picked me up at the Bahnhof and we had stopped to get something to eat then went on back to the BOQ. Mary Ann was there, and she came over and talked. She and Harold had gone to Switzerland and did some sight-seeing. Sara brought her up to speed on the last part of her parents visit.

"How did it feel to meet the parents?" Mary Ann asked.

"It was okay; survived, I think," I replied, laughing. "Sara could probably answer that better than I can," I said.

Mary Ann looked at Sara. "He did fine, I think. Mom said they thought he was a fine young man."

Maybe it was just my sensitivity, but I sort of flinched at the term, "young man." I thought it sounded like they were talking about a high-school kid. Sara hadn't used that word "young" when she told me what they had said before. Now I was wondering what they really said.

The conversation was running down, and I wanted to do something besides just talk, anyway.

"Anyone up for some cut-throat pinochle?" I asked.

"It sounds good to me," Mary Ann said.

"I'll play, where are the cards?" Sara asked.

"Sugar, it's your apartment; if you don't know where the cards are who does?" I joked.

"You had them last. What did you do with them?"

"I put them on top of the dresser, I think."

I got up and walked over to the dresser and found the cards under some clothes that hadn't been put in the drawers yet. I couldn't bitch, they were my clothes. I took the cards back to the bed, Sara brought over some paper and pen to keep score on.

"Let the games begin!" I shouted and began dealing out the cards.

We played cards; we drank wine, cokes and smoked cigarettes until around midnight and finally called it a night. Mary Ann said good night and returned to her room.

I went in and took a shower. Sara was next in the shower and after she was finished we heard Mary Ann in the shower singing at the top of her lungs. I think the wine finally hit her. Sara and I laughed at her singing, she was only slightly better than I was and I was friggin' terrible.

Sara on the other hand was a very good singer, I think. I had only heard her humming and singing with some of her records around the apartment and that sounded very nice to me. One Sunday morning we decided to go to church. Then we came to that first hymn, Sara almost burst my right ear drum. I'd never heard anyone sing so loud. Now I didn't know if she was good or just loud. The person she reminded me of most was Ethel Merman. I guess Sara must have been good; after all, Ethel Merman was a star.

We started off Saturday morning with breakfast. Sara scrambled some eggs on her little hot plate and made some toast and coffee. I don't know why I was always so hungry when I was in K-Town but I always ate a hearty breakfast. I could handle three or four eggs with some bacon and a glass of milk. Sara might eat one egg, one piece of toast and drink some coffee.

After breakfast, Sara washed the dishes in the little sink in her room, dried and put the dishes away. I sat down and did some touch up work on my duty boots. Sara sat at the desk and wrote some letters. I think one of them was to my parents. She had said earlier that she had not written them since her parents had arrived. Knowing my parents I was pretty sure they hadn't even noticed.

Sara had heard of some little shopping area in K-Town she wanted to explore; she was building up quite a collection of those little figurines or statuettes, I think they were generally referred to as "Hummels," but I'm not sure that's the right word or if it's an English or German word. Anyway she wanted to go check out some of the shops in this particular area.

Sara had checked it out on the map of K-Town and pretty much knew where she wanted to go. The particular street she was looking for was just off the Hauptstrasse, a couple of blocks over. She had no trouble finding the street and we parked in a small park platz, locked the car, and walked over to the corner of the street and just began strolling and window shopping. It was a great day for the last part of June and there were a lot of people on the streets.

We walked in and out of several stores up one side of the street. Sara found one figurine she really liked and bought it. She gave it to me to carry. I knew my role I was the official package carrier. We made all the little shops down the other side of the street and Sara found one more she liked and bought it too.

At the end of the street there was a little bakery. We went in and looked at all the goodies. Sara wanted to try some Apple Strudel and a cup of coffee. I thought I would try the German Chocolate Cake and a glass of water. I should have gone with the Strudel too. I knew the cake would be dry and grainy. Oh, well, I thought, I'll know better next time. We finished our dessert, went back to the car and drove back to the BOQ.

When we got back to the BOQ, Mary Ann was gone. Sara put her new figurines away. I popped a coke and sat back on the bed.

"Last week when you took me to the train you said your mother said she thought I was a nice man. Last night you told Mary Ann she said I was a nice young man. Which was it?" I asked.

Sara looked at me for a minute and asked, "What difference does it make? She said she thought you were nice."

"It makes a difference to me as how they saw me. Did they see me as a man or a high-school kid?"

"Rick, she said young, but that's just my mother. Everyone is young to her."

"What did you father have to say?" I asked.

Sara laughed, "He said he thought you were awfully quiet."

I had to laugh at that. "Like he is such a big talker. I don't think he said a dozen words the whole time we were around each other."

"What else did your mother have to say?" I inquired.

"Nothing much, really; she asked if you had plans after your Army tour was up."

"What did you tell her?"

"I said I didn't know, that we had never really discussed it. What did you think of my parents?"

"I thought they were very nice people. Pretty straight-laced and pretty Victorian in their thinking."

Sara looked at me in as if she were surprised. I don't think she thought I knew words like "Victorian."

"You're right; that pretty much describes them to a T. I know my mother cringed every time we kissed in public or even just in front of them."

"I guess you had a pretty sheltered life when you were growing up then, huh?" I asked.

"I wasn't allowed to have any male friends over to my house unless we stayed right in the living room or parlor where my mother could watch over me. I didn't have a date until my senior year in high school. I think I told you that I had to come straight home from school and get supper ready, because my mother was at the store helping my father. So I didn't have a lot of free time. On the weekends I cleaned house and helped out in the store." Sara had told me about the little super market her parents owned. Apparently they turned it into a little gold mine. He had just retired, and that was the reason they came to Germany. Her father had sold the store to her cousin, who had also come to America after escaping from the East Zone, and had helped his uncle in the store until he bought it.

"Back to this Victorian upbringing you had; I need to ask you about last weekend. I'm definitely not complaining, I enjoyed the hell out of it; loved it, but I really didn't expect that from you. I really didn't expect us to have any time to ourselves until your folks left the country. I got the feeling that they really intimidate you. I got to thinking about it on the train ride home, and I had to wonder what brought that on. It was just so not like you. I didn't know if you were just really horny and happy to see me or if you were, in your own way, being rebellious."

Sara sat quietly for a few minutes. I didn't know if she was trying to formulate an answer or was trying to figure out and understand what her own motivations were last weekend. She lit a cigarette and finally said, "I think it was a little bit of both. I knew you weren't happy and comfortable with my parents visiting, and I felt like you thought I was ignoring you. And they do intimidate me. I felt uncomfortable every time we kissed in front of them, but I just made up my mind I wasn't going to let them do that to me anymore."

"So you made up this plan about getting me a room at the Guest House and talking me into coming back here, knowing Mary Ann wouldn't be here, just so you could jump my bones to get even with your parents?"

"Yes, I guess that was part of it; but I wanted to spend time with you, too, because I missed you."

I sat there smoking my cigarette for a long time with out saying anything. Finally I put my cigarette out, got up and walked over to Sara, put my arms around her, gave her a kiss and said, "Good plan. You should get rebellious more often. And feel free to jump my bones anytime."

Saturday evening Sara and I went to the Club at Ramstein for supper. I was in the mood for some seafood, so I ordered fried shrimp with French fries and coleslaw. Sara had scallops with coleslaw and something else. She had wine; I had ice tea.

"What are you plans for the rest of the summer?" I asked.

"I really haven't made any; I would like to do some traveling. Do you have any leave time coming?"

"Yeah, I have a lot of leave time built up. I'd like to go somewhere, too. Maybe get outta Dodge for a couple of weeks."

"Where would you like to go?" she asked.

"I'd kinda like to go to Spain."

"I would like to go to Paris," Sara said.

"That's on the way to Spain," I replied.

"That would be a long trip to do both of them. I don't think we should try to do them at the same time."

"Okay, which one would you rather do?"

"Paris is closer; we can do that in less time. Let's make the most of the summer and do Spain first," Sara said.

"I can squeeze about 16 days out of a 12 day leave if we leave on a Monday. Would that be enough?" I asked.

"That should be plenty of time," she said.

"I have to put in my request at least ten days in advance to give the first sergeant time to adjust the duty roster. So if I put in for it when I get back on Monday that will make it somewhere around the 15th of July."

"That sounds fine. I need to get the car in for a check up and get some gas coupons. I should be able to get that done by then. I don't see any problems."

"Okay, I'll put in for leave Monday when I get back. I don't think there will be a problem in getting the time off."

We finished our meal. Sara had a second glass of wine; I got a refill on my tea. We smoked a cigarette and played footsies under the table. When we finished our drinks and cigarettes we asked for our bill and paid the waitress. We didn't wait for change; we just got up and left.

It was a nice warm night out, and there was a picnic table just down the hill a little way from the BOQ, so when we got back we walked down to the table and sat out under the stars. It was good to get out of that little room for a while. You could get claustrophobia if you didn't get out of there every once in a while.

While we sat at the table smoking, we checked out the stars and tried to pick out some of the constellations but that was kinda hard since the trees around the picnic table got in the way. I probably wouldn't have recognized one anyway; astronomy wasn't big on my list of things I like to do. I turned and straddled the bench by the picnic table and Sara turned her back to me leaned back against me and I put my arms around her.

"You remember all that stuff we talked about this afternoon; about how you were brought up and stuff?" I asked.

"Yes," she replied.

"Well, that was the first time we ever really talked about anything like that. Now I've suddenly realized that I really don't know much about your upbringing."

"What do you want to know?"

"Well, you said you weren't allowed to date until your senior year in high school. Did you not have a boyfriend when you were in high school?"

"Nope, no boyfriends, and my cousin took me to my senior prom," Sara said.

"How about college? Did you have a boyfriend in college?"

"I didn't have time for a boyfriend. I went to class, came home, cooked supper, and studied. On weekends I helped clean the house and worked at the store sometimes."

"So you're telling me you didn't have a boyfriend all through high school and college and lived at home the whole time you were in college?"

"That's right," Sara said.

"What about after college? Did you continue to live at home? And still no boyfriend?"

"Right again," she said.

"So are you telling me you never had sex before…before me?"

"You're batting a 1000 so far, cowboy."

I had to have a cigarette. Somehow I kinda suspected I might be the first, but I never really believed it. I mean, come on now, how many twenty-five-year-olds are still virgins these days?

Sara sat up, turned around, and looked at me. "You don't believe me?"

I told Sara what I had just thought. "It's not that I don't believe you; you have never given me any reason not to in the past. But it's just like

I said, you just don't expect to find many twenty-five-year-old virgins these days. As I said, I thought maybe I might be your first, but I really figured that somewhere along the way you had at least been with one other guy."

Sara lit a cigarette. "There was this one guy that I went out with a couple of times. We fooled around but never went all the way. That was as close as I got until I met you."

I was really having some mixed feelings here. On the one hand it made me feel kinda good that I was the one and only. But at the same time it was kind of scary. I had never been "the first" in any previous encounters in my young life. So the girls in my past at least had some experience to draw on, some more than others; and most more than me. In my mind that sort of explained why Sara was a little timid and less imaginative about some things. Obviously she could be a little devious if she put her mind to it. She proved that to me last weekend. But that was a different type of imagination.

"What are you thinking?" Sara asked. Her voice brought me back to the present here and now.

"I'm thinking you have been deprived too long and we need to practice. And there is no time like the present to start." I took Sara by the hand, helped her up off the bench, and led her back to the BOQ. Time was wasting.

We slept in late Sunday morning. I didn't wake up until around 1100 hours. Sara was up brewing coffee but not dressed yet. I sat up on the edge of the bed and lit a cigarette.

"Good morning," Sara said.

"Is it still morning?" I asked.

"For about another hour."

"Have you had your shower yet?" I asked.

"No, not yet. Go ahead if you want to. I'm going to drink my coffee."

I got up and headed for the bathroom. I noticed Mary Ann' door was shut. I wondered if she had company or just still sleeping. I turned the water on in the shower and let it run waiting on the hot water to make up to the top floor. I brushed my teeth while I was waiting. By the time I was finished the shower was hot and I hopped in. I didn't take a lot of time, not wanting to use up all the hot water. I washed quickly and turned the water off and got out and toweled off. I walked back to the room with a towel wrapped around my waist.

"Okay, sugar, it's all yours," I said.

Sara took one more sip of coffee and headed for the bathroom. I got some clean clothes out of "my" drawer, dropped the towel, and slipped into them. I still hadn't gotten used to having a drawer all my own. It was almost like we were living together. I guess we were, weren't we, at least part time? I kinda liked it.

I was dressed and on my first coke by the time Sara got out of the shower. I sipped on my coke and smoked a cigarette and watched her get dressed. I always enjoyed watching her get dressed; or undressed.

Sara got something out of her desk drawer and came over and sat down beside me on the bed. She had a small wall calendar in her hand, she opened it to July and we figured out when would be the best time for us to take off for Spain. Allowing ten days for me to get my leave in and approved if I put it in on Monday, we could leave about the 20th of July.

Mary Ann came out of her room but shut the door behind her and went into the bathroom. Sara and I looked at each other and kinda grinned. I think we both strongly suspected that Mary Ann had someone in her room and she didn't want us to know who it was. This meant it probably wasn't Harold.

We decided to go down to the cafeteria and see if they still had the breakfast buffet going or if it was too late. We just barely got there in time before they broke the buffet down. They still had plenty of eggs, and your choice of meats left and a few biscuits. We filled our plates and found a table.

After we ate, we walked over to the PX and walked around Sara had already replaced her camera so neither of us really needed anything and ended up walking out without buying anything. We got back in the car and drove back to the BOQ. Mary Ann and whoever was with her had left by the time we got back.

"I guess that's a secret we'll never hear about," I said, pointing to Mary Ann's room. Sara just laughed and said, "Well, it's her business."

The afternoon passed rather quickly, Sara put on some music, wrote some letters and I played cards. About 1700 I told Sara it was time for me to head for the Bahnhof to catch my train. We slipped on our shoes and walked down to the car. Just as we were leaving Mary Ann was pulling in, by herself. Sara and I both chuckled and waved as we left.

We didn't talk much on the way to the Bahnhof. There wasn't a lot left to say this weekend. Sara pulled up in front leaned over and gave me a kiss and reminded me to put in my leave request on Monday.

"I will; I love you."

I leaned over and gave her a kiss, got out of the car, and walked into the Bahnhof. The train ride back to Heidelberg was uneventful, as usual.

GERMANY
Chapter 56

The first thing Monday morning before I went on duty I put in my request for leave. There had been some personnel changes over the past couple of weeks. We had lost a few of the old guys and picked up a couple of new 'cruits. One guy named Shumaker and one named D'Angelo were now in the Snake Pit. Also a guy named Billy Stearns had just reported in.

Everybody dropped by the Pit to check 'em out and introduce themselves. It seemed like only yesterday I was the one they were coming to check out. Now I was doing the checking. They all seemed like nice guys. Shumaker and D'Angelo were a little bit older than the normal 'cruits we got in. We found out they were draftees (US) and not Regular Army (RA). I never did know what that US stood for but I knew if a guy's service number started with RA he had enlisted, and if it started with US it meant he was drafted.

Draftees presented a little different attitude about things. For the most part they were just there to get in their military service and get it out of the way so they could return to their chosen field in the civilian world. Some made good soldiers, some didn't. Almost all that came to the 529th made good soldiers if not excellent ones.

I used to listen to these guys talk. They all seemed to have come from a different background, upper to middle class families, not all but most had some college if not their degree, and most were already set with a civilian job when they got their military service obligation out of the way. You could always hear them say things like, "Yeah, when I get out I'm going back to my old job at such and such, and I'll be making $100,000.00 a year in the next couple of years." Back in those days that was a lot of money.

The draftees didn't have a monopoly on this kinda talk; a lot of the regular army guys had the same plans. None of this was new; I had heard it from the first day I was in basic training. I just always wondered how they knew this and had this all planned out already. I didn't have the slightest idea what I was going to do when I got out. I wasn't even sure I was going to get out. But I didn't let that get around. I didn't want guys thinking I was a "lifer" (a career military guy).

The work week was more of the same. Nothing exciting happened. There were a couple of Honor Guard ceremonies during the week. I was able to watch them both since I had duty at Campbell Barracks. I really did enjoy watching those guys. I really would have enjoyed being one of them. Sometimes I really wanted to go ask Sgt. Shire if I could go to drill call with them sometime. Of course that wasn't going to happen anytime soon. Every once in a while I would be going to chow early and catch one of the guys waiting for the drill call to start and he would let me borrow his rifle so I could practice and see if I could still handle one of those things. I enjoyed just being able to handle the weapon again.

I spent the next weekend in K-Town. My leave had been approved, Sara and I got out the map and the tour guide book to see where we wanted to go in Spain. We chose three places, Madrid, Valencia and Barcelona. That covered a pretty good distance in Spain.

Mary Ann had taken off for parts unknown. She just told Sara she would be gone for a few days but didn't say where she was going or who she was going with; or going to see. Sara and I suspected she had a new boyfriend but for whatever reason she didn't want us to know about it, or who he was.

It was definitely summertime now; but for the most part Sara's apartment was not too bad. I think being up high allowed us to get some of the breeze that the apartments below didn't get because the trees were actually in the way. We would open the three windows wide open and we had a small rotating fan that kept the air moving. The nights actually got a little bit chilly sometimes and we would have to shut the windows or at least close them a little bit.

Other than going out to eat a couple of times we stayed pretty close to home. I think we were both looking forward to the following weekend when we would actually be on the road for Spain.

I returned to Heidelberg on Sunday evening. When I got back to the barracks I went straight to my room. When I walked in everyone was there. Dietz, Harry, Rizzo, Tom and Roach were all in the room.

"Hey, guys, what's up?" I asked.

"All these guys got tossed out of the club last night," Rizzo said.

I looked at Roach and then all the rest of 'em, and they all just had this little shit-eating grin on their faces, so I knew it must be true.

"All of you?" I asked.

"All of us," Roach said.

"What the hell did you do?" I asked.

"It wasn't our fault!" Harry bellowed out.

Roach bummed a cigarette and began to explain. "These assholes from Mannheim came over here and got drunk and started messing with our WACs. They asked us if we would get these guys to leave them alone. So we asked them nice the first time and they kept on messing with the girls. I told them if they didn't stop I was going to get the manager. They said some not so very nice things to me then, and that pissed me off, and I got in the guy's face. He shoved me, and Harry shoved him, and then all hell broke loose."

"To make a long story short, Roach continued, all the guys on duty came down, plus Sgt. Deavers and some of the guys just getting ready to go on duty came over. They took us all to the station. Deavers put the guys from Mannheim in the D-Cell and made us sit out in front of him at the desk."

"So are you guys restricted now or what?" I asked.

"Yeah, Deavers had to call the first sergeant, and he told Deavers to put us all on restriction until he talked to us on Monday morning. He called the 382d MPs in Mannheim to come get those guys and take them to their unit and release them to their duty officer."

"So I take it this is a rehearsal to be sure you all have your stories straight for the first sergeant in the morning?" I asked.

"Yeah, we wanna be sure we're all on the same page," Tom said.

"I don't think we will be in any big trouble, the girls already wrote statements saying those guys were bothering them, and they started the fight," Harry added.

"Well, I'm glad I wasn't here; I'd have probably been right there with you. And I'm going on leave next week," I said.

"You're going on leave again? You just got off leave," Rizzo said.

"That was back in March," I said.

"Where you going this time?" Roach asked.

"We are going to Spain."

"That's a long trip." Dietz said.

"You're right, it is. Now if you clowns don't mind I'd like to get some sleep, so you guys get your butts off my bunk," I said, pointing to Tom and Roach.

They got up and stretched and decided they had rehearsed enough for tonight anyway. If they didn't have their stories straight by now they never would have. Roach and Tom left. Rizzo and Harry started getting ready for the midnight shift. I got undressed, lay down on the top of my bunk and lit a cigarette. I really was glad I wasn't part of all that I had no idea what Top would do or even if the commander would let him handle it. I knew if the commander got involved the guys were in big trouble.

Finally Rizzo and Harry left for work and turned the lights out on their way out. Dietz was already asleep and I wasn't far behind.

Monday morning I went to work as usual but I was wondering what was going on back at the company. I hoped the guys weren't in too much trouble. I asked CPL Mapes a couple of times during the day if he had heard anything, but he said no. We finally got relieved and headed back to Patton Barracks.

I turned in my weapon and headed up to my room. Roach was just coming out of his on the way to the mess hall.

"Hey, wait up. Let me change clothes, and I'll walk over to the mess hall with you," I said.

Roach followed me into my room.

"Well, what happened? What did Top have to say?" I asked.

"We are all restricted from going to the club for a week. We also got our passes pulled for a week, and he said from now on we were to let the club manager handle the girls' problems."

"That's it?" I asked, a bit surprised.

"That's it," Roach said.

"Sounds like you got off easy."

"Top had statements the girls made to Deavers Saturday night. And even the club manager said the other guys had been acting up all evening. So Top cut us some slack."

"Well, a week's restriction ain't bad, and you're just starting your mid-shift duty, right?"

"Yeah. I can deal with it," Roach said, laughing. "At least I didn't get busted again."

We walked over to the mess hall and had supper. All the excitement and anticipation was over now and everybody was pretty quiet. We walked back over to the barracks, Roach stopped by the day room to shoot some pool. I went on up to my room and put my uniform on a hanger. I lay down on my bunk, lit a cigarette, and thought: four more days and I was out of here for a couple of weeks.

GERMANY
Chapter 57

Friday night found me on the train to K-town. Sara picked me up at the Bahnhof and we headed for the BOQ but had to make a side trip to the PX to pick up a couple of cartons of cigarettes.

Sara asked if I needed anything else while we were in the PX but I couldn't think of anything. I hadn't brought a lot with me from Heidelberg; I had almost as many if not more clothes at Sara's than I had back in my locker. Since I had left all my stuff in her car when we returned from Vienna, I had just replaced what I needed in Heidelberg and as a result I pretty much had two of everything. It made traveling back and forth between Heidelberg and K-Town a lot easier.

We left the PX and went on up to the BOQ. Sara had bags out all over the place; some half packed some still empty. I looked around trying to figure out which ones were mine.

"You really think you're going to get all these bags in Blue Bird?" I asked.

"Depends on how many you pack," she said.

"Me! I can get by on one if I have to; you're the one that has to have a half dozen, and that's before you pack any clothes." I snorted.

"Well, girls need things."

"No, they don't; they just think they *might* need things."

"Shut up and pack your one suitcase and leave the rest to me," Sara growled.

"Okay, I'll do my one suitcase, but first I want a coke," I said as I walked over to the little refrigerator, grabbed a coke and kicked off my shoes.

We worked quietly for a long time, each lost in our own packing arrangements. Sara had her music going. I had picked up the *Blue Hawaii* Album in the PX, so we had a little change of pace in music when it came on. Finally about 2200 we had more bags packed than were left unpacked.

"You lied," Sara said.

"What do you mean, I lied?"

"You have two bags," Sara said, pointing at the two bags I had packed.

"You can't count the little one. That is equal to your cosmetics and makeup—one bag," I declared.

"It's still more than one," she teased.

"Okay, sue me. I got two bags. It's still half of what you have, not including your makeup shit."

Sara and I sat on the bed, smoked a cigarette, and discussed our options. "Do you want to pack the car tonight?" she asked.

"Well, we could, but with our luck someone would decide to steal the car or break into it and get our stuff," I replied.

"I guess we should wait until morning."

"I think that would be a wise decision."

"Okay, then, I'm going to take my shower; I'm tired," Sara said.

"Hurry up, and save me some hot water."

Sara got up stripped and slipped on her robe. I always enjoyed watching her get undressed or dressed. But I think I said that, didn't I? I lay back on the bed, smoked a cigarette, and sipped on my second coke while I waited for Sara to get out of the bathroom.

When Sara came out of the shower, I got up stripped and headed for the bathroom.

"You need a robe," Sara said.

I stopped and struck one of those Greek god poses I had learned from Rizzo.

"What? You don't like my Greek god body?" I replied.

"Your Greek god body has been eating too many French fries."

"Humph! Just for that you're not getting any tonight."

"Oh, good. I can just go right to sleep for a change." She laughed.

"Make that two nights," I said as I pranced off to the bathroom in my all together.

I took my time and enjoyed the hot shower. I got out and toweled off, brushed my teeth, wrapped the towel around my waist and went back to the room. The only light that was on was a candle burning by the bed; Sara was big on candles. I locked the door, in case Mary Ann decided to put in an appearance, blew out the candle, crawled over Sara to my side of the bed, and slid under the covers.

Sara had her back to me when I came into the room, so I tuned over with my back to her. I hadn't got comfortable yet when I felt Sara move over close to me, and felt her hands begin to roam. I rolled back over on my back and looked at her.

"Oh, no you don't. I told ya, you ain't getting any tonight."

Her hands kept roaming. She snuggled her head into my neck and nibbled on my ear lobe.

"You don't like this Greek body. Too many French fries, remember?"

"I lied," she said as her leg crossed over mine.

"You lied, huh?"

"Yes," she whispered.

"Okay, I'll forgive you this time," I said as I slipped my arm around her.

I don't know what time the alarm when off, but it had to be wrong. It was too early to get up. At least I thought it was, but Sara was up, out of bed and on her way to the bathroom. I tried to go back to sleep, but I knew that wasn't going to work. I sat up, lit a cigarette and took a swig of the warm coke left over from last night. I couldn't decide which tasted worse, the cigarette or the coke.

Sara came out of the bathroom and I jumped up and headed right in. I needed another shower to get my day started. I turned on the water, brushed my teeth while I let the shower water get hot. I tested the water when I was finished brushing my teeth, it was hot and I stepped in and let out a sigh as the hot water streamed down over my abused body. Okay, maybe it wasn't abused, just slightly used.

I didn't spend too much time in the shower. I was coming alive now and was getting anxious to get our trip started. I climbed out of the shower, toweled off, slipped on some shorts, walked back to the room and finished dressing. Sara was already dressed and putting on her makeup up with her mug of coffee close at hand.

"Are all your bags packed and ready to go?" I asked.

"All except my makeup bag," she said

I grabbed as many bags as I could carry and headed for the car. Sara followed shortly with the rest of the bags. While I arranged the bags Sara went back up stairs and got the cokes and snacks she had made. By the time she got back all the bags were packed, she put the snacks in the back seat with the cooler of cokes and we were on our way to Spain.

GERMANY
Chapter 58

During the week prior to our departure for Spain, Sara had mapped out a route for us to follow. We crossed the German-French border at Saarbrucken, Germany. It didn't take very long after crossing into France to recognize that there was a distinct difference in the two countries.

In my travels through Germany I never saw trash along side the road and I never saw people making bathroom calls along the side of the road. We no more than crossed the border into France and we saw both. I have to admit I was a little taken back by the sights and smells of France.

Our trip through France was to take us through Dijon, Lyon, Saint-Etienne, Toulouse and then into the Pyrenees mountains where we would cross the border into Spain at Andorra. We pushed hard the first day and stopped for the night in Lyon. Lyon wasn't on our list of attractions so all we did was find a hotel for the night. We didn't even bother to find a place to eat, instead ate a sandwich Sara had packed and drank a coke. It had been a long day so after dinner we smoked a cigarette and went to bed.

The alarm went off the next morning at some ridiculous hour. Sara got up and dug out her instant coffee and found some of those rolls she bought. I went through my morning ritual, cigarette, shower, dress when necessary and then eat. It worked out well, Sara had her coffee and a roll with honey while I showered and then I ate while she showered. We packed our bags and were on the road before 0900.

The roads in France at that time were not exactly Autobahns and travel could be slow as hell sometimes and you passed at your own risk most of the time. Needless to say when we got an open stretch of road in front of us we tried to make the most of it. We pushed hard again and finally made it to Toulouse and pushed on through the Pyrenees Mountain range to Andorra. Once we crossed the Pyrenees we drove on through to Madrid.

With Sara's handy travel guide book we found what was classified as a four star hotel near center city. We parked the car and checked in. The main entrance and the lobby area looked very elegant. I wasn't sure we could afford this place. But that feeling didn't last past the first floor. Once we got off the elevator on our floor, it looked like the place was falling apart. Wall paper was hanging off the wall, and there were ladders and scaffolds stretched out down each side of the hallway.

In my best Spanish, English and any other language I asked the bellman that was bringing our baggage as politely as I could. "What the hell is going on here?"

The best answer I got from the bellman, "No Habla Ingles, Señor."

Using some simple sign language I managed to get a simple response. "We fix."

I was not too happy with the looks of this place, but I will say, once we got to our room it apparently had been fixed already, at least on the surface. The surface was as far as it went; water from the sink only trickled out, there was no pressure, and you could hear air in the pipes. The water in the shower was the same. I was afraid to try the toilet.

"Do you wanna stay in this place?" I asked Sara.

"Not really, but I'm too tired to try to find another one now. I saw they had a restaurant downstairs; let's just go get something to eat and then decide in the morning what we want to do," she said.

"You're braver than I am if you wanna try to eat in this dump."

"Maybe the food is better than the accommodations," Sara replied.

"Ah, yes, the eternal optimist." I snickered.

We made our way down to the dining room. It was after 10 p.m. Spaniards didn't eat supper before 9 p.m. so we were running fashionably late. We entered the dining room, either we were early, or there weren't a lot of people eating in this place. We had our choice of tables, it seemed, so we picked one near the sign that said "Baños" (Bathrooms). I mean, let's be real here. You didn't know what was coming out of that kitchen, but I was pretty sure it wasn't going to be tacos, with enchiladas, rice, and refried beans.

A waiter finally arrived with menus. I didn't read or speak any more Spanish now than I did when I was in Spanish class with Charlene. Surprisingly, or maybe not so surprisingly, the waiter spoke German. He and Sara went over the menu together. She translated for me. Nothing she said sounded very appetizing to me so I asked her, "What are you having?"

"I think I'm going to have a rack of lamb, with a spinach soup," she said.

Lamb was a meat, and I like spinach. "Okay, I'll have the same thing," I said.

Sara ordered, and off the waiter went. A few minutes later he was back with some wine for Sara and ice tea for me. That was the last we saw of the waiter until around 11 p.m. Finally he showed up with our Spinach Soup. I should have known better. The waiter set that bowl in front of me without using any thing to protect his hands from burning; I knew that wasn't a hot dish I was getting. I looked down and saw this green slimy stuff floating around in a darker green soup; with some other white stuff mixed in with it.

I leaned across the table after the waiter left and whispered to Sara. "What is this shit?"

"That is your spinach soup," she said.

"No, really. What is it?" I insisted.

"The green is spinach, and the white is egg white," she said.

I sat there for a minute and then thought, *Well, maybe it tastes better than it looks.* I picked up my spoon and took a bite. I was wrong; it didn't taste any better than it looked. It was ice cold and tasted like shit. I pushed my bowl to the side and lit a cigarette just to get the taste out of my mouth. Sara, meanwhile was just spooning away. I should have known; she can eat anything.

Shortly after Sara finished her soup the waiter came over and picked up her bowl. He looked at my bowl and then looked at me like he was insulted I didn't eat that crap. I flicked my hand at him to take that bowl out of my sight. He picked up the bowl swiftly turned and waddled off back to wherever he came from. A short time later he returned with our rack of lamb. He was nice to Sara and refilled her wine glass; he didn't offer me anymore tea. The lamb he sat in front of me at least looked edible. Wrong again! I cut into that lamb, and it started to bleed. I was beginning to wonder if every country in Europe only ate raw and cold food. Sara was just eating away.

After Sara finished the waiter was back to pick up the dishes. He got Sara's plate walked over to get mine, hesitated, gave me a dirty look. I flicked my hand at him again to get that crap off the table. He picked up the plate, rolled his eyes at me, and waddled off again.

Sara and I sat and had a cigarette while she finished her wine.

"I take it you didn't like the soup and the lamb?" she asked.

"Where did you get your first clue, Sherlock?" I said smugly.

"Somewhere between the face you made when you tasted the soup and when you tasted the lamb," she laughed.

"'Tain't funny, McGee; I'm hungry," I snipped.

"Aw, poor baby. You're going to have to go to bed with no supper tonight," she teased.

"As long as it's just supper I'm going to bed without I'll get through it." I grinned.

Sara smiled; the waiter brought our check and slammed it down on the table near me.

"Gracias, Señor," I said curtly.

He walked off without reply. *Rude bastard,* I thought. *You people need to learn how to cook.*

Sara and I went back to our room kicked off our shoes. She sat on the sofa, and I lay on the bed. I smoked a cigarette and she looked through the guide book. After a little while Sara put the book down, lit a cigarette and said, "There are a lot of palaces and museums right around this area to see. Plus a market area not too far from here. I wanted to see a bullfight, but I didn't see anything in the guide book about it."

I turned around and opened the night stand next to the bed and found some literature and began to thumb through it. To my surprise they had some things written in English as well as Spanish. I found a section on bullfighting. I read it out loud to Sara. "'Madrid hosts the largest Plaze De Toros (bullring) in Spain, Las Ventas, established in 1931. Las Ventas is considered by many to be the world center of bullfighting and has a seating capacity of almost 25,000. Madrid's bullfighting season begins in March and ends in October. Bullfights are held every day during the festivities of San Isidro (Madrid's patron saint) from the middle of March to the middle of June, and every Sunday, and public holiday the rest of the season. The style of the plaza is Neomudejar,' whatever that means."

"So that means we missed the season?" she asked.

"Sounds like it to me, and we missed one today, since they only have one on Sunday this time of year," I said.

"Shit!"

"What did you say?" I asked

I said, "Shit!"

"Ummm, I'm telling your mother. She'll wash your mouth out with soap."

Sara got up and walked over to the bed and pounced on top of me. Straddling me she looked down and said, "Just wait until I tell my daddy what you have been doing to his little girl, and he will cut your dick off."

"Ouch! Okay, I won't tell if you don't tell," I said.

We laughed, rolled over on the bed and forgot what time it was. Tomorrow could wait.

GERMANY
Chapter 59

We slept in late the next morning. Sara as usual was up first, having her first cup of instant coffee. I groaned and rolled off the edge of the bed and grabbed my cigarettes.

"Good morning," Sara said.

"Morning," I mumbled as I lit my cigarette.

Sara was munching on one of those hard rolls as she drank her coffee and reading through the guide book. I got up off the bed and headed for the bathroom. "I take it you haven't tried out the bathroom yet, huh?" I asked

"Not yet, I figured I'd let you have first crack at it."

"Chicken!" I said.

"Cluck, cluck, cluck," Sara replied.

I turned on the shower; a small cold sprinkling of water came dribbling out. I left that on and walked over to the sink and turned it on. Same results. It couldn't be put off any longer; I had to go to the bathroom. I walked over and raised the seat on the toilet. At least my plumbing worked. I attempted to flush the toilet and only got about a half a flush. I walked back to the sink; the flow had picked up some so I figured I could at least get my teeth brushed.

By the time I got my teeth brushed the water in the shower was stronger and actually getting warm so I hopped in real quick while I could. I didn't stay long, figured I would save some warm water for

Sara. I stepped out and she was waiting to step in, I was tempted to stay but thought better of it so I stepped out and toweled off and went in to get some clean shorts and T-shirt.

By the time Sara was out of the bathroom I was dressed and gobbling down one of those hard rolls and drinking a coke. I was starving; I couldn't remember the last time I had some food I could actually eat. Sara dressed quickly; we smoked a quick cigarette and then headed out the door to see what we could see of Madrid.

We strolled around the city, Sara following some directions out of the guide book and we eventually ended up at some King's Palace. I think it was called Palacio Real de Madrid, and it is the official residence of the King of Spain. I didn't even know they still had a king. That's one huge place; we spent a lot of time just walking around the outside of it.

Once we finished the Palace we wandered back to the center city. I noticed that most of the stores were closed; only a few remained open. It took me a minute then it dawned on me it was siesta time. I think this was the first time I had ever been in a country that actually observed siesta. I know they didn't in the border towns along the Texas Mexico border. Or maybe they did and I just never noticed. Sara and I found a little outdoor stand in a park that had ice cream and cokes. We got some ice cream and sat down at a small table and enjoyed our ice cream while it lasted, which wasn't long since it was definitely warm out.

Ice cream has a way of making me thirsty so I went back and got a coke. Sara said she would have one too. We sat and drank our cokes, smoked a cigarette and just watched the people strolling by in the park. Somehow I always imagined that all Spaniards were dark skinned and dark haired. I was surprised to see some rather light-complected blonde haired women walking about. Okay, so some of them could have been bottle blondes but there sure were a lot of them.

"Do you think that blonde sitting over there is a natural blonde?" I asked Sara, pointing to a particular blonde lady sitting a couple of tables down.

Sara turned slightly, looked at the woman for several moments, then turned back to me and said, "I don't know; it's hard to tell from here with her sitting in the shade. If I saw her up closer and out in the light I might be able to tell. Why do you ask?"

"I was just curious. I've noticed a lot of blondes down here, and I always thought of Spaniards to be dark complected and dark haired."

"Why don't you go ask her?" Sara asked.

"Right, I'll just walk right over there and ask her if she is a natural blonde. First of all she probably won't understand me; second of all what if she does, and says she is? What am I supposed to do then? Just take her word for it?"

"Maybe you'll get lucky and she'll prove it to you," Sara said as she sipped her coke.

"You're a dirty old woman," I said, "but I like your thinking. You think she would prove it right there or have to take me back to her place?"

"If she takes you back to her place don't expect me to be sitting here waiting for you when you get back," Sara said.

"Why shouldn't you be here? It was your idea. Don't you want to know the answer?"

"Just because it was my idea doesn't mean I want you to do it. And I really don't care if she is blonde or not," Sara replied.

"Then why did you suggest it?" I insisted

"You wanted to know; I was just giving you an option to find out."

"So you were helping me try to do something you really didn't want me to do in the first place?" I asked.

" Something like that." Sara grinned.

"That doesn't make sense."

"Sure it does. Think about it," Sara replied.

I sat there for a minute trying to decipher this little bit of female logic. I sat there squinting my eyes, looking at Sara. "You were testing me. You wanted to see how I would act. If I actually went over there you would have been really pissed no matter what happened. You were testing my loyalty or some shit like that, weren't you?"

"You're catching on, cowboy." Sara smiled.

"Not only are you a dirty old woman you're a tricky one too," I said.

Sara stood up, leaned over the table, and gave me a kiss, I mean, a real lip-locking, tongue-sucking, spit-swapping kiss, right there in front of God and everybody.

"What was that for?" I asked

"For not letting me down and being smart enough to understand it," she smiled.

We got up and through our cans in the trash can and strolled hand and hand through the park on our way back to the hotel. I was feeling pretty proud of my self but worried at the same time. Okay, so I got this one but how many more of these little tricks did I have lying ahead of me? What if I missed the next one? Would she tell her daddy? Or just do it herself?

When we got back to the hotel I walked over to the desk clerk and asked if he spoke English and he said that he did. I asked him if there was a restaurant in the vicinity that he could recommend that served American style food. He immediately recommended one, the name of which I can't remember anymore. I asked him where it was and he said it would be best if I took a taxi rather than him giving me directions. He said the doorman would be delighted to get me a taxi when I was ready. I thanked him and we went up to our room. Since it was siesta time, Sara and I decided we might as well join in, so we stretched out on the bed and took a nap.

I don't know how long we slept since I didn't have any idea what time we laid down; but when I woke up it was about 6:30 p.m. Sara was still asleep. I got up, lit a cigarette and grabbed a coke out of the cooler and moved over to the sofa. Since they didn't serve dinner around here until 9 p.m. there was no hurry, so I let Sara sleep.

My mind kept wandering back to that little episode back in the park. I had heard guys, usually married ones, talk about how women think different than guys and how they seemed to always get pissed about something and you never knew why and no matter what you did you were wrong. I realized this one was kinda far out, but if it was any indication of what I was in for I might be stark friggin' crazy before I was twenty-five.

Sara finally stirred and woke up. It was about seven p.m. She asked what time it was; I told her, and she immediately headed for the bathroom muttering she had to get ready to go out to dinner. I just kinda shook my head; she had two hours before they even started serving dinner and she had to start getting ready. Something else to get used to.

About 8:45 we walked down to the doorman told him our destination and asked him to hail us a taxi. The taxi was there immediately, I tipped the doorman, we got in the cab, and were on our way.

It was about a 20 minute ride to the Café. The taxi pulled up in front and a doorman opened the door for us. I tipped the doorman as Sara and I started inside. We were seated at a table for two near some windows that overlooked a courtyard with a lighted fountain in the middle. The waiter was there quickly with menus and greeted us in English. *I wonder how he knew?* The waiter poured us some water and disappeared.

I opened the menu and started to drool. The first thing I saw was a hamburger with all the trimmings and onion rings. As I wiped my chin I looked further down the menu and saw such things as BBQ Pork Ribs, BBQ Chicken and a bunch of other stuff. This was going to be a tough decision. But I was holding back. I remembered that rack of lamb also looked good the other night too.

When the waiter returned I had some questions for him. I did have a little bit of knowledge about BBQ since that was my daddy's specialty; remember, I dropped a brick on his head helping him build his BBQ pit. When I was satisfied that they actually cooked their meat I decided to go with the BBQ ribs, although I really could have eaten a hamburger. Sara opted for the BBQ chicken. Sara had a white wine for a change and I stuck with ice tea.

"If these ribs are any good, we're coming back here tomorrow for a hamburger and onion rings," I said.

Sara didn't have any objections so supper tomorrow night was already settled. We smoked a cigarette while we waited on our ribs and chicken. It was a short wait; the waiter was there just as we put out our cigarettes. The only problem with eating ribs is, they are sloppy. But I didn't care; I tucked my napkin into my shirt, asked the waiter to bring me another one, and dug in. I was starved for something American. Sara sat there all prim and proper cutting that chicken off the bone with a knife and fork. *If she ever gets to Texas we'll teach her how to eat this stuff,* I thought.

Sara looked over at me and burst out laughing and had to put her napkin over her mouth to cover up her giggling.

"What's so funny?" I asked.

"You look like you've been playing in my lipstick," she said.

"Well, darlin', that's just the joy of eatin' BBQ ribs. You need to get used to it," I said, wiping my mouth with the extra napkin the waiter had brought me. And if you really wanted to enjoy that chicken you'd put that knife and fork down and pick it up and eat it with your hands.

"I'm not going to do that," she said. "That would be impolite."

"Suit yourself," I said as I stuffed more ribs in my mouth.

We finished our meal in silence. I couldn't talk; I always had a mouth full of ribs. Naturally I was finished way before Sara. She was still trying to cut the meat off that chicken.

"If you would pick that up and eat it, you would be finished already," I said.

"Are you in a hurry?" she asked.

"Not anymore. I'm full now," I said.

Sara finally finished. The waiter came over and took our dishes away and asked if we wanted dessert; we declined, but Sara had another glass of wine. I sipped my tea and Sara her wine while we both had a cigarette. The waiter brought us our bill. I took a peek, it wasn't as expensive as that place in Vienna, but it wasn't cheap either. When Sara finished her wine, I slipped some money in the folder with the bill, and we walked out front, and the doorman got us a cab back to our hotel.

When we got back to the hotel there was a small band playing in the park across the street from the hotel so Sara and I walked over and listened to the music for a while. It wasn't a Mexican Mariachi Band like you might see in Texas but it was similar. We listened for about 30 minutes and then walked back across the street to the hotel.

It was after 1 a.m. when we crawled in bed. Despite the little siesta we had, we were both tired and full. We were asleep in about two minutes.

The next day we spent walking around the city. We toured a museum, found a little market. Sara found some of those hard rolls we had been eating for breakfast and bought some since we were all out. She found another little place that sold jewelry and trinkets. I think she bought a spoon to add to her collection.

We walked back to the park across the street from the hotel, sat and had some ice cream and a coke again. I didn't ask Sara about any blondes I saw sitting around this time. I wasn't going to push my luck. The stores were closing down for siesta already. We lingered around the park and sipped our drinks and smoked. The park was a pretty nice place; you could sit in the shade of the trees or out in the sunshine if you chose to. No one bothered you; it was a pretty peaceful place.

We got back to our hotel room and kicked off our shoes. Sara was putting away the rolls and whatever else she bought. When she was finished I stepped over to her, put my arms around her, gave her a kiss and began to unbutton her blouse.

"What are you doing?" she asked.

"I'm going to find out if you're a natural brunette," I said.

"You already know that."

"One can never be too sure in these matters," I said as I continued to unbutton her blouse.

I kissed her again and slid her blouse off her shoulders. My hand slid down to the zipper of her shorts and as the shorts fell to the floor she stepped out of them and I led her over to the bed. The Spaniards could siesta if they wanted to. I had other plans.

GERMANY
Chapter 60

Sara and I woke up in the same position we fell asleep after our afternoon interlude; her with her head on my shoulder and arm across my chest and one leg over mine. We must have awakened about the same time. She stirred and rolled over on her back as I was starting to move my arm out from under her head.

She sat up and looked at her watch it was almost 7 p.m.

"I need to start getting ready for supper," she said.

How did I know she was going to say that? Sara rolled off the bed and headed for the bathroom. I lay there and stretched and thought about going back to sleep but decided against it. Instead I sat up, lit up and got a coke from the cooler. For once I was actually looking forward to going out to eat. I could taste that hamburger with onion rings already.

Sara came out of the bathroom around eight. I never could figure out what took so long for a woman to spend an hour in the bathroom. Especially when her hair wasn't done and she didn't have makeup on yet. She walked out and I walked in. I turned on the shower and was surprised that there was actually a little water pressure this evening and it was even hot. I lingered and enjoyed the shower for longer than usual. Afterwards, I shaved, brushed my teeth, walked out and got dressed.

We walked down to the doorman; fortunately it was the same guy that was on last night because Sara and I had forgotten the name of the Café we went to. He called up a taxi for us, told the driver where to take us and I slipped him a little bigger tip tonight. I figured his memory was worth something, otherwise we wouldn't know where to go get our hamburgers with onion rings.

The head waiter at the restaurant also remembered us and took us back to our little table by the windows that overlooked a little plaza with a fountain in the center or it. The waiter arrived and brought us a glass of water. He started to hand us the menus but I stopped him and told him what we wanted. He nodded and trotted off to wherever waiters trot off too.

We waited, watched the people stroll around the plaza and smoked a cigarette. Our hamburgers arrived in short order. I was drinking a coke with mine Sara was having a beer. The hamburgers were great. The onion rings had a little different taste than what I was used to but they were great also. One thing I liked about these hamburgers, they came ready to eat. You didn't have to "build" it. All the lettuce, tomatoes, onions, and pickles or whatever you ordered was already on it.

"How is your burger?" Sara asked.

"Outstanding, makes me almost believe I'm home," I said

"You have hamburgers in Texas?"

I looked at her. "Of course we have hamburgers in Texas. What kinda friggin' question is that?" I asked in amazement.

"I thought you took all those cows with great big horns and drove 'em up the Chisel Trail to Kansas City," Sara said with this little shit-eatin' grin on her face.

"That's Chisholm Trail, not Chisel Trail, and it went to Abilene, Kansas, not Kansas City, Kansas, and those cows with great big horns are called longhorns," I replied. "Are you pulling my leg, or is this a test, Miss Teacher?"

"I was just wondering if you had hamburgers in Texas." She laughed.

"How many beers have you had? " I asked.

"Just one," she replied.

I had to laugh at her; I think she was enjoying messing with me here the past couple of days; either that or this Spanish air was getting to her.

She had come up with some weird shit the past couple of days. But that was okay; I was having a good time with it all.

We finished our supper, lingered over a cigarette, then I paid the bill and we walked out and caught a taxi back to the hotel. Again we walked across the street to the park and listened to some of the music. A couple of times the band played a couple of slow numbers and we danced our way around behind the crowd watching the band. We weren't by ourselves; a few other couples were dancing too.

About midnight we returned to our hotel room. We decided it was time to move on and leave Madrid. We looked at the map and decided we would go to Valencia next and then work our way back towards France through Barcelona. We packed everything we weren't going to need in the morning and were in bed by 1:30 a.m.

GERMANY
Chapter 61

We awoke early, showered, ate one of those hard rolls and were on our way to Valencia bright and early. We stopped on the way out of Madrid and gassed Blue Bird.

When we packed the car before leaving I noticed that the sunroof was not actually locked it only looked locked. I tried a couple of times to lock it but the latch kept popping out. I could tell there was a great day ahead; the sun was out, and the sky was clear; we would probably be driving with the sun roof open most of the day, so I just left it open for the time being.

The road to Valencia was a two lane winding, up and down road. And it was loaded with trucks hauling everything from chickens to manure, or at least it smelled like manure. We had no choice but to take our time but we did pass everything in front of us when the opportunity presented itself.

Despite the traffic and the curving road it was a rather enjoyable trip so far. There wasn't a cloud in the sky, except for one; just this one tiny little cloud that seemed to be traveling about the same speed as we were and moving in the same direction.

Sure enough we started feeling raindrops coming from this one tiny little cloud that was traveling about the same speed as we where and moving in the same direction.

I reached up and pulled the sunroof shut; I tried to lock it in place but it wouldn't latch, but I figured it would hold. Suddenly a gust of wind picked the sun roof up and blew it clear off the car. It landed in the middle of the road behind us. Drivers were swerving to miss it some were running off the road and some just ran over it.

Now it was pouring down rain out of this one tiny little cloud that was traveling about the same speed we were and moving in the same direction. Sara pulled the car over, I got out ran back and picked up the sun roof and got some dirty looks and gestures from some of the other drivers. Screw 'em. I didn't have time to respond. I was getting soaked. I figured Sara was getting soaked too but while running back to Blue Bitch (I told you her name was going to change) I noticed Sara's umbrella sticking out above the sunroof opening. Well, kiss my ass I thought, I'm getting soaked and she is sitting there high and dry!

I got back to the car and worked at sliding the sun roof door back on its runners so it would at least slide back and forth. Of course in order for me to do this Sara had to take her umbrella down. Ha! I thought now she can enjoy this little down pour from that one tiny little cloud, moving about as fast as we were and in the same direction. I finally got the roof on its runners so that it would slide forward but it still wouldn't lock. We didn't have a shoe string between the two of us and nothing we could use to try to tie the top down. Even if we had, I'm not sure what we would have tied to what. That meant that I had to hold the damn thing in place to keep the rain out even if the rain stopped I had to hold the roof down to keep it from blowing off again. I never did like that car. Now I really hated it.

We drove all the way to the outskirts of Valencia about 200 miles before we came to a place that could possibly fix the car. We were both still wet and worn out from the drive. We decided to find a place to stay and then find a car repair place. We found a nice little hotel, nobody spoke much English it seemed but we managed to get a room and some directions to a car repair place. We got the bags out of the car and took them up to our room.

"You stay here and get dried off and cleaned up. I'll go see about getting the car fixed," I said.

"Okay, good luck," Sara said.

I walked out the door and got in the Blue Bitch. I drove at a snail's pace down the street and held the top down between shifting gears. I found an auto shop and pulled in.

A scruffy-looking guy with really dirty hands walked up and said, "Si, Señor?"

I gave my high-school Spanish my best shot. "Habla Ingles?" I asked.

"No, Señor," he replied.

"Figures," I said.

"Como?"

"Never mind. Come over here," I said as I walked towards the car and motioning him to follow.

He came along, and I climbed inside the driver's seat and showed him the problem with the lock on the sun roof. He walked around to the passenger side and got in and looked at the lock on the door. By this time we had a crowd around the car, all peeking in at the problem. All seemed to have an answer or at least and idea; which was more than I had right at that moment.

After much conferring with his staff, which I think by this time, included every male in the village, the guy came over and brought along another guy. It seems the other guy spoke at least some English. After a lot of talking in broken English on their part and some broken Spanish on my part they got the point across that they couldn't fix the roof here and now; they would have to order parts, which would take about three days to get.

Well, that sucked. I knew I wasn't ready to spend three days just waiting on parts and then no telling how many more days to actually fix the damn thing. And I knew they would be taking their siesta every day. I had an idea. I saw one of the guys using a welding torch when I came in.

I walked over to the torch pointed to it and said, "Use this," and made a circle with my hand indicating I wanted 'em to use it all around.

The little Spanish guy mimicked my gesture, and I said, "Si, all around. How long will it take?" I asked.

The guy looked at his partner and his partner translated for him I guess, he turned back around to me and said, "Mañana"

"Bueno; mañana is good enough for me," I said. "How much?"

Again he referred to his partner then turned to me and said, "Twenty-five dollars."

"Twenty-five dollars American?" I asked.

"Si, American," he replied.

"Bueno, hasta mañana," I said and walked out of the shop.

I walked back to the hotel and was trying to decide if I should tell Sara now what was about to happen to her car or just wait and let her discover it tomorrow. If I waited I could always say there was a lack of communication, and I didn't know they were going to weld it shut. Or I could just tell her now and explain that it was the only choice we had unless she wanted to sit around this little town for a week or so. I knew either way she wasn't going to be happy.

I got back to the room; Sara had already taken a shower and was brushing out her hair. She looked startled when I walked in.

"Did I scare ya?" I asked.

"No, I just wasn't expecting you back so soon."

"So soon? You already had time to take a shower and wash your hair. You got some guy hiding under the bed?" I walked over and looked, knowing there would be no one there.

"He just jumped out the window," Sara said.

I walked over to the window and stuck my head out. "Hey, I see you down there; come back and fight like a man!" I hollered at no one in particular.

Sara was laughing, "You're crazy; you know that?"

"You think that's crazy, wait 'til you hear what they are going to do to your car," I said.

"Oh, shit. Do I want to know?" she asked.

"There you go with that language again. You know, I'm writing your mother when we get home."

"Funny, I was just thinking: it's about time I wrote my daddy," Sara replied.

"Okay, forget the letters. You wanna know about your car now or just wait and see for yourself?"

"Sock it to me," she said.

"That will have to wait. Right now I wanna tell you about your car," I replied.

"Smart ass," Sara quipped.

"They can't fix the roof of the car without waiting for three days or so for parts and then no telling how long it will take them to fix it. I didn't figure you wanted to sit around this place that long, so I told them to weld the top shut, and we can pick it up in the morning."

"Weld it shut? As in, there will be no more sunroof?" Sara asked.

"Yep, that's about it. Sorry, but I didn't see any other alternative."

"It's okay; we don't use the sunroof all that much anyway, and at least we don't have to worry about someone breaking in through the sunroof anymore," Sara said.

"I didn't even think about that breaking-in thing. Good point," I said as I started to undress and head for the shower. "Is there any hot water in this joint?"

"I had plenty when I showered."

"Does that mean you used it all and now there is no more?"

"I guess you'll just have to find out for yourself."

"There better be some hot water," I snipped.

"Or what?"

"Or I'll just sit around here naked until there is some," I said.

"Wow, that sounds exciting."

"Hey! I hollered at Sara. She looked at me, and I shot her the finger as I walked into the bathroom. I heard her laughing as I closed the door.

I turned on the shower and waited a couple of minutes, and the hot water started pouring out. I stepped into the shower and was thinking that Sara was really acting out of character this trip. Not that I minded; I thought it was great. It just wasn't the same Sara I was used to.

GERMANY
Chapter 62

The next morning we grabbed a roll, Sara had her instant coffee, and I had a coke. We made short work of breakfast and with bags in hand went down to the check out desk. While Sara paid the bill I walked on down to the garage.

I was kind of surprised when I got there; I really didn't expect the car to be ready yet, but there she sat; roof all welded together ready to go. I checked out the welding job and couldn't find any problems; like I would have known one if I had. I paid the scruffy little guy, thanked him and drove back to the hotel. Sara was waiting outside with the bags; so it was a quick packing job and we were off to Valencia.

It was only about an hours drive to the center city of Valencia. Using the handy tour guide we managed to find a nice little hotel located only about 3 minutes from the beach. We checked in and immediately left to find something to eat. Those hard rolls didn't go a long way. We walked around and eventually found ourselves down near the ocean; actually I guess that is the Mediterranean Sea.

We found a little place there that served an almost American hamburger. They didn't have any mustard at least anything I associated with the mustard I was used to. I wasn't sure what the meat was, and wasn't going to ask. But along with the lettuce, tomato and a large dose of salt and pepper it wasn't bad. Oh, and the bread was good. At least with that and a coke we satisfied our immediate hunger.

We sat outside at a little table with wooden chairs. The day was hot but there was a breeze blowing in off the water, and that cooled things down considerably.

"How is your hamburger?" Sara asked.

"Not as good as we have in Texas," I said sarcastically.

Sara grinned and replied. "Well, I'm glad you like it."

"Well, it's edible, and right now that works for me," I said. "Wanna go for a dip in the Mediterranean?"

"I didn't bring a bathing suit."

"Neither did I, but we could go skinny dipping," I suggested.

"No way, cowboy. I'm not getting naked in front of all these Spaniards."

"We could come back tonight," I said.

"I don't think you can swim in the nude here anyway," Sara said.

"You're such a killjoy," I replied.

"Fine. You go jump in there naked, and I'll watch out for the cops. If you don't get arrested, maybe I'll join you."

"No, you won't." I said.

"You're right, but it sounded good, didn't it?" Sara laughed.

We finished our cigarettes and walked around the town for a while. The further away from the water we got the hotter it got. We stopped in and visited some museum which really didn't hold any interest for me but Sara seemed to enjoy it.

When we came out of the museum I noticed the shops were starting to close down. I asked Sara if she wanted to keep walking around or head back to the hotel and join the natives in a siesta.

"A siesta sounds good to me; it's getting too hot to be out here now anyway."

The room had a ceiling fan and a small window unit. We hadn't thought to turn them on before we left and the room was a real sweat box when we walked in. We turned on the fan and the window unit and came out of our clothes in a hurry. It was too hot to move. We both stretched out on the bed and just lay there; within a few minutes we started to feel some cool air coming our way.

I lit up a cigarette, offered one to Sara. She asked if I would get hers out of her purse, I walked over got the cigarettes, lit one for her and handed it to her.

"Find anything really exciting in or about Valencia in that travel guide?" I asked.

"Not really. Lots of museums around. There is a tomato fight in August, but we'll be gone before that takes place," she said.

"A tomato fight?" I asked.

"It's some kind of festival or something. It's over there in the book if you want to read about it."

"I'll take your word for it," I said as I crawled over her back to my place on the bed. I lay back, smoked my cigarette, and wondered what we were going to do for supper. Sara must have been reading my mind. "Did you see any place that looked like it might serve some decent food for supper?"

"No, I didn't. I think this place has a little restaurant around the corner behind the desk. We can check it out later if you want to," I said.

"Sounds like a plan to me," she said.

"Hey, that's my line," I quipped.

"So it is; I guess I'm gonna have to start hanging out with a better crowd."

"Screw you!" I snorted.

"You would like that, wouldn't you?"

"Humph! Never happen," I replied.

Sara turned over towards me and started nibbling on my neck. "You sure about that?" she asked.

"Forget it. I'm not interested."

Her hands began to roam while she continued to nibble on my neck and ear lobe. "Are you sure?" she asked.

"Yeah, I'm positive."

"Ummm, something tells me you're lying."

There are some things a guy just can't keep to himself no matter how hard he tries.

GERMANY
Chapter 63

By the time I woke up the room had finally cooled down to the point of actually being chilly. Sara was curled up next to me in a little ball. I reached over and pulled the covers up over her as I climbed out of bed and slipped on my jeans and shirt. I walked over and turned the window unit down to low, then went to the sofa and lit a cigarette.

I checked my watch it was only 6:30 pm. Still a long time to go before supper time around this place I thought. I saw Sara stir and come awake.

"Where did you go? What time is it?"

"I just got up. It's about 6:30," I told her.

"Will you bring me a cigarette?"

"Say please," I said.

"Please."

I got up got her cigarettes and lighter out of her purse and carried them over to her. She pursed her lips, making that little "kiss kiss" sound. I bent down and gave her a real one then returned to the sofa. We were both silent as we smoked our cigarettes.

"I think I'll take a shower," Sara said as she put out her cigarette.

"I think that's a splendid idea; it's only two hours before they start serving supper, and we don't want to be late."

"Okay, smart ass, no more afternoon delight for you," she stated.

"Hey, that wasn't my idea. You started it," I snapped.

"See if I ever start it again then."

"Yeah, right; you can't stay away, and you know it," I quipped.

Sara threw her panties and hit me in the face as she headed for the bathroom.

"See, what did I tell ya? There you go again, throwing your panties at me already." I laughed, as she slammed the bathroom door.

I went over to the cooler and got a coke, which was warm, since we hadn't put any ice in the cooler for a while; but it was still wet, anyway. I sat back down on the sofa and smoked another cigarette, waiting for Sara to come out of the bathroom.

About 7:30 Sara finally came out of the bathroom with a towel wrapped around her and another one on her head. I got up, stripped and headed for the bathroom. I turned on the water, it was hot right away and I jumped right in. The hot water felt good as always. I closed my eyes and just stood there. Every time my skin adjusted to one temperature I would turn it up a notch until it got as hot as I could stand it and then I just totally relaxed.

I don't know how long I was there, but the next thing I knew Sara was peeking around the shower curtain and asking if I was all right. The bathroom was all steamy and the mirrors all fogged up.

"Yeah, I'm fine, just totally enjoying the shower," I said.

"Well, you steamed up the mirrors, and I still need to put on my makeup, and I can't let my hair down. It will frizz up."

"Frizz up? What kinda word is frizz up? Is that some Yankee kinda word?" I asked as I turned the water off.

"Just get out! I need the bathroom again."

"I'm not finished yet," I said.

"You can come back later," Sara snapped as she popped my butt with a towel.

"Ouch! Damn it, that hurt! I screeched. "You realize you're in big trouble when we get back from supper, don't you? I said.

"I'll worry about that then," Sara said as she slammed the bathroom door in my face.

I walked over and grabbed some clean clothes out of the suit case, *Damn women,* I thought; *they need a bathroom just for them.* I got dressed and finished my warm coke while I smoked another cigarette.

Sara finally came out of the bathroom with her hair and makeup done and began getting dressed. I just sat and watched: this had become one of my favorite pastimes. She was almost finished dressing when she looked over at me.

"Are you going to shave?" she asked.

"Nope."

"Why not?"

"'Cause I couldn't get in the bathroom," I replied.

"You can get in there now," she said.

"No way; I'm already dressed now. You're just going to have to go to supper with an unshaved heathen tonight," I said smugly.

"When do you plan on shaving then?"

"I dunno; mañana, maybe, maybe not," I replied.

"Well, you ain't getting any until you shave," Sara stated.

"That's blackmail!" I cried.

"Well, it's up to you," Sara replied.

"Humph! We'll see," I said as we walked out the door on our way to the dining room. The dining room was small and cozy, definitely not crowded; it was just barely 9 p.m. We found a table in the corner for two with a wine-bottle candle. I hadn't seen one of those in a long time.

The waiter brought menus which was pretty much a waste of time since our Spanish wasn't good enough to read it. He came back shortly with some water, and in very good English said, "May I assist you with the menu?"

"Oh, yeah, we can use a lot of assistance," I said.

He went down the list of options on the menu. One was some kinda veal. Instantly my Wiener Schnitzel came to mind. I didn't hesitate with that one. I told the waiter that's what I wanted. Sara ordered the same. It came with some black rice and beans. Sara rolled her eyes at the beans but didn't say anything. We drank our usual wine and tea.

"What are we going to do tomorrow?" I asked.

"I don't know. What do you want to do?"

"Go skinny dipping," I said.

"Well, you can do that if you want to, but I'm not going with you. I'll go look at some more museums," Sara said.

"Okay, okay, so we don't go skinny dipping, but I can't get excited about those museums either."

"They are pretty boring," Sara admitted.

The waiter brought us our veal with beans and rice. The veal wasn't breaded, but it was cooked; I'm thinking pan fried, so I was happy with that. Sara and I ate in silence. She pretty much skipped over the beans.

"Can I have your beans?" I asked.

"Haven't you had enough?"

I put my elbows on the table, leaned forward, looked her in the eye, grinned and said, "I just wanna be sure you have a real good night tonight."

She put her elbows on the table, leaned forward, looked me in the eye, grinned and said.

"If you lay off the beans and shave, I promise you will have a real good night tonight."

A counter offer. I wasn't prepared for that. I had to think about it for a minute. "Okay, you got a deal."

We finished our drinks and decided to stroll back down towards the water and walk off some of our dinner. It was cooler down by the water naturally and the beach was pretty crowded. We took off our shoes and strolled arm and arm along the shore line for a while.

On the return route we found our little wooden table and chairs outside the little place we got our hamburgers earlier. It was closed now. We sat down in the chairs and smoked a cigarette.

"How would you feel about driving on to Barcelona tomorrow?" Sara asked.

"Suits the shit outta me," I replied.

"It's only about 220 miles, and I would like to get there and see what they have to offer and then hit some of the small towns and villages along the Costa Brava."

"I think that's an excellent idea," I said.

"Okay, we'll leave in the morning then. You ready to go back?" she asked.

"You in a hurry to get back?" I asked.

"You have to shave don't you?" Sara grinned.

"By George, I do believe you're right," I said.

We got up and walked hand and hand back to the hotel. As soon as we hit the door I took my shirt off and headed for the bathroom. It didn't take me long to shave, when I was finished I stepped back out into the living room and Sara was already in bed. I took off my jeans, turned out the lights and crawled into bed beside her. I guess we can pack in the morning I thought.

GERMANY
Chapter 64

We were up early the next morning. We packed, checked out of the hotel and were on our way to Barcelona before 9 a.m. Sara played navigator and I drove we were on the open road in about 20 minutes.

We followed the coastline all the way to Barcelona. It was a beautiful drive; the scenic and rugged coastline was a succession of coves, cliffs and mountaintop lookouts. We stopped a couple of times to take in the views and once to eat a late breakfast which basically consisted of various fruits.

We arrived in the City just before noon. Sara consulted her guide book and picked out a hotel. With a little help from an English-speaking policeman we found the hotel rather quickly and checked in. It was not far from the center city. Barcelona is the second largest city in Spain, and there was a multitude of things to see.

This was actually a pretty nice hotel. Our room had a balcony and since we were on the north side of the building we didn't have a lot of sun. Once we settled in, we opened a can of coke, sat out on the balcony, and just enjoyed what little view we had. Besides, it was almost time for siesta, and we couldn't see any sense in going out to watch the stores close.

Taking siestas can get addictive. It seems the more siestas you take the more you miss it if you don't take one. Sara got up and said she was going to the bathroom. I stayed on the balcony, drank my coke and smoked a cigarette. When Sara hadn't returned in a reasonable amount of time I went in to check on her. There she was stretched out on the bed sound asleep. Damn! She could have told me she was going to take a siesta I thought. I got out of my clothes and joined her on the bed. It didn't take long and I was sound asleep.

By the time I woke up Sara was awake and in the bathroom. I got up found my cigarettes, lit one up, grabbed another coke and moved back out to the balcony. It had cooled off some, and it was nice out there. We were on about the 5th floor, I think, which was high enough for us to have a rather decent view. You could just barely see part of the ocean between some of the other buildings. Occasionally a pigeon would fly by stop and sit on the railing around the patio. I think people must have fed them. They would look at me and make noise like they expected me to give them something and when I didn't they would fly off in a huff.

Sara came out and joined me on the balcony dressed in nothing but her towel carrying a bottle of nail polish, a coke and her cigarettes She sat down in the chair across from me; pulled a small end table up in front of her, put the cigarettes down on one side, the coke on the other side and propped her foot up between the two and began polishing her toenails.

I sat there taking all this in, waiting for the coke or the cigarettes to end up on the balcony floor, but somehow she seemed to make it all work. "You have big feet, you know that?" I quipped.

"The better to kick your butt with," she snapped.

"You know there must be something in this Spanish air; you sure have gotten sassy since we crossed the border," I noted.

"You complaining?" she inquired.

"No, I just thought I should point that out to you before you let your alligator mouth overload your hummingbird ass," I grinned.

"And what will you do if I do get overloaded?"

"I might have to spank you," I said.

"Oh, please, spank me, spank me." She laughed.

"You'd like that, wouldn't you?"

"I dunno; I've never been spanked."

"I can see you have a lot to learn," I said.

Sara put the top back on the nail polish, set the bottle down, lit a cigarette, picked up her Coke, and propped both feet on the little table in front of her. She turned towards me, smiled, and asked, "You gonna teach me, cowboy?"

"I'll certainly give it my best shot," I replied.

"When do I get my first lesson?" Sara asked, smiling.

"I guess we have to at least wait until your nail polish is dry," I said.

We sat looking out over the city that we could see from our balcony, smoking our cigarettes and drinking our cokes. The sun was fading fast now and the night was fast closing in on us.

Sara got up and headed back in towards the bedroom. She stopped at the door, dropped her towel, said, "My nails are dry now," and walked on into the room. I put my cigarette out, got up and picked up Sara's towel. I walked in the bedroom and laid it across the sofa. Sara was lying on the bed, obviously ready for lesson number one. I took off my jeans and walked into the bathroom.

"Where are you going?" she asked in surprise.

"I need to take a shower," I said.

"What about my lesson?" She pouted.

"This is it. Lesson number one: patience," I said as I closed the bathroom door.

I took my usual hot shower, got out, shaved, brushed my teeth, then walked into the bedroom and crawled up on the bed next to Sara. She had her back to me and didn't move as I slid closer to her. I started kissing her shoulder, moving up to her neck and then lightly nibbling on her ear. I let my hands begin to wander.

"What are you doing?" she asked as if she were mad.

"This is lesson number two," I whispered in her ear.

"I'm still practicing lesson number one," she snapped.

"Okay, lesson number one is important," I said as my hands continued to wander, and I kept kissing her on the neck. I could feel her body begin to more beneath my touch. Slowly she began to stir with more energy. I had the feeling lesson number two was about to commence.

After lesson number two was completed to everyone's satisfaction we both just lay on the bed, neither of us saying anything. I think it's called after glow. I got up and got our cigarettes and brought them back to the bed. I lit one up for each of us.

"You know what I want to do?" Sara asked.

"Lesson number three?" I inquired with a smile.

"No! Well, not here and now," Sara said.

"Then I give up."

"I'm tired of the cities. I want to go visit some little villages along the Costa Brava," she said.

"I know; you said that yesterday, or was it today?" I replied.

"I mean I want to go now," she stated.

Right this minute? But you're not dressed!" I said.

Sara hit me with a pillow, "No, you dummy, not this very minute, but let's leave in the morning," she said.

"That's fine with me, but you're not gonna be sorry later, are you, and wanna come back?" I asked.

"No, I don't think so."

"Okay, then, we can leave in the morning. But in the meantime I'm getting hungry."

"Me too. Let's just go down to the hotel restaurant for supper," she said.

We rolled off the bed and began to get dressed. Naturally Sara had to do her hair and makeup so I was dressed and sitting around twiddling my thumbs while she finished. Finally she was ready to go and we left the room and took the elevator down to the lobby.

We found a table, the waiter brought us a menu; I looked for that veal stuff I had before with the beans and black rice. With a little help from the waiter I discovered that I had made the right choice. Sara ordered fish of some kind. She was braver than I was when it came to food.

The food and drinks came quickly we hardly finished our cigarettes before it was there. We ate quietly, each lost in our own thoughts I guess, or just starving to death. I gobbled my food down but then I usually did. It was the Army way. Sara took her time as was her way. So while she finished, I smoked another cigarette. After Sara had finished, the waiter came by with a dessert tray; we both passed on dessert, and the waiter left the check. I slipped some money in the folder and we left.

"Wanna go down and walk on the beach for a while?" I asked.

"Sure, need to walk off some of that supper anyway."

Hand in hand we headed for the beach. It took us about 10 minutes to get there. We slipped off our shoes and felt the sand squeeze in between our toes; it was still warm from the day's hot sun. The more we walked towards the water, the cooler the sand became. We turned and walked just beyond the edge of the tide as it rolled in and then back out again.

As we walked we passed other couples, some were walking, and some were not. Sara tried to ignore those that weren't walking but I could see her glace over that way every now and then. I just had to grin. They really weren't doing anything, yet; but I couldn't help but wonder what we would see on our return walk. Maybe Sara was wondering the same thing. "Let's go back now, okay?" she asked.

"If that's what you want to do, then by all means, let's turn around. Who knows what we might see on the way back?" I grinned.

"I won't see anything," she said.

"Well, if I see something interesting I'll point it out to you."

"I'm not looking," she snapped.

I laughed, slid my arm around her waist, kissed her cheek and said, "Okay, Miss Prude."

We walked back the same way we had came, and much to my disappointment there was nothing going on that I could point out to Sara. When we got back to the street, we sat on a little bench and dusted the sand off our feet and slipped our shoes back on and returned to the hotel.

When we got back to the room I grabbed a coke, went out on the balcony and smoked a cigarette. Sara joined me for a cigarette and then went in and began packing what little there was to pack. I think Sara and I without really talking about it had come to the conclusion that we were both out of the sightseeing mode and preferred to just walk around, see whatever we saw and watch the people.

I went in and packed away what little I had to pack, got undressed and climbed in bed. It must have been the sea air, but I was asleep in no time and don't even remember Sara coming to bed.

GERMANY
Chapter 65

We left Barcelona early the next morning, sticking around only long enough for Sara to have her cup of instant coffee and me to drink a coke. We were on the highway such as it was along the eastern coast of Spain.

The Costa Brava started just a short distance outside the City of Barcelona and ran to the southeastern border of France. The Costa Brava is a beautiful, rugged region with miles of sandy beaches. You could see signs that tourism had begun to catch up with it as construction of high-rise hotels and resorts began to be seen alongside the fishing villages, sheltered rocky coves and medieval towns with ancient castles.

Sara and I stopped at some of the small villages and walked the streets, visiting the various shops that were available. The people were very friendly and helpful, they actually seemed happy to see us. We bought a few trinkets, sat outside at a small café, and had a drink. There weren't many places you could stop and not have a view of the ocean.

While it was only about a 100 mile drive from one end to the other, Sara and I took so much time at the various shops we were just slightly more than half way when it was siesta time. We returned to the car and continued our trip at a slow pace, not in any hurry to leave this area.

"I really like this area," Sara said.

"I do too; it's really pretty and a really laid-back place. All the villagers seem like really nice people."

"Let's spend at least one night here," Sara said.

"Pick a spot. Sounds like a good idea to me," I replied.

A few miles up the road we came to another village, I can't remember the name of it but we stopped. We just parked the car in front of a café on the main street and sat outside under the covered porch. We ordered a drink and the young lady brought it to us right away.

"Do you speak English?" I asked the young lady. Actually she was a young girl.

She held up her hand as if to say, "Wait a minute," turned and left. A few minutes later she returned with an older woman. "May I help you, Señor?

"Is there a hotel in this town with a view of the ocean?" I asked

"Si, Señor, at the end of this street, turn to the right. My daughter will show you if you like?" she said.

"That would be very nice of her. She can ride with us," I said.

"No, Señor, she will walk in front of you; you can just follow her when you are ready to go."

"I think we are ready now," I said as I looked at Sara, and she nodded in agreement.

We paid our bill, thanked the lady for her help and walked back to the car. The young girl was in front of us waiting for our signal that we were ready. I waved to her and she waved back and began walking. I let her get several feet in front of me and then began to follow. It was only a couple of blocks down the road before we turned to the right; we drove to the end of the street where the young girl stopped and pointed to a door. I parked the car almost right in front of the door, got out, and tried to tip the young girl for helping us.

"Gracias, no, Señor," she said, waving her hand back and forth.

"Are you sure?" I asked.

"Si, Señor," she said and ran off back down the street.

Sara and I went inside and found a rather portly lady sitting behind a desk reading a magazine. She looked up as we approached her and smiled. "Buenas dias." She smiled.

"Buenas dias," I said. "We are looking for a room with a view of the ocean. The lady down at the café said you had such a room.

The lady smiled, then in English said, "I do have such a room; it is not too large, but it has a patio with a very beautiful view of the ocean."

"May we see it please?" I asked.

The lady turned and took a key from a wall hook, walked out from behind the desk and motioned for us to follow her. There was no elevator so we walked up three flights of steps. I was wondering how bad I really wanted to stay in this room. When we got to the third floor there were only about four rooms on the whole floor that I could count. The lady picked the one right at the top of the stairs. She unlocked the door, stepped aside, and let us walk in. But without leaving the front door I could see onto and across the patio to the ocean.

"We'll take it," Sara said without even consulting me. I looked at her and smiled.

"Good choice, darlin'," I said with my best Texas accent.

We went back down the three flights of stairs, registered; then went out to the car to get our bags. Before we could get them unpacked, the lady from behind the desk came out with a young boy at her side and told us he would get the bags and bring them to our room for us. I wasn't about to argue with that. Sara and I grabbed a few small items and went on back up to the room. The young boy was not far behind with the bags. When he finished I offered him a tip; this time it wasn't refused.

The boy smiled said, "Gracias, Señor," bowed slightly, and left.

I walked out on the patio with Sara. There were no buildings to our right, none to our left and only the Mediterranean Ocean in front of us. Right at that moment I don't think there could have been a more peaceful place on earth.

GERMANY
Chapter 66

Sara and I unpacked a few things and made ourselves comfortable. We sat out on the patio for a while and just enjoyed the view. The beach down below us was not particularly active, a few people here and there. The beach was divided into sections separated by huge boulders; some of the boulders were surrounded by smaller ones. Some extended out some distance from the actual shore line and you could hear the crashing sound of the waves against them.

"I'd like to live on the coast like this," Sara said.

"I like this too, but I would have a tough time choosing between this and the mountains."

"I didn't know they had mountains in Texas."

"Humph! I'll have you know that Castle Peak out near Merkel, Texas, which is in Taylor County and only about 20 or so miles from Abilene, reaches a majestic height of about 2500 feet!" I said with some indignation.

Sara laughed. "Excuse me, that's really a huge ant hill, isn't it?"

"Actually we have some ant hills bigger than that," I replied.

"There are some bigger mountains out further west. I think they are called the Guadalupe Mountain Range."

"So have you ever lived there?" Sara asked.

"Lived where?"

"In these huge mountains you claim Texas has."

"Nope, I never lived in them, just passed through them or by them a few times."

"Then how do you know you would like to live in the mountains?" Sara asked.

"Damn! You ask a lot of questions. I spent a couple of weeks in a place called Glorieta, New Mexico; it's located in the mountains. I really liked that. It was nice and peaceful like this," I said.

"What were you doing there, camping?" Sara asked.

"Well, not exactly. I went there with a church group. There was a Southern Baptist encampment there. There were about forty or so of us that went up and spent a week during the summer. Liked it so much went back the next summer," I explained.

"I can't believe you went on a church retreat." Sara smirked.

"Well, would you believe I went because there were girls there?" I asked.

"Now that I would believe." Sara laughed.

"So, did you score?" Sara grinned.

"What kinda question is that? What do you mean, did I score?" I snapped.

"You know what I mean. Did you get laid at this church encampment?"

"I don't kiss and tell. What kind of a person do you think I am?" I replied.

"Don't answer that!" I said.

"Well, did you?" she persisted.

"NO! Well, not at the camp anyway," I said.

"What does that mean?"

"Remind me never to discuss the mountains with you again," I replied.

"Are you gonna tell me, or am I gonna have to get out the garden hose and beat it out of you," she threatened.

"That's rubber hose, and you don't have one." I laughed.

"Whatever. Are you going to tell me or not?"

"I met this girl up there. She was from Tucumcari, New Mexico. We hung out together, but nothing happened. We played a little kissy face and smacky mouth a couple of times when we could sneak off," I explained.

"So you didn't get any *at the camp;* that implies you got some another place."

"Another time and another place." I sighed.

"How did that happen?" Sara persisted.

I couldn't help but think Sara would have made a good cop. Or was this just a woman thing?

"Between my junior and senior year in high school, I ran away from home. I couldn't think of any place to go besides Tucumcari, so that's where I went," I said.

"You must have really liked her to run away and drive all the way to New Mexico just to see her."

"If you want to look at it in those terms, think about this. I run away to K-Town every weekend, holiday, and any other time I can get off to see you."

I think that caught Sara off guard. She got a surprised look on her face. She got up out of her chair came over and sat in my lap, smiled, gave me a kiss, and said, "Yes, you do, don't you? I love you, cowboy."

"I love you, too, but you gotta get up or adjust your position; you're killing my leg."

Sara got up and said, "I need to go take a shower. I'm getting hungry. Are you?"

"Yeah. I could eat something. Save me some hot water," I said.

She walked in, undressed and went into the bathroom. I stayed on the balcony smoked a cigarette and drank my warm coke. Sara had never asked about my past before, I wondered what brought that on. I really didn't have a problem telling her. After all I had inquired about hers. It just seemed a little out of character for her, but then she had been out of character this whole trip. Maybe she was inventing a new character. I was beginning to really like this one. I wondered if it would stay.

Sara finally came out of the bathroom wearing nothing but a smile. It was all I could do to just sit there, but I kept my composure. "Are you finished in there?" I inquired.

"Yes."

"Are you sure? I don't want you coming in there running me out again!" I hollered at her.

"It's all yours. I'm done in there this time," she assured me.

I got up, stepped inside, slipped out of my clothes, and went to the bathroom. By the time I was finished with my shower, Sara was already dressed and sitting on the balcony smoking a cigarette. I dressed quickly and moved out to join her. I sat down and lit up a cigarette. "You got ready in a hurry this evening," I said.

"I know; I wanted to come out here and just relax," she said.

"You really like this place don't you?"

"I really do," she replied.

We both sat quietly for a while, just enjoying the view. You could see lights of boats out in the Mediterranean, and the stars were beginning to shine on a very clear night.

"You ready to go find something to eat?" I asked.

"Yes. Let's do that so we can get back here," she said.

We walked down the stairs. I asked the lady at the desk about a place to eat. She suggested we go back to the place the young girl had brought us from when we checked in. We thanked her and walked out to the car.

"Can't we just walk?" Sara asked.

"Sure we can; it's not that far," I said.

We strolled hand in hand back up the street and around the corner then headed for the little café we had stopped at earlier in the day.

I guess we really didn't notice during the day since we never went inside but the place was really a nice little cafe. The lady that spoke English was there, along with her daughter. There were a few other people in the place, they appeared to be locals. We sat at a table near the front so we could look out at the street.

The lady brought over some menus. I had really been in the mood for some fried shrimp but had been afraid to order them but figured this would be as good a place as any to try. I asked the lady if they had fried shrimp and attempted to explain to her about them being breaded.

She just smiled and said, "Si, Señor."

Sara asked for the same, and the lady headed for the kitchen.

We ordered drinks. Sara had her usual wine. I thought I would try something different and ordered a rum and coke. Not that I had never had one before, but just never ordered a mixed drink before or with dinner. The young girl delivered our drinks and disappeared.

I didn't notice immediately, but there was a straw in my rum. It wasn't an ordinary straw, it was made of wood. I rarely drink anything from a straw so I took the straw out of my drink and laid it aside. Sara and I drank our drinks and smoked a cigarette.

There was something different about Sara tonight. I couldn't really put my finger on it but whatever it was I was certainly aware of it. It seemed to be radiating directly to me. Well, I hoped it was directly to me, anyway. We didn't talk much, but there seemed to be a lot being said.

Our food came, and we ate in silence. At least there was no talking. I ordered another drink, and for some reason asked the young girl if she could sell me a bottle of this rum. She went back and checked with her mother, returned with a bottle in a paper bag and set it on the table.

We finished our meal. I ordered another drink. Sara wanted some more wine, and we smoked a cigarette while we sipped our drink.

"I've never seen you drink more than one drink," Sara said.

"I know. I don't usually drink at all, and this is my second one already," I said.

"Third. That's your third drink, sweetie." Sara smiled.

"Really? Well, who's counting anyway?" I laughed.

"Are you getting drunk?" Sara asked.

"If I am, it's your fault," I said.

"Why is it my fault?" she asked in surprise.

"I dunno, but it is," I replied.

"In that case I better get you home before you pass out, and I have to carry you."

"You wouldn't carry me; you'd get a couple of these Mexicans to carry me back to the hotel." I laughed.

"Spaniards, baby. This is Spain, not Mexico." Sara grinned.

"Close enough," I insisted.

"Okay, let's get out of here; pay the lady while you can still walk. You can still walk, can't you?"

"Of course I can," I said as I put some money on the table for the bill.

I stood up and for some reason I picked up the wooden straw and put it in my shirt pocket. I grabbed my bottle of rum, and out the door we went, among a bunch of "Buenas noches," from everyone in the café.

We made it back to the hotel and up the three flights of stairs. The room was cool with the sea breeze blowing in through the balcony doors. Whatever little buzz I had from drinking was just about gone from the walk back from the café. But I was still feeling pretty good. I opened the bottle of rum I had bought and fixed myself another drink. Sara opened a bottle of wine she had purchased back in Valencia and poured herself a glass.

I took the little wooden straw out of my shirt pocked and stuck it in my drink. I got undressed, all the way down to my birthday suit, grabbed my drink, and headed for the balcony.

Sara laughed. "What are you doing?"

"I'm going to enjoy the balcony," I said.

"Like that?"

"Why not? Who is going to see me? There is no one else out there on either side of us," I said, as I turned and walked out and sat down on the balcony.

Sara came out and joined me, fully dressed. I moved my chair over closer to her and sat down so that I could put my arm around her. We sat there quietly, enjoying our drinks, the sea, the breeze, the stars and each other. Sara got up.

"I'll be right back. I need to go to the bathroom."

I sat thinking, *This is the life. Here I am, sitting on a balcony in some small Spanish town on the Costa Brava over looking the Mediterranean Sea drinking a rum and coke through a wooden straw. Who would have ever thought it?*

I finished my cigarette and my drink. I got up out of my chair walked over to the railing of the balcony. I was just taking in the view when I felt Sara gently slip her arms around me from behind and kiss my shoulder. When I turned around to return her kiss; I realized that the only thing between us was only about two ounces of silk and lace. We stood there in each other's embrace for what seemed like an eternity but in reality was only a few minutes; then she turned, took my hand, and led me back inside to the bed.

GERMANY
Chapter 67

Sara and I spent the next two days, walking the beach below, sitting on the balcony sipping wine and rum and coke and just totally relaxing and enjoying life.

In between strolls on the beach and time on the balcony we walked the streets of the little village and stuck our noses in every little shop along the way. I'm not sure but I never saw any other Americans or anyone else that appeared to be foreign to the area so I think we were the only strangers in the village.

One evening after we had supper we decided to go for a moonlight walk along the beach. We were pretty familiar with the beach by this time and had no problems walking around the large boulders to the beach area on the other side. One evening we stopped just past one of the boulders and had a cigarette.

"Let's go swimming," I said

"We don't have any bathing suits," Sara reminded me.

"Who cares? There is no one here but us. We don't have to go out too far, and we can stay pretty much behind this big-ass boulder," I stated.

Sara looked nervous and undecided. I figured one of us had to make a move one way or the other.

"Okay, you stay here if you want," I said as I began to undress. "I'm going swimming."

I stripped completely and headed for the surf. The water was cold at first but warmed up quickly and was really pleasant. A few minutes went by and then I saw Sara come running naked out from behind the boulder and watched her plow into the water. The water was just barely waist deep where I was standing; Sara swam up to me, stood up and put her arms around me.

"If we get caught I'm gonna cut your balls off!" she said.

"You may have to wait. You might not be able to find 'em by the time we get out of here." I grinned.

"You idiot!" Sara laughed then gave me a kiss.

We played around in the water for a good hour or more before we swam back to shore. We lay out on the beach above the shore line to dry off and smoked a cigarette. It occurred to me while I was lying there, smoking my cigarette, that I had never made love on a beach before. I was almost positive that Sara never had, considering she had never even gone skinny dipping before. No way I could just let this opportunity pass by without at least giving it a shot. Just the thought of it was doing wonders for me; now all I had to do was transfer some of that enthusiasm to Sara. I rolled over on my side and faced Sara. I took the cigarette from her hand and pitched it aside.

"Got something on your mind, cowboy?" She smiled.

"As a matter of fact, I do," I replied.

"I wonder if you're thinking the same thing I am?" she asked.

"I think I am."

"You better show me in a hurry before I get wet feet." She laughed.

It took a while, but I believe she did get the point. We stood up afterwards and brushed as much sand off each other as we could, got dressed and walked slowly back up to the hotel. This was the latest we had ever been out and weren't sure if we could still get in the hotel without having to wake someone up. As it turned out Felipa was still behind the desk. She looked at us and smiled as if she knew where and what we had been doing.

Back at the room, Sara and I shared a shower and helped get the rest of the sand off each other and out of our hair. We stepped out of the shower toweled each other off and went directly to bed. In a matter of minutes we fell asleep with Sara's head on my shoulder and her legs draped over mine.

The next morning instead of going for our usual stroll along the beach we went to town and to the café. We were really starving. I was in the mood for some eggs, toast and some kind of meat, as long as it wasn't goat meat. I asked Blanca that was the ladies name that ran the café. If I could get some eggs, toast and some kind of meat. Preferably some ham or bacon.

"Si, Señor, I give you very good huevos with toast, honey, butter, jelly, and some jamon (ham)."

"Señora, for you?" Blanca asked.

"I'll have the same thing," Sara said.

Blanca nodded and headed for the kitchen. Her daughter brought out the coffee. I asked if I could have orange juice and she nodded and came back shortly with a large glass of orange juice.

"Did you sleep well last night, Sugar?" I asked Sara.

She smiled. "I slept like a baby, cowboy. How about you?"

"Never better," I said. "I don't think I moved all night."

"You didn't move, but you snored your ass off." Sara laughed. "You shouldn't sleep on your back."

"You should talk about snoring," I snapped.

"I don't snore," Sara said, kicking me under the table.

"Ouch! Okay, tonight I'm gonna make a recording, and we'll see about that."

"You don't have a recorder," Sara said.

"I'll buy one then."

Blanca brought out our breakfast, and it looked fantastic. This was the first decent breakfast we had had on any of our trips.

"Enjoy," Blanca said, and moved off to the kitchen.

Enjoy we did; the breakfast was great. Both of us were starved and didn't waste time talking. We were too busy eating.

After breakfast we both sat back very satisfied. Sara drank another cup of coffee and we smoked a cigarette. Blanca came over and asked if everything was okay. We thanked her for the best breakfast we had had on our whole trip. She smiled and took our plates away I paid the bill and we left the café.

Every place we went the people smiled and said hello. There weren't many places in the village we had not been already, it was almost like we had been long time residents. As we walked I asked Sara, "When do you want to leave?"

"Never," she said.

"I know, but unfortunately we have to. My leave is up in four days, not counting my day of grace," I said.

"I guess we should leave tomorrow and give ourselves some driving time in case something goes wrong," Sara offered.

"Now you're starting to think like me. This is getting weird," I said.

"I know; scary, ain't it?"

"Now you're even talking like me!" I sighed.

"Okay, I'll stop it," Sara said.

"No, don't do that. I am just starting to understand you now," I quipped.

Sara stopped, stood on her tiptoes, and whispered in my ear, "Fuck you."

I burst out laughing. "Now I really understood that," I laughed.

I'm not sure Sara had ever used that word before. She was laughing, but her face was red as a beat.

"Wait until I tell your mother about that!" I joked.

By this time we had reached the hotel, and as we passed the desk I told Felipa that we would be leaving tomorrow.

She smiled and said, "Si, Señor," but she really looked a little sad.

We made it on up to our room and got comfortable, which means we stripped down to our unmentionables. We fixed ourselves a drink and wandered out on to the balcony. We sat for a while smoked our cigarette and finished our drinks then went in and had a siesta.

I didn't sleep very long; I think I slept so well last night I didn't need a long siesta. Sara was still asleep so I just let her sleep and I headed for the bathroom and from there I grabbed a coke and went to the balcony. As I sat out on the balcony, I thought; if I ever lose my memory I hope

I don't lose this one. This is one part of my life, especially these past few days, I never want to forget. I don't have a clue as to what had come over Sara but I wasn't going to complain. She had just really lightened up a lot. It wasn't that she hadn't always been fun, but this trip she was just different.

For the first time since we left I wondered what the guys back at the company were doing and what kind of trouble they were getting into; who had left and had we got any new guys in? This was the first time I had really missed them since we left. Maybe because it was the longest I had ever been away at one time or maybe it was because I was just having such a good time.

I felt Sara's arms go around my neck and felt her lips nibble on my ear.

"Whatcha doing out here by yourself, cowboy?" she asked. She came around and sat down beside me and lit a cigarette.

"I'm just sittin' here waiting on you, darlin'."

"I was tired, I guess," Sara said.

"How could you be tired after the way you slept last night?" I asked.

"Too much fun, I guess." She smiled. "Have you been in the shower yet?"

"Nope, figured I'd let you get in there and get all your stuff done, and then I would have it all to myself."

"Okay, I'll go." She put out her cigarette and walked off to the bathroom.

I heard her close the door and turn the shower on. The next thing I heard was her singing one of her German songs she always played on the record player. I'd never heard her actually sing a song out loud like that before, except that one time in church. I lit another cigarette and settled down in my chair; I had a feeling I was in for a long wait.

Finally she walked out of the shower with her usual two towels wrapped around her and came out on the balcony. There was something different about the way she was wrapped in those towels this time. The one around her hair was the same, but the one around her body was just wrapped around her waist, not under her shoulders. I wondered if we could buy this place and just live here. I certainly was enjoying being here.

It was hard to just get up and go take a shower but I managed. I took advantage of the hot water and just let it beat down on me for a while. Eventually I stepped out of the shower and toweled off. I shaved, put on some Old Spice, brushed my teeth and stepped out into the bed room. Sara was still sitting on the balcony brushing her hair.

"I thought you would be all dressed and ready to go by now," I said

"I just hate to leave this spot," she said.

"I know; it's kind of addictive, ain't it?"

"Yes, it is."

"Well, you enjoy. I'm going to get dressed."

"Since when are you so anxious to get some clothes on?" Sara laughed.

"I'm not; just don't want you getting all hot and bothered right now, though." I smiled.

"What if I want to get all hot and bothered?" Sara asked slyly.

"Remember lesson number one," I said.

"What if I run out of patience?"

"Well, I hope I'm around. If not I hope you'll be able to take care of things yourself." I grinned.

"I see," Sara said. "I'll keep that in mind."

Sara came in and began to get dressed. We left the room and headed for the café. We took our time walking down the street. All the villagers smiled and said hello. When we walked in the café there were more people than normal, but we were led to our usual table. Blanca was there to greet us.

"Buenas noches, señor, señora."

"Buenas noches, Blanca," I said as we sat down.

"Would you care for your Rum and Coke tonight, Señor?" Blanca asked.

"Bueno, gracias y vino por la Señora," I said

Blanca smiled and hustled off to get the drinks. Her daughter was back almost before we could light a cigarette. She set the drinks down, smiled and hurried off. Blanca came back and asked if we had anything special we would like for supper this evening.

"Blanca, you know what would be really good this evening?

"Que, Señor?"

"A really nice beef steak. Comprende?" I asked.

"Si, Señor, dos?"

I looked at Sara. "How does that sound to you?" I asked

"I think it's a great idea."

"Si, Señora, dos," I said.

Blanca smiled and went back to the kitchen giving orders as she was moving that way. Hardly with out notice a couple of the men in the café' moved over to one corner of the room and began playing their guitars. Sara turned to look at them and then changed chairs so she could watch them play.

They played a variety of music, some songs I recognized, most I didn't but it was nice music. Not too loud and not too fast. We smoked a cigarette and had our drinks while listening to them play. Our steaks arrived along with a surprise, French fried potatoes. We got a refill on our drinks and began to eat. The steaks were great, cooked medium well and not a lot of fat.

After we had finished our meal, Blanca brought out a small cake with a candle in it and set it on our table. Sara and I were both surprised and had no idea what to say.

"What is this for, Blanca?" I asked.

"Señor, we have heard that you will leave tomorrow. We wanted to show you and your Señora, how you say, our apreciación for your visit to our village."

Blanca's daughter brought two paper sacks tied in red ribbon over and set them on the table.

"We would like you to take these with you and perhaps you will remember us when you have a drink," Blanca said.

Talk about surprised and raising a lump in your throat. I couldn't talk, and I don't think Sara could. The best I could do was stand up and give Blanca and her daughter a hug.

"Thank you very much," I looked at Sara and she had a tear in her eye.

But she managed to get out a soft, "Thank you very much," also.

"Now you and your señora dance, please. We have a little party this evening."

Blanca motioned and the band began to play a slow song and the other patrons in the place led by Blanca began to applaud. Sara and I didn't really have much choice but to take to the dance floor which had mysteriously appeared sometime during the evening.

I danced once with Blanca and then once with her daughter. Sara danced with some guy; it was either the cook or Blanca's husband, maybe both. Then the music picked up and got faster, definitely not my style but Blanca grabbed me and led me around while Sara followed the other guy around the floor. We had a great time.

Sometime around 1 a.m. Sara and I excused ourselves promising to come by for breakfast in the morning. We walked back to the hotel arm and arm. It had been a really great evening. I hadn't had anymore to drink but Sara had a couple more glasses of wine and I think she was a tad tipsy. We managed to make it up the steps to our room and let ourselves in. I set the bottles of booze down on the table and began coming out of my clothes. As soon as I was down to my shorts I headed for the balcony. Sara was right behind me. We sat and smoked a cigarette. The fresh, cool sea breeze in our face helped to clear our heads some.

"That was some evening," I said.

"Yes, it was," Sara agreed.

"You know we don't even really know these people, and I feel like I'm leaving my family tomorrow."

"I know what you mean. They are thanking us for visiting their village, and we should be thanking them for treating us so nice and being so friendly," Sara said.

"You're right. We should do something for them. Got any ideas?" I asked.

"I noticed they had a little church down the other end of the street that looked like it could use some work. We could make a donation to the church," Sara suggested.

"You got any money?" I asked.

"I have some."

"How much is some? I asked.

"I could give them about $100.00. But you might have to get us home or at least to the next place there is American Express," Sara said.

"I think I have enough money for gas. We may have to sleep in the car. Be sure to eat a big breakfast in the morning." I laughed.

Sara got up, walked over to my chair, gave me a kiss said good night, then walked back in the room.

"Good night? Just like that? Good night?" I asked, surprised.

"I'm still practicing lesson number one," she said.

Damn, I thought, *I'm sorry I ever taught her that lesson.* I got up and followed her in and climbed in bed beside her. Truth be known, I was too tired to fool around myself.

We climbed out of bed about nine a.m. the next morning. It was later than we planned on sleeping. We both hurried through our bathroom activities and packed our bags. As soon as we were sure everything was packed we walked down to the desk. Felipa smiled and said good morning.

"We are going to the café and eat breakfast, could you have someone bring the bags down from our room and put them in the car for us?" I asked.

"Si, Señor, I will do that."

"Thank you, Señora."

Sara and I showed up at the café to a bright and cheerful Blanca. She said good morning and showed us to "our" table. She asked what we would like for breakfast. I asked if she had any more of those eggs. She smiled and said, of course. Sara nodded in agreement, and off Blanca went to get breakfast.

We sat quietly and smoked a cigarette; Sara drank her coffee, I sipped on my orange juice. We looked out the window and watched the villagers go about their business; no one seemed to be in any particular hurry. Time moved very slowly it seemed.

Blanca brought our breakfast; we thanked her and began to eat. We didn't rush through our meal it was almost as if we were eating particularly slowly; putting off our inevitable departure. Finally we finished our meal and were smoking a cigarette when Blanca came over to clear the dishes.

"Blanca," I said.

"Si, Señor?"

"You and your family and the whole village have been very nice to us, and we have enjoyed our stay in your village more than any other place we have been during our travels."

I handed Blanca a $100.00 dollar bill. "We would like to make this small donation to the church down the street to show the village our appreciation and for accepting us into your village."

Tears rolled down Blanca's cheeks and she gave me and then Sara a big hug, said a bunch of stuff in Spanish I didn't understand, thought I got the gist of it. Her daughter came over and gave us a hug, and the man in the back came out and shook our hands.

We paid our bill, waved to everyone as we left the café, and walked back to the hotel. As we rounded the corner we saw two young boys washing Blue Bitch off with buckets of soapy water. By the time we got to the car they had finished and disappeared into the hotel. We checked to see that all the bags were in the car, and then went inside to pay our bill.

After paying the bill I gave Felipa $10.00 and told her to buy the boys something they would like. After a mild protest; she shook our hands and said, "Muchas gracias."

Sara and I walked out to the car, I turned the car around, and we headed back down the main street as we had come in. Everyone waved. Blanca and her clan were standing on the porch of the café, and I honked the horn, and they all waved until we were out of sight.

We drove for several miles before either of us said a word.

Finally Sara said, "I think that has been the nicest vacation I've ever had or will ever have."

GERMANY
Chapter 68

In less than two hours we had crossed the border back into France. You didn't need a sign to tell you when you crossed the border. We were no more than 100 yards inside France when we saw some guy was squatting along side the road.

"You would think he would at least have the decency to walk off among those trees over there, wouldn't you," Sara said, shaking her head in disgust.

"When you gotta go, you gotta go, I guess."

Sara held her nose as we passed by the guy. Of course he didn't see her, and I doubt that he would have cared if he had.

"Does this mean you don't want to go to Paris?" I asked.

"Well, I don't want to go now. We don't have time."

"I didn't mean now; I mean anytime," I said.

"No, I want to go to Paris. Surely the city isn't this crappy," she offered.

"Good choice of words," I laughed

Sara laughed. "That's just the way it came out. I didn't really think about it."

"I knew that," I replied.

"Are you saying I can't make a joke?"

"Oh, no, darlin'; I wouldn't say that," I replied.

"But you would think it, right?"

"I'd never tell you if I did," I laughed.

"I feel a siesta coming on," Sara said. "Can you handle it by yourself for a few minutes?"

"I think I can stay awake for a while without your company," I replied.

"Are you saying I'm bad company?"

"Oh, hell no, sugar; I love your company," I said, "most of the time."

"What was that last part?" Sara asked.

"Nothing, just go ahead and take your siesta. I'll let you know when I can't go anymore."

Sara took a little pillow we had brought along and turned her back towards me stuffed the pillow under her head and was asleep in moments. I lit a cigarette and let my mind wander. I wondered if Roach and Bobbie Jo were still together. Chuck was getting to be a real short timer. I hope he hadn't gone home yet. I wondered what it would be like to go home.

On a different note I wondered if Sara would extend her contract and stay in Germany. Maybe she could get transferred to Heidelberg. She had never said anything about staying in Germany any longer than her contract with the government called for. Of course I hadn't mentioned to her that I liked my assignment and would like to stay right where I was. I guess it was something we were going to have to talk about one of these days pretty soon. But I still had about eight months before I was due to rotate back to the states.

I checked the gas gauge, it was near empty. I started looking for a gas station. I finally found one about twenty miles on up the road; I slowed down and pulled into the station and stopped at the pumps.

Sara woke up and asked where we were. I told her I had no idea except to say that we were at a gas station somewhere in France. She got out while I filled the gas tank. When it was full she went inside and paid for it. I followed her in and found a coke machine and picked up a few cold cokes and some chips.

When we got back to the car I told Sara it was her turn to drive and my turn to take a siesta. She frowned at me but got in behind the wheel.

We moved back on to the highway and I lit a cigarette and popped the top on one of the cold cokes I just purchased.

"I thought you were going to take a siesta?"

"I am, just as soon as I smoke this cigarette and drink my coke," I said.

Sara gave me a dirty look but didn't say anything. We continued on down the highway, it didn't take long for my road hypnosis to start to set in. I finished my cigarette but had to set the coke in a cup holder. I grabbed the pillow turned over stuffed the pillow under my head as Sara had done and I was asleep even faster than she had been.

I dunno how long I slept, but when I woke up we were just passing a sign that said Dijon 10K. I looked at my watch; it was only 1600 we had made good time. We could be back in K-Town tonight if we wanted to push on through.

"Are we going to push on through and get back to K-Town tonight?" I asked.

"I don't see why not. I'm kinda looking forward to sleeping in our own bed tonight, to tell you the truth," she responded.

I didn't say anything, but I was thinking that I liked the way she referred to it as "our" bed. I leaned over and ran my hand up Sara's thigh. "I kinda like the idea of sleeping in our own bed tonight, too." I grinned.

"Don't get any ideas, cowboy; I'm still practicing lesson number one," she shot back as she slapped my hand and moved it away.

"Shit! I knew I should have skipped lesson number one and gone straight to lesson number two." I pouted. I reached in the glove compartment and took out a pencil and pad Sara kept in there and started writing.

"What are you doing?" she asked.

"I'm making myself a note," I replied.

"And what does your note say?"

It says: "Remember to never teach lesson number one and always go straight to lesson number two."

"You plan on teaching someone else, do you?" Sara snipped.

"Well, no," I mumbled.

"Then why do you need a note?" she asked.

"Well, I may pass it on to our son," I said, trying to work myself out of a jam.

"Nice try, cowboy, but that shit won't fly," Sara replied. "Who said I was going to have kids with you in the first place, and even if I do, what if they are all girls?"

I tore up the note and threw the pieces in the air. Sara laughed, reached over and pulled me by the arm over towards her.

"You're so cute. I love you," she said and gave me a kiss.

"You're only saying that 'cause it's true," I quipped. "And you need to keep both hands on the wheel and both eyes on the road while driving. I would hate to have an accident before I got the chance to pass on all the wisdom I have learned to our son."

"Yes, dear." She smiled.

I reached down and got my warm coke, lit a cigarette, and felt this little smile creep across my face. I was enjoying this give-and-take banter Sara and I had developed on this trip. She really seemed to come alive. I hoped it would last.

About 2030 we pulled up in front of the BOQ. Sara shut the engine off, and we just sat there for a minute. I think we were both dreading carrying all the bags up those three flights of stairs. I opened the car door, got out and stretched. Sara did the same. We both just walked around for a few minutes.

"Okay, shall we start unloading the car?" I asked.

"I suppose we have to."

Sara popped the trunk and we each grabbed as much as we could carry and started up the walk to the BOQ. Just as we were about to go inside, Mary Ann came out.

"Hi, you guys, just getting back, I guess, huh?"

"That would be a good guess, Mary Ann," I said kind of sarcastically.

"Can I help?"

"Yes, grab anything that's not tied down to the car," Sara said.

We stumbled up the steps and finally made it to the room. Mary Ann followed behind us with what was left inside the car. We all just dropped stuff wherever there was a spot.

"I was just going down to the pizza place and get a pizza. You guys want some?" Mary Ann asked.

"Sounds good to me," I said.

"Me too," Sara added.

"Okay, pepperoni all around sound good?"

"Yes, that would be great," Sara said.

Mary Ann waved and was out the door. Sara and I looked at each other and you could tell both of us were thinking; we wanted to go back to Spain. She started putting things away and separating the dirty clothes from the clean ones, then decided they were all dirty and threw them all in the laundry basket. As she emptied the suitcases I put them away in the closets.

"You're not going to wash tonight are you?" I asked.

"Hell, no; it can wait until tomorrow. What is tomorrow, anyway?"

"I looked at the calendar. It's Saturday," I said.

"You don't have to be back until Sunday night, right?" Sara asked.

"Right, Sunday night," I said with some disappointment.

"Good. Then we can wait and do laundry tomorrow."

We sat and waited for Mary Ann to return with the pizza. It seemed like it was hours, but actually she was back rather quickly. She came over to Sara's side of the room with the pizza and some beer. We each took a slice of pizza and the girls had beer. I stuck with my coke.

"So how was Spain? Did you have a good time? Where did you go?" Mary Ann was full of questions.

"We went to Madrid, Valencia, and Barcelona," Sara offered. She looked at me and smiled, as if to say the village was just between us.

I smiled to signal that I understood, and to be honest, I really didn't want to share it with Mary Ann. I knew at some point I might tell the guys when I got back to the company. I let Sara handle the inquiries by Mary Ann. I just ate my pizza, drank my coke and kept my mouth shut. I figured this was one of those times best suited for me to just shut up. Women know how to talk to each other and not really say anything.

Mary Ann finally ran out of questions; or sensed that Sara wasn't going to really tell her anything interesting anyway and decided it was time for her to say goodnight. We said goodnight and she moved on over to her side of the apartment and closed the door.

After Mary Ann left, Sara asked me, "Do you know the name of that village?"

"I was going to ask you the same thing. I don't think I ever saw the name of that village the whole time we were there, except maybe on the road sign when we exited, but I can't remember what it said." I laughed.

"That's the only place I remember seeing it, too, and I think it started with an E, but I'm not sure. I've looked on the map and in the guide book but can't find it, or maybe I did but don't know what I was looking for."

"I guess it will always be a mystery then. Maybe we were in the twilight zone?" I grinned.

"Maybe so. I wonder if we can go back?"

"I dunno, but right now I'll settle just for the memories," I said.

Sara smiled. "Me too."

We were both really tired. I got up and shut the door to Sara's room and got undressed and climbed in bed. Sara undressed, turned out the lights and followed right behind me. We were by the time our heads hit the pillows, in our usual position; Sara's head on my chest and her leg draped over mine.

GERMANY
Chapter 69

Sara and I spent the rest of the weekend just unwinding from the trip and putting things back in their place. Sara did a couple of loads of wash. I helped separate the clean ones into my stack and her stack. When I was finished with that I put my stack in "my" drawer. I was going to fold her clothes but the first time she saw me folding a pair of her panties, she snatched them out of my hand and politely told me that wasn't the way she folded them and she would do her own stuff. I just shrugged and thought, *How many ways can you fold a couple of ounces of lace anyway?*

We didn't even go out for a meal on Saturday. We just ate whatever Sara had in her little fridge or what was left of anything we managed to bring back with us from the trip.

"If you wanted to could you extend your contract with the government and continue to teach over here?"

Sara looked at me in surprise. "Where did that question come from?"

"I was just curious if you could do that," I said

"I suppose I could, but I'm not really sure I want to do that."

I didn't say anything else. We just continued to eat the ham sandwiches Sara had fixed. I could tell she was wondering why I asked that question. But she didn't say anything right away.

Mary Ann dropped in to say she was going out. She didn't say where or with whom but kinda beat around the bush that she had an exciting evening planned but didn't give us any details. Sometimes I wondered if she was jealous of the relationship that had developed between Sara and me. She didn't stick around long before she flew out the door as though she was late for wherever she was going.

After we finished our sandwiches, Sara washed and put away the few dishes and utensils we used. She went over and sat in the chair at the desk, and I sat on the bed, finishing my coke.

"Are you going to tell me why you asked me that question earlier?"

"I was just wondering if you could do that or if you would be interested in doing it if you could?" I said.

"Are you thinking about staying in Germany instead of going home?" Sara asked.

"I've thought about it," I admitted.

"Is that what you want to do?" Sara asked.

"It's something I've thought about. I don't know that is what I want to do. I have some time yet to decide."

"Well, I don't think the military would be the type of environment I would want to raise a family in," Sara said.

"The last time we talked about a family, you said you weren't even sure you were going to have kids with me," I reminded her with a grin on my face.

"Well, if you're going to be going around giving other women lessons, why should I?"

"I didn't say I was going to be giving other women lessons," I replied.

"You were writing yourself notes even."

"I tore 'em up, even," I snipped.

Sara got up, walked over to the bed, and pushed me back and jumped on top of me.

"Listen, cowboy, if you're even thinking of teaching someone else lessons you can start walking back to Heidelberg right now," she growled.

"Okay, okay, I won't give anyone else lessons. Are you ready for lesson number three?"

"What is it?" she asked.

"Go shut the door and lock it, and I'll show you."

Sara got up, walked over, shut and locked the door, turned around, looked at me with a sultry look. She started walking towards me while unbuttoning her blouse.

"Teach me lesson number three."

By the time we were through with lesson number three, we were both dripping wet from sweat and grasping for breath. I got up, staggered over, opened all the windows, and turned the little rotating fan so it was blowing directly on us. Then as I returned to the bed I grabbed our cigarettes and flopped down beside Sara. I lit us a cigarette and handed one to Sara.

"How many lessons are there?" Sara asked.

"I dunno. I've been making 'em up as we go," I said.

"Let me know when you think up the next one."

"Trust me; you'll be the first one to know," I replied.

Sara started laughing. I rose up and looked at her with a quizzical look on my face. She put her hand behind my head and pulled me down to give me a kiss.

"If you were taking my class in creative arts, I'd give you an A+ + + + +," Sara said.

"Would I have to bring you an apple to class every day?" I asked.

"No, but you might have to stay after class and clean the chalkboard and erasers," she quipped.

"Is that it?" I asked in surprise.

"Well, we might have to go over your lesson plans sometime," Sara laughed.

I laughed and lay back down. I lit another cigarette. Sara lit one also. We just lay there and finished our cigarettes. When she was done Sara rolled over towards me, put her head on my shoulder, draped her leg over mine, and within minutes she was breathing softly and easily, sound asleep.

GERMANY
Chapter 70

Sunday we went to the cafeteria for brunch. Just to be different I had some pancakes and sausage. I think Sara had French toast. I hate that stuff. Of course she had her coffee.

We found a table and ate quietly. I think we were both still recovering from our trip. Or maybe it was lesson #3. Whatever it was, neither of us were running on all cylinders yet.

"What time are you going back today?" Sara asked.

"I just have to be back in time to sign in before midnight," I replied.

"Does that mean you're going back late?"

"Are you trying to get rid of me?" I asked.

"No, I was just wondering if you wanted me to drive you back," Sara said.

"That would beat riding the train back, but I don't want to go back too late and have you on the road by yourself," I said.

"I don't mind," she said.

"I do."

We continued to eat in silence for a few minutes. I would prefer to have her take me back; it was quicker, but I just didn't like the idea of her being on the Autobahn late at night. And I really didn't like getting in at the last minute, anyway. I'd rather have some time to get adjusted to being back and finding out what was going on.

"Okay, I'll tell you what. I'll go back later this afternoon, and you can drive me back; then you have time to get back before dark, and I get a chance to settle in and take my time signing in. How does that sound?"

"If that's what you want to do," she replied.

"You don't sound too excited about it?"

"No, it's okay. Actually, it's a pretty good idea. I can get back in time to take care of some letter writing I've needed to catch up on," she replied.

We finished our meal and left the cafeteria. We walked over to the Main PX and picked up a few things. Sara got some food supplies to restock the fridge with and I picked up some cigarettes for both of us.

We paid for our purchases, walked back to the car then drove back up the hill to the BOQ. Once we got things put away, I kicked off my shoes, lay back on the bed, and lit a cigarette. A few minutes later Sara came over and joined me. It seemed neither of us had a lot of energy today. We lay there, smoked our cigarettes until they were done, not speaking a word, just enjoying the moment. Siesta time must have kicked in automatically, we both fell asleep.

Neither of us slept very long. I looked over at Sara; she was awake but not saying anything. I got up, walked over to the fridge and got a coke.

"You want one?" I asked Sara.

"I'll drink some of yours," she replied.

"Humph! You will, huh?" I grinned.

I walked back over to the bed, sat down, popped the coke, took a swig and passed it to Sara. She took a couple of sips while I lit a cigarette.

"What time is it?" Sara asked.

I reached over and got my watch off the record player. "It is now 1605," I said.

"What time is that in English?" she asked with a smile on her face.

I knew she was screwing with me now. I had used military time around her so much I knew she knew damn well what time it was. "For you non-military types, that is five minutes after four in the afternoon," I said sarcastically.

"What time do you want to leave?" she asked.

"We should start thinking about it," I said.

Sara got up off the bed. "I need to go throw some water on my face to wake up here," she said, as she walked off to the bathroom.

I thought that was a little strange. If all she was going to do was splash some water on her face, she could have done that in the sink in her room. But maybe that was another one of those, "I need to go powder my nose," things that women use when they have to go to the bathroom. I never did understand that. I mean, when one woman says she has to go powder her nose and every female in earshot jumps up and has to go to, sometimes I wonder what they all do in there; I know there ain't enough stalls for all of 'em.

Sara came back out looking more refreshed. "Okay, cowboy, you ready to ride?" she asked.

Oh, shit, I thought, *I could live with the cowboy thing, but now she was starting to add to it.*

"Why, sure 'nuff, Miss Kitty. I'm just really chompin' at the bit to get started," I replied in my best Texas accent.

"You're a smart ass, you know that?" she stated.

"You started it."

"But I was being cute. You were being mean and making fun of me." She pouted.

I got up, walked over to her, put my arms around her, kissed her, and said, "You're right; it was cute. I shouldn't have made fun of you."

"Well, just don't do it again, or I won't let you wear your spurs to bed anymore," she grinned.

"Shucks, ma'am, it's hard to break a buckin' bronco without yer spurs," I replied.

She laughed and began tickling me.

"You're so crazy sometimes," she said as she continued to tickle me, driving me back towards the bed.

"Stop it!!" I yelled to no avail.

She continued to tickle me until I fell back on the bed, with her falling on top of me.

"You better stop!" I warned. But she just continued.

"You're askin' for it," I said.

"What are you going to do about it?" she asked, daring me to make a move.

I rolled her over and lay on top of her, pinning her hands down, spread away from her body. I looked down at her and could see her eyes begin to smolder and feel her breasts begin to rise and fall under me. I leaned down and kissed her. She returned my kiss and the tickling party was over.

"What time is it?" she asked as she put her clothes back on. I looked at my watch.

"It is now 1710," I said.

"That's ten minutes after five, right?" she replied.

"Very good for a civilian," I quipped.

"We could have almost been to Heidelberg by now," she said.

"That's okay; personally I think the hour delay was well worth it, myself."

She looked at me, walked over, gave me a kiss and said, "So do I."

We finished dressing. I checked to make sure I had everything: wallet, watch, ID card, money, etc. When I was satisfied I had everything we walked out of the apartment and down to Blue Bitch and headed for Heidelberg.

There wasn't much talk during the trip. I guess we were both thinking about what was ahead of us for the next week and beyond. It was August already; not long now before Sara had to start thinking about getting ready for school to start again. I was thinking about going back to work on those boring gates but mostly I was getting anxious to see the guys again and see what changes if any had taken place. It seemed like I had been gone for a year.

We were in Heidelberg and driving in the gate at Patton Barracks before I even really realized it. Rizzo had the gate. He let out with one of his, "Hey, lover, welcome home," thing as he waved us through the gate.

Sara laughed. "That's Rizzo, the Greek god, right?" she asked.

"Yeah, that's Rizzo."

Sara drove the car past the company entrance, around the side of the building and parked. I always hated saying goodbye. Part of me wanted to just sit there, and the other part just wanted to jump out of the car and get on inside the building. I don't think Sara was much at good-byes either.

"So are you coming up next weekend?" she asked.

"I planned on it. Why? You have some plans?" I inquired.

"No, I just wanted to know if you were coming."

"I'll be there," I said.

"Okay, I'll see you then. Call me during the week if you get a chance."

"Okay, I will." I leaned over and gave Sara a kiss. "I love you," I said as I opened the car door.

"I love you too. See you next weekend," she said.

I stepped out of the car. Sara backed up and headed off back down the way she had come in. I waved until she was around the corner and out of sight. I walked back around the side of the building to the main entrance. In a way it was kinda nice to be back home. In a way it wasn't.

GERMANY
Chapter 71

The first thing I really noticed when I finally looked at the building was the scaffold they had put up all around the building. I had no idea why since it was a brick building and I knew they probably weren't going to paint it. Maybe they had to replace the mortar or some of the bricks. I didn't have a clue. It was a high scaffold that ran right under the windows on the second floor. That meant they were right outside our windows.

I walked in the building, down to the sign-in book by the Orderly Room and signed in. I walked back up the stairs to my room. So far I had not seen a soul, and there was nobody in the room. I knew Rizzo was on the gate but he was the only one I could account for.

I took my shoes off, lit a cigarette, put my cigarettes in my wall locker and lay down on my bunk. I was beginning to wonder if something really big wasn't going on. It wasn't normal not to see anyone from the basement to the second floor. I had been lying there about twenty minutes or so when Horse Face Harry walked in. He didn't even see me. He walked over to his bunk, opened his wall locker by the open window with the scaffold outside it and began to strip.

"Hey, Harry, what's up?" I asked.

He turned and looked over at me and said, "Heyyy, Bonesy, when did you get back?" Harry was drunk as a skunk.

"I just got in about half hour ago. Where is everybody?" I asked.

"Bunch of guys at the club, supposed to be a band with a stripper over there tonight," Harry said.

As long as I had been there, there had never been a stripper at that club, and I didn't believe there was gonna be one there tonight. But apparently Harry did. "What are you doing here then, Harry?"

"I'm gonna take a shower then go back," he said as he stripped to the bone. "You should come over, Bonesy."

Harry grabbed his shaving kit threw his towel over his shoulder and stepped out on to the scaffold.

"HARRY!" I shouted. But before I could get up off the bunk Harry had made a right turn, and I guess in his mind he was headed for the shower. I ran to the window, stuck my head out, and saw Harry down around the Snake Pit windows. I think he realized now that he was definitely not in the right place but was not sure exactly where he was.

He was drawing a crowd. Guys with their dates were walking to the club or the movie theater across the little park. Harry was just standing there with his bare butt hanging over the scaffold. I couldn't see from where I was but apparently the windows in the Pit were not open.

"Harry," I yelled, "Stay right there; I'll come open the door for you."

I turned and ran out of the room and down to the Pit. I rushed into the room, and sure enough, there stood Harry in front of the closed windows. I opened the windows and reached out and took his arm and said, "Get in here, you fuckin' idiot, before you hurt yourself."

Harry just gave me a dirty look, whinnied at me, and marched out the door and across the hall to the showers. I hurried back to my room and grabbed my cigarettes and lighter and then went back to the shower and posted myself as Harry's personal guard.

A few minutes later Roach and Tom came running up the steps. First they headed down to my room. "Hey, you guys, down here!" I yelled.

They turned and came down the hall. Roach said, "There was a story going around the club that there was some naked guy running around the scaffold outside our barracks."

I pointed over my shoulder with my thumb. "It was Harry. He is/was as drunk as a skunk. He got undressed to take a shower and walked out the window instead of the door. He made it down to the Pit and then, I guess, he realized he was in the wrong place. I got him back in. He is takin' a shower now. I figured I better watch him for a while."

Roach and Tom both laughed their ass off. "I don't suppose you had a camera, did you?" Roach asked.

"No, but there were a lot of people moving around in the park. I wouldn't be surprised if one of them did."

Harry came walking out of the shower. "Hey, what are you guys doing here?" he asked as if nothing was wrong.

"Oh, nothing, Harry. You just tried to take the scenic route to the shower, using the scaffold. Bones just probably saved your naked ass from falling off the damn thing," Tom told him.

"I wasn't on the scaffold," Harry replied.

"Harry, do you always suffer short-term memory loss when you're drunk?" Roach asked.

"How would I know?" Harry asked.

Nobody had an answer for that.

"Go get some clothes on, Harry; you look obscene," Roach said.

We all escorted Harry back to his room. Tom was the first one in. He walked over and shut the window by Harry's wall locker.

"You guys going to see the stripper tonight?" Harry asked as he put his shaving gear away and began to get dressed.

"There ain't a stripper, Harry. Somebody just started a rumor," Roach told him.

"Are you sure?" Harry asked. "I heard it from one of the bartenders."

"I asked the manager. He said it was against the club rules to have a stripper perform in the club," Roach said.

"Damn! Then why am I getting dressed?" Harry asked no one in particular as he sat down on his bunk. "I wasn't really out there on that scaffold, was I?"

"Yes, you were, Harry," I replied. "You walked out your window and down to the Pit windows. They were closed I went down and opened them for you so you could get in."

"Did anyone see me?"

"Only everyone that was going to the club or the movies about that time," I said. "Your picture will probably be in *The Stars and Stripes* this week."

"Shit, I bet Top will be all over my ass in the morning."

"So what? Everybody else has already seen it," Tom quipped.

Rizzo came storming in the room. "Hey, lovers, what's up? Hey, Harry, I hear you were out on the scaffold buck-ass naked this afternoon?"

We all laughed. Rizzo had been working the main gate, and there was no way he could have seen Harry. News does travel fast on a small Caserne.

"Bones, how was your trip, buddy? When did you get back?" Roach asked.

"Yeah, lover, how was Spain? Lots of señoritas down there? Can I bum a cigarette?" Rizzo chimed in.

Some things never change, I thought as I handed Rizzo a cigarette. "I'm guessin' there were more señoritas than mademoiselles, Rizzo," I quipped.

Rizzo gave me a dirty look. "Shit head, you know what I mean."

"Okay, well, the one thing I noticed that I wasn't aware of before, there seems to be a lot of blonde-haired Spanish women. I expected 'em all to be dark haired like you, Rizzo."

"Where all did you go?" Roach asked as Dietz walked into the room.

"Hey, Bones, welcome home," Dietz said.

"Thanks, Dietz. We went to Madrid, Valencia, and Barcelona. We walked around and saw stuff, museums and famous castles and palaces and shit like that," I said.

"Oh, hell. That sounds exciting," Harry pitched in.

"Well, we had our moments," I said.

I wanted to tell them about the little village, but then I didn't. I just didn't want to share it with everybody. I told them about the sunroof blowing off the car in the middle of a rain storm and how I had to put the thing back on and hold it down until we could find a place to get it fixed. And how we, rather I fixed it. They all got a laugh out of that.

Rizzo and Dietz had just got off work; they were headed for the shower room and then the club to see the stripper that wasn't going to be there. Roach and Tom said they were going down to shoot some pool and asked if I wanted to come along. I said I might be down later. Harry had quietly passed out on his bunk.

I lit a cigarette and lay back on my bunk. It had been a little more exciting return than I had planned on but things worked out okay. I laughed to myself thinking about Harry running around that scaffold naked as a jaybird. He was lucky he didn't fall off there and break his neck. I was glad everything turned out okay. I bet Harry was right; the first sergeant would have something to say to him tomorrow.

GERMANY
Chapter 72

Part of my orientation when I reported into the Company was about our mission if we had an alert. We were supposed to have one a month, but according to the people that had been there for a while that never happened.

At that point during my time there we had exactly two. The mission of the MP Company was to get out as fast as we could and establish Traffic Control Points (TCP's) at major intersections other units would be passing through along the route to the new designated rendezvous point. Our job was to make sure that all other traffic yielded to the convoys as they came through our intersection and also be sure the convoy was going in the right direction.

The first one happened shortly after I got there. The balloon went up (that's what we said when the alarm when off) about 0230. I was working at Campbell Barracks on the midnight shift. The shift on duty stayed on duty until the rest of the company had been posted to their alert assignments. The oncoming day shift was the last to get posted, which meant we were getting relieved early. But as soon as we were returned to the barracks we had to switch to our combat uniform.

I got dressed in combat gear, grabbed my duffel bag, secured my weapon and reported to my squad leader. He put us all in a truck and we headed out the gate. Somewhere along the line I got dropped off in the middle of a road in some little town and told to stay there until someone came to pick me up. I have no idea what the name of the town was. What I was most aware of was I was freezing my ass off.

I had very little traffic coming through my check point. I was beginning to wonder why I was even there. About 0500, this little old Putzfrau (cleaning lady) came walking up to me and handed me a big mug of coffee. I started to tell her I didn't drink coffee but I figured what the hell she took the time to bring it to me and besides it was cold as shit out there. I took a swig of the coffee and almost choked on it. It wasn't that it tasted bad; I was just taken by surprise, about half the mug was filled with cognac. That was the only cup of coffee I have ever enjoyed.

About 0900 Pappy Altman came through my checkpoint, stopped and asked me what I was doing here. "This is where they put me, Pappy."

Pappy just shook his head and motioned for me to get in the jeep. As it turned out I was put at the wrong check point. I was supposed to be two blocks up and one block over.

We didn't have another alert until the early morning hours of August 14th, 1961. This one was different. We didn't move out to any particular place. We just stayed in the barracks. Apparently the day before the Russians and East Germans had begun construction of the Berlin Wall between East and West Germany. We were told to put on our combat gear; including the day shift going to work. The rest of us were to standby our rooms with our duffel bags ready to go. For three days we wore our combat gear to work and were restricted to the caserne. Married members were required to move into the barracks and find a "bunk." All the other units were under the same restrictions. After about four days I guess they decided we weren't going to be attacked or attack anyone so we got the order to stand down and things went back to normal.

I had just got back from K-Town Sunday night and didn't have a chance to call Sara to tell her what was going on. I called her and told her after things settled down. She asked if I was coming to K-Town the following weekend and I told her to plan on me being there; if I heard anything different I would try to call her.

Things settled back into a normal routine, we got out of our combat gear and went back to regular duty uniform. Bill Schumacher had got a company basketball team together. This was something I could get excited about. Billy Stearns and I had been asked to play for the USAEUR team, but the company refused to release us since, that meant we would be TDY to HQ and not available for duty, and the company was a little short on man power at the time.

By playing on the Company team we could be available to perform our regular duties and play basketball when we could get off. Headquarters company, the transportation company and a couple of other units in the general area put a team together so we had ourselves a regular little basketball league going. We practiced and tried to put an offense and defense together until after Labor Day when the season officially began.

Working straight days I was available all the time for games and practice. If we had a game on the weekend Sara would drive down for the game and then we would go back to K-Town.

From September until the beginning of November I was working, practicing, or playing basketball; or in K-Town. Since we were just about a six team league we played each other often. An intense rivalry developed between us and Headquarters Company. With both of us living on Patton Barracks there was a lot of trash talk going on all the time. We started packing the little gym over on Campbell Barracks every time we played.

By the time it got down to the playoffs towards the end of October the intensity was extremely high. The coaches had worked out a double elimination playoff round. Headquarters was in one bracket and we were in the other and as expected we both won our brackets and were going to play for the Championship.

It was surprising how much attention our little league drew. The first sergeant and company commander were there along with almost every guy in the company that could get off. Even some of the general staff came to watch us play. For the first playoff game there was standing room only in the gym.

Whoever said basketball was a non contact sport never played in one of our games. The referees did the best they could, but it was basically every man for himself. The back of my hands and arms were scratched and bleeding in some places from where this little shit named Billy something or other kept scratching me with his fingernails trying to knock the ball out of my hands. Everybody had bumps and bruises. We lost the first game by a basket.

We had two days to lick our wounds and rest up. The second game was on Friday and Sara was going to drive down and try to get there in time to see the game. In fact she was planning to stay over because if we won the Championship game would be Sunday afternoon. I didn't get to see her before the game started in fact I didn't even know when she got there. We managed to win the second game by one point.

Sara waited for me to come out of the dressing room by the door to the gym. I had on some sweats since it was starting to get just a bit chilly and I was still sweating from the game. I saw Sara and walked over and said hi and gave her a kiss.

"Hey, cowboy, you had a good game, I think." She laughed. Sara admittedly didn't know a lot about basketball.

"I did okay; missed some shots I should have made," I said.

"It looked like that little guy guarding you kept slapping you on the arms. Isn't that a foul or something?

"Well, in most games it might be, but not in these games." I laughed. "Since we won tonight we play again Sunday. Have you found a place to stay yet?" I asked.

"I stopped by that little hotel we stayed at before and got a room. Is that okay? That's why I was a little late getting here; and not being able to fine a place to park. I didn't think there would be such a crowd."

"Yeah, that's fine. Let's just go there. I have some clean clothes in my bag here," I said.

We walked to the car. I threw my bag in the backseat and climbed in. Sara got in behind the wheel and drove us to the hotel. We locked the car and went straight to the room. The first thing I wanted was a hot shower so I headed straight for the bathroom. I got in as soon as the water got hot and just let it run over my aching muscles. It had been a rough game. The hot water burned the fresh scratches on my arms but it helped relieve the aches in my shoulders and neck. I must have stayed in there for 30 minutes. When I felt like I was alive again I turned off the water and climbed out, toweled off, wrapped the towel around my waist and stepped into the bedroom.

"Oh, my God!" Sara gasped when she saw my arms.

The hot water had made them bleed more, and I didn't realize blood was still trickling down my arms. I looked down, whipped the towel off, and put it over my arms to catch the blood. Sara got a hand towel and ran it under the cold water, then came over and started dabbing and rubbing my arms with the cold towel. Slowly the bleeding began to stop.

"What happened to you?" she asked as she continued to wipe my arms with the cold wet towel.

"That little guy guarding me has some fingernails," I said.

"Isn't that against the rules?"

"To have fingernails?" I grinned.

"You know what I mean, smart ass," Sara snapped.

"You asked that already; and yes, it can be if he gets caught or the refs wanna call it," I explained.

"Does it hurt?"

"No, not really. It stings a little bit sometimes. I'm going to wrap my arms just above the wrist for the game on Sunday so he won't have such a big target," I said.

"Do you have to play against him? Can't you play against someone else?" Sara asked.

I had to laugh. "Honey I can't pick who I want to guard me. That's the other team's choice."

"Well, then they need to make him cut his fingernails," she demanded.

"It's not like I'm the only one that has a few bumps and bruises. I know the other team has a few also."

I took my free hand and reached for my cigarettes and lighter and fired one up. It actually felt good to smoke; I hadn't had one since way before the game.

"Are you hungry?" Sara asked.

"I could eat something. Do they have Wiener Schnitzel and Pomme Frites at the Bahnhof?" I asked.

"I'm sure they do."

"Okay, let me get dressed, and we'll walk over there and have supper. Or would you rather go some place else?" I asked.

"No, that's fine with me; unless you want to drive to Spain?" She grinned.

"It's a tempting thought, but I don't think we could be back in time for the game on Sunday."

I got dressed and we walked over to the Bahnhof, found a table, and ordered supper. "How is school going?" I asked.

"It's going pretty well; everyone is pretty much back into the routine now. I have some pretty smart kids this year," Sara explained.

We had discussed doing something over the Thanksgiving holidays but hadn't made any definite plans. "Have you been thinking about Thanksgiving?" I asked.

"I have thought about it. I will be off Thanksgiving Thursday and the following Friday. I can take a personal day the next Monday. That will give us five days. I think we can do Paris in five days, don't you?"

"I think we can. If that's what you want to do then I need to put in for leave," I said.

"That's what I want to do."

The waiter brought our supper and we sat quietly and ate with little conversation. We finished our meal, smoked a cigarette then moved over to the bar after paying our bill and had a drink. I had rum and coke Sara has some Kula or some shit like that I think. We sat and sipped our drinks, smoked a cigarette, then walked back to the hotel.

I was really tired. I got undressed and lay down on the bed on my stomach. Sara came over and massaged my shoulders and upper arms. That was the last thing I remembered that night.

GERMANY
Chapter 73

Saturday started out slow and we kept it that way. We got up late; walked over to the Bahnhof and had breakfast. We took our time eating at a leisurely pace. When we finally finished we sat back, Sara with her coffee and me with my orange juice, smoked a cigarette while watching the hustle and bustle of the crowd moving about the Bahnhof.

We left the Bahnhof and made the short walk over to the Hauptstrasse. We strolled up one side of the Strasse stopping in a store or shop every now and then to browse. Of course Sara can't just browse. She found one of those little figurines she was collecting and just had to buy it.

After doing one side of the street we returned via the other side of the street, more stores, more shops, more browsing, but no more buying. We crossed over the streets to get back to the hotel; and walked up to our room. Sara had brought the cooler, and even though there was no ice left in it, there were still some cokes. I grabbed a coke, kicked off my shoes and sat down on the sofa. Sara grabbed a coke and joined me.

"You have anything special you want to do today?" Sara asked.

"Not really, we could take in a movie at the Caserne, I guess, but I don't have any idea what is playing."

"You want to drive out and see?"

"Naw, I can call and get one of the guys to check it out and let me know if you really want to do that," I said.

"Actually I'm in the mood..."

"All right, I'm in the mood too!" I said cutting her sentence off.

"Let me finish, you dope. I was about to say I'm in the mood for a siesta."

"Oh," I said rather dejectedly.

I had to laugh. Here we are, back from Spain for three months, and still taking siestas.

"But who knows what kind of mood I may wake up in," Sara added with a smile.

"Okay, a siesta sounds pretty good to me too."

I got up and walked over to the bed, stripped down to my shorts and climbed in bed. I watched Sara do the same, and pulled her over next to me until I could feel her body next to mine, with her arm around my waist. I took her hand in mine and quickly dozed off to sleep.

When I woke up Sara and I had reversed positions. She was lying with her back to me and I was next to her with my arm draped over her waist and she was holding my hand. I couldn't help but wonder how and when that happened. I kissed her on the shoulder and whispered.

"Are you awake?"

No response. I ran my lips up her shoulder and along her neck. "Are you awake?"

"No, but I will be if you keep that up," came her sleepy response.

"Good. Now that you're awake hand me my cigarettes, please."

Sara sat up in bed, grabbed a pillow, and started beating me on the head with it. "Asshole!" she said.

"Lesson number one, lesson number one! I screamed as I fended off the pillow attack.

We both were laughing as I took her pillow away from her and pulled her down and gave her a full tongue in the mouth, lip locking kiss. After a minute or two went by, she pulled away and sat up in bed; reached over and got my cigarettes and handed them to me.

"What are you doing?" I asked in surprise.

"Practicing lesson number one," she replied with a wicked little smile on her face.

"Bitch!" I muttered.

"What did you say?" She threatened.

"Nothing….I didn't say anything," I lied.

Sara sat up in bed and lit one of her cigarettes, the sheet falling to her waist. "How are your arms?" she asked.

"They are okay."

"When are you going to wrap them?" she asked.

"Tomorrow, before the game," I replied.

"They really look bad," Sara stated.

"They don't look any worse than my back does sometimes."

"But I'm afraid I'll hurt you." She pouted.

"Oh, hurt me, please hurt me!" I said mockingly and laughing.

Sara climbed over on top of me and glared into my eyes. "Okay you asked for it," she said. "I'll make you bleed like a stuck pig."

"Well, you can't right now," I said.

"Why can't I?" she asked.

"Because I have a ball game to play tomorrow, and we still have clothes on."

Sara glared into my eyes; I could see the wheels in her head turning. She slid down my waist, over my legs and grabbed the top of my shorts as she moved downward until she got them off over my feet. Then she sat back and removed her panties and climbed back on top of me.

"Now we don't have any clothes on, and I really don't care if you have a game tomorrow. You can explain any scratches on your back any way you want to," she whispered.

"I'll come up with something," I said as I took her head between my hands and pulled her down closer to me.

I escaped with only minor scratches but I had some deep finger nail marks on my sides. After we rested for a while Sara raised up on her side.

"Turn over." It was more of a command than a request. I turned over and could feel Sara's eyes going over my back and feel her hands running smoothly over me. I thought for a few minutes there I was going to get away with the fingernail marks but she finally spotted them and let out a little gasp.

"I did it again didn't I? She pouted.

"Do you hear me complaining?" I asked

"No, but that must hurt," she said.

"Only for a minute," I said.

Sara flopped back down on the bed like she was upset. I leaned over and gave her a kiss and told her again it was all right. I grabbed my cigarettes and offered her one. She took it and I lit hers then mine.

We decided we were hungry but didn't want to go to the Bahnhof again for supper. Neither of us were that hungry anyway. After careful thought and consideration we decided to just drive out to the little snack bar on Patton and grab a hamburger.

Sara parked the car and we walked down to the snack bar, ordered a couple of hamburgers with fries and a couple of cokes. We waited for our order, and then when they were ready we found a table and sat down to eat. We managed to eat in peace, meaning no one came in that we knew that wanted to talk.

By the time we finished it was already dark outside. We hopped in the car and drove straight back to the hotel. Someone had taken our place right in front of the place and we had to park a few doors down but it was only a short walk back to the hotel.

We hadn't really paid much attention before but we had a room with a view out the front of the hotel which meant we could see the Bahnhof and the surrounding area. We opened the window and watched the traffic and people coming and going while we smoked a cigarette. I swear I never understood why there weren't more traffic accidents the way those people drove. That wasn't to say they didn't have their share and when they had one it was usually a big one with more than just two vehicles involved.

It was starting to get a little chilly and the afternoon activities were beginning to take a toll, at least on me. We closed the windows, I got undressed and climbed back in the already rumpled bed. Sara got undressed in front of me. I swear she did that on purpose. But did I really care? She turned out the overhead light, walked over to the bed, climbed in and turned out the lamp next to the bed. I rolled over on my side with my back to her. I wasn't being mean; I just always slept on my side. A few seconds later I felt Sara move over next to me and drape her arm over my waist. I was comfortable and went right to sleep.

GERMANY
Chapter 74

I woke up early Sunday morning. My mind was already on the game. It wasn't like we were playing for the State Championship or anything but to me and I knew to the other guys this was an important game. A game we really wanted to win. I was already starting to get those butterflies in my stomach like I did when I played in high school.

I crawled over Sara grabbed my cigarettes and moved to the sofa. I checked my watch, it was only 0600. Damn! I thought I hate it when I wake up early like this with nothing to do. It was okay when I was going to work or if Sara and I were getting ready to take a trip.

I got up, got a coke out of the cooler and moved back to the sofa. I tried to be quiet and let Sara sleep but I guess she heard me pop the top on the coke can.

"What are you doing up so early, cowboy?" came a sleepy voice from the bed.

"Sorry, sugar, didn't mean to wake you up," I said.

"It's okay; I think I've been sleeping too much lately anyway," Sara said as she got up and headed toward the bathroom. A few minutes later she came back out and ran back to crawl back under the covers. She sat up in bed with the covers pulled up around her as she lit a cigarette. "Aren't you cold?" she asked.

"I wasn't until you mentioned it," I said. I got up, walked over to the bed, and crawled under the covers with Sara.

"What time is it?" she asked.

"It's about 0630."

"What time do you have to be at the gym today?" Sara asked.

"The game starts at 1500; I should be there by 1400, so I guess we should leave about 1330 or so," I replied.

"You wanna give me that in civilianese? It's too damn early in the morning for me to understand all that army talk," Sara grumbled.

I couldn't help but laugh. "We need to leave about 1:30, the game is at 3:00," I said

Sara leaned over put her head on my shoulder and said, "Thanks."

"Are you going for a shower first or am I?" she asked.

"Go ahead. You like to take all day in there. I can sleep for another couple of hours," I said.

She smacked me with a pillow as she got up and hustled into the shower. I watched her walk away, her butt wiggled when she walked fast I thought. But I don't think I'll tell her that. I took the pillow she hit me with and propped myself up in the bed, Just when I got comfortable I remembered my cigarettes and warm coke were over by the sofa. *Shit!* I thought. I threw the covers back, got up, hurried over and got my coke and cigarettes and jumped back in the bed and got comfortable again.

Sara finally came out of the shower all wrapped up in towels. "It's all yours," she said.

I climbed out of bed and headed straight for the bathroom. I got the hot water going and immediately climbed in. If Sara hadn't said anything about it being cold I probably wouldn't have noticed. But now the hot water felt even better than usual. I wasn't in a hurry and I let the water beat on my shoulders and neck. As I washed I noticed that some of the little scratches on my arms were starting to bleed again. I figured I had had enough of the hot water.

I climbed out of the shower, dried off and wrapped the towel around me. I stepped over to the sink and brushed my teeth. Then I got the hot water going again and shaved even though I really didn't feel like it. I knew Sara wasn't a fan of facial hair.

By the time I stepped out of the bathroom Sara was dressed. I didn't waist anytime. For now I slipped into my jeans and sweat shirt. I planned on changing into my uniform after we came back from breakfast.

"Are you ready to go eat?" I asked.

Sara, with instant coffee in hand said, "Sure. Where to? The Bahnhof?"

"They do have a decent breakfast, and I don't want to eat a big meal later before the game."

We walked over to the Bahnhof, into the restaurant, found a vacant table, and ordered breakfast. We took our time; it was still early, so there was no hurry. We lingered for a long time over coffee, orange juice, and cigarettes. About 10:00 a.m., we paid the bill and took a walk around the Bahnhof just to kill sometime. Finally we walked back to the hotel.

When we got back to the hotel it was about 11:15 or so. I pulled off my sweatshirt and walked over to my bag and got out a couple of ace bandages and some tape. Then I walked back to the sofa.

"You wanna wrap my forearms for me?" I asked.

"Sure, I'll do that," Sara said.

She sat down on the sofa beside me, and I gave her the ace bandages and tape. "Don't wrap them too tight. I need some flexibility; I'm just trying to keep his fingernails out of my skin."

"Yes, sir!" she said with a left-handed salute. Before she could wrap my wrist and forearms she had to go get a cold towel and wipe them off. Finally she was satisfied and began to wrap my arms. She took her time and did a good job. She didn't wrap them too tight but made sure they were well taped.

"There, how does that feel?" she asked.

I leaned over and gave her a kiss. "That's perfect," I said.

I got up and took off my jeans, walked over to my bag and got out my uniform. I dropped my shorts and started putting on my athletic supporter.

Sara started laughing. "What is that thing?" she asked.

I looked at her in surprise. I thought surely she knew what a jock strap was. "This is a jock strap!" I snorted.

"You have to wear that…thing?" she asked.

"I don't have to, but I might wish I had if I get kneed in the balls," I said. "You, too, might wish I had if I get kneed in the balls," I added.

"Oh, well, in that case, by all means wear it." She snickered.

I finished putting on my uniform and put my sweats on over it. I walked over, grabbed the last coke, went back to the sofa, sat down by Sara, and lit up a cigarette. I was ready to go. We had about half hour before we had to leave.

We arrived at the gym a few minutes before 2 p.m. Most of the guys were there already, warming up on one end of the court. I walked over and set my bag down by our bench, grabbed a ball and went out to warm up with the rest of the guys. There wasn't a lot of talking going on. Everybody had their game faces on. But then so did HQ Company.

There is no way I could give a play by play of the game. It was close all the way through; neither team could get more than a three or four point lead. That little shit Billy whatshisname was still slapping at my arms every time I had the ball but thanks to the wraps I was wearing there wasn't as much scratching with those fingernails of his.

To make a long game short it came down to the final 30 seconds or so. Billy Stearns had the ball and we had a one point lead. One more basket and we would probably win this game but Billy lost the ball when he hit a loose board in the old floor of the gym. The guy that was guarding me scooped up the ball and was headed for an uncontested layup. There was no way I was going to let that happen, he had quicker hands but I was a head taller and faster. I ran him down from behind and when he went up for his shot I blocked it from behind him and "accidentally" put my knee in his back and helped him find a seat in the over flow crowd behind the basket at that end of the floor.

I got called for a foul; but I figured that was our best shot at winning the game. Either he would miss them both and we win, or he misses one makes the other and we are tied with still a chance to win. He came limping out of the crowd and gave me a dirty look as we lined up for his free throw attempt. He made the first one and the game was tied at 59 all. I knew when he let the second shot go he had missed it and Hill came down with the ball and we called time out. We had 14 seconds to win this game or go into over time.

Normally we went to Hill since he was the biggest and tallest guy we had but HQ company had a black guy just a little shorter with legs like tree trunks and wasn't easy to move. We decided to let Billy try to rub his man off Hill at the high post and if he got past his guy, and the black guy didn't switch to pick Billy up; then he had a clear path to the basket for a lay up. If the black guy picked him up he dropped the ball off to Hill who would be trailing him to the basket. Got it? Basically it's a pick and roll, if you're a basketball fan you have surely heard that term before.

That was our plan. When play resumed I got the ball into Billy and just hung back as a defender just in case something went wrong. Billy played it perfectly, he took his man to the left then went right and ran his man into Hill the black guy was quick and moved in to block Billy's shot. Billy went up for the shot but instead of shooting he dropped the ball back off to Hill and Hill slammed it home. We were ahead 61-59. They had 6 seconds left to try to tie the game. They called a time out to try and set up a play.

They had that little shit that was guarding me throwing the ball in. I guarded him and blocked his view as best I could. Everyone else dropped back since they had to bring the ball the length of the court we didn't want to take a chance on fouling anyone. They got the ball into a guy in the corner. I ran over to him and kept him trapped along the sideline and they never got the ball up the court far enough to even get a shot before time ran out.

The crowd went wild. We went wild. We may not have been playing for the state championship but it felt like it. So it was just some little no nothing league that would be forgotten and eventually lost in the grand scheme of things. At that time and that place it was the biggest thing that happened around USAEUR Headquarters since I had been there.

Sara and I drove back to the hotel and I got a quick shower. The team was going to meet at the club and celebrate our hard earned victory. Sara wanted to come but she couldn't stay long; she had to drive back to K-Town tonight because she had school tomorrow. I tried to talk her into calling in sick but she declined.

We were the last ones to arrive at the club. We got a big cheer when we walked in and someone stuck a beer in our hands. We all congratulated each other and went over every play in the game. Guys from the company came over and joined in our celebration. It was something really great to be a part of.

Sara tugged at my arm and said she needed to get on the road. I walked her out to the car. Gave her a kiss goodbye and told her to drive careful. She gave me a kiss and congratulated me on our win, got in the car and drove off down the street. I kinda wished I was going with her; but on the other hand I wanted to stay and party with the guys too.

GERMANY
Chapter 75

For the next couple of weeks everybody was still talking about the game; actually they talked about the whole series. It really was a balls-to-the-wall series. Nobody gave an inch and made the other team work for everything they got. Even HQ Company got some kudos just for playing a great series. And they deserved it. I ran into little Billy whatshisname in the snack bar one day while I was on break. We shook hands, there were no hard feelings.

"I should arrest you for possession of a dangerous weapon," I said.

"How so?" he asked.

"Those fingernails of yours. You kept ripping my hands and forearms to shreds," I replied.

He held out his hands, he didn't have any fingernails left; they were all cut back to the end of the finger.

"So you just grew those for the games this season huh?" I inquired.

"Yep, makes people think twice sometimes."

"Tell me about it," I said, "You were ripping me to pieces. That's why I wore those ace bandages the last game."

"Smart move and by the way, I still got bruised ribs where you kicked me into the bleachers." He laughed.

"I didn't kick you, just gave you a little nudge," I replied.

"Well, probably had something to do with me missing that last free throw."

"Well, that game and either of the other two games could have gone either way. It was fun to play. I'd say we'll have to do it again next year, but I probably won't be here," I said.

"I know I won't be, I'm a single-digit midget now," he replied.

"No shit! When is the big day?" I asked.

"I leave Patton Barracks, the day after tomorrow," he said.

"Well, good luck; maybe I'll see you around again before you leave."

We shook hands and I went back to work. *A single-digit midget,* I thought. That meant he had less than ten days left. I didn't think to ask if that was in country or until he was home and discharged. I was happy for him, if that's what he wanted to do, but somehow the idea of me ever being a single-digit midget didn't brighten my day any.

I had put in my request for leave the Monday following the basketball game. The first sergeant was there when I turned it in. First thing he did was congratulate me on winning the game. He noticed I had a leave request in my hand and asked to see what I was asking for.

"You and Sara going away for the Thanksgiving holiday?" he asked

"Yes, we are," I said, shocked as hell that he even knew Sara's name. How the hell would he know that? I never told him. I just had to shake my head; the guy was amazing. There wasn't a thing going on in the company he didn't know about, or who was doin' what to whom.

He bent over the clerk's desk, picked up a pen, and signed the leave. "To the victor go the spoils, Tommy."

"Thanks, Top," I said and turned around and walked out before he told me something else I didn't think he should know about, like maybe lesson number three.

That had been a little over two weeks ago. Now all I had to do was finish this week through Wednesday, and we were off to Paris. I was kinda looking forward to this little trip there were actually some things in Paris I had heard about; like the Eiffel Tower, The Arc De Triomphe and the Champs-Elysees.

Tuesday Roach and I were both working Campbell Barracks. He was the relief guy and I had gate #6, the slowest gate on the caserne. Whenever he wasn't relieving someone else Roach came back and spent time with me. We hadn't had much time to talk lately. He did make the basketball games with Bobbie Jo but we didn't get a real chance to get together afterwards and until just recently our schedules conflicted. He was working nights and sleeping days and I was working days.

Chuck was a double digit midget; he should be home maybe for Christmas. He was looking for someone to buy his car but so far no takers. Roach was as unsure about his future as I was he was considering extending his tour of duty to be able to stay in country until it was time for Bobbie Jo's father to rotate. I still wasn't sure I even wanted to go home. I liked what I was doing.

I told Roach I had something I wanted to tell him but not now, I thought maybe we could get together after we got off work and go find a nice, quiet place to talk. He said he knew just the place and we could go down after supper.

Roach hanging around Gate #6 with me made the day go faster. He had to leave and go open the pedestrian gate by 1630 so people could walk home and if he was lucky he would see Bobbie Jo for a few minutes.

As soon as the swing shift showed up and relieved us we were on the truck back to Patton. Roach and I changed clothes before we went to the mess hall for supper and as soon as we were finished we left the caserne and caught a taxi. Roach told the guy where to go and we headed straight down the road in the direction of a little village called Schwetzingen.

It wasn't like I had never been to Schwetzingen, when I first arrived in the company they had a short timer's party out there for someone I didn't even know. It was one of those big ones where everybody showed up. There had been five of us 'cruits in the company at the time. All five of us got a ride out there, and all five of us got carried back in, one way or another. I got drunk and puked all over the end of one of the tables, or so I was told. Chuck brought me back. That's how we got to know one another. Waterhouse put his fist through the front door and required stitches; he came back in an ambulance. I can't remember who the other three were now; Horse Face Harry may have been one.

Roach had the taxi pull up in front of this little guest house. He paid the driver we got out and went into the guest house. Apparently Roach was not a stranger, seems everyone there knew him. We found a table in the corner, the Fraulien brought Roach a beer and me a coke. We both lit up a cigarette.

"Okay, Bones, what's this big secret you got on your mind?"

"It's not really a secret; it's just something I didn't feel like sharing with everybody."

"Wow, I feel so privileged."

"Shut up, asshole, and let me tell you before you make any wise-ass comments."

"Okay, sorry."

"You remember when Sara and I went to Spain?" I asked.

Roach nodded and took a swig of his beer.

"I think we found the twilight zone," I said.

"Excuse me?" Roach said in surprise.

I told Roach about our experiences in this little town and that Sara nor I could remember the name of the town and couldn't find it on the map. That we spent about three days there, and there were no other Americans or other foreigners in the whole village. I gave him in detail how well the villagers treated us and always seemed to have whatever we asked for; that we couldn't even find in the cities we stopped in. I also told him how Sara was while we were there. I'd never seen her so relaxed for lack of a better word. And how relaxed I was, as far as that went. Neither of us wanted to leave.

Roach snatched one of my cigarettes instead of smoking one of his own.

"Christ, you're getting as bad as Rizzo," I said.

After lighting the cigarette, Roach ordered another beer and coke. "And you don't know where this place is?" he asked.

"Only that it is between Barcelona and the French border," I replied.

"You looked on the map, and you don't know the name of it, right?"

"Right. I wanna say it started with an "E" on the sign I saw when we turned off the road, but I could be wrong. When we went back out the same way we didn't even see a sign. If I had time I would go back and look for it. That was the greatest vacation I ever had in my life. Everything was perfect. There were no cars except ours and a couple of other beat up old things that I never saw running. The beach was great, Sara was great. The people were great. I'd go back in a heartbeat," I said.

"Sounds like you two found the perfect place, Bones."

"I know. It's almost too perfect. That's one reason I really didn't want to tell everybody. You know how people are," I said.

"Yeah, I know. I wouldn't tell 'em either," Roach agreed. "So where are you two off to over Thanksgiving?"

"Paris," I said.

"Now that's where I would think you would find the perfect place," Roach said.

"Have you ever been to France?" I asked skeptically.

"Nope."

"Well, trust me, you can tell you're in France as soon as you cross the German border, and you don't need a sign to tell you. The roads are lousy and the countryside is dirty. We didn't get half a mile down the road and some guy was takin' a dump right there alongside the road. Sara and I are just hoping things are cleaner inside the city."

"I hope you're right." Roach laughed.

"So, you got anything else on your mind?" Roach asked

"Naw; that was my Shangri-La story," I said. "How are things with you and Bobbie Jo?" I asked.

"Same as always, great one minute and fighting like cats and dogs the next."

"I think you both like it that way. Maybe that's what keeps the excitement going for both of you?" I said.

"You could be right, but every once in a while it just gets old, and I need a break," Roach confided.

"I think we all need a break every once in a while, no matter how good or bad things may be."

"Speaking of Bobbie Jo," Roach said, "I'm supposed to call her tonight. I need to get back to the barracks and do that."

I called the Fraulien over and paid the bill. We walked out and caught a taxi back to the barracks. When we got back to the company, Roach went down to use the phone I went on back to my room. I kicked off my shoes, lay down on the bunk, and lit a cigarette. It wasn't that I felt bad before but I always felt better after Roach and I talked. I guess that's what friends do for each other.

GERMANY
Chapter 76

Wednesday night about 1900 I arrived in K-Town. I didn't bother to call Sara, I knew she would be busy packing; I just grabbed a cab to the BOQ.

When I arrived at the BOQ, I let myself in with my own key. I was right; Sara had shit all over the place, suitcases here, clothes there. You couldn't find a place to walk or sit. I just stood in the doorway of her room surveying the place; she hadn't even noticed I was there yet.

"Hey, you!" I said a little loudly. Sara jumped and dropped some clothes she had in her hands.

"You scared the hell out of me," she said sternly. "How long have you been there?" she asked.

"Just a few minutes; been trying to find a way to get past all this crap you have all over the floor," I said.

"Those nearest you are just empty suitcases I dragged out. You can put them back in the hall closet/ I don't think we are going to need them. We won't be gone that long.

Are you going to take your suit?" she asked.

"You think I should?"

"Well, if we go out some evening you might need it," she replied.

"Okay, I'll take the suit. Don't forget to pack a shirt and tie with some socks that go with it," I said.

"You can pick out your own shirt, tie, and socks. I'll fold the shirt for you."

"Right, I pick 'em out, and then you look at 'em and say, 'Are you really going to wear that?'"

Sara laughed and said, "I would never do that."

"The hell you wouldn't," I replied.

I picked up the empty suitcases and put them in the hall closet, took off my sweater and hung it up while I was there then walked back in the room. Sara had her German Music on. I was getting pretty good at recognizing at least the names of the songs, even knew a few words to some of them. But I never sang. Sara laughed the first time I tried to sing along with some of those songs. Of course I have to laugh at myself trying to sing in any language. I can't carry a tune in a bucket.

I walked over to the fridge and got a coke. "Have you eaten anything?" I asked.

"I had a bowl of soup earlier. Are you hungry?" she asked.

"I think I'll just fix myself a ham and cheese sandwich while I'm here. You want one?"

"No thanks. I want to finish packing," she said.

"Did you pack any of my stuff?" I asked as I fixed my sandwich.

"I put some shorts and T-shirts in that case over there. I have your jeans laid out on the bed; you just need to fold them and put them in the suitcase. Your dress shoes are still in the closet. If you'll pick out what shirts you want to take, I'll fold them for you."

Sounded like a good idea to me. I walked over to the closet and picked out three or four shirts and a couple of sweaters, lay them on the bed for Sara to fold, then got my shoes out of the closet and put them in the suitcase with my shorts and T-shirts.

"Did you pick out a tie and a pair of socks to wear with your suit?" Sara asked.

Shit! I got back up off the bed, went to the closet. I only had like three ties and any of them would go with that bland gray suit I had. I picked out a yellow one with some kinda little gray thingys on it. I got a pair of gray socks out of "my" drawer and got my silver tie clip while I was there and clipped it to the tie. I couldn't think of anything else, so I walked back to the bed, sat down, and started to eat my sandwich and drink my coke.

"Do you have all your shaving gear and stuff ready to go?"

"Holy shit, woman! Let me eat this sandwich, and I'll get my shaving gear," I snapped.

"Hey, screw you. If you forget your razor you're not using mine, and you know I don't like beards and whiskers and such, so you know what that means," she snapped.

I got up off the bed again and headed for the bathroom, mumbling to myself.

"That's fuckin' blackmail, you know that?"

"What did you say, dear," she said with a little lilt in her voice.

"Nothing!" I shouted.

I entered the bathroom and put my shaving gear and toothbrush in my shaving kit. I walked back out to the room, threw the shaving kit in with the shoes and sat back down to eat my sandwich and drink my coke in peace. I hoped.

I finished my sandwich and lit a cigarette; Sara just about had everything in a suitcase by then. She came over and sat down beside me and lit a cigarette.

She leaned over and gave me a kiss and said, "Hello, cowboy."

"Hi, yourself," I said.

"Little testy this evening aren't we? Did you have a bad day?" she asked.

"Naw, guess I'm just a little wound up and anxious to get out of here for a while. Sorry," I said as I leaned over and gave her a kiss.

"I think I just about have everything in the suitcase now. We just need to double check. I took the car down today; had the oil and filters checked, the tires checked, and gassed it up, so that's done. We're ready to roll in the morning as soon as we get it packed. Oh, and I went to the PX and got some cokes, snacks, and ice for the cooler. I have the ice stuffed in this freezer and in Mary Ann's. Don't let me forget that in the morning."

"You have been busy today; you got all that done after school?" I asked.

"I don't have a last period class so I left early," Sara said.

"If I had known you had last period free, I could have come up and done some of that, had the bags packed, and we could have left already."

Sara put her arms around me. "Cowboy, I've seen you pack. The most I'd trust you to pack for me is my panties."

"Sweetie, that would be the one thing I would figure you could do without and not pack 'em at all," I said.

Sara laughed. "Why do I believe that?"

"I'm tired. I'm going to take a shower. I think we just have to make one last check in the morning before we leave," Sara said.

"I took a shower before I left the company. What time are we getting up in the morning?"

"I set the alarm for 0530. You think that's early enough?" Sara asked.

I grinned. "I'm gonna make a soldier out of you yet. Did you hear what you just said? I asked.

She thought about it for a minute. "Oh, shit, I'm starting to talk like you more and more. Worse than that, I'm starting to understand you." Sara laughed as she got up and headed for the bathroom.

I laughed with her, stripped to my shorts, and climbed in bed. I lit a cigarette grabbed my almost empty coke and just waited for her to get out of the shower. Despite being one of those guys that really didn't like to travel around looking at old churches, museums and shit like that; I was kinda looking forward to seeing Paris. I think some of those old movies I used to see about Paris make it a little more appealing.

Sara came out of the shower in her robe and hair done up in the usual towel. She lit a cigarette, took the towel off her hair and began to brush it out. I lay quietly and watched her go through her ritual. When she finished her cigarette, she put it out, put her hair brush away; took off her robe which was all she had on. Then she walked over, turned out the over head light, turned out the lamp, and then climbed in bed. She knew I was watching her. I think she did that shit on purpose. She rolled over and put her head on my shoulder kissed my neck and said good night. I played like I was almost asleep already and mumbled a good night back. Lesson number one, I thought, as I drifted off.

GERMANY
Chapter 77

The alarm went off right on time; I groaned, Sara jumped up and headed for the bathroom. I reached over grabbed my cigarettes and lit one up. I had just taken a few drags when Sara came out of the bathroom.

"Come on, lazybones, we need to get a move on here," Sara snapped.

I rolled over and got my feet on the floor, took one more drag on my cigarette then put it out and walked to the bathroom. I jumped in the shower real quick just got get my blood pumping again and hopped right back out. I brushed my teeth with my extra tooth brush and walked back to the room and put on some clothes.

"Would you get the ice from Mary Ann's fridge for the cooler?" Sara asked.

I walked over to Mary Ann's room and got the ice. I wondered where Mary Ann had been keeping herself lately; she hasn't been around much. I got the ice, took it back to Sara's room, and along with the ice in her fridge put it in the cooler around the cokes.

Sara had suitcases lined up by the door ready to be taken down to the car. I grabbed a couple of the bigger bags and headed down to the car. I was on my way back up the stairs when I saw Sara coming down.

"Is that all the suitcases?" I asked.

"This is all the cases. The cooler and the bag of snacks and my purse are still up there on the floor by the bed," she said. "If you get those and lock the door we should be ready to go."

I continued on up the stairs got all the stuff Sara mentioned, walked out of the apartment, locked the door and headed back down the stairs. Sara was fussing around the car making sure everything was just like she wanted it. I put the cooler, snacks and her purse in the back seat. I looked at her, she looked at me.

"Are we ready to roll?" I asked.

"I think so," she said as she got in the car. I climbed in the passenger side, and we were off. The sun wasn't even up yet.

Once again we crossed the border into France at Saarbrucken, and once again you didn't need a sign to tell you that you had just entered France. The only thing missing this time was the guy taking a dump along side the road.

Other than it being a little chilly, it was a bright sunny day and traffic was light. It made me wonder if the French celebrated some kinda Thanksgiving too; of course I knew that wasn't true. Well, at least they didn't celebrate our Thanksgiving but what do I know maybe they had one of their own.

We made good time and arrived in Paris mid-afternoon. I had to admit it looked a lot cleaner the closer to the city we got. Our plan was to find a hotel reasonably close to the places we wanted to see and take a taxi to those places that weren't so close; thereby avoiding having to drive in the city traffic. That plan didn't work out at all. Before we knew it we were precisely at one of the places we wanted to see. We just didn't want to see it from the car driving around in circles.

Somehow we managed to end up at the Arc De Triomphe with all its many traffic lanes. If I remember there are about twelve of the damn things. I don't understand how it works; no matter how hard you try to stay on the outside lane so you can exit....someplace you always seem to end up closer to the Arc. I don't know how many times we drove around that damn thing before we finally managed to get to an outside lane and just get the hell off. We had no idea where we were or what street we were on. But at that particular time we really didn't care we were just happy to be off that traffic merry-go-round.

"I dunno about you, but I've got a friggin' headache!" I said.

"You should have been driving," Sara said as she reached over and slapped me on the shoulder.

"I think you did just fine, darlin'," I said.

"Don't you darlin' me. I was ready to just stop right in the middle of that damn circle and pull my hair out," Sara said, "and all you could do was tell me to watch out for this car or that car. I was watching out for all those friggin' frog idiots."

"Temper, temper, now," I said.

She hit me on the shoulder again.

We drove straight down some street we were on until we were definitely sure we had cleared that traffic circle. Sara made a right turn which we thought would take us back to the Champs-Elysees; which it eventually did. Before we got back on that road we pulled over and Sara consulted her handy little travel guide book. She found a four star hotel which was just off the Champs-Elysees on Rue something or other.

"What street are we on now?" she asked.

"You're asking me?" I quipped.

"Yes, damn it, I'm asking you," she growled.

"I don't have the foggiest dammed idea," I replied.

"Well, get out and look," she demanded.

I looked in the glove compartment, got the pen and paper out, then climbed out of the car and walked up the street until I found a street sign. I wrote down the name of the street and took it back to Sara. I handed her the piece of paper and lit a cigarette.

"What's this?" she asked.

"That's the name of the street we are on," I said.

She snatched the paper out of my hand and started looking for the street on the city map she had. After a few minutes she said, "Here it is; I found it."

"I'm so happy for you."

She gave me a dirty look then went back to her map. I got the flashlight out of the glove compartment to shine some light on the map since it was starting to get a bit dark where we were parked under a bunch of trees. I would have turned the overhead light on in the car, but since Blue Bitch no longer had one, a flashlight would have to do.

"You realize, if this hotel is on the other side of that big-ass road down there, and you have to go left, the only way you're gonna be able to do that is to go back to that merry-go-round again and then come back this way," I just casually mentioned to her.

"I know, but I can do it. I know where the hotel is now. We are just a couple of blocks away," she said, "We just need to remember the name of this street and then go up two blocks past it."

"So you're going to go tackle that friggin' circle again?" I asked.

"Yep, hang on, cowboy; here we go," she said as she put the car in gear and moved out.

Sara turned right and headed for the Arc again. I prayed. She moved into the circle like she knew what she was doing and flew around that thing with the best of 'em. She honked and moved and pushed her way where she wanted to be. I prayed with my eyes closed. When I finally peeked she was back on the Champs-Elysees going the other way.

I sat up in my seat looked around, eased my grip on the edge of the seat and stopped trying to stop my side of the car with my legs.

"That was easy. Nuttin' to it; I knew you could do it," I said.

"You had your eyes closed the whole time," she said.

"How do you know that?" I replied.

"I looked. You had your eyes shut so tight I thought I would have to pry 'em open when we got to the hotel," she said.

"What are you doing lookin' at my eyes when you're supposed to be watching the road?" I snapped.

"I decided I didn't have to watch the other cars; they had to watch me."

I didn't have any come back for that one. How do you argue with logic like that? We passed the street we had been looking at the map on across the street, Sara slowed down and on the second street she turned right; went up one more block turned left and right on the far corner was the hotel she was looking for.

We found a place to park close to the door, locked the car, and went in and registered. I asked the desk clerk if they had a bellman to get our luggage and bring it up to our room.

"Oui, Monsieur." He hit the little bell on the desk and this guy in a uniform just like you saw in those old movies appeared. I felt like asking him where his monkey was but thought better of it since I was about to give him the keys to the car and access to all our luggage.

The desk clerk gave us a room key and told us our luggage would be up momentarily. We walked to the elevator and rode up to the sixth floor. Our room was just about two doors down from the elevator. I opened the door to the room and to my surprise it was a pretty nice room. Larger than most we had stayed in and very nicely decorated. More old movies I thought.

A few minutes later there was a knock at the door, I knew it was the bellman with our luggage I walked over to let him in. He brought the luggage into the room, put it on the little luggage stand, then walked around doing whatever it is bellboys in a fancy hotel do. He asked if there was anything else he could do for us in fairly good English. I said no thanks and slipped him five American dollars as he left. He just sneered at me and pranced out the door. *See how much he gets the next time he comes around,* I thought.

Sara checked out the room including the bathroom and gave it her stamp of approval. Having learned that they don't eat anywhere in Europe early; I kicked off my shoes, flopped on the sofa and lit a cigarette. Sara came over, moved my feet off the sofa and sat down with her cigarettes

"Are we going to supper?" she asked.

"Well, let's see; what are our options? We can go out to eat, pig out on snacks, order room service, or just forget supper and go to bed. Take your pick," I offered.

"I didn't come to Paris to eat in the room, so forget room service and snacks. That leaves going out to supper or not eating and going to bed."

"I vote for going to bed," I said with a grin.

"Is sex all you think about?" she asked.

"Yeah, pretty much." I smiled.

"Well, forget it; we're going out to eat," she barked.

"Damn, I knew you were going to say that. You know, I have a problem finding anything I like in these places," I cried.

"You seem to do all right in Spain," she reminded me.

"That was different," I said.

"Yes, it was, wasn't it?" she sighed. "But it doesn't make any difference; we are going out to eat. Let me re-phrase that. I'm going out to eat, you can do what you want to."

"You mean you would go out to eat and leave me here to starve to death?" I asked.

"You wouldn't starve; you could have all the snacks to yourself," she said.

"That wouldn't be any fun, sitting here eating alone."

"So go get your shower so we can get ready to go eat," she said, leaning over to give me a kiss.

I tried to pull her back down on the sofa but she wasn't having any of it.

"Lesson number one," she said.

I let her go and sighed. *Damn, I wish I had never taught her that lesson.* I got up, stripped, and headed for the shower.

This was my first excursion into the bathroom; it had the standard stuff, sink, shower/tub, toilet and this other thing that looked like a toilet but different.

"Hey! I hollered. Do they have men and women's toilets in France?" I asked.

"No, they don't," came her laughing reply.

"Then what is this other thing that looks like a toilet?" I inquired.

"It's called a bidet." I could hear her laughing harder.

"What the hell is a bidet?" I asked becoming rather frustrated at this point.

"Try it and find out for yourself," Sara said still laughing.

"I ain't trying it," I mumbled.

"It will make you feel better," she said.

I stood there and looked at that thing. I could think of a lot of things that would make me feel better, but sittin' on one of those things wasn't one of 'em. I decided to just ignore that bidet thing and just use what I knew. I turned the water on in the shower, got it nice and hot and jumped in. I didn't stay long in the shower. I was still thinking about that bidet thing. I toweled off, walked around it a couple of times, then went to the sink, shaved and brushed my teeth.

"Did you try the bidet?" Sara asked with this big grin on her face as I walked out of the bathroom.

"No! I did not," I said sarcastically.

"Well, I'm going to take my shower now. I'll probably use it while I'm in there," she said with that smart-ass grin on her face. She got undressed and pranced into the bathroom. I was tempted to go peek and see if she used it but changed my mind. I decided it was probably a woman thing anyway, and I didn't need to know about it.

I got dressed while Sara was in the shower. After dressing I grabbed a coke from the cooler, lit a cigarette, and walked over to the window in our room. There wasn't much of a view. The street outside our room was not very well lit but over the tops of some of the other buildings you could see the glow of more well lighted areas.

Sara walked out of the shower wrapped in one of those big, heavy, white robes. "Where did you get that?" I asked.

"It was hanging on the wall behind the door," she said. "There were two. Why didn't you use yours?"

"I didn't see it," *I said, probably 'cause I was thinking about that damn bidet thingy*, I said to myself. I watched Sara go through her ritual, brushing her hair while she smoked a cigarette and then getting dressed. This was one of the most enjoyable parts of our trips together for me, watching her get dressed. But I think I mentioned that before, didn't I?

When she was all dressed we left the room, took the elevator to the lobby and walked out the front door.

"Do you have any idea where we are going?" I asked.

"No, but I think we need to walk over that way." Apparently she had looked out the window too.

Just as we turned the corner onto this dimly lit side street in Paris France; I swear I felt like I had just stepped into one of those American in Paris movies. Walking straight toward us was this woman with the longest, reddest hair I had ever seen with a red beret cocked to one side of her head. She was wearing a red-and-white-stripped, off-the-shoulder, long-sleeved blouse with a black leather mini-skirt, fishnet stockings, and at least four inch stiletto-heeled shoes.

"Bonsoir, Monsieur et Madame," the red-headed lady said.

"Good evening," I replied, as I turned to watch the redhead walk away.

Sara punched me in the ribs with her elbow.

"Hey, I couldn't help it. She looked like something out of one of those American in Paris movies, you know with Gene Kelly and Leslie Caron."

"She looked like a hooker," Sara growled.

"Well, that too, but that's just the way they would have dressed one in the movies," I replied, "I just thought it was kinda unreal or surreal, whichever one applies," I said. "Besides, you're the one that picked this area; if there are hookers in the area don't be poking me in the ribs if I look at 'em," I said.

"I won't poke you in the ribs for looking at them, just as long as you don't stare at them and talk to them."

"I was just being nice," I replied.

"Well, be nice to me. I guarantee it will be more worth your while, and cheaper, too," Sara said, as she reached up and kissed me on the neck.

"Does that mean you're paying for dinner?" I grinned.

Sara punched me in the ribs with her elbow again. I was sure I was going to have a bruise in the morning.

We walked on down to the street which turned out to be the Champs-Elysees. We turned left and just walked past the shops and stores, and a ton of cafés and restaurants. Finally Sara spotted this little Bistro looking place. We looked in the window and it looked inviting so we decided to give it a try.

The head waiter led us to a small table towards the back. The lighting was low, and there was a small candle mounted on the wall just above our table. The wine waiter came around with a menu. Sara already knew what she wanted so she ordered without looking at the menu. I nodded to the waiter that was good enough for me too. So he hurried away. Sara and I lit up a cigarette while we surveyed our surroundings. The guy with the wine was back quickly. I took a sip after the waiter left. It was a white wine that seemed to have a little bitter taste to me; but what do I know I'm not a wine drinker anyway.

Finally another waiter showed up with some menus. He gave one to each of us and then disappeared. I opened it up but have no idea why.

I didn't read anymore French than I did German. After a couple of minutes I asked Sara if she saw anything she recognized.

"I think I'm going to have this Cordon Bleu," she said.

"What the hell is that?" I asked.

"It's chicken rolled up in breaded dough with some other things inside," she said.

"Just what are those 'other things'?" I asked.

"It depends; sometimes it's ham and cheese, but it could be something else. Depends on the chef, I suppose."

I thought I could handle the ham and cheese, it was those "other things" that would be a deal buster. Finally the waiter showed back up, pen and paper in hand.

"Is Monsieur and Madame ready to order?" he asked rather smugly.

Right away I didn't like this guy.

Sara ordered the Cordon Bleu. Since I didn't have any idea what anything else on the menu might be I decided, what the hell? I might as well give it a try.

"I'll have the same," I said.

"Oui, Monsieur," said the waiter and headed back to the kitchen.

The waiter was back rather quickly with what I assumed was supposed to be a salad. It was made up of some dead lettuce, a strip of red bell pepper, a couple of slices of tomato, some cucumber, and what appeared to be a slice of limp pickle.

Sara dived right in. I doctored mine with everything they had on the table but still wasn't too crazy about it, but managed to eat a good portion of it. When we finished our salads the waiter came by and took our dishes away. I thought the main course would be right behind the salad, but that was a mistake.

The wine guy came back buy and refilled our glasses. We smoked another cigarette while waiting on the main course. Finally the waiter came over.

"Are you ready for your dinner now, Monsieur?"

"Oui, Garçon, I believe we are," I replied.

I knew I didn't like this guy; I wanted to punch the smug bastard right between the eyes. He departed quickly; I think he knew I wanted to hit him.

He was back just about as quickly with our cordon bleu. He set Sara's in front of her first then took his time getting mine off the tray and on the table in front of me. Or maybe it was just my imagination

"Bon appétit," the waiter said and sauntered off to wherever waiters saunter to.

To my surprise I actually liked the Cordon Bleu. It had the chicken and ham with cheese in it along with some other spices that just added to the taste.

"How do you like your Cordon Bleu?" Sara asked.

"It's really pretty good. Better than I thought it would be. I wonder if they make this in anything besides chicken."

"You can ask the waiter when he comes back," Sara suggested.

"I ain't askin' that asshole nuttin'," I said.

Sara laughed, "I got the feeling you didn't like him."

"So far I've only seen two French people I like. The desk clerk and the hooker," I said.

"Watch it, buddy," Sara warned.

We finished our meal. The waiter, Mr. Friendly, offered the dessert tray, but we declined, even though some of that stuff looked pretty good. Then he slipped the bill on the table in that little folder thing they use. I took a peek at the bill; it was in Francs! Now the guy had really pissed me off.

"Do you still have that currency converter?" I asked

Sara nodded that she did.

"Figure out how much this is in American money and then figure out what 15 percent is, would you please," I asked as I slid the bill across to her.

She dug into her purse, got out the converter and the little pocket calculator she carried, then began to put the figures together. When she finished she slid the numbers across to me.

After looking at the figures I was satisfied that if I left the guy 15 percent he wasn't going to get too much, but on the other hand he wasn't getting' anything more, either. I put enough money to cover the bill and the tip. Sara and I got up and walked out the door to the nods of the waiter and head waiter. I kinda wanted to wait and see the look on the waiter's face but decided against it.

We left the Bistro and strolled along the Champs-Elysees. I thought this was great, the lights, the Arc all lit up in the distance. A couple of sidewalk cafés were still open. In case you haven't figured it out I was a fan of all those old '50s musicals. If it had rained I probably would have busted out with a chorus of "Singing in the Rain" and danced down the street. Of course that would have happened right after pigs learned to fly.

Sara and I walked a few more blocks up the street then turned around and walked back, passed the Bistro and down to the street we needed to turn on to get back to our hotel. I was hoping we'd see the redheaded hooker again but no luck. I couldn't help but wonder if she was visiting a client right in our very hotel.

Back in our rather fancy hotel room I kicked off my shoes, stripped to my shorts, grabbed a coke and lit a cigarette. Sara went in the bathroom came out a few minutes later wearing one of those big heavy bathrobes. "That's not my robe you're wearing, is it?" I asked.

"What if it is?" she replied.

"I may want to wear it," I said.

"Too bad, I got it now. You'll just have to run around in your drawers." She snickered.

"That's all right; I don't plan on doing much running around. I'm tired." I yawned. "In fact, I think I'll just go climb in the bed. It's been a long day, and you drove me crazy and gave me a headache driving around that Arc."

"Fine. From now on you drive." She frowned.

"I'm kidding; you done good, sugar. But right now I'm too tired to talk about it."

I got up, walked to the bed, pulled the covers back, climbed in and rolled over to my side of the bed and waited for Sara.

"I'm tired, too. I'll be right there."

She went in the bathroom, came right back out with the other bathrobe, and put it on the end of the bed on my side. "There. Now you'll have something to put on when you get up in the morning," she said.

She walked over turned out the overhead lights, came back to the bed; took off her robe which left her wearing nothing but a smile, put it on the end of the bed on her side and crawled under the covers. She moved over next to me, put her head on my shoulder, threw her leg over mine then gave me a kiss and said good night.

GERMANY
Chapter 78

I think we both must have slept like babies. We woke up in the same position we went to sleep in. I had no idea what time it was, but I really didn't care. I was comfortable and felt like I could just lie there all day.

That idea didn't last long, Sara nudged me and said, "Get up and tell me if it's cold in here."

"Humph! Get your own ass up and see if it's cold," I replied. "Besides, you have that heavy robe at the foot of the bed you can slip into right way."

"You never had any problems getting up first in Spain," she whined.

"It never was cold in Spain. It was fuckin' August," I responded.

"You just don't love me anymore," she continued to whine.

I relented. "Okay, I'll get up and see if it's cold."

I crawled out from under the covers and pranced around the room naked. "Okay, you satisfied now? It's not cold."

"Then how come little Charlie is all shriveled up?" she observed.

"Because that's Charlie's natural state when he isn't excited, or I don't have to go pee real bad, and right now I am neither excited nor do I have to piss," I said, rolling my eyes.

"Okay, come get my robe ready to put on me just in case I'm cold," she asked.

"You're such a baby sometimes, ya know that?" I snapped.

I walked over got her robe and held it open for her to step into when she climbed out of bed. She threw the covers back, stepped gingerly on the floor, turned around and I slipped the robe on over her shoulders.

She turned back around and put her arms around my neck. "I know," she said, "and I love it when you treat me like one sometimes."

She gave me a long, slow, tongue-twisting kiss. Sometimes it was worth treating her like a baby, I thought.

She rushed into the bathroom. I went over grabbed my own robe, slipped it, on and walked over and grabbed my cigarettes and a coke. I walked over to the window and looked out. The street didn't look any different in the day time than it did at night. I was wondering if the redheaded hooker lived around here some place. Or maybe she had a client in this very hotel last night.

Sara came out of the bathroom in her robe with a towel around her head. I was thinking it was a good thing she couldn't read my mind when she said.

"Looking for your redheaded hooker?"

"NO!" I lied. *How the hell did she know that?* I wondered; I can't even have any thoughts all my own anymore.

"Are you through in the bathroom?" I asked.

"It's all yours, cowboy; the hot water is great," she said.

Now I was leery, she never told me the hot water was great before. What did that mean? Was it really great or was there no hot water at all? Damn, she was making me paranoid, reading my thoughts and shit. I walked into the bathroom, immediately turned on the shower. The water was extremely hot. Okay, well maybe I really was just being paranoid.

I slipped out of the robe and hopped in the shower. It didn't take long for the hot water to make me feel really human again. A good hot shower was always my jump start in the morning. After about 15 minutes in the steam and I was ready to get out. I turned the water off, stepped out and grabbed the terrycloth robe and put it on. I took a towel and dried off the places the robe didn't reach. I shaved and brushed my teeth and proceeded out to the bedroom. I was drying my head with the towel when I walked out of the bathroom when I heard this sultry voice saying, "Bonsoir, Monsieur."

I looked up and about swallowed my tongue. There stood Sara over by the bedpost wearing this little fedora hat I had been wearing around since Spain down over one eye. She had a sheer blouse and nothing else on under it. It was unbuttoned to the waist. She wore an emerald-green, short leather skirt that barely covered the top of her sheer, skin-colored stockings

"Hoooly Shiiit!" I uttered in total disbelief. "Do I know you?"

Sara propped one leg up on the bed frame, which only raised that short skirt higher, leaned forward on her elbow, and propped her chin in her hand. "You liked the lady with the red hair last night, oui, Monsieur?" she said with her best French accent with a little German thrown in.

"Oui, I mean yes; I mean, she was okay. Your tryin' to trap me here, aren't you?" I said. If she was it was working, I thought. Charlie wasn't standing still for any of this.

Sara motioned me to come over to her with her finger. I walked tentatively towards her. She reached out and grabbed the belt to my robe and pulled me up against her. "You like to give lessons, oui, Monsieur? she asked. "I think this morning we go over your lesson plans, oui? Only this morning Monsieur we skip lessons one and two and go directly to lesson number three," she said in her best French accent.

She undid the belt to my robe and pushed if off my shoulders until it hit the floor at my feet.

"Damn, I've created a sex maniac," I mumbled as she pushed me down on the bed.

Gawd! I hope I didn't leave anything out of the lesson plan, I thought as she climbed on top of me with this wild look in her eyes.

If I had forgotten anything Sara did some great improvisations, I thought as I lay back huffing and puffing and sweating trying to smoke a cigarette but lacking enough air to puff. Sara was lying next to me with this little shit-eatin' grin on her face, not saying a word. You could see the ringlets of sweat running down between her breasts and off her forehead. I hoped she never asked me to teach her lesson number four.

Finally Sara sat up, looked at me and said, "Now see what you've done? I need another shower."

I just raised my limp arm and waved to her to let her know I heard her. She hopped off the bed and headed back to the bathroom. I just lay there ready to take a nap.

By the time Sara got out of the shower this time I had somewhat recovered and was ready for another shower myself. I followed her immediately into the bathroom and took another not-quite-so-hot shower. I finished, threw on my robe, and before walking out into the bedroom this time, I peeked out and carefully surveyed the area. Sara was sitting on the sofa in her robe brushing her hair and smoking a cigarette. I walked over to the sofa grabbed a coke, lit a cigarette and sat down beside her.

"Sometimes you're just full of surprises; you know that?" I said.

She smiled, took a drag on her cigarette, put it out and said, "Did you like it?"

"Yeah, well, it was pretty good," I said matter of factly.

"Pretty good! Just pretty good?" Sara hissed as she slapped me on the leg with her hair brush.

"OUCH! That hurt!" I cried as I rubbed my leg.

I reached over and grabbed her, gave her a kiss, and said, "Sugar, you were great. You surprised and shocked the hell out of me. Feel free to do it again anytime you want to." I put my arms around her and hugged her.

"Are you sure it was okay?" she asked. I could hear some self doubt creeping into her voice.

"Baby, it was terrific, you were great. Might wanna work on your accent a little bit, though." I laughed.

She smacked me with her hair brush, lightly this time, and grinned. "Remember, I'm German, not French."

"German, French, American, hell, it was all good," I said. "Okay, what are we gonna do the rest of the day, and how much of the rest of the day is left?" I asked.

She looked at her watch. It was 12:30; we still had most of the day left. "Wanna go to the Louvre and see the Mona Lisa? I know museums are not your favorite thing to do."

"That sounds like a plan to me; we can stop and get something to eat at one of those out door cafés. For some reason I'm starved."

We both got off the sofa and began to dress. A short time later we were on the Champs-Elysees, sitting out in the fresh, air eating some kinda ham and cheese sandwich thingy, which was either really good, or I was starving to death. We finished quickly and hailed a taxi to the museum. We weren't actually that far from the museum so it was a short ride.

Upon arrival we were told that for some reason the museum would be closing early today so we did a whirl wind tour. We found the Mona Lisa; I thought it looked like Sara's mom, minus the smile. She didn't think that was funny but she laughed anyway. We saw a few other things that I will never remember as we worked our way back towards the exit.

Once outside a little wind had picked up and it was a tad chilly. We grabbed another cab and went directly back to the hotel. Once there I went over and talked to the only Frenchman I liked at the hotel and asked him about a couple of places we could go for dinner and a show in the evening. He suggested the Lido and the Moulin Rouge. I asked how we could make reservations and he offered to make reservations for us. He suggested we have dinner and make the late show. I thought that sounded great so I told him to go ahead and make the reservations. I gave him a tip for his services. More than I gave that snooty bellhop.

Sara and I went up to our room to relax since we didn't have anything to do now for several hours. I was sitting on the sofa when the phone rang. Sara looked at me and I looked at her. Who would be calling us? She was closest so she answered the phone, listened for a few minutes and then said thank you and hung up.

"That was the front desk. Our reservations have been confirmed at the Lido for dinner and the late show. There will be a taxi here to pick us up at 8:30."

"Well, now, ain't that the cat's meow," I said.

In the meantime Sara dug around in the drawers of the night stands and found some literature on some of the local nightlife. For the Lido, formal attire is requested, jacket and tie is appreciated. No casual clothes such as jeans, tennis shoes or sports wear.

"I guess that meant I wear my suit tonight, huh?" I asked.

"I think you better if you want to get in." Sara laughed then she got to the good part about topless girls running around on stage.

"Now that's my kinda show." I grinned.

At 8:15 we were waiting just inside the lobby for our taxi when the doorman came in and motioned to us that the taxi had arrived. The doorman opened the door for us and as we got in I slipped him a few Franc's for his help. The Lido was on the Champs-Elysees and besides scaring the shit out of us the taxi driver got us there all in one piece. I paid the fair and we were ushered in by a doorman, met by a head waiter and let to our table; which turned out to be a really big table with room for lots and lots of people. But that was okay.

Actually we were early arrivals. There were no other people at our table when we first arrived. The waiter brought us our complimentary bottle of burgundy and some gal with a camera came around and wanted to take our picture. I figured what the hell how many times does a high school drop out from a small Texas town get to go to the Lido Café in Paris France with a pretty woman at his side.

I can't tell you what we ate, but it wasn't bad, I will tell you I stayed away from the escargots though. No way I'm eating snails. None the less the food was pretty good and the floor show was great. I had never seen so many costumes in one place on so many pretty women. Not to mention the costumes they weren't wearing. That was the part I liked best naturally. Sara would kick my shins every once in while under the table if I started to drool.

The show lasted about two hours and we left the Lido sometime after midnight. Since we weren't far from our hotel we decided to walk. I have to tell you, walking down the Champs-Elysees is a walk worth taking, especially at night when it's all lit up. It's definitely the who's who of avenues. I can tell ya this: poor folk may walk the street, but poor people don't live on the street. No telling what an apartment on that street would cost you.

We walked all the way back to the hotel; still no red headed hooker. We went straight to our room. Besides being a little tired from the walk, I think we were both a little tipsy from the Burgundy. We both undressed quickly and hopped in bed.

Sara rolled over, said, “I love you, thanks for taking me to the Lido tonight,” And gave me a kiss.

“I love you too, sugar, and the pleasure was all mine,” I said as I put my arm around her and pulled her over close to me

GERMANY
Chapter 79

We were off early the next morning. Sara had her usual cup of instant coffee but once we hit the Champs-Elysees we couldn't resist stopping at another outdoor Café. The weather was a tad brisk but the sun was shining and it was a nice day. We had a European breakfast some rolls with jelly, honey and some fruit.

"What's first on the agenda this morning?" I asked.

"How about the Eiffel Tower?" Sara asked.

"I think that's and excellent choice. I might even ask you to marry me while we are up there," I grinned.

"You did that already, cowboy," she replied.

"I did? What did you say?" I teased.

"If you don't remember I'm not going to tell you."

"I see you're wearing an engagement ring, so I assume you said yes," I said.

"Maybe this isn't your ring," she suggested.

"Aha, so you're here in Paris, fooling around on your fiancée with me then?" I said.

"What he doesn't know won't hurt him," she said.

"You brazen hussy!" I snorted.

Sara laughed. "You're so crazy, sometimes. You asked me to marry you, I said yes, and now I'm pregnant."

"Whoa! Whose is it? Mine or is it your fiancée's?" I asked in nervous anticipation.

"It's my fiancée's," she said.

"Whew; for a minute there you had me worried." I laughed. "You ready to go to the Eiffel Tower?" I asked.

As we got up to leave, I had one more question. "Uh, you're not really…you know… pregnant, are you?"

"I'll tell you after the Eiffel Tower. I wouldn't want you jumping off." She laughed, and walked off towards the curb to hail a taxi.

"Damn, woman! I'd tell you if I was pregnant!" I hollered at her. Heads of other customers at the café turned at that comment.

I paid our bill at the café and hailed a taxi. We arrived at the tower and I think at that time it was the tallest building or structure I had ever been in or on. We went to the observation tower and Sara walked around with her camera and took a bunch of pictures. We got some guy to take a picture of us together. I figured we were safe letting him use our camera. Where was he going to run? The view from the top of the tower was spectacular. You could see so much of the city and the Seine River seemed to be endless.

After doing the Eiffel Towner thing, we took a river tour up and down the Seine. You could see the Tower of course and the Notre-Dame Cathedral among other things. Of course you could see the right and left bank, one of which was supposed to be where a lot of painters got their inspiration, but I can't remember which one it was.

After our tour we returned to the Hotel, my favorite Frenchman was working the desk. I walked over and asked him if he could get us reservations to the Moulin Rouge for the evening. He looked at his watch and kinda cringed as if to say it was kinda late. But he said.

"I shall try, Monsieur."

I thanked him and slipped him some money. *He better come through*, I thought as I walked away. He was getting expensive.

About an hour after we got back to our room the phone rang. It was the desk clerk. He informed us that we had reservations for the late dinner and show at the Moulin Rouge, and a taxi would be available for us. I thanked him again and hung up. We had a few hours before we had to get ready. Sara was already snoozing on the bed; I kicked off my shoes went over and joined her. All that fresh air made me tired.

I woke up about 6 p.m. Sara was already up and in the bathroom. I rolled over, grabbed my cigarettes and fired one up. I got up, walked over got a coke, and parked my butt on the sofa. I thought about today, visiting the Eiffel Tower and taking a boat tour on the Seine. I'm normally not much of a sightseer but today had been fun.

Sara interrupted my thoughts when she came out of the bathroom in her big heavy robe, brushing her hair.

"The bathroom is all yours, cowboy, and the water is hot," she said.

"I'm on my way as soon as I finish this cigarette," I replied.

I took a couple more drags on the cigarette, put it out and headed for the shower. I love a hot shower; I think I said that already, didn't I? But I had taken so many since we had been here in Paris I was beginning to feel like a prune. I didn't stay as long as I normally would. I grabbed my robe, toweled off my hair and stepped over to the sink to shave and brush my teeth.

When I came out of the bathroom Sara was just pulling on those long silk stockings I like. I stopped and watched for a fleeting second then thought better of it. I wasn't about to take another shower; besides we didn't have time. We both continued to dress quietly and then smoked one more cigarette before we went down to get our taxi.

We arrived at the Moulin Rouge and were immediately ushered to our table in the cabaret theatre. We had relatively good seats about center stage and not too far back from the stage. The waiter immediately brought us our complimentary ½ bottle of champagne. Sara ordered some kinda fish, and I had some beef fillet something or other with some kinda screwed up potatoes in a wine sauce. What I really wanted was a hamburger. For dessert we had a choice of a fruit cocktail kinda thing or something else that looked like very dark chocolate.

The floor show was great. There must have been a few hundred dancers and other type of performers on the stage at anyone time. I've never seen so many feathers, rhinestones, sequins and tits in my life. Sara was sitting next to me, so she couldn't kick me but I think she broke two ribs with her elbows. Of course the best dance of the evening was the Cancan. These girls could Cancan like nobody else can….can.

Sara and I both really enjoyed the show. We had a smile on our face all the way back to the hotel. When we got back to the hotel my favorite desk clerk was still on duty, I walked over and thanked him for his help.

He nodded and said, "You re very welcome."

I had to wonder if he was actually French. The snooty bellman was there, too, but I just stuck my nose in the air and walked right on past him.

When we got back to the room, we kicked off our shoes and came out of the rest of our clothes, and slipped into our heavy white robes. I grabbed a coke, and our smokes, and then Sara and I cuddled up on the sofa and just relaxed.

"You know this was almost as much fun as Spain, but in a different sort of way," Sara said.

"You're right. It was fun, but different. Which one did you like the best?" I asked.

"It's hard to pick one, but I think if I had to I would pick Spain," she said.

"Why?" I asked.

"Spain was just like another world. It was slow paced, almost like time stood still, and there was just you and me. We didn't have to hurry to do anything."

"I liked Spain the best, too. Spain seemed to bring out this change in you that has been so great. You've just been a totally different person and so much fun. I like that. So I vote for Spain too. This has been fun, and I have enjoyed it, but I think that was because it was the first place we have been where I actually knew something about the place and what the attractions were that I would like to see. And for the most part we did that, but we didn't have enough time to see it all. We might have to come back."

Sara sat up and looked at me. "You mean I wasn't fun before?" She pouted.

"You were fun, but now you're just a different kind of fun. You're not so uptight, it seems," I said.

"So you're saying before Spain I was an uptight, boring bitch?" she queried.

"I wouldn't go as far as to say that now," I replied, feeling I was about to stick my foot in my mouth here.

"But you would think it?"

"How did I know you were going to ask that question?" I sighed. "Look, I just think you suddenly, for whatever reason, broke away from your Victorian upbringing given to you by your parents and just now realized it's okay to have fun and enjoy some things you were taught weren't supposed to be fun. And I'm glad I was here to see it, be a part of it, and see the change in you, and I love you even more because of it."

Sara locked those deep brown eyes of hers on me and just sat there staring at me for what seemed to be forever. Finally she leaned forward and gave me the most tender, gentle kiss I had ever gotten from her.

"For a small-town Texas high-school dropout you're pretty damn smart, cowboy, and I love you for lots of reasons, but mostly for teaching me it's okay to have fun."

I pulled her back down in my arms and said, "The pleasure has been all mine, sugar."

I don't remember going to bed that night, but I know I woke up feeling great. Sara was still asleep. I got up and went to the bathroom. When I came out I walked over, got my cigarettes and usual morning coke, and flopped on the sofa. I was trying to remember what happened last night after our little talk. Slowly I started to remember bits and pieces and by the time I had the whole picture I could feel this huge smile on my face. *What a night,* I thought, *for our last night in Paris.*

I saw Sara begin to stir and watched her wake up. She climbed out of bed slipped on her robe and headed for the bathroom.

"Good morning," she said on her way by. She was in the bathroom and had closed the door before I could respond. It wasn't long before I heard the shower running.

Sara came out with the usual towel around her head. She kissed me on the cheek on her way to the instant coffee. Once the coffee was fixed, she grabbed her cigarettes and came over and sat down beside me. "I don't wanna leave," she said.

"I know; me neither, but we really don't have a choice," I replied.

I got up and headed for the shower. By the time I was out Sara was pretty much dressed and had the suitcases out on the bed. The good thing about returning from vacation was that you didn't really have to pack, you just threw shit in a suitcase, figuring it was all dirty and you were gonna wash it when you got home anyway. Therefore packing didn't take very long at all.

Once all the suitcases were stuffed, we called for a bellman and Mr. Snooty showed up. I told him to take our bags down to the desk, we were going to the restaurant in the hotel for breakfast then we would be checking out. He returned my nose-in-the-air attitude and said, "Oui, Monsieur."

Sara and I left the baggage in his charge and walked out of the room and down to the restaurant across the lobby from the desk area. We both ordered the American Breakfast which was a couple of eggs with ham and toast. It wasn't bad, or maybe we were just hungry.

We finished breakfast I walked over and checked out of the hotel. There didn't seem to be a bellman in sight. I'm not sure if that was on purpose or not but Sara and I just grabbed our bags and walked out, the car was just down the street and around the corner. We packed the Blue Bitch, hopped in and we were off. I kinda hated leaving Paris because there were still things there I would have enjoyed seeing.

We got out of Paris without having an accident and back on the road to K-Town. The drive home didn't seem to take as long as the drive to Paris. We were in K-Town before dark. We pulled up at the BOQ and unloaded the bags. I had a decision to make.

I could go on back to Heidelberg tonight which technically I needed to do since my leave was up at midnight but I had a day of grace which means I could wait and sign in on Monday. Sara and I talked about it; she offered to drive me to Heidelberg in the morning if I wanted to stay over. It didn't take much arm twisting to get me to stay.

GERMANY
Chapter 80

I don't know what I was thinking when I agreed to stay with Sara in K-Town when we got back from Paris. The next day was Monday and she had to go to work. I don't remember if she set the alarm before we went to bed or if it was set from before and had been going off every morning we had been gone but it went off on Monday morning and I jumped straight up. Sara rolled over to turn the alarm off.

"Get up and get moving," I said. "You have to go to work this morning."

"I'm taking you back to Heidelberg this morning, remember? she said.

"No, you need to go to work; I can catch a taxi to the Bahnhof and catch a train."

"I don't wanna go to work; I wanna play hooky," she whined, as she sat up and stretched.

"If you keep doing that we'll both be late," I said.

Sara grinned and shook her shoulders from side to side.

"Stop it!" I said.

She pulled the covers down below my waist. "I don't think you want me to stop," she said, grinning bigger.

"I have to go pee," I said.

"How do I know that? You could be lying," she insisted.

I pushed her back down on the bed. "If you get in trouble for playing hooky, you're on your own," I said as I kicked the covers to the foot of the bed.

Sara reached up and pulled me down on top of her. "I'll stay after school one day to make up for it," she said.

Sara called the school office and said she had developed a little sore throat and wouldn't be in today. I lay there smoking a cigarette, nodding my head and smiling as though I could understand that. Sara hit me in the groin with a pillow.

Sara got up and fixed her instant coffee, then came back to bed. She sat crossed legged on the bed drinking her coffee and smoking a cigarette while I sipped on the coke she had brought me. Basically we were waiting to hear Mary Ann leave so we could get up and move around and get in the bathroom.

Finally Mary Ann said, "Goodbye," and slammed the door on her way out.

"Wonder how she knew we were here?" I asked.

"I'm always up and moving before she gets out of bed, and the door is closed," Sara said.

Sara finished her first cup of coffee and headed for the shower. I turned on the radio to the Armed Forces Network and listened to some good old American music until Sara came out of the bathroom wearing a heavy white robe.

"Where the hell did you get that robe?" I asked suspiciously.

"I got it from the hotel. Yours is hanging on the back of the door," she said.

"You're a little thief!" I laughed.

"I wanted more of a souvenir from that hotel than just a postcard. Something to remind me of the times we spent there," she said with a melancholy tone in her voice.

I got up and walked over towards her on my way to the bathroom. I put my arms around her.

"You may be a little thief, but you're my little thief, and I love you, so I won't tell," I said.

She grinned, kissed my check and I continued on to the bathroom. I brushed my teeth while the shower got hot. I put shaving cream on my face and stepped in the shower with my razor. I figured I would kill two birds with one stone and shave while the hot water beat down on my shoulders and neck. Since we were apparently in no hurry I stayed in the shower a little extra time but when I finally got out I stepped into my big heavy white Terrycloth bath robe.

Since Sara called in sick we didn't want to be seen hanging around in the snack bar/cafeteria area, she fixed us some eggs with ham and toast on her little hot plate. We took our time eating. I think we were both really dreading the drive to Heidelberg but we didn't have much choice.

"I'm not pregnant," Sara said.

"What?" I replied with a mouth full of eggs.

"I told you I would tell you after the Eiffel Tower," she said.

"Oh, well, I'm glad you finally told me. I was about to go jump out the window." I laughed.

"Is it too late?" she asked.

"Too late to what? Tell me or get pregnant?" I asked.

"Both or either," she said.

"Well, it's a tad late to be telling me, since I asked you yesterday. And it's not too late to get pregnant, but it is definitely way too early to even be thinking about it," I stated.

"So that means you don't want to have any kids now?" she asked.

I put my fork down, wiped my mouth and looked her straight in the eye. "I don't know what brought on this conversation now, but to answer your question as plainly as I can; no I do not want any kids now. I'm still a kid myself. I am not ready physically, emotionally, mentally, and especially financially to handle the responsibility of a kid. Why the hell are you asking me this now anyway?"

"I just wanted to hear you tell me that, so I knew for sure we were on the same page," she said.

"Sugar, sometimes you have a hell of a way of getting to the point," I said. "You could have just asked me if I wanted kids."

"I was afraid you would just tell me what you thought I wanted to hear and not how you really felt," she said. "Are you mad at me?"

"No, I'm not mad at you, but I thought yesterday when you said you were pregnant you were just going along with my joking around, I didn't know you had really been thinking about this."

"I'm sorry. I don't know why I thought you may have been thinking about having kids, but all of a sudden I just needed to hear you tell me what you wanted," she stated.

"It's okay; now you know," I said.

I finished my breakfast, Sara drank her coffee, and we were both very quiet. I was uncomfortable and I think she was too. This was no good. I think she felt badly about the way she went about things and she shouldn't. It upset me when she didn't feel good about things. I needed to do something to change the mood.

I pushed my little tray aside stood up and pulled Sara up off the bed and in my arms. I kissed her and began to unbutton her blouse.

"What are you doing? she asked.

"I wanna have sex."

"I don't want to get pregnant," she replied.

"I don't want you to get pregnant either, but we need to keep in practice so we don't forget how when the time comes," I said.

"You're so crazy," she grinned. "Besides we already had sex once this morning. You think you can do it again?"

"Humph! Are you questioning my abilities as a man to be able to perform more than once a day?" I asked.

I slid her blouse off her shoulders and let it drop to the floor, reached around behind her and unsnapped her bra; it too fell to the floor. I took her hand and put it between us.

"You tell me what you think," I said.

"I think I need a closer examination of the evidence," she said as she unzipped my jeans.

I've heard women say that men think sex fixes everything. Sometimes they get one right.

GERMANY
Chapter 81

Sara and I arrived at Patton Barracks just about 1430. Shep Williams was working the gate. As we pulled in he had a smile on his face from ear to ear. I stopped just to say hi.

"Hey, Shep, what's happening?" I asked.

"Hey, Bones, Ms. Bones," Shep said, tipping his hat to Sara. We both had to laugh. Sara had never been called Ms. Bones before, or Ms. anything as far as I knew.

"You seem awful happy to be working the gate, Shep?"

"This is my last one, Bones; I got my orders. I'm leaving in a week. I'm going home." Shep beamed.

"Hey, man, that's great. You're not short anymore. You're next," I said.

"You got that right," Shep replied.

I had to move on. Traffic was stacking up behind us. "Okay, Shep, I'll catch you again before you leave, man. Have a good last tour," I said as I drove on through the gate.

"Well, Ms. Bones, there is the next guy to leave the company," I laughed.

"I don' think I wanna be called Ms. Bones." She giggled.

We pulled up in front of the company and drove on around to the parking area on the side. I put Blue Bitch in park and turned off the ignition. I turned to Sara and said, "I'm sorry I upset you this morning."

"I think you got that backwards, cowboy. I upset you, because I was afraid to just come out and ask you a question. As I recall you made it all better," she smiled as she leaned over and gave me a kiss.

"Well, okay, I accept your apology." I snickered.

"I'm not apologizing, you shithead," Sara said as she punched me on the shoulder.

I laughed and gave Sara a hug. "That's my girl," I said. "But I have to ask you one serious question and I need a straightforward answer."

"Okay."

"Why were we even talking about your being pregnant and kids and shit?"

"You talk in your sleep," Sara said.

"I do not," I replied.

"Yes, you do. In Spain one night you were just talking away."

"And what did I say?" I asked.

"You said you were afraid she would be too old to have kids when you were ready."

"I did not say that," I insisted.

"Honey, I heard you just as clear as a bell," Sara said.

"Well, I have never had a conscious thought like that, ever…not before I met you or since; so I have no idea where that came from," I said.

"I just thought it must have crossed your mind at some time; otherwise why would you dream about it?"

"I don't know. How many times have you had dreams about stuff you never had a conscious thought about before?" I asked, a little pissed.

"I'm sorry; now I've made you mad again," Sara sighed.

"No, I'm not going to get upset over this. I refuse to let this become an issue between us. I don't want kids now, you don't want kids now, end of story. I don't give a fuck what I said in my sleep. Got it?"

"Yes, sir, I got it, sir," she said and gave me a left handed salute, with a grin on her face.

I couldn't help but laugh, she was just too damn cute with that look on her face and that left handed salute thing.

"Okay, I'm going in now. Drive carefully on your way back to K-Town, and I'll call you one night during the week. And yes, I will be there next weekend, before you even ask," I said.

We got out of the car I waited by the driver's side to help her in. She came around and I put my arms around her waist and gave her a kiss. "I love you," I whispered.

"I love you too," she whispered back.

She climbed in behind the wheel and adjusted the seat. The car started right away and she put it in reverse. Neither of us were big on good byes, she backed the car out and started off down the road; I waved until she was around the corner.

I walked back around to the main doors to the company area and walked down to the Orderly Room and signed in off leave. I stuck my head in the door of the day room to see if Roach was around; nobody had seen him. I walked on up to my room, it was empty. Maybe all the guys were working over at Campbell Barracks today, I thought as I sat down on my bunk. I ran my hand under my dust cover and found a couple of letters from my mother that someone had picked up for me. I wasn't in the mood to read them now so I just pitched them on my footlocker.

I slipped out of my shoes, lit a cigarette and just sat there thinking. This had been a real confusing day for me. I was still confused about all this pregnant talk stuff. Even if I said that in my sleep why would she think I was serious? And she had already said that she didn't think the military life was the place to raise a family. That was something she had come right out and said and I couldn't shake that out of my mind. At some point I needed to decide what I was going to do. I liked my job, I liked where I was stationed and I didn't have any real desire to go home.

Sure enough, all the guys came walking in at once; they had all worked Campbell today. They all said hello and welcome back.

"Hey, Bones, how long are you staying with us this time?" Rizzo asked.

"I just dropped by to pick up a change of clothes," I told him.

"Did you get your mail, Bones?" Harry asked.

"Yeah, thanks, Harry."

"Was Roach workin' with you guys today?" I asked.

"Yeah, he should be down in his room or in the mess hall," Dietz said.

I got up and walked down to Roach's room. He was just changing clothes as I entered the room.

"Bones!" he shouted. "Glad you're back; how was Gay Pareee?" he asked.

"Hey, it's good to be home, and Paris was great. You should go if you ever get the chance I said.

"Are you on your way to the mess hall?"

"Yeah, you coming with me?" he asked.

"If you're waiting on me you're walking backwards," I said.

We left his room, down the stairs and out the door together.

"So Paris was a ball, huh?" Roach asked.

"The thing about Paris, I knew a little bit about what was there and what I would like to see, you know stuff like the Mona Lisa, the Eiffel Tower, stuff like that and we went to places I had actually heard of like the Moulin Rouge and Lido Café'. That made it more interesting."

"So you had a great time then?" Roach said.

"Yeah, until we got home," I said.

"Uh oh, what happened?"

"I'll tell you when we get inside if there isn't a whole table full," I said.

We entered the mess hall; it wasn't too crowded most of the day shift was already there.

We had finished our supper by the time I finished telling Roach everything that had happened and were smoking a cigarette. We just sat there for a while, then Roach said, "You know what, Bones? Sometimes women are just fucked up. They can't help it; it's in their genes. Bobbie Jo does this kinda shit to me all the time; she pulls something out of the air I said a month ago just in passing and makes a whole big deal out of it when it didn't mean anything at all. Of course Bobbie Jo is still a kid compared to Sara, no offense intended, but I guess they just start thinking that way when they are born."

"Well, no offense taken. But can you imagine going through life with this kinda shit? Whatever happened to going out, having fun, getting drunk, and getting laid? They wonder why men die earlier than women."

"I agree, but let me ask you this. Can you imagine going through life without it? How boring would that be?" Roach ventured.

"Humph! Sounds like we're fucked either way," I said. "I guess you just gotta figure out how to make it work for you."

We both laughed, got up and left the mess hall. We were the last ones out, and the KPs had already come and picked up our trays so they could finish cleaning the place up and get outta there.

"You going down to Stadt Hall tonight?" Roach asked

"Why would I want to go down there tonight?" I asked.

"Fasching is still in full swing; there are parties every night," Roach said.

"Well, I'm not going tonight. I'm too tired. You going?" I asked.

"No, I'm not going tonight either. I'll wait until after payday."

We walked back to our respective rooms. Roach said he was going to read for a while and I had some mail to read. When I walked in Dietz, Rizzo, Harry, Tom and Hobbs were all on their way to town. I wished them all good luck as they hustled out the door.

Fasching is like the Mardi Gras in New Orleans. It's one big party, depending on which part of Germany you're in it starts at different times. Germans call it the pre-lenten Carnival season. It is usually considered to start on the 11th of November on the 11th hour at the 11th minute. This is the one time of year when many normally staid Germans loosen up and go a little crazy. The closer to Easter it gets the wilder it can get in some areas.

I got the letters from my mother, sat on my bunk with a cigarette, and read through them. Maybe looked at 'em would be a better term. My mother never wrote anything I was interested in reading. Except the one time she sent me a picture of Carlita Siegler when she was voted Miss Abilene. Carlita and I used to have chemistry class together and dated a couple of times. She sure didn't look back then like she did in the picture my mother sent me. Ain't that the way it always works out?

GERMANY
Chapter 82

It seemed like I just woke up one morning and it was Christmas already. Sara of course had off for the holidays until after the first of the year. I, on the other hand, wasn't so lucky. As is customary it seems they split Christmas and New Years in half; half the company got off Christmas and the other half got off New Years.

I asked for Christmas which wasn't a problem for me. My straight day schedule worked in my favor. Other guys had to change shifts in mid stream to cover the time off the other guys were taking.

Just after payday I had gone to the PX after work to look around for something for Sara. I had already picked out a couple of personal things but I wanted to get her something else. For some reason I was back in the little furniture section they had in the PX and I spotted this really cool coffee table. It was a light blonde color, don't ask me what kinda wood it was; I have no idea. But the table I thought was unique, recessed in the middle of the table was this carving or a little German farm house complete with barn, a couple of people, a stream running near by, trees, and mountains in the back ground and a couple of deer grazing in the fields. The table had a glass top so the carved picture was always visible. I thought that was neat as shit. I figured Sara would like it so I bought it, if nothing else it could and did become our new dining room table when we "ate in" at the apartment. On my first weekend off before my Christmas break, I hauled that table up to K-Town on the train. Actually it turned into a combination Anniversary and Christmas present, since the 19th of December was the day we became engaged. It was hard to believe that we had been engaged a year already.

One evening during my week off the teachers and staff were having a party. I really, really, really didn't want to go to this party. This was where I felt the most uncomfortable and I guess all my insecurities showed. But I knew Sara not only wanted to go but was pretty much expected to attend, so I had to just suck it up and make the best of it.

I did okay as long as Sara was right there by my side; she could field any questions and fend off anyone that started talking above my grade level. And she was real good about that, she rarely left my side, and on the couple of occasions that she did nobody bothered me. I wondered if Sara put out a warning or something. Those that did come around and chat were friendly enough and were pretty down to earth. There were these couple of guys I would have liked to have punched out. Not so much because of what they were saying to me but the way they were coming on to Sara. Maybe it was just me, but I got the feeling they were trying to hit on Sara. It was a game they were playing to see if they could take her away from me that evening. I think I was surprised because I thought only guys my age played those kinda games.

She would be holding my hand and feel me get tense when these guys started talking their shit and she would just squeeze my hand and lean over and give me a kiss and whisper some sweet nothings in my ear, like..."Lesson number three." I couldn't help but smile or just laugh and I think the other guys got the idea she was talking about them so they didn't stick around long. I noticed at least one of them try to run her down when she went to get a fresh drink or a plate of those little finger sandwiches and whatever other stuff they had to offer. She kept moving, not giving him a chance to get her involved in any conversation.

The party finally broke up and I was ready to leave. Sara said her good byes and we walked out together arm and arm. It was getting cold so we hurried to Blue Bitch and drove quickly back to the BOQ.

When we got inside, got out of our coats and got comfortable. I walked over to Sara as she was pouring herself a glass of wine, slipped my arms around her waist from behind, kissed her neck and said, "Thanks."

She leaned back into me and asked. "For what?"

"For not leaving me hung out to dry down there at that party tonight," I said.

She turned around put her arms around my neck.

"I know you're uncomfortable at those kinds of functions. I'm not really sure why, but I wouldn't leave you alone for very long. I know some of those people; especially the men can be real jerks. I don't even like the majority of them."

"I'm uncomfortable because some of them want to come up and try to get me in a conversation about politics or some shit that I have no idea at all what they are talking about, and I feel like an idiot, and I become an embarrassment to you when that happens. If it was just me, I'd tell 'em to go fuck themselves, and let it go."

"Well, next time one of 'em does that you just tell 'em to go fuck themselves, and don't worry about me," she said.

I burst out laughing, I couldn't help it. That was the second time she had used that word and it was so totally not her, completely unexpected and the look on her face and how red she turned when she said it; I just couldn't help but fall in love with her all over again right there, just as I had the first time in Spain. I laughed so hard I made her laugh and we both must have laughed for ten minutes and the more we laughed the redder she got.

When we finally calmed down enough, I lit a cigarette and said, "You gotta stop hanging out with me, I guess. I'm teaching you naughty things."

"But I like hanging out with you and being naughty," she replied.

"But it's so unladylike for you to be naughty."

"That's the whole point. With you I don't have to be a lady. That's all I was ever told growing up; be a lady, don't do this and don't do that. Act like a lady, and you'll be treated like a lady."

"Well, that's pretty much how it works; you get respect and treated better when you act like you expect it."

"I know, and I'm tired of it. I don't want to be disrespected, and being a lady in public is one thing, and I'll do that, but when I'm alone with you I like the way you treat me, like a woman, like a friend, like a lover, and you're never mean to me."

We had been lying on the bed when we put out our cigarettes. I reached over put my arm around Sara and pulled her close to me. She put her head on my shoulder with her arm resting across my chest. We just lay there quietly. I was thinking about what she just said. On the surface it sounded simple enough. It sounded easy. But the more I thought about it the more it occurred to me, maybe there was more to it than that. Maybe she wasn't just asking me to be a friend and lover and treat her like a woman; maybe in her round-about way she was telling me she was putting all her faith and trust in me to take care of her to be there when she needed me to be, in whichever capacity she needed at any particular time.

I tried to clear my head, maybe I was reading too much into all this. But I was suddenly feeling a great responsibility for this sometimes child-like woman that lay in my arms. Listen to me, I thought; I'm calling her child like, and she is five and a half years older than I am. Who is really the child here? Still I couldn't help but feel this overwhelming responsibility to protect and provide for the welfare and needs of this woman. That was a pretty scary thought.

I tried to look down at her face but I couldn't see it however her deep even breathing told me she had fallen asleep lying on my shoulder. I knew my arm was going to go to sleep soon enough but until I had to move it I was just going to let her sleep.

Sometime during the night, she must have waked up, got undressed and crawled under the covers. When I woke up I found myself still in my street clothes covered with a blanket and Sara curled up behind me with her arm around me holding my hand. It made me wonder who was taking care of whom here.

GERMANY
Chapter 83

After the first of the year there were a couple of surprises. I was supposed to go home in March 1962, but my tour of duty had been extended until 25 May 1962. It made sense to me, if I went home in March the Army would have reassigned me for three months and wouldn't have gotten much out of me by the time I took leave and reported in to my next assignment. This way I would get home about three weeks early and they could just give me an early discharge.

That little bit of information didn't break my heart at all. I was still torn between staying and going. The way things were going I was getting to be one of the senior Sp4's around there and while Top didn't come right out and say it, he had indicated that I would be considered for promotion if I stayed around there. This was another very good reason for me to re-enlist for my own vacancy. It was getting nut crunching time. I had to make a decision. My biggest draw back was Sara. She didn't want to stay in Europe and she wasn't in favor of a life in the military and that weighed heavy on my mind.

The second surprise was the company had been given a mission to provide two 12 man squads plus one officer to join another MP Company in K-Town for two weeks while the regular MP unit assigned to K-Town went on field exercises. Of course I was the first to volunteer for that assignment. I figured this would be a great time for

Sara and me to spend sometime together. It was a short notice assignment and I had barely enough time to call Sara and tell her what was happening and that we would be there before week's end.

Those of us that volunteered or "selected" packed our field gear, winter uniforms and loaded it all on a deuce and half. Some were selected to drive every jeep we had in the unit which was only about seven or eight. Not being a field unit we didn't have many field type vehicles.

I don't remember the other unit we joined up with when we arrived but they put us all in a big cold two story barracks that was not normally used. The boilers hadn't been used in no telling how long, they had to get someone over there to fix them and get them in working order, then get them up and running. In the meantime we froze our asses off. We were issued cots to sleep on. If you have ever slept on one you know they aren't the most comfortable things.

I don't know if I mentioned this but back in the old days before computers and such, there were manual typewriters and carbon paper and whiteout. If you could type more than 10 words a minute without making a mistake you were considered most desirable by any and everybody in need of a typist. As soon as they asked if anyone could type I raised my hand. I had learned long before that if you could type you got the best jobs. As it turned out I got assigned as day shift desk clerk. Things couldn't have worked out better.

Sara would drop me off at work in the morning and pick me up in the afternoon when I got off. The girls in the back office loved me because I was a good typist and they didn't spend all their time correcting what I typed. I could even do a Serious Incident Report (SIR) which required a ton of copies (usually you had to make two originals just to get sufficient readable copies to go to everybody that should get one).

For two weeks Sara and I played house. While the other guys were freezing their butts off sleeping in that rat trap they called a barracks and from what I heard eating lousy mess hall chow, I was staying at the BOQ, which in case of emergency was close enough to were I worked I could walk to work in about 20 minutes cutting through the woods and down the hill.

Sara and I naturally had a lot of time to talk. On a couple of occasions I tried to point out to Sara this is how it would be if we got married and stayed in Germany. I didn't push it but I was hoping it would sway her ideas of what family life could be like in the military. She always had a response to the contrary; bringing up things like shift work; moving around a lot and kids, if we had any, never being able to stay in one school or making any friends.

I really didn't have any come back at the time for any of that stuff and she seemed to pretty well have her mind made up; so I guess my mind was made up too. I would be going home in May.

The two weeks went by quickly. It seemed we no more got there than it was time to leave. Actually the Administrative Officer, who knew about my relationship with Sara, like everyone else knew, asked me if I would consider transferring down to K-Town to work in his admin section. I told him I was short, would be rotating in May and I really liked Heidelberg and the unit I was in. He understood and wished me luck.

The last night we were in K-Town I had to spend the night with the rest of the unit in that cold lousy barracks so I could be there bright and early the next morning when we took off. I didn't know this until halfway through my shift; so I didn't get a chance to tell Sara until she came to pick me up.

Needless to say neither of us were too happy about it; but we had no choice but to go along with it. The good thing about it if there was one; was that I didn't have to be back at the barracks until midnight. We decided to make the most of it and go to supper at the club. I was a little concerned that I might run into some officer I knew since I had been working around there now for a couple of weeks. We stuck to the dining room, which wasn't very crowed, and didn't have any problems.

"What time do you leave tomorrow?" Sara asked.

"I'm not sure. I heard roll call was at 0500 in the morning, but that doesn't mean we will leave right away," I said.

"Who's going to keep my feet warm tonight?" She pouted.

"Well, I'm sure there are a lot of guys in the club over there that would be more than happy to volunteer to do that for you," I replied.

"Screw you!" she said as she threw a piece of ice at me. "That's not what I want. I want you to keep my feet warm," she whined.

"Well, I see you're trying to clean up your language anyway," I laughed.

She grinned, "Only because there are other people sitting within earshot, and I said I would be a lady in public. And I'm so pissed I want to scream. Isn't there any way you can stay one more night?"

"I wish I could, sugar, but they aren't going to take a chance on leaving someone behind. I know there will be bed check tonight and roll call in the morning. I can't afford to miss either one of those things and hope to stay out of trouble. They have been overlooking me not living in the barracks for the past two weeks because they know about you, or us, I should say. And if I had missed one day of work or even just been late they would have had my ass back in the barracks before you could bat an eye."

Our supper came and we ate pretty much in silence, both lost in our own thoughts. I know Sara was dreading me going back to the barracks tonight as much as I was. We paid our bill and left the club right away. I still had some stuff at the BOQ I had to pick up to take back to the barracks with me. I wasn't looking forward to getting back out in the cold and spending the night in that barracks. I'm not sure I could even still find the bunk I was assigned.

As soon as we got back I rounded up all my stuff and put it in a bag and set it by the door. Mary Ann was in her room but before she could come over to Sara's room; Sara shut and locked the door. I was sitting on the bed smoking a cigarette. Sara walked over, took the cigarette out of my mouth, put it out and straddled me, putting her arms around my neck, her skirt sliding up over her thighs. "We have time for a refresher course on lesson number two, cowboy?" she asked as she leaned down and nibbled on my ear lobe.

I kissed her neck. "We might even be able to review lesson number three if you study real hard," I said as I pulled her down on top of me.

"'I'll study. *Real hard*, is your part," she whispered.

"In that case I've almost accomplished my part already," I grinned. "I might miss bed check tonight."

GERMANY
Chapter 84

By the time we got back to the company, Chuck had left; he had gone home to Mississippi. I was disappointed that I had missed him. I knew he was leaving but I thought I would be back before he departed. I talked to Roach, he said D'Angelo had bought Chuck's old Mercedes and he gave me a piece of paper with Chuck's name and address on it. I looked at the paper.

"Maurice C. Lane?" I said out loud. "Who the hell is Maurice C. Lane?"

"That's Chuck," Roach said. "That's his real name, Maurice C. Lane. He hates Maurice and didn't want everybody calling him "Reecie." That's why he never told anybody until the day he left, and he told me you were the only one I could tell. But only if you promised to keep it to yourself."

"Reecie. I laughed. I can understand why he never told anyone. What about the rest of the address?" I asked as I looked at the piece of paper; it only says Maurice Lane, Magnolia, Mississippi?"

"He told me that was all you would need. If you ever get to Magnolia just ask for Maurice Lane, and they would know who you were talking about," Roach said.

"I wonder what they do in Magnolia on a summer night; watch the june bugs fly around?" I said to no one in particular as I put Reecie's address in my wallet.

"So how was K-Town?" Roach asked as we lit a cigarette and sat down in his room. I assumed you stayed with Sara while you were there?

I gave Roach a general rundown. I told him I stayed with Sara all except the last night and that I got a job offer down there if I wanted it. I also told him about trying to sway Sara over to staying in Germany and getting married while we were here and how well that didn't go over; and that I would be going home in May.

"What's been going on back here?" I asked.

I looked over at Chuck's old bunk that was empty now and asked if anyone else left while I was gone.

"Shep left, but you knew that, right? Truman is outprocessing now and leaves the end of the week, I think. We have a couple of new 'cruits down in the Pit. They seem like nice guys. I think they'll fit in once they get the hang of it."

"So what are you gonna do?" I asked.

"I'm going to extend my tour about six months I think. Bobbie Jo's dad doesn't rotate until August, and I thought I would stay and try to leave about the same time he does. I'm hoping I can get orders for the same place he gets assigned when he rotates."

"What are the chances of that?" I asked.

"I talked to the sergeant over in personnel in charge of assignments. He told me if I could give him enough lead time he could try but couldn't promise anything. But I figure it's worth a shot," Roach explained.

"Can't hurt to try," I replied. "You going to chow?"

Roach and I walked over to the mess hall and joined Tom, Hobbs and a guy named DeLaney. DeLaney had been around the company for sometime but he had been working back in the operations section and seemed to be a nice guy but had never really mixed with the other guys until we started getting short of personnel, and they hired a civilian to fill his position and brought him back out to do regular MP duties with the rest of us.

About the second weekend in February, I got a three day pass. Sara and I drove up to Bonn, Germany which was at that time the capitol of

West Germany. Sara wanted to see if she could locate a distant cousin she had that lived there. Actually she was trying to do her mother a favor, it seems they had lost contact with this guy and wanted Sara to see if she could find him with the last address they had for him. Sara had tried to contact him by phone, but there was no listing for him. That didn't mean he didn't live there anymore, just that he didn't have phone.

We drove up as soon as I got off work on Friday afternoon and arrived in Bonn late evening. We found a place to stay and hustled out to find someplace to eat. We found a little bistro type place just before it closed. In fact they let us in, and we were their last customers for the evening. Sara talked to the lady that waited on her getting some directions to the address she had for her cousin and the lady was very helpful. We finished our meal, thanked the lady for her help, left and went back to the hotel.

Bright and early Saturday morning we were up and after our showers, Sara's cup of instant coffee we were out the door. It didn't take long to find the address. Sara knocked on the door and talked to the lady that answered. They didn't know her cousin, they had lived there for about a year and the place was empty when they moved in.

Not one to give up easy, Sara asked some of the neighbors, a couple knew of him but didn't really know him. They said he had moved a little over a year ago but nobody knew where he had gone.

About lunch time we decided this was pretty much a lost cause and decided just to look around the city as long as we were there. Sara got on her shopping kick and we hit all the little shops along the Hauptstrasse; she found one of those figurine shops and bought a couple of those she liked.

As we were driving around we saw a sign for the US Embassy. We decided to follow the signs and see what the Embassy had to offer. There was a US Marine Guard at the gate. We asked him about what there was to do around Bonn and recommendations for places to eat. He kinda laughed and said there wasn't much more to do in Bonn than any other German town. They had some clubs and so forth. He did mention that the Embassy had a little movie theater that showed

American Movies and they had a really nice club that we could use as American citizens. We thanked the Marine and headed back to our hotel.

"What do you want to do?" I asked Sara.

"Well, I don't want to spend any more time looking for my cousin. I think he has just moved somewhere and hasn't bothered to tell anyone," Sara replied.

"Okay, what about tonight? Want to go to that movie at the Embassy and maybe their club?" I asked.

"We should have asked what movie was showing and what time it started."

"Yeah, we should have. We could check this evening on the movie, and if it isn't something we want to see we could just go to the club and get something to eat," I suggested.

"Okay, that sounds like a good idea. Right now I'd like to get back to the hotel and take a good hot shower," she said.

"Want some company?" I asked with a sly grin on my face.

"No."

"No?" I asked in surprised. "Why not?"

"Because you hog the hot water, and I have to stand out in the cold," she said.

"Awww, but baby, I'll keep you warm," I promised.

"You always say that, but I still always end up standing in the cold," she snipped.

"Okay, but this time I really promise to let you stand under the hot water," I said.

"Well, we'll see, but if you make me stand in the cold I'll squeeze your balls off!" she swore.

"But baby, if I stand in the cold you won't be able to find 'em to squeeze," I laughed as I leaned over and gave her a kiss.

We arrived back at the hotel, immediately stripped and headed for the shower. It took a few minutes for the water to start to warm up. I let her step in and get in under the hot water. As soon as she was wet all over I stepped in behind her and put my arms around her. "See? Now we are both under the hot water," I said. She turned around and put her arms around my neck and gave me a kiss. "You better not move if you know what's good for you," she threatened.

"I promise, I'll wash your…back from right here," I said with a grin as my hand slipped between us.

"That's not my back," she grinned.

"Well, I have to start somewhere and work my way around," I replied.

"You're such a liar," she said as she kissed me and pressed her body closer to mine.

We enjoyed our shower until the water started getting cold and then hopped out of the shower and toweled off. I wrapped a towel around my waist and stepped out into the bedroom, got a coke from the cooler, lit a cigarette and sat down on the sofa. I let Sara have the bathroom first; it was still steamy in there, and you couldn't see in any of the mirrors anyway, and I needed to be able to see to shave.

Sara finished in the bathroom; I went in, shaved, brushed my teeth and threw on some Old Spice. By the time I finished she was almost dressed. I got dressed and then waited while she did that last minute touch up stuff women do. Finally she was ready to go.

We arrived at the Embassy; naturally there was a different Marine Guard on duty. We showed our identification and told him what the other guard had told us. He said that was correct and gave us directions to the little movie theater and the club.

I parked the car, Sara got out and I locked it up. We walked down this little outside walkway following the signs to the movies. There was a schedule of current and coming movies. The current was Beach Blanket Bingo or some shit like that. Sara and I both passed on that and continued to follow the signs on down to the Club.

To say I was surprised when we walked in the club would be an understatement. I had only been in a few NCO and Enlisted Clubs and the one Officer's Club at Ramstein, but none of them even came close to this place.

As you stood in the entrance way the whole wall to your left was solid glass and looked out over a grassy sloping area that led down to what I presumed was the Rhine River. You could see the boats moving up and down the river and barely make out some of the buildings across the river. Of course that could have been from fog rolling above the river.

The club itself was two tiered. The lower tier was the dining room, very plush in a thick dark blue carpet, with obviously heavy solid wood tables, and soft leather chairs that rolled smoothly on the carpet. The upper tier which was two or three steps up from the dining room was the bar. It too was covered in the dark blue heavy carpet. It was separated from the dining room by a solid glass wall. You could sit at the bar in tall soft padded stools or sit at one of the tables with similar chairs as those in the dining room.

And last but not least in the far corner of the dining room in the right corner was a small dance floor with a four piece band playing music you could actually talk over without having to yell.

As usual we were rather early for dinner and had no trouble getting the head waiter to give us a table near the glass windows over looking the river. We took our seats, with the head waiter helping Sara into her chair before he left. He had no more than left and I was getting comfortable before Sara cracked my shins with the toe of her high heels.

"Ouch! I almost yelled. What the hell was that for?" I asked in disbelief.

"That's for the first time you look at that blonde sitting at the bar," she said.

"Shit, I haven't even looked in that direction yet," I said rubbing my shin. "But since I've already paid for it I'm gonna look now."

I moved my legs so my shins wouldn't be in the same location as they were then turned and looked towards the bar. Damn I thought Sara may have to kick me again. Sitting at the bar on one of the high stools was this very long-legged, long-haired blonde with a very short skirt on and some really skinny high heels. I couldn't tell what color her eyes were but I knew she had legs just like I like 'em, feet on one end and pussy on the other.

I kept that last thought to myself as I slowly pulled my gaze away from the blonde and back to Sara.

"Not a bad-looking woman," I lied. She was gorgeous but there was no way I was telling Sara that.

Sara leaned towards me. "Sweetie, you're such a liar when it comes to women. She is a very pretty woman. But I love you for lying to me about it."

I just sat there and stared at her. My mind was a total blank. I wasn't even going to try to figure that one out. I thought maybe in twenty years the answer will come to me. The waiter from the bar came over to our table to see if we wanted drinks about the time my mind started to function again. I ordered a rum and coke Sara had her usual glass of wine.

Our waiter came over about half way through our drinks with menus, laid them on the table, and then moved off. I picked up the menu, opened it and I could read every word, it was all in English. It was just like any menu you might find in a very nice up scale restaurant back in the states.

After looking it over for a few minutes I decided I wanted a tossed green salad with blue cheese dressing, a combo plate of steak and shrimp and a glass of ice tea. I laid my menu down and just like magic the waiter appeared. Sara ordered a seafood platter with a tossed green salad with blue cheese. I gave the waiter my order and he moved off to the kitchen.

"This is a pretty nice place, ain't it?" I asked.

"Isn't it?" Sara said.

"I think it is," I said.

"No, you said, 'ain't it;' you should have said 'isn't it,'" Sara said.

I wasn't sure if she was correcting my English which she had never done before or if she was just screwing with me. "Well, either way it's a nice place," I said, rather irritated. I motioned to the bar maid to bring me another drink.

Sara turned and looked at me. "You're upset with me, aren't you?" she asked.

"Sugar, I love it when we banter back and forth. I don't even really get upset when you kick my shins or punch me in the ribs. It tells me how you feel about me, but I'm not one of your students, and in Texas 'ain't it,' is an acceptable phrase. And sometimes I let a little Texan slip into my vocabulary."

"I'm sorry; I won't ever do that again," she said as she reached across the table and squeezed my hand.

The waiter brought my other drink, set it on the table, and moved over to another table. I lit a cigarette and offered Sara one. She took it, and I lit it for her. The place was starting to fill up a little and the little quartet began to play some soft music.

"Would you like to dance?" I asked noticing that a few other couples had taken to the dance floor.

"Yes, if you promise not to get even by stepping on my toes."

"I ain't promising nuttin'." I grinned.

Sara laughed, as I helped her from her chair and we walked to the dance floor. She glided into my arms with ease, our bodies molded together. Her being so tall made it a pleasure to dance with her. Most of the women I had ever danced with had been rather short, and it got a little uncomfortable sometimes.

We danced to a couple of songs and then returned to the table. We no more than got back than our food arrived. There was a lot of everything. We took our time eating. We watched the boats with their lights on moving up and down the river and watched other couples on the dance floor. Someone had that tall blonde out there, but I pretended not to notice. I didn't wanna go through that again.

We finished our meal, ordered another drink, danced a few more times and then finally left the club. It was a very enjoyable evening all things considered. Sara made it difficult for me to stay mad or upset with her for very long. And as I was driving home she was making it extremely difficult to be upset with her. When we got back to the hotel she made it totally impossible to be mad at her. I couldn't help but think I should get mad at her more often.

GERMANY
Chapter 85

The first of March I took three days leave. We were going to go to Luxembourg. Actually we were going to Brussels, Belgium but you had to pass through Luxembourg to get there. Driving through Luxembourg took all of about 30 minutes I think. It is one of the smallest countries in the world. There really isn't much to see there except museums and stuff like that which I think I have said I really don't enjoy very much unless there is something there I am familiar with.

Our goal in Brussels was a particular statute called Manneken Pis, which loosely translated, as I understand it, is peeing boy. It's a statue of a little boy peeing. One story is he used to pee beer instead of water. Roach would have loved that. One of the stories as to how the statue came to be is that a little boy peed against the door of a witch living where the fountain stands now. To punish the little boy, she turned him into a statue. What a bitchy witch. They say the statue is sometimes dressed in seasonal costumes.

I was expecting to see a big statue in the middle of a square somewhere in the center of town but instead the actual statue is stuck next to a building and not really all that big. I was a little disappointed but at least it was a little different. It's not every day you see a statue of a kid pissing. On the other hand if you drive through France you can see a real kid pissing along side the road.

We weren't too impressed with Manneken Pis and only spent one night in Brussels and then took our time driving back to K-Town. Sara seemed to be awfully quiet throughout the whole trip so far. Finally I had to ask. "You seem awfully quiet this trip. You have something on your mind? Something you want to tell me?" I asked

Sara hesitated for a few minutes then said, "Yes, I do need to tell you something."

"Okay, I'm waiting, and don't you dare tell me you're pregnant again. Well, not again, again, I mean like you weren't when you told me you were before but weren't."

Sara laughed, "You want to say that again?"

"No, you know what I mean. Just tell me what it is you have to tell me," I replied.

"I thought you were going to be going home around the 15th of this month like you had told me, so Mary Ann and I signed up for a tour to Switzerland over spring break with a bunch of the other teachers. I can't get my deposit back, but I won't go if you don't want me to go," she offered.

I sat there quietly for a while thinking about this new development. Actually it wasn't all that bad, except it was time we wouldn't be spending together. Tom and Hobbs and DeLaney were trying to rent a car to take on a vacation to Berlin and then to Denmark. "When is spring break?" I asked.

"The last week of March, but we would leave the Saturday before and not return until the following Saturday," Sara said. "I can tell you're upset. I won't go. I'd rather spend time with you anyway," Sara stated.

"Wait a minute, I want to spend the time with you, too, but the only way we would get to spend more time together would be for me to take leave when you're off; otherwise I would only see you on the weekends, and you would be stuck in K-Town by yourself. Right?"

"Yes."

"Okay, you can't get your deposit back, it's not right you should have to lose that money, and I don't want to have nothing to do on the weekends while you're gone. Tom, Hobbs and a guy named DeLaney are looking for a car to rent because they want to go to Berlin and Denmark and a couple of other places I think. Since you're going to be gone Blue Bitch will just be sitting at the BOQ or I'll take it back with me. I could take her back and go on leave with those guys and make them pay for the gas. It would be a cheap vacation for me. So you go on your trip, and I'll go with the guys on one. How does that sound to you?"

Now she was quiet again. I could see her thinking. "I'd almost rather lose my deposit and go somewhere with you," she finally said.

"Sugar, you must have wanted to go on this tour; otherwise you wouldn't have signed up for it. And I know you don't like losing money."

"I guess you're right. I was looking forward to it, but that was before I knew you were still going to be here," she said.

"It's okay; you made a decision on the information you had available to you at the time. That's all you could have done, or all I could have done. But now that you have made your decision; I can make one based on what I know. If I take Blue Bitch it will give me a chance to see some other parts of the world I've never seen an probably won't ever get a chance to see again, and it will be pretty cheap trip since all the other guys will be buying the gas."

Sara didn't say anything else about it the rest of the trip home. Neither did I. We just made some small talk until we pulled up in front of the BOQ. We unloaded the car and took everything up to the apartment.

Mary Ann was home for a change, and she came over and asked about our trip. Sara told her all about it. I just kinda took care of my own stuff and then sat back, smoked a cigarette, and drank a coke.

Mary Ann didn't want to seem to leave, and I could tell Sara wasn't really interested in talking to her. Mary Ann asked if we were hungry; I wasn't really hungry, and Sara didn't seem all that interested either, but when Mary Ann volunteered to go get pizza, Sara saw it as an opportunity to get rid of her for a while, and maybe after we ate she would go to bed, so we agreed to buy the pizza if she would go get it.

Mary Ann threw on her coat and hustled out the door to go get the pizza. Sara came over, lit a cigarette, sat down beside me, and leaned her head on my shoulder.

"I feel like shit now. I don't want to go to Switzerland," she said. "Why don't you come with us? I'll bet there is room for one more, and I'll pay your deposit. I'll pay for it all."

"Oh, come on now; you know I don't feel comfortable around those people you work with. I'd be miserable the whole time, and I don't ski or any of that other winter sport stuff. You just go and have a good time," I said. "It's just a bump in the road; we'll both get over it, and besides we'll both be busy so the time will go by fast."

"You sound like you're anxious to get rid of me." She pouted.

"Don't start that with me now. You know that's not true," I said.

"What if you see some pretty blonde Scandinavian women?"

"I'll make sure Tom knows he is supposed to kick my shins or punch me in the ribs if he catches me looking at any blonde Scandinavian women," I said.

Sara laughed, put her arms around me, gave me big lip locking kiss and said, "I love you, Bones."

Mary Ann was back with the pizza much quicker than we wanted but the mood had lightened up some since she left so it wasn't so bad that she was back. We ate pizza, the girls drank beer, I had a coke and we played some three handed cut throat pinochle. After I had whipped their butts in a couple of quick games the girls decided they had had enough. Mary Ann went back to her room leaving Sara and I alone.

We were tired from our trip so we closed up shop relatively early and went to bed. Sara blew out the candle and slipped in bed beside me. She didn't waste any time crawling right over and into my arms. I rolled over and gave her a kiss and told her I loved her. She put her finger on my lips and said.

"Can we just lie here like this for a while and not talk? I just want to feel your arms around me tonight."

I kissed her on the forehead and said, "Sure."

That was the last thing I remember.

GERMANY
Chapter 86

I got back to the company on Monday morning. It was my day of grace so I didn't have to go to work. I signed in, went upstairs to Tom's room. He and Hobbs had worked the midnight shift and were in bed already. DeLaney was working Campbell Barracks. I would just have to wait to talk to them about the trip.

Roach was off; I went in and caught him actually working on his boots, which was different; Roach didn't work on his boots a lot. "What happened? Someone step on your toes?"

"No, I just decided I needed to do some work on 'em," he said.

"How long you been here now? And you're just figuring that out?"

"Fuck you, Bones. Don't start with me this early in the morning," Roach snapped. "And why aren't you working? This is Monday morning, isn't it?"

I could tell Roach had a good weekend if he wasn't sure what day it was.

"Yeah, it's Monday, but it's my day of grace. I just got back off leave."

"You go on leave more than any person I know. You spend more time on leave than you do working. How do you get away with that?" Roach inquired.

"I dunno, I just ask for it. I think everybody else tries to hang on to their leave in case of emergency or they want to get paid for it when they get out. I'd rather use mine if I have it coming. And I'm fixing to use some more if Tom and Hobbs are still looking for a car to rent."

Roach gave me that quizzical look, like "What the hell are you talking about?" so I explained to him about those guys looking for a car and Sara going to be gone to Switzerland, and I would have Blue Bitch.

"You wanna go with us?" I asked. "I'd rather have you go than DeLaney. There is something about that guy that just doesn't fit."

"I'd like to go, Bones, but I don't have the money, and I need to be around here for Bobbie Jo."

"You wanna explain that?" I asked.

"It's nothing, really; she is just having problems with her parents. She wants to move into a place of her own. She can't afford it, I can't afford it, and together we can't afford it, so I just try to keep her on track so she doesn't do something stupid."

"I thought you and Chuck had that little studio place you shared?" I asked.

"We did, but with Chuck gone I can't afford it by myself, and I don't trust anyone else enough but you to share it with, and you don't need it," Roach said.

"You going to noon chow?" I asked.

"I was thinking about the snack bar. I'm in the mood for a hotdog with chili. Wanna go?"

"Why not? That sounds pretty good. I haven't had one of those in a long time," I said.

Roach put up his shine gear, and we headed for the snack bar.

We ordered our chili dogs and found a table in the corner away from the jukebox. A chili dog really hit the spot; I hadn't had one of those in so long I forgot what one tasted like. We ate like we were starved. Roach got up and went to order another one; I hollered at him to get me one too. He came back with the two chili dogs and we gobbled them up too.

After knocking off the second one, we sat back, lit a cigarette, and sipped on our cokes. We just sat there and shot the shit for a while; he asked me about this trip Tom and the guys were planning. I told him I didn't have all the details but I just saw it as a way to get to see some more of Europe that I wouldn't ever get a chance to see again and with me providing the ride and them buying the gas it would be a cheap trip for me. I tried to talk him into going. He said he would like to but he just needed to stay close to home as he put it.

Finally we strolled back over to the company, he went down to the day room; I went back up to see if Tom was awake yet. Tom was sitting on his bunk in his boxers smoking a cigarette when I walked in. "Hey, Bones, you back already?" he asked.

"Yeah, this was a short trip," I replied.

"I got a couple of questions for you if you're awake enough to talk yet."

"Oh, yeah, I'm awake. Shoot, what're your questions?"

"Are you, Hobbs, and DeLaney still planning a trip up to Berlin and Denmark?" I asked.

"If we can find a car we can rent cheap, we are."

"How does a fee of gas only sound to you?" I asked

"No rental fee?" Tom inquired.

"No rental fee. You just have to put up with me tagging along," I said.

I explained to Tom about Sara having made some plans, and her car being available and she was just going to give it to me to watch anyway and wouldn't expect any payment for it, just as long as we didn't wreck it. I told Tom I needed him to get a civilian drivers' license if he didn't have one already so he could relieve me of some of the driving. He agreed.

I told Tom the car would be available the last week of March but we could pick it up the Friday night before and be ready to leave the next morning.

"Okay, I'm in," he said as he picked up a boot and threw it at Hobbs, who was still asleep in his bunk. The boot bounced off his butt and he rolled over still half asleep.

"What the fuck you throwing shit at me for?" he sleepily mumbled.

"I got us a car for our trip," Tom said. "Bones is gonna have his girl's car, and we can use it."

Hobbs finally realized I was in the room and said, "Hey, Bones, that's cool; you going with us?"

"You don't think I'd let you clowns take the car by yourself, do you?" I asked.

"Well, all right then, now we just need to get DeLaney lined up. When are we leaving?"

"Get your ass outta bed, and let's go eat, and I'll tell you about it then. You going to chow, Bones?"

"Naw, Roach and I went to the snack bar already. I'm going back to my rack and just kick back for a few minutes then go take a shower. I have to get ready for work tomorrow anyway. We'll all get together and talk later," I said as I walked out the door.

I went back to my room, kicked off my shoes, lay back on my bunk, and lit a cigarette. *I guess we are all set,* I thought, *just have to tighten the screws a little bit and we'll be on our way in a couple of weeks.*

GERMANY
Chapter 87

The next couple of weeks the guys and I spent fine tuning our trip. Tom went down and got a civilian driver's license. DeLaney, I found out already had one so in a pinch he could drive but to be honest I didn't like that idea. We were a little concerned about our leave request being approved in time since each leave had to be approved by some higher authority before we could actually leave and drive across the Helmstadt Autobahn.

Finally our leaves came back approved and the following Friday as soon as Tom and I got off work at Campbell Barracks we hustled down to the Bahnhof and grabbed the first train to K-Town. Tom was impressed with the train ride but that was only because he didn't do it every week and he was flirting with the girl sitting across the isle from us.

We arrived in K-Town and took a cab straight to the BOQ. Sara was expecting us and opened the door right away, almost before I knocked. She had met Tom before so they said hi and no introductions were needed. She had her suitcases out and was beginning to pack for her trip.

Sara offered us a coke as she continued to pack. She acted as though she was excited about her trip but I got the feeling that she really wasn't. She gave me her gas coupons for the rest of the month since she wouldn't need them.

Tom and I drank our cokes and smoked a cigarette. I was uneasy, I really wasn't crazy about Sara going on her trip anymore than she was crazy about me going on mine but we had already made our plans.

"When are you leaving?" Sara asked.

"We hope to get out as early as we can in the morning," I replied.

"And where are you going? Berlin and then Denmark?"

"And then over to Amsterdam," Tom said.

"Sounds like a fun trip," Sara said.

"Tom, has Rick told you what you're supposed to do yet?" Sara asked grinning.

"You mean about punching his ass out if he looks at another woman?" Tom answered.

"You understand perfectly," Sara said laughing.

"No sweat; I'll keep him straight," Tom laughed.

We finished our cokes, Tom sensing that Sara and I needed some alone time said he was heading downstairs. I told him I'd be right down. I pitched him the keys as he headed for the door and told him to warm the blue bitch up. He nodded and exited the apartment.

"Well, guess I'll see you in about a week. Don't break your leg skiing or whatever it is you're going to do," I said.

Sara walked over to me put her arms around my neck and gave me a kiss. "I'll be careful, and you stay out of trouble," she threatened.

"Getting in trouble doesn't even sound exciting anymore if it's not with you," I replied.

She punched me in the ribs and said, "You better mean that."

I leaned forward put my arms around her and gave her a kiss. "I better get going so you can pack, and we need to get back and get our act together. I love you," I said.

"Okay, I love you, too; drive careful."

I kissed her again then turned walked out of the apartment and headed downstairs. Tom had the car running and ready to go.

I hopped in on the passenger side and said, "You might as well get used to driving this thing so let's go."

Tom slipped the car in gear backed out, and we were on our way back to Heidelberg.

Tom did well on the drive back; he didn't have any trouble with the German road signs and found his way back to Patton Barracks once we got back in the city. Billy Stearns waved us through the gate at Patton and we drove straight to the parking area on the side of the building. We exited the car, Tom locked it up and pitched me the keys and we walked inside. First thing we did was find Hobbs and DeLaney to let them know we were back and had the car.

We all agreed to be up by 0600, go grab some chow and be on the road by at least 0730. Everybody went their separate ways and started packing. I had told them all to try and keep it down to one bag if possible but no more than two if necessary. I had gotten pretty good at packing for these little trips, but I was used to packing at Sara's and always getting some help from her.

I was packed by 2200 hours; I sat down on the bunk and lit a cigarette. Tom came in and said he was ready to go. Roach stopped by and said he wished he was going with us. He didn't say it but I got the impression that he and Bobbie Jo had been arguing again. I told him we could squeeze one more in if he wanted to go, knowing that he really wouldn't accept.

Hobbs and DeLaney stopped in to let us know they were ready. Rizzo followed them in to get ready for the midnight shift, he was running late. We didn't even get a "What do you say, lover," out of him, and he didn't even try to bum a cigarette. Those had to be a sure signs that he was having women troubles. After a few minutes Harry and Dietz came in with a big bottle of Double Bach German Beer, a sure sign they made a last-call stop at The Last Chance Saloon, just outside the gate. They weren't feeling any pain, and were more than happy to share their beer. Between all of us except Rizzo it didn't take long to finish off the bottles.

By the time the beer was gone so was everybody else. I got up, got undressed and crawled in the sack. I really wasn't sleepy but knew I needed to try to get a few hours sleep before we hit the road tomorrow.

I guess I was more tired than I realized because the next thing I remembered was the CQ coming in to wake up Dietz and Harry to get ready for work. It was 0530 I climbed out of the bunk, slipped on some clothes and walked down to Tom's room. He was dressed and putting on his shoes; Hobbs was not far behind. The three of us walked down to Delaney's room to check on him. He was dressed, so we all headed for the mess hall.

We all ate quickly and by 0630 we had returned to the barracks, grabbed our bags, signed out on leave and had blue bitch loaded and ready to go. I slid in behind the wheel and Tom hopped in as my navigator. Hobbs and Delaney took the back seat. I started the car, backed out, put it in drive and we were headed out the gate on our boys only adventure.

GERMANY
Chapter 88

Once we got out on the Autobahn it was every man for himself. Germans have never been known for driving the speed limit, even if they had one. Blue Bitch wasn't exactly the fastest thing on the road so we stayed in the right hand lane and waved to all the other traffic as it passed us by.

There wasn't a lot of chatter in the car. Hobbs and DeLaney fell asleep. Tom and I made some small talk smoked and drank cokes. Being the experienced traveler in the bunch I had brought the cooler from Sara's and filled it up with cokes and ice before we left Heidelberg.

By the time we reached the beginning of the Helmstadt Autobahn Tom was driving as we arrived at the American Check Point. We all exited the car and went inside the little information center, where we received a briefing from an MP sergeant. He showed us two blowup pictures of the autobahn we were to travel. There was to be no deviation of any kind allowed. If we took a wrong exit more than likely we would be arrested or at least detained by Russian or East German troops.

We were told we had a certain amount of time to cross the autobahn. It if took us too long to cross the autobahn they, meaning the Russians or East Germans would come looking for us and it was not too unreasonable to expect to get a speeding ticket if we crossed it too fast. The sergeant gave us two pieces of paper written in English and

German which, should we have car trouble, we were to give to a passing motorist going in both directions and then just sit and wait. We were also given instructions as to what to do if we saw any sort of troop movement along the way.

Finally he checked out leave forms to be sure they were in order and told us that when we proceeded to the next check point, which I believe was the East Germans they would not talk to us and we should be alert for a soldier to come out and lead us to the Russian Check Point, where our papers would be checked. The sergeant made a point that we should only show our paperwork to a Russian Officer. We would be directed as to where to park and only the driver would be allowed to exit the car so he should be sure he had the paperwork and ID cards for all of us before he got out of the car.

"Okay, you guys got any questions?" the sergeant asked.

We all looked at each other; no one seemed to have any questions.

"Okay, good luck, and enjoy your leave," the sergeant said.

We went back out to the car. Tom got in behind the wheel since he had the keys, and we drove up to the checkpoint and waited for the East Germans to raise the gate. Finally the gate was raised and we drove through then given a hand signal by an East German soldier to halt. We stopped. We waited. Finally the soldier in front of us stepped aside but didn't give us any signal to move so we stayed put. A couple of minutes later another soldier came out of the little house they had and began walking down towards the Russian Check point.

"That's him; there he goes. Follow that guy!" Hobbs was hollering from the backseat.

"I see him, Hobbs, I see him. Cool it," Tom replied.

Tom followed the soldier down the road a couple of hundred feet or so. When the soldier reached the Russian Check Point, he walked inside and disappeared. Tom pulled the car up in the closest parking place to the door, I handed him all our paperwork and he got out and walked inside the building. From where I was sitting I could see inside the building and the room Tom was in appeared to be empty. Tom was just standing there when all of a sudden this little widow opened up and a hand reached out.

I could tell what was going through Tom's mind. "Do not show your papers to anyone but an officer." Tom moved closer to the window, bent down, and looked up inside the window. I couldn't help but laugh and expected that hand to reach out and slap Tom upside the head any minute. But Tom apparently was satisfied that he was looking at an officer and put our paperwork in the hand. The hand retreated and the window slammed shut. All Tom could do was stand there.

After a rather lengthy wait a Russian soldier came walking around the corner and past Tom, not saying a word. I could tell he had our paperwork in his hand and Tom saw it too. He rushed out to the car and got in and started following the soldier down to the gate. When we got to the gate the soldier handed our paperwork to another soldier who took his time looking at each piece of paper and then looking at each one of us. Finally he seemed satisfied and motioned for another soldier to raise the gate and motioned us on through. We all let out a simultaneous sigh of relieve and got the hell out of there.

Sara had told me prior to our trip that a good place to stay in Berlin was a place called Wannsee, located southwest of the city of Berlin. Wannsee is basically a summer resort with two lakes and nice beaches and lush surroundings. It wasn't exactly swimming weather yet, and since it was still off season we figured we should get some pretty good rates.

I read the map, Tom navigated through the traffic and we didn't have any problems finding Wannsee. Sara was right about it being a really pretty place. Everything was turning green and flowers were starting to bloom. We found the office and checked in. We got two rooms with double beds; Tom and I in one room and Hobbs and DeLaney in the other. After we got settled in we realized we were hungry. They had a dining room that was open; we figured that was as good a place as any to get something to eat.

After our meal we walked around the area, it really was a pretty place; I would have loved to have a place like that to live. We settled in on a table not far from one of the lakes to talk over our options. None of these guys had ever done any traveling around the country so they didn't have a clue about some things. They thought we should get downtown early and check the places out we might want to see.

"Places don't start hopping until late; there is no need to rush down there now, and everything will be dead. Most people don't even eat until around 2100," I said.

"What about curfew?" DeLaney asked.

"I don't think we have to worry about curfew up here since we are on leave."

"Well, I'm with Bones; he has done more traveling around than any of us. I don't know about the rest of you, but I'm tired and could use a nap, so I'm going back and sack out for a while," Tom said as he put out his cigarette and got up from the table.

"I'm in for a nap myself," I said.

Hobbs and DeLaney agreed and we all went back to our rooms to sack out for a couple of hours. Despite how tired we may have been I don't think any of us did anymore than doze for about an hour. I know I didn't. When I looked over Tom was lying there smoking a cigarette.

We checked with the other guys and they weren't sleeping either so we decided to go ahead and drive into Berlin. Our first target was Check Point Charlie which was located on the other side of town from where we were. For the most part we just followed Potsdamer Strasse almost all the way to the other end of Berlin and then easily found the then famous check point.

Check Point Charlie was located in the American zone of Berlin, the city being divided into four different sections, Besides the American Zone there were the French and British Zones, and I believe the other zone belonged to the Russians. It wasn't a problem to climb up in the tower and look across the wall into East Germany. We got there just about sundown and the buildings on the other side of the wall which appeared to be deserted were casting long shadows making it look almost like it was midnight already. The place looked like a ghost town, no one on the streets, occasionally you might see movement in the shadows and in some places you could see a single low wattage bulb burning some place off in the distance.

It didn't take but a few minutes of looking across that wall to make you want to get outta there. If that was the way the rest of East Berlin looked it certainly made you appreciate being in West Berlin. We climbed down off the tower, asked the MP on duty for some directions to this club we had heard about. He gave us some general directions, we thanked him and off we went.

We found the club we were looking for, I thought I would never forget the name of it but now I can't think of it to save my soul. The unique thing about this club was that each table had a phone on it. Above the table was a tall pole that could be seen from almost anywhere in the club despite its size. You could be sitting at table #36, and if you saw someone you would like to talk to at table #75 you could call 75, and it would ring at that table, but the people at table 75 would never know who was calling them.

We were led to a table for four, and I got the seat next to the wall dividing the table area from the dance floor; which I suspect had an ice rink under it. My seat put me right next to the phone. We all ordered a drink and sat and marveled at the size of this club and watched the people dancing. It wasn't long before our phone began to ring. Since I was the closest I ended up answering the thing. Most of the time the person spoke German and my little bit of German didn't seem to impress them and they would hang up. After a couple of calls I turned the phone answering duties to Tom. He didn't have any better luck than I did.

We were just enjoying the place and our drinks and the phone kept ringing. I answered one and the lady asked me in German if I danced. I understood that and said yes, but a slow dance is best for me. Then she said in English I will come get you at the next slow dance and hung up. I hung up and told the guys what that call was all about and none of us believed it so we just went on about our drinking and just enjoying ourselves.

I was looking around at the various tables over on our side of the dance floor and had my back slightly turned away from the floor when I suddenly realized that the guys were all looking at me. I had no idea why, and then I felt the presence of someone to my right which would have put them on the dance floor. I turned; there stood a rather tall, blonde-haired young lady looking at me. Smiling, she asked, "You dance slow dances, no?"

"I dance slow dances, yes," I said.

"OUCH!" I shouted, startling the young lady. Tom had kicked my shins under the table.

Tom looked at me and grinned. "I'm just following instructions," he said.

"Fuck you!" I said in a whisper.

I turned back towards the young lady who had this really strange look on her face. I smiled at her and told her I would meet her at the entrance to the dance floor just a few tables behind us. She nodded okay and walked back towards the entrance.

Hobbs and DeLaney had no idea what the hell was going on and just sat there with this blank look on their faces. I squeezed out of my chair and walked back to the entrance and met the young lady, and we danced a couple of dances.

Through my broken German and her broken English we managed to learn each other's names. She was called Inga; she was not from Berlin but someplace close by. I told her I was on holiday with my friends from Heidelberg. After a couple of dances we parted ways. She went back to her table, and I went back to mine.

When I got back Tom and Hobbs had apparently found a couple of girls to dance with, and DeLaney was there by himself. "How come you're not dancing?" I asked.

"I'm not much of a dancer," he replied.

I sat back down and a few minutes later Hobbs and Tom came back. They didn't hold out any hope of doing anymore than dancing with the gals they had just been with. We had a couple more drinks and then decided to call it a night and went back to our rooms.

Getting back to Wannsee was a trip. Potsdamer Strasse is a series of traffic circles, each one looks like the last one. We were starting to wonder which one we were supposed to take since we really didn't pay any attention when we went downtown. DeLaney didn't make anything easier. Every time we came to a traffic circle he would say, "I think this is it."

"Why do you think this is it?" Tom asked

"I remember that green light," DeLaney replied.

"Delaney, at the last traffic circle you remembered the red light. Did it ever occur to you that all these fuckin' traffic circles have red and green lights?" Tom growled.

Delaney shut up and slid back down a little further in the backseat. Finally we saw a sign for Wannsee and found our way back to the hotel without further assistance from DeLaney.

It didn't take us long to pass out once we hit the rack. The long day and a few drinks took its effect on us right away.

We slept in late the next morning and had brunch at the hotel restaurant. We discussed what we were going to do during the day over coffee, and cigarettes. We finally decided we would just drive into town, find a place to park and just walk the streets to see whatever we saw.

We jumped in blue bitch and headed back into town along Potsdamer Strasse with no help from Delaney. When we figured we were about half way down the road we found a place to park near an American Express office. We figured that would be something DeLaney could recognize if we got lost again.

We walked the streets and found the Brandenburg Gate, one of the remaining gates to the city. Further north of that we found the Reichstag, which is headquarters for the German government. At the time that was the East German government, I guess, because when we started walking up towards it some soldiers with rifles at the ready started walking towards us. We decided we didn't want to see the Reichstag that damn bad, so we turned around and went the other way.

We worked our way back to Potsdamer Strasse and found a place to eat. We decided it was too late to go back to Wannsee now and then come back to town, so we decided to stay and see what kinda trouble we could get into. We stopped in a few clubs to check them out but it was still early for there to be any real action going in the clubs. We did however run into some British soldiers and got to talking to them. They were stationed there and told us there were some pretty nice clubs in the French sector we might want to check out later in the evening.

After really just killing a lot of time and sipping on a few drinks we finally decided that it was about time to find the French Sector. We asked for some directions from some American GIs and they were more than happy to tell us where to go. We made it to the French Sector with only one minor detour, found a place to park and began to check out the various clubs.

Maybe we didn't know where to go or what to look for; or maybe it was just the wrong night, but there didn't seem to be much going on in the French Sector either. We did find this one club that was a pretty nice club and they had a stripper dancing the whole time. Actually they had more than one stripper, one would perform then another one would come out and take her place. It was pretty low key, nobody standing up and whistling at the girls or throwing money at them, actually it didn't seem that people paid too much attention to them at all. Except for four GIs from Heidelberg but we kept our distance.

We sat at the bar when we first walked in; it was a pretty posh club. The chairs we sat in were just that chairs not bar stools. The chairs sat on a platform that elevated you to the height of the bar just like a bar stool would. Hobbs and I sat side by side and both ordered a cognac and coke. There happened to be two girls working behind the bar at the time, one waited on Hobbs and one waited on me.

Our drinks got there about the same time, when Hobbs asked how much the girl said, "That will be four Mark, seventy Pfennings." That was slightly over a dollar.

I asked when my drink arrived and was told by the nice young lady. "That will be Four mark eighty Pfennings."

"Wait a minute. My friend just ordered the same thing I did, and his drink was only Four mark seventy Pfennings. Why is mine four Mark eighty Pfennings?" I complained.

The girl looked at me then said, "You see the line here on the bar? She asked as she pointed to what appeared to be a break or joint in the bar.

"Yes, I see it," I replied.

Waving her arm towards the other girl she said, "That side of the bar is hers, this side of the bar is mine. She has her prices, and I have mine; that will be four Mark eighty Pfennings."

I had to laugh. The difference in ten Pfennings is maybe two cents. But I had to act indignant, so after paying four Mark eighty Pfennings for my drink I got up and moved to a chair on the other side of Hobbs. Then I stuck my tongue out at my former waitress. She was a good sport and just laughed.

We drank our drinks and watched the strippers strip. After the second stripper stripped, we decided we had seen enough and decided to go on back to Wannsee. Tom drove, once we got on Potsdamer Strasse he couldn't help but ask DeLaney at every traffic circle if there was anything there he recognized. DeLaney just kept his mouth shut and shot Tom the bird every time he asked.

We decided we would leave in the morning and head for Hamburg.

GERMANY
Chapter 89

We were on our way to Hamburg early the next morning. It was a relatively short drive compared to some we had. We had to stop along the way and re-load the cooler since we forgot to do that before we left Berlin. There was a little café where we stopped so we decided to get something to eat, we had left Berlin in a hurry and besides not filling the cooler we didn't take time to eat breakfast.

The guy's primary objective in Hamburg was to visit the Reeperbahn or red-light district in Hamburg. I don't know where the guys heard about that place. But I may have mentioned it when Sara and I had returned from visiting her cousin Karl. But I don't remember ever saying anything about it. If you remember Karl spoke a little English and I got Karl's phone number from Sara before we left, promising I would call him when we got to Hamburg.

We got into Hamburg about mid afternoon. I didn't remember where Karl and his family lived but had a general idea of the section of town. I didn't ask DeLaney for directions. I went as far as I thought I could without getting lost then we found a Gästehaus and stopped in for a beer.

I didn't know what time Karl got off work. I didn't want to call him too early but I didn't want to call him too late either. We sat around and had a couple of drinks.

Finally I decided to call Karl, I wasn't even sure he would remember me, and if he didn't there wasn't any sense in us just sitting there. I dug out the piece of paper I wrote his number on and used the phone in the Gästehaus. A male answered the phone, I figured it had to be one of three things, it was Karl since he only had two daughters or I had the wrong number or three, his wife had a visitor.

"Karl?" I asked.

"Ja," came the reply.

"This is Rick, your cousin Sara's friend from Heidelberg," I said hesitantly.

"Ja, Rick, how are you? Are you here in Hamburg?" Karl asked.

"Yes, I am here with three of my friends. We are on holiday and on our way to Denmark," I said.

"Where are you now?" Karl asked.

I had no idea where I was so I called the waitress down to the end of the bar and asked her if she would please tell the man on the phone where we were. She nodded she understood and took the phone.

After a short conversation she handed the phone back to me. I thanked her and continued to talk to Karl who said, "I know where you are. Stay there. I will be there shortly, okay, Rick?"

"Okay, Karl. I am not going any place. I will wait here for you," I said and hung up.

I walked back to the table and explained to the guys what was happening and that Karl should be here shortly. In the meantime we continued to drink our drinks and waited for Karl.

About thirty minutes later a guy walked in; I hadn't seen Karl in almost two years, but it looked like him. He seemed to be looking around so I raised my hand when he looked in our direction. He seemed to recognize me and smiled, waved back, and walked over.

"Rick, how are you?" Karl asked, extending his hand.

"I'm good, Karl. Nice to see you again," I said, shaking his hand and motioning for him to sit down with us. I introduced all the guys to Karl, and he was excited to meet us all, I think.

The waitress brought Karl a beer, and he didn't waste anytime putting it away and ordering a second. "So Rick, how long will you be in Hamburg?"

"Just tonight, Karl; we plan on leaving for Denmark tomorrow."

"Have you found a place to stay?" Karl inquired.

I was afraid to say yes and afraid to say no. I didn't want to disappoint Karl because we didn't wait for him to offer us a place to stay and didn't want to say no, afraid he would. But I told him we had just arrived and hadn't had a chance to look and thought perhaps he could recommend a place.

Thankfully Karl didn't offer us a place at his house but did make a couple of suggestions. He said he would take us down to one that he thought would be best because it was closer to the autobahn and we could get out of town faster when we were ready to leave in the morning. We all agreed that would be a good idea. Finally he asked us all what we were waiting to hear.

"Would you like to go to the Reeperbahn this evening?"

It didn't take us long to make up our minds on that decision. Once that was settled, Karl told us to follow him and he would take us to a hotel. We all finished our drinks and followed Karl out to the parking lot.

Before we left I told Karl. "Karl, remember we are Americans; we don't drive like the Germans do so don't forget we are behind you okay?"

Karl laughed, "Okay, Rick, I will wait for you and make sure you don't get lost."

He got in his car as we piled into blue bitch and we proceeded out of the parking lot with Karl making sure we were right behind him.

The hotel wasn't far from the Gästehaus so it was a short trip. We all went inside but Karl did all the talking he got us two rooms with twin beds and helped us carry our baggage up to the rooms. Tom and I were in one room again. When Karl was satisfied that we were comfortable he suggested that we go to a restaurant right down the street and eat something, we would need something in our stomachs if we were going to the Reeperbahn. Karl said he would be back to pick us up about eight p.m. to take us to "die sundige Meile," the sinful mile.

We agreed and waved goodbye to Karl and said we would be waiting for him when he got back. None of us were really starved but figured we better do what Karl said so we went down to the restaurant down the street from the Hotel and grabbed a bite to eat. The food was pretty good and the service was fast so we were in and out in a short period of time.

"I dunno about the rest of you, but I'm going back and take a nap," Tom said as he lit a cigarette.

We all agreed that was a good idea and after joining Tom in our after dinner cigarette, we paid our bill and walked back to the hotel. It didn't take long for me to fall asleep and I'm sure the other guys didn't have a problem either.

About 8:15 we were awakened by a pounding on our door. I got up and answered it. Karl came smiling into the room and asked were Hobbs and DeLaney were. Tom went next door and woke them up and they joined us in our room. I'm not sure if Karl was excited about having some American friends with him or excited about going to the Rapperbahn, but he was definitely wound up. I kinda chuckled to myself and thought, maybe old Karl needed a boys' night out.

We all hopped in Karl's car and we were off. It was only about a 20 minute drive to the Reeperbahn, at least the way Karl drove. But we arrived safely and he found a place to park without any problems. We got out of the car and looked up and down the street. It seemed like there was everything you wanted on this street, Discos, hundreds of bars, restaurants, strip clubs, a sex museum and brothels. I wasn't about to ask what a sex museum was and I guess none of the other guys were either, we just kinda ignored that.

We walked up and down the streets for a while. If you wanted a woman there were plenty to choose from. We went into a strip club and had a drink and watched the show. The girls on the stage were definitely not bashful and neither were the girls working the customers in the club. They would just come sit in your lap and whisper sweet nothings in your ear, and what it would cost you to get all that sweet nothing was nothing. When you told them you didn't have any money they would just get up and say something like, "Sorry, no money, no honey," and move on to the next possible customer.

I'm not sure what was going on with the other guys. I don't know if they just didn't find a girl they liked or they were a little leery of taking off with one while they were with Karl. I'm not sure but what Karl wouldn't have picked up a girl if I had not been there; or if I had picked one up he might have felt more inclined to do the same. But I wasn't going to pick one up, one because Karl was Sara's cousin and two none of these women interested me; I was only interested in being with Sara.

We all left Reeperbahn with our virginity still in tact and went back to our hotel. We thanked Karl for his hospitality. He wished us a safe trip to Denmark and stop in again on the way back if we wanted to. We all walked quietly back to our rooms. Although we were quiet I didn't get the impression anyone was disappointed.

Tom and I got back to our room and lit up a cigarette as we sat on our beds.

"Well, that was pretty much a waste," Tom said.

"Why was it a waste? What were you expecting?" I asked.

"It was pretty much what I expected, I guess, but when you get right down to it, there isn't much difference between it and Heidelberg; it's just more out in the open here. The girls are all the same, just more open about it all. Basically we could have stayed in Heidelberg and had as much fun," Tom said.

"I think you're right."

"You're lucky you travel around with Sara. She takes you places to see things, and I don't mean boys town either," Tom laughed.

"Yeah, I know, I'm not much of a sightseer as far as museums and old churches and shit like that goes, but it beats just going out to strip joints and bars. And Sara can make things interesting when she puts her mind to it," I said.

"Didn't you say she had a roommate?" Tom asked.

"Yeah, she shares an apartment with another teacher, but I don't know what she is up to. We don't see much of her anymore. I'm not sure if she has some guy she is seeing or what. I know at one time she had found some guy she knew from college stationed somewhere in Germany, and the four of us went on a vacation a couple of years ago.

But since then I haven't seen the guy but a couple of times and haven't seen him recently at all," I explained.

"I was talkin' to Roach the other night, and your name came up. You know what Roach said about you?" Tom stated.

"I don't have a clue. What did Roach say?" I asked.

"He said every guy in the company thinks you're the luckiest son of a bitch in the company."

"What does that mean?" I asked.

"It means, you found an American girl in Germany who speaks German fluently, who has a car, and a job, and is in love with your boney ass. And you two travel all over the place together. You're gone more than you're here anymore, and you two have seen everything; things most of us will never see, and done all those things you've been doing."

Tom lit a cigarette and blew a smoke ring in the air. I lit a cigarette and blew smoke in the air. Never did learn how to do the smoke-ring thing.

"And Roach is right. Shit, look at us. Here we are in Hamburg, Germany, already been to Berlin, and going to Denmark and Amsterdam, and for what? To get laid; hell, we could have done that in Heidelberg," Tom rambled on. "And I'm just talking about me, Hobbs and shit head DeLaney over there are probably dying to get laid somewhere along the line. I dunno what you're doing here. But if you hadn't come along, I wouldn't have gone to the Brandenburg Gate in Berlin, or known what the Rieichstag was or about that place we stayed. None of us would have known about the Reeperbahn if you hadn't told us and would probably never have found the place if you didn't know Karl."

"You sound like you're mad at me," I said.

"I'm not mad at you. I'm jealous, you dummy. You've done something with your tour over here; all the rest of us have done is work, shoot pool, play ping pong, get drunk, and chased some pussy every once in awhile. I'd trade places with you any day, and I know if you asked them other guys they would too."

"Well, I can't argue with you, I got lucky when I met Sara and that things have worked out the way they have; otherwise I'd be in the same boat with the rest of you. But as far as this trip goes, from here on I've lost my edge. I don't know anything about Denmark or Amsterdam. We are all on our own in those places," I said. "And on that note I'm going to bed; I'm tired and I can't stand to hear a grown man cry."

"Fuck you." Tom laughed as he threw his shoe at me. "If you had been living with those other creeps over there as much as I have you would be crying too."

I stripped and turned out the light by my bed and was asleep in no time, but I was aware of the smile I had on my face. It was nice to know that the other guys noticed.

GERMANY
Chapter 90

We checked out of the hotel in Hamburg, stopped by the restaurant Karl had pointed out to us, ate breakfast and then hit the autobahn for Puttgarden, Germany, where we would catch a ferry across the Kiel Bay into Denmark.

It was a relatively short ride to Puttgarden; but we had to wait for the ferry, wait to board the ferry and then wait for the ferry to take off; so we lost a good part of the day just hanging around waiting. It was actually late afternoon or early evening before we actually got underway.

There were a lot of interesting passengers on the ferry, Hobbs and Delaney were almost drooling but unfortunately none of the ladies they met spoke English and neither of them seemed to have the patience to try and communicate. Or maybe they just didn't get any positive vibes from the girls. Tom and I wandered around the ferry; we saw some attractive ladies but looking was all I was allowed to do; Tom reminded me with a punch in the ribs a couple of times. I never really expected him to take Sara's instructions seriously.

The one big thing on that ferry that was missing was something worth eating. They had a buffet laid out and everything on it was some kind of raw fish. We were told they had food aboard the ferry so none of us ate before we got under way. Never having ridden a ferry before no one thought to ask how long it would take to cross the bay. When someone finally thought to ask we learned it was about a 4 to 6 hour trip depending on the weather. From what I could tell looking out the windows, the weather wasn't very good.

We finally docked in Denmark; it took about an hour for us to disembark and clear customs. The first thing we did was find a place to eat that severed something besides raw fish. I think we all had a sausage with some rolls and something to drink. We also learned that it was about 200Km to Copenhagen. We gassed blue bitch and hit the road, we guestimated our time of arrival in Copenhagen as somewhere around 2400 hours.

We were right on with our estimation, we hit the outskirts of Copenhagen right about midnight. We had no idea where we were or what we should be looking for as far as a hotel goes. Surprisingly, it seemed as though shops and businesses were still open at this late hour. As we were driving around downtown trying to figure out what we were going to do, I saw a sign in the window of a shop in German that said, "Zimmer, um zu vermieten." I was pretty sure that meant rooms to rent, so I suggested we stop and go check it out.

Tom parked the car and we all went in. There was an elderly lady behind the counter and I guess we stuck out like sore thumbs because she immediately said in English, "Yes, Gentlemen, may I help you?"

"I surely hope so," I said. "We just arrived in town and need a place to stay for a couple of nights. We really don't know where to go or the best place to be."

"You want a place not too expensive, yes?" she asked.

"Yes, not too expensive."

She started looking through some books she had, then after a few minutes she picked up the phone and made a phone call. She talked to the party on the other end and then hung up.

"I have a place for you down by the waterfront; it is a nice place not far from the old Palace. It is a bed and breakfast run by a very nice couple; and it will only cost $20 American dollars per room. She has two rooms left."

I looked at the guys they all were nodding their heads, yes, so I told the lady we would take it. She wrote down the name of the place, address, the phone number, and gave us a strip map with the route we should take to get there. We offered to pay her for her services, but she said we were nice young men and she would not charge us this late at night. I thought now if we could only find some young women to think we were nice young men we would be all set to go. We thanked her, went back to the car and headed for the bed and breakfast.

It took a little bit of doing but I was navigating and Tom was driving and we made a pretty good team. DeLaney had long since learned to keep his mouth shut and Hobbs didn't give a shit as long as we got there. About 30 minutes later we arrived at our destination.

It didn't look like much from the outside. It appeared to be no more than a two story A Frame building. We got out of the car and went in. An older guy was behind the desk and he was very friendly and asked if we were the gentlemen the lady had referred. I said yes we were.

We registered and he gave us two keys, asked us to follow him. We went down a narrow hallway and out the back door. Across the courtyard sat another small building similar to the one we had just come out of. We walked in and the old guy opened a door on the right and said this is one room. Then he proceeded upstairs and showed us the second room. The upstairs room had one huge double bed while the room down stairs had two single beds.

Now this presented a dilemma; which two guys were going to sleep in that double bed together? I just knew one thing; it wasn't going to be me and DeLaney. There was only one fair thing to do. Flip a coin, two heads got the single beds down stairs, two tails got the double bed.

If I didn't have bad luck I wouldn't have any luck at all. I got half the double bed but on the bright side, Tom got the other half. If I had to share a bed with anyone of those guys it would be Tom of course. It was too late that night to do anything; at least as far as we were concerned so we just grabbed our bags out of the car and moved into our rooms.

Actually the double bed room wasn't such a bad deal after all, what none of us noticed until Tom and I brought our luggage up was that there was a small day bed against the far wall. We figured we could take turns on that especially if one of us got lucky at one of the bars. I took the little day bed the first night; I was used to sharing one not much bigger than that anyway so in a way it was like having my own bed since I was the only one in it.

Around 0900 the next morning there is a knocking on our door, figuring it was Hobbs and or DeLaney I got up in my shorts and answered the door. To my surprise there was this heavy-set lady with a big smile on her face, and a big tray full of rolls, jams, jellies, honey and all sorts of fruit and some coffee. Shortly after she came in, Hobbs and DeLaney followed her in; apparently she had stopped off and got them on the way up. She was a nice lady and just smiled and jabbered away and poured everyone a cup of coffee. She looked surprised when I turned mine down. I told her I wasn't a coffee drinker I preferred orange juice. She nodded her head that she understood and left the room. A few minutes later she returned with a very large glass of orange juice.

Over breakfast we weighed our options for the day. Hobbs and DeLaney were anxious to explore the bars. They had found out from the old man at the desk that the bars in Copenhagen were open 23 hours a day, closing only one hour to clean up and they had a rotating schedule so that all the bars were not closed at the same time. There was always a bar open. I wasn't too excited about that idea. I meant it wasn't even noon yet and these guys wanted to go to the bars already. I didn't say anything; I just kept my mouth shut.

"I think we should look around the city some and see what else is here. I'm sure there are more than bars in Copenhagen," Tom said.

Delaney and Hobbs kinda looked at Tom like he was crazy then looked at me.

"I'm inclined to go along with Tom. Guys, it's not even noon yet. We have all the time we need, and if what you say is true I'm sure there are women in those bars all the time."

"It's a nice day out, and I'd like to see some sunlight before getting locked up in one of those bars all night," Tom said.

"We could drop you guys off at a bar and then meet you back there later," I suggested.

Hobbs and DeLaney both lit a cigarette and thought about it for a little bit. Tom and I joined them in a smoke and waited for them to decide what they wanted to go.

Finally Hobbs spoke up. “We don’t know where any of this stuff is, we could spend all day looking for shit.”

“We don’t know where the bars are, either but I bet we find ’em before nightfall,”

Tom countered, “You guys do whatever you want to. I just don’t wanna spend all day and night sitting in some dark old bar.”

“I bet if we check with the people at the desk they can tell us what some of the tourist sights are and how to get there; they can probably tell us where to find a guide book if we want one,” I offered. “Besides, did you guys ever think that you might pick up some pretty nice gals somewhere besides a bar?”

“Guess that’s always a possibility,” DeLaney chimed in. “And actually, I kinda agree with Tom; it’s a long time to spend sitting in a dingy bar somewhere.”

“Hell, let’s do it then. I’m up for it,” Hobbs agreed.

We all finished what we had to do to get ready to go out for the day. I showered and shaved and put on some fresh clothes. Hobbs and DeLaney went back to their room. When I finished I told Tom I was going down to talk to the people at the desk and see what we could come up with to do.

Both the man and woman were at the desk. I asked them if they had any information on some of the main tourist attractions in Copenhagen and they were more than helpful. They had a little tour guide book they gave me which was all in English. I offered to pay for it but they declined. There was also a map in the book with the location of each attraction so when you were at one it told you how to get from there to the other.

I took the book back up to the room. Hobbs and DeLaney were waiting along with Tom. After looking over the book for a while we found out that we were almost at the statute of the Little Mermaid in the harbor just a few blocks away. There was even a little synopsis of the story. The thought crossed my mind that it might be a good story to read to my kids. I have no idea where that thought came from. We counted at least 4 palaces and one castle; we figured we would be bound to run into at least one of them along the way so we didn’t mark any of them down for places to visit. After looking through the guide we decided to go look at the Little Mermaid Statute and then go to Tivoli Gardens. The Gardens seemed to offer the most to do in one place.

We hopped in the car and drove down to the harbor and drove around until we found the statute. We parked, got out, Tom took a few pictures; he was the only one with a camera. Once we had enough pictures we were back in the car and on our way to Tivoli Gardens.

Tivoli Gardens is actually more of an amusement park than a garden. It has a number of rides including a wooden roller coaster whose workers ride in the last car to brake the train when it goes downhill so as not to pick up too much speed. I had second thoughts about riding that thing but everybody else was going for it so I went along too. It was fun but I kept looking over my shoulder to be sure those guys were still in the last car.

Restaurants and cafés abound in Tivoli, and the choices are as varied as the international flavors of visitors. Snack and drinks carts are just as plentiful. Prices vary depending on what you're looking for in a dining experience.

There is a variety of music at the park. The have a concert hall that hosts international stars from Jazz to Opera. In addition there is other music being played throughout the park. We wandered over the park, stopping to eat or get something to drink and just watching the people. DeLaney and Hobbs even met a couple of girls and shared a drink with them while Tom and I stayed to ourselves. It was a good time of the year to be there all the flowers were in bloom all around the lake which I was told use to be part of the moat surrounding the castle. Don't ask me what castle I couldn't tell you. Strolling through the park and around the lake I kept thinking I wish Sara was there to see this. I know she would love it.

At dusk lamplights came on and illuminated the vast gardens at Tivoli. Now I really wished Sara were there. The landscapes are almost like a botanical garden and you get a completely different perspective from the daytime strolling. Streams gurgle in the moonlight, moths come out for you to see their markings, some as colorful as any butterfly.

The time finally came that the guys had their share of nice and quiet and pretty flowers, they were ready to get down to some serious drinking and girl hunting so it was off to the bars. We found an area that had several bars within walking distance of each other. The first one we went into was an upstairs bar. This was one huge club with the longest bar I had ever seen. If you wanted to buy a girl a drink at the other end of the bar you would have to send it FedEx overnight. It had a large dance floor and some nice comfortable chairs around little tables. Even if this place was packed you couldn't tell it because it was so big.

We found a table and sat down. A waitress was there almost immediately and took our order. Looking around, you could see some couples and a lot of single females alone or in groups of two or three. When we first sat down we were pretty much in an isolated little spot in the bar just around the corner from a jukebox. By the time we ordered our second drink; we were beginning to get surrounded by young ladies in those groups of two or three I mentioned. Before long, all the guys were engaged in conversation with some of the ladies that had surrounded our table.

I was talking to a nice looking young lady when I felt a tap on the shoulder. I turned around and it was Tom.

He leaned down and whispered in my ear. "Don't make me have to kick you in the shins again." He laughed and returned to his chair.

I glared at him for a few minutes then said, "Nobody said you actually had to follow those instructions, ya know."

He just laughed and nodded as if to say, "Oh, yeah, somebody did."

This bar thing got to be bigger than all of us. We stayed in that club from the time we got there until it closed down at five in the morning to clean up. Somehow we all got separated; but all ended up back at the hotel. Not being a regular drinker it didn't take too many drinks for me to just forget everything. I am sure one of the guys, probably Tom made sure I got back to the hotel. The next thing I remember after leaving the hotel was waking up when the old lady brought us breakfast around 1000. She just waltzed right in with a big good morning to everyone.

Everyone included me and Tom and two girls in the big double bed and DeLaney and Hobbs crawling up the steps with two more girls right behind them. As embarrassing as that may have been to us, it didn't seem to bother the old lady or the girls. They sat up in bed and helped themselves to the coffee and rolls. I grabbed my orange juice before anyone else got any ideas.

I sat up in bed drinking my OJ, smoking a cigarette and visually surveying the room. Clothes were thrown everywhere; there were cans of beer and a bottle of Cognac rolling around on the floor. I have no idea where those came from. Why would we bring all that stuff back to the room?

My head was beginning to clear; the OJ and cigarettes were replacing the bad taste in my mouth with the bad taste I was used to. There wasn't a lot of talking going on, at least among the guys; the girls seem to chatter back and forth a little. My only question was what do we do now?

I leaned over the girl between me and Tom. "How did all this happen? How did these two girls end up in this bed?"

"I brought 'em. They are from out of town and needed a place to crash," Tom said.

"I can't believe you fell for that line. How much is this going to cost us?" I asked.

"Nothing. I made sure before I brought 'em up here," Tom responded.

"Well, I certainly ain't paying one of 'em. And how come my ribs and shins don't hurt? I snorted.

"You don't have to pay any of 'em anything, and your shins and ribs don't hurt 'cuz you were too drunk to even find the bed, much less do anything." Tom laughed.

I leaned back on my pillow. Humph! I thought that's kind of embarrassing. Too drunk to do anything? I ain't ever been that drunk before.

"I leaned back over towards Tom. "Okay, now how do we get rid of these gals?"

"We just have to give 'em a ride to the train station; they need to get back to wherever it is they live," Tom replied.

"And when does this happen?" I asked.

"That one said she needed to be at the train station by 1230. I guess she has the furthest to go. We are just gonna take 'em all at one time, and get it done in one trip."

"Good, sounds like you got a plan, so you can get it done since you have the car keys anyway. You do have the car keys don't you?" I asked.

"Yeah, I got 'em somewhere. I guess we should start getting this thing moving; it's after 1100 now."

Tom clapped his hands and got everyone's attention and explained that all the girls needed to start getting dressed so he could take them all to the train station. Hobbs and DeLaney immediately grabbed the girls they were with and hustled back downstairs. Tom got out of bed and headed for the bathroom but got stopped at the door by one of the girls, who smiled at him and said, "Me first, please."

Tom came back to the bed and lit another cigarette. Eventually Tom and the two girls upstairs got dressed and ready to go and they walked out the door to get the group downstairs. I told Tom I wasn't going anywhere; I'd get cleaned up and dressed after they left. As soon as they were gone I hopped in the shower and took a very long and hot shower. My head hurt and I generally just felt like shit all over.

Tom and the other two got back about 1230. They all seemed to be holding up pretty well. I guess I was the wuss of the bunch. They all had some story to tell. I listened to all of them and I could remember some similar stories but they all seemed like so long ago. I could have told them some more recent stories but I wasn't about to share those memories with these guys anytime soon.

We all decided we were hungry but nobody had any suggestions as to what to eat. We jumped in the car and just drove around looking for something or someplace to find something that sounded interesting to eat. Finally we saw a Chinese restaurant and that caught our fancies; so Chinese food it was.

I ordered my usual Chinese dish, Shrimp Fried Rice with a couple of Egg Rolls. I think everybody else ordered egg foo yong. As usual you get more than you can eat but we all made a good stab at it. I don't think any of us realized how hungry we were.

After we ate, it was time to make some plans. We lit up our cigarettes and considered our options. How long did we want to stay in Copenhagen? Did we want to go on to Amsterdam? We finally decided to stay in Copenhagen one more night and then move on out to Amsterdam the next day. We also all agreed tonight wouldn't be a repeat of last night. I agreed even though I didn't really remember much of last night.

After we left the Chinese Restaurant we went back to the hotel. The maids had been in and cleaned the place up. We were all tired and before long we were all snoozing away. It was dark before I opened my eyes. I finally felt better, I was rested and my headache was gone. I reached over, grabbed my cigarettes and lit one and exhaled, damn I thought still no smoke ring. Tom had been sleeping on the little day bed and he began to stir.

"What time is it?" he asked.

"It's about 1930," I said, still trying to blow a smoke ring.

"Well, I feel better; last night was a hell of a night," Tom said.

"I don't wanna hear about it," I snapped.

Tom laughed. "Bones, I've never seen you so drunk. We had to pour you into the car and then into bed."

"Did that gal I woke up next to try to seduce me?" I snickered.

"I dunno about that; I was busy doin' some seducing of my own."

"So I could have been sexually ravaged and violated, and you wouldn't know about it?" I asked in shock.

"It coulda happened," Tom said.

"Damn, I could have had great time and don't even remember it; getting drunk sucks!" I quipped.

DeLaney and Hobbs banged on the door and then let themselves in. They looked well rested and ready to go again.

"You guys ready to go back to the club?" Hobbs asked.

"I'm ready to go get something to eat first," Tom replied.

"Damn, son, you just ate a few hours ago," DeLaney chimed in.

"You know what they say about Chinese food," Tom shot back.

"How about you, Bones?" Hobbs inquired.

"I could eat a bite, I'm not starved, but something small would be good," I replied.

"Where do we wanna go eat?" DeLaney asked.

"I noticed a little restaurant just down the street from the Chinese place. We might be able to get a sandwich there," I said.

We got in the car and headed back towards the Chinese place. There was a parking place right in front of the restaurant I was talking about. We left the car and moved into the restaurant. It was a pleasant little place and the waitress spoke English and asked us if we wanted a drink while we looked over the menu. I got a coke the rest of the crew got a beer. I found a ham and cheese sandwich on the menu and that sounded perfect to me so that's what I ordered. Everyone ordered a sandwich of some sort.

Hobbs and DeLaney were just full of stories about there escapades last night. They talked and laughed at each others stories; Tom and I mostly sat and listened and had to laugh at some of their portrayals of things. Eventually they realized that Tom and I weren't providing any input to the conversation and when they asked, Tom said.

"We both just fell asleep."

"You lyin' ass; you didn't just fall asleep," Hobbs said.

"I did, I swear, and Bones was passed out by the time he hit the bed," Tom lied.

We ate our sandwiches, smoked a cigarette while we finished our drinks and then headed back to the only club we had bothered to find while we were there. When we arrived at the club we found a spot very near the place we had started out the night before. The waitress came by and we placed our order. I asked for a coke, plain, no rum, no cognac.

We had been there about half an hour when Tom tapped me on the shoulder and nodded towards a table just down from us. Lo and behold, there sat the two girls that had been in our room the night before; the ones that had to catch a train and go home. Tom pointed them out to Hobbs and DeLaney and they got up and started looking around the club and sure enough they found the two girls they had been with. One was with another guy and one was sitting alone at the bar.

Some navy guys came in and sat down at a table near us. One of them was a short timer and they were out to party. We got to talking to them and mentioned our experience last night with some girls that stayed at our place and said all they wanted was a ride to the train station the next day. One of the navy guys enlightened us. Apparently the girls came in from small towns on weekends to party but didn't have a place to stay so they would find some guy to shack up with for a bed to sleep in. Then tell them they had to catch a train home but really all they did was go to a locker in the station and get their bags so they could change clothes in the bathroom and then they were back in the bars.

So the girls were telling the truth, sorta. They just left out the part about not actually going home but coming back to the clubs instead. OH well, seems like it was a good deal for everyone involved.

We hung around the club until about 0100 and then decided to call it a night. We drove back to the hotel and went straight to our rooms. Tom and I kicked off our shoes, he hopped on the big double bed and I sat down on the little day bed and leaned back against the wall. I lit a cigarette and exhaled, no smoke ring again, damn it.

"Well, Bones, you have made it through three stops so far, and your virginity is still intact. Of course I may have to report back to Sara about that little blonde you danced with in Berlin, and that gal you passed out on last night without getting laid," Tom threatened.

"You make it all sound so lurid and cheap," I countered.

"You better be glad I like you, 'cuz I think if I really told her, she would actually cut your balls off." Tom laughed.

"No, she wouldn't, because she hasn't learned lesson number four yet," I said.

Tom looked at me with this quizzical look on his face. "Lesson number four?"

"Never mind," I said with a grin on my face.

"Well, fuck you anyway. Why did you mention it if you aren't going to tell me?"

"Because I get excited thinking about it," I said.

"Maybe I want to get excited too?" Tom said.

"Then make up your own lessons," I replied.

"Obviously this conversation isn't going anywhere. I'm going to bed. See you in the morning. What time are we getting up?"

"When we wake up, I guess, or when Frick and Frack come wake us up," I replied.

Tom and I both stripped and climbed in bed. I was sleepy but didn't get right to sleep. I shouldn't have mentioned lesson number four. That made my mind start wandering, and I couldn't wait to get back to K-Town.

GERMANY
Chapter 91

Our trip back from Denmark to Amsterdam was long and tedious. I think if anyone had even suggested that we just turn it around and go back to Heidelberg we all would have voted in favor of doing just that. But I guess we were all thinking that we had agreed to go to Amsterdam so that's what we had to do.

There was only one reason we were going to Amsterdam: to go visit De Wallen on Canal Street, Amsterdam's answer to Hamburg's Reeperbahn. I guess it's just in the nature of young men to go check things like that out.

We hit center city of Amsterdam about noon after driving all night from Copenhagen. While sitting at this huge intersection a guy pulled up beside us and began speaking to us in English. "Good day, gentleman, are you new to Amsterdam? he asked.

Of course we nodded yes.

He continued, "It appears you have just arrived after a long journey, are you looking for a nice place to stay? Not too expensive and close to the local night clubs in the area?"

I guess you didn't have to be a mind reader to figure that out by just looking at us, but we agreed to all of the above.

"Perhaps I can help you out. If you will follow me I can show you such a place not far from here."

We didn't have anything to lose since we didn't have the slightest idea where we were or where to go anyway. So we agreed and told the guy to lead the way. We proceeded followed the guy through the intersection and down several streets, making only a couple of turns before he pulled into a parking place and moving up enough for us to park behind him.

"You know what? I bet this son of a bitch owns this place," I said as we piled out of the car.

The guy led us in the door, walked around behind the counter, put on a little visor and said. "Now gentlemen, what kind of accommodations would you prefer?" I almost laughed out loud.

We got our usual, two rooms with two double beds; located up on the second floor. We walked out to the car and grabbed our bags.

"I told you this guy owned the place. I bet he has a list of girls he can fix us up with too if we ask him," I said.

The guys laughed and continued to grab their bags and we proceeded back inside and went on up to our room.

As I said the drive had been extremely long and we were tired, too tired to even think about eating right at the moment. Tom lay on his bed and was out like a light. I lit a cigarette and kicked off my shoes and just sat there smoking and wishing I was home already. I put out my cigarette, lay back on the bed, and I was gone.

We must have slept for three maybe four hours. I woke up to the sound of voices. Tom, Hobbs and DeLaney were all sitting around gabbing away. I sat up and grabbed my cigarettes.

"Welcome back to the land of the living, Bones," DeLaney remarked.

"I'm not sure I'm ready to be back yet," I said as I exhaled. Still no smoke ring.

"We were just talking about what we wanted to do," Tom explained. "You got any ideas?"

"Has anyone thought about something to eat?" I inquired.

"Yeah, we all seem to be in favor of that first," Hobbs added.

"Okay, well, I'm sure the guy at the desk can recommend a few places. He probably owns 'em," I said sarcastically.

"Well, let's go ask him," Tom suggested.

We all got up and walked down to the desk. There was our man with the visor reading the paper. He looked up and smiled as we came down the stairs.

"Good evening, gentleman. I bet you're hungry, yes?"

A friggin' mind reader, I thought. I wanted to reach over and slap him, just to see if he could see that coming.

"Yes, we are; do you have some suggestions on places to eat?" Tom asked.

Mr. Know It All, rattled off a few places; advising that this particular one catered to Americans and served many American dishes. I just knew he must own it or have an interest in it; but it sounded like what we would be interested in so following his directions off we went.

We found the restaurant without any problems. We found a table for four, and an attractive young lady came over to take our order. DeLaney popped off immediately and said he wanted a Sheep Herder's dinner.

Before he could finish, I shut him up. "DeLaney! Knock it off; she probably won't get it anyway," Delaney slumped back down in his chair and kept looking at his menu. I guess everyone else figured I was in a pissed off mood so they just ordered their meal and didn't say anything else until the waitress left.

"Okay, I give up. Tom said. What the fuck was that all about?"

"Yeah, what's a Sheep Herder's Dinner?" Hobbs asked.

"It's nothing really bad; I shouldn't have jumped in your case, DeLaney; I just thought it was the wrong place and wrong time I guess. Sorry about that."

"It's okay, Bones; you're probably right," DeLaney said.

"Well, what the fuck is it?" Tom insisted.

"The waitress comes over, and you order a Sheep Herder's Dinner; she doesn't know what that is so you tell her you want a glass of milk and a piece of ewe. Get it?"

"That's it? Sounds kinda lame to me," Tom scoffed.

"Yeah, I still don't get it," Hobbs said, looking confused.

Tom and I broke out laughing at Hobbs. What a dunce he could be sometimes, but I guess that's what we liked about him.

"Think about it Ray; you'll get it sooner or later," I said.

Delaney leaned over and whispered in Hobbs's ear.

Ray's eyes lit up and he broke out laughing. "Okay, I get it now," he said. "That's pretty cool."

Tom and I just looked at each other and did the best we could to keep from laughing. We got our meals, pretty much ate in silence and then fired up cigarettes and figured out what our next move was. Still no smoke ring, damn it.

Tom suggested we go back to the hotel and ask Mr. Know It All about some clubs in the area and how far from Canal Street we were. Nobody had any better suggestions so that's what we did. We walked back to the hotel and Mr. Visor was still there, still reading the paper. We posed our questions and got some very specific answers. There was a very nice little bar around the corner about half way down the block and Canal Street was only three Canals over. I thought it was interesting that was the first time I had ever received directions by canal.

We went down to the bar the guy recommended. It was a nice little pub; it had a pool table in the back and a jukebox that didn't play the music so loud you couldn't talk over it without having to shout. We ordered our drinks and Tom and I put our bid in for the next pool game.

While we were sitting there watching the guys before us play. I was sitting on the end of a booth just minding my own business. There was a guy sitting behind one end of the pool table that seemed to be engrossed in some sort of project. I really didn't pay much attention to the guy until he got up to leave. On his way past the booth I was sitting at he laid a piece of paper on the table and kept on walking. I just glanced down at the paper at first figuring it was some kind of advertisement; but as I looked closer I could see that it was a picture. I picked it up and looked closer. It wasn't just any picture; it was a sketch of me, with my hawk nose and all. Mostly my hawk nose, it was a caricature drawing. Before I could catch the guy he was out the door and gone. I had a really ugly nose but I thought it was a pretty good likeness.

I showed it to Tom and told him what had happened and where I got it. He looked at it.

"Yeah, that's you, Bones." He laughed. That's pretty good though. The guy just laid it on the table and left?"

"That's it, he just walked by and dropped it and kept on walking."

"Maybe he was afraid you would get up and punch his lights out?" Ray chimed in as he looked in over my shoulder. "Are we ready to go to Canal Street yet?"

"Apparently you are," Tom said. "Let Bones and I finish our game, and then we'll go."

It didn't take long to get the game over with, I sunk the 8 ball on the next shot and Tom won so we left. We followed the directions we were given and sure enough we found Canal Street, right were the guy said it would be.

The unique thing about Canal Street it was like going window shopping. The girls lived in these little rooms, in front of the room was a platform and each room had a store front window, just like you would find in any department store. The girls sat on a chair or sofa or whatever on the platform to display their wares. On the outside of the windows on either side was a rear view mirror. With those the girls could see if a potential customer was approaching from either direction and put down their book or needlepoint and make themselves more presentable for the business at hand.

We walked both sides of the street, window shopping. Most of these gals were fairly attractive, but occasionally you would run across a real sweat hog, and you had to wonder what kinda business she attracted.

After walking both sides of the street a couple of times it was beginning to get a little cold with a brisk little wind blowing off the canals. Hobbs and DeLaney had spotted a set of twins that seem to catch their fancy. We were on one of the over passes on one of the canals at the end of the street when they decided they wanted to go visit the twins. Tom and I told them to hurry up, we would wait for them right here on this bridge so they wouldn't get lost.

And hour and a half later her come these bozos walking and grinning back towards the canal. Tom and I had been freezing our asses off waiting on these shit heads. We figured it was time to get even.

"You guys done now? Did you have a good time?" Tom asked in a thinly disguised pissed-off tone.

"Oh, yeah, it was great. We had tea and little cakes while we talked about price," Ray volunteered.

"Okay, well, now that you guys have had your fun you wait for Tom and me. It's our turn now," I said as we headed off back towards the shopping area.

Tom and I already had a plan. There were a couple of little bars in the middle of the block on either side of the street. We were going to go have a drink, or two, or three while Hobbs and DeLaney waited for us.

After a little over an hour had passed we decided they should have had enough by now so we went back to the bridge. There they were, hands in their pockets, shoulders all scrunched up, stomping their feet, you could almost see their breath; apparently it had gotten a little colder since we left.

"Hey, where the hell you guys been? It's cold as hell out here," Hobbs whined.

"Yeah, we've been waiting over a fuckin' hour already," DeLaney chimed in.

"Gee guys, were sorry, we had tea and crumpets while we negotiated prices," I snickered.

"My gal was so good I had to go a second time," Tom lied.

We wasted no time in getting off that canal and almost double timed back towards the hotel. Nobody said anything about it getting this cold in Amsterdam this time of year.

It was about 1 a.m. when we got back to the hotel. I don't think any of us could wait to get in bed and get under those big down comforters they had on the beds to get warm. At least I know I couldn't. I didn't go to sleep right away but at least I got warm enough to sit up and have a cigarette. I tried again…still no damn smoke ring.

The next morning we went back to that American style restaurant and had breakfast and decided what we wanted to do for the rest of the day. Everybody mentioned wooden shoes, tulips and windmills. That's what we thought we were gonna see in Holland. Nobody talked about going back to Canal Street.

We finished our breakfast and went back to our resident know it all and asked him about those shoes and tulips and windmills. He said there were a couple of places we could go and gave us some directions. These were actually small villages outside the city, in fact from the map he showed us they were pretty much along the way we would be taking to get back to Heidelberg.

Someone had the bright idea that maybe we should go ahead and check out now and we could stop by these places on our way back to Germany. I think that was me. Anyway we all agreed so we hustled upstairs and grabbed our shit, stopped by the desk on our way out, paid our bill and we were off. I think this was really the happiest we had all been in a while despite some quasi conjugal visits by a couple in our party; we realized we were actually heading back home.

We found a couple of villages that we stopped and visited, we saw the windmills and dykes but none of them had holes in them. We tiptoed through a few tulips and tried to walk around in some of those wooden shoes. I was surprised at the tulips, never thought much about them as a flower but these were really pretty. I also thought tulips only came in yellow, wrong again.

We found this one place where they made a variety of cheeses. Ray bought a big role of this cheese to take back with us. In fact we all bought some sort of cheese, we each got a different type, since money was beginning to get a little tight we figured we could eat some cheese with some crackers we had picked up to kinda curb our appetite along the long trip home.

We didn't spend a lot of time in any of these places, we really were anxious to get back to Heidelberg, none more than me. Tom and I kept the car gassed and only stopped when we had to fill up. Everybody grabbed a coke or two and whatever else they wanted and went to the bathroom all when we stopped for gas.

The cheese we bought kept us from getting hungry until Hobbs opened up that big role of shit he bought. That was the stinkiest shit I had ever smelled. We had to roll down the windows to help make the smell go away. Ray said it was pretty good once you got past the smell.

None of us really cared because we weren't having any of it. We made him throw it out the window.

We pushed hard and finally about 2 a.m. arrived in Heidelberg. Tom didn't even wait for Charlie Waters to wave us through the gate at Patton Barracks; he just beat feet for the parking lot. He pulled into the first parking place he came to. Since we still had a couple of days left on our leave they better get their stuff out of the car because I was headed for K-Town the first thing in the morning. They moaned and groaned but grabbed their bags, and we all headed up the stairs to our rooms.

I didn't know who was working and who was asleep in my room so I didn't turn on any lights and tried to be as quiet as I could. I just dropped everything on the floor, stripped to my shorts and t shirt and crawled in my bunk and was out like a light with one last thought going through my mind. No more vacations without Sara.

GERMANY
Chapter 92

I slept a little later than I had wanted to but I got off to a pretty early start. I wanted to get to K-Town as soon as I could and be there shortly after Sara got back or before if I could.

It was good to just be alone in the car without the other three. I liked all those guys, well maybe DeLaney not so much as the others but still he wasn't all that bad; just a bit of a dip shit every now and then. Ray was just....Ray. He was okay, not the sharpest tack in the box but okay. And Tom, I could see his attitude changing, especially after this trip together. I think he really wished he hadn't wasted so much of his tour over here and got out and done more than hang out in the bars.

I arrived at K-Town and pulled up in front of the BOQ. Mary Ann's car was there, but then that didn't mean a lot. Where else would it be if she went on the trip with Sara? I parked Blue Bitch, grabbed a few things out of the car, and headed on up to the apartment. I knocked a couple of times, but no one answered, so I let myself in with my key. I dropped my bag, walked over and grabbed a coke from the fridge, plopped on the bed, and lit a cigarette. I exhaled after every drag. Still no damn smoke ring. I think my tongue must be deformed or something.

I hadn't finished my cigarette yet when I heard a key in the lock. Mary Ann came in, said hi, and walked over to her side of the apartment. Sara was right behind her. She had a big smile on her face when she saw me even with an arm load of bags and stuff. I got up and walked over and took some of the stuff from her and set it on the floor. I put my arms around her waist and gave her a big kiss and said welcome home.

"Thank you. It's good to be home. When did you get here?" she asked.

"Just about 30 minutes ago maybe, not long."

She went about putting some of her things up and getting out of her clothes and slipping into something more comfortable. If she would have been looking she would have noticed how happy I was to see her.

"How was your trip?" she asked.

"Sugar, it was okay, but I wish you had been with me instead of them guys, and I never wanna go traveling around the country without you again," I confessed.

"Awww. Did you miss me?" she asked as she came over and gave me a kiss.

I leaned into her slightly and asked, "Can't you tell? How was your trip?"

Her eyes got wide and she got a mischievous little grin on her face. "My trip was okay but not as good as my homecoming is going to be in a little while," she said, rotating her hips against me. "Are you hungry?" she asked. "Want to go get something to eat?"

"If you want to go out and eat then that's what we'll do, but personally I'm really tired of eating out. Don't we have anything here?" I asked.

"How about this? I really want to get a hot shower. How about I take a shower, then I'll fix us some sandwiches for now, and we can decide later what we want to do for supper?"

"At last," I said, "someone else that can come up with a plan besides me."

"Ah, so you were the brains of the outfit, huh?" she asked.

"Let's just say I had more travel experience than the other guys did. And by the way, your cousin Karl in Hamburg said to say hello."

"You saw Karl?" Sara said in surprise. "Wait, let me get my shower and then you can tell me all about it, okay?"

She hustled off to the bathroom and within minutes I heard the shower running full blast.

I sat down and lit another cigarette. Mary Ann walked over and said, "Hey, how was your trip?"

"Great," I said.

"Good," she replied, and walked out the door of the apartment.

A few minutes later Sara came out of the bathroom in her usual after-shower attire, the heavy white bathrobe she stole from the hotel in Paris and a towel wrapped around her head. She picked up her cigarettes, walked over, and climbed up on the bed beside me.

"Okay, so tell me about your trip. Where did you go, what did you do?" she asked all at once while she lit a cigarette.

I told her we went to Berlin and about crossing the Helmstadt Autobahn. I told her about the neat café, restaurant, bar or whatever it was with the table to table phones with the poles over the tables with the number of the table on it so you could call that particular table.

"Did you get any calls?"

"Yesss, we got some calls," I replied.

"No, did YOU get any calls?" she demanded.

"Yes, I got a few but nothing ever happened except once when this girl asked me to dance. I had forgotten about her call until she showed up at the table."

"Did you dance with her?"

"Yes, I did, but only after Tom crushed my shins under the table."

"Oh, goodie, he did what I asked him. He is a good man. I'll have to give him a kiss for that," Sara said with delight.

"You ain't kissin' Tom," I said sternly.

"Okay, maybe just a hug then."

"How about just a handshake?" I suggested.

"Okay, just a handshake," she agreed as she put my arm around her and laid her head on my shoulder.

"What else did you do?"

I told her about the rest of the stuff we did in Berlin; we saw the Brandenburg Gate and tried to visit the Reichstag but some German soldiers with guns didn't want us to get very close so we blew that off.

And how we went to Check Point Charlie and looked across into East Germany and it was like looking into a ghost town. I probably could have left that part out; I forgot that she still has some distant relatives living in East Germany. I changed subjects and told her about the strip club in the French sector and how Hobbs paid ten Pfenning less for the same drink than I did.

"Where did you go next? What did you do?"

"What is this? Twenty questions, and you expect me to play on an empty stomach? I thought you were going go fix us some sandwiches?" I said.

"Oh, all right. You're such a grouch. But I can listen while I'm fixing the sandwiches, so keep talking," she said as she got up off the bed.

I told her after Berlin we went to Hamburg. And that I called Karl using the number she was sure I had, and that he took us out to the Reeperbahn.

"What's the Reeperbahn?"

"It's Hamburg's red light district where all the prostitutes hang out," I said.

She turned and looked at me with that little knife in her hand. "You didn't," she snapped.

"No, I didn't, but I could have, but even if I had wanted to I wouldn't have 'cuz I know you gave me Karl's number for a reason, and you probably called him and told him to keep an eye on me if I showed up," I surmised.

"I did no such thing. I just thought it would be nice if you called him if you passed through Hamburg," she replied.

I knew she hadn't had that in mind when she gave me the phone number, but I just liked yanking her chain every now and then. She was cuter when she got riled up a little bit. I told her about the Reeperbahn and that we just walked around and checked out the clubs, watched a couple of strip shows, and then left.

She brought the tray of sandwiches and drinks over to the bed and climbed back up next to me with the tray in her lap. "Where did you go next?" she asked.

I told her we then went to Denmark and about crossing the bay on a ferry with nothing to eat but raw fish and the long drive to Copenhagen. I explained to her about finding a bed and breakfast hotel near the harbor and the statue of the Little Mermaid and some of the story that I could remember. I told her about going to Tivoli Gardens and how pretty it was and that I wished she had been there with me to see it; especially at night.

"You didn't go to any bars?" she asked.

"Yes, we went to one bar. I think it had the longest bar in the world. This place was huge."

"Were there lots of girls there?" she inquired.

"Yes, there were tons of women in the place," I replied.

"Did you sleep with any of them?" she asked rather tentatively.

"Yes, I slept with at least two, maybe three, I'm not sure," I replied.

Sara slammed the tray on the coffee table, pushed me back on the bed and straddled me, pinning me down with her knees. "I'm going to cut your balls off, cowboy! What do you mean two, maybe three? You have a lot of explaining to do, so you best get with it."

It was all I could do to keep from laughing, but I knew I dared not laugh now. "Okay, okay, let me up, and I'll tell you everything I remember."

"What do you mean everything you remember? You tell me, and then maybe I'll let you up."

"Okay, we went to the bar early, and those bars stay open 23 hours a day, closing only one hour to clean up, but when they close another one is opening up. Anyway, we stayed until this one closed down, about five in the morning. I really don't remember much after that until the little fat lady brought us our breakfast the next morning. When I woke up there were two girls in bed with me and Tom, and another girl was on a small day bed, and DeLaney was passed out on the floor. (I was stretching the truth a tad here to save my own balls.)

"So there were three girls and four guys in one room?" Sara asked.

"Yeah, that's right, three girls and four guys," I replied.

"Who didn't have a girl?"

"I didn't."

"Then why were there two girls in the bed with you and Tom?"

"I think the other girl in bed was Delaney's, but she must have kicked him out because there wasn't enough room for four."

Sara was looking down at me through those little squinting eyes; you could almost see the wheels turning in her mind, trying to put it all together; making sure she had all the facts straight in her mind. After what seemed like forever, she leaned down until we were nose to nose, still staring at me with those deep brown eyes. Finally she said, "I love you, cowboy. And I love you for telling me the truth when you could have lied about the whole thing. Most men I know would have just danced around that part and hoped they got away with it." Then she gave me a really long, wet, tongue-sucking kiss.

When she let me come up for air and climbed off my chest, I sat up on the bed, took a deep breath and said, "Can I have the rest of my sandwich now?"

Sara laughed and reached over and picked up the tray and put it back in her lap so we could finish eating.

"And just for the record, how many men do you know?" I asked.

"Ha, you think I'm going to tell you that?" she scoffed.

"Well, you already did unless you were fibbing to me then," I said.

"There was one guy on my trip that kept trying to get close to me, wanted to buy me drinks all the time, kept asking me to dance and gave me the key to his room."

"And what did you do?" I asked.

"I didn't drink any of the drinks he sent over to me, I refused to dance with him, and I dropped his key in his drink as I walked by his table while he was talking to some other woman."

When we stopped laughing, I reached over and gave her a kiss and told her she was my favorite teacher ever. "If I was one of your students I would fail every class you taught me just so I could take it over again to be near you."

"You're such a liar sometimes," she said, "But not about the really important things. Now what did you do after you left Copenhagen?"

I shook my head and laughed. "You just never give up, do you?"

"Nope," she grinned.

I lit a cigarette and leaned back against the wall and told her about Amsterdam. I told her how DeLaney and Hobbs left me and Tom standing out in the cold for almost two hours while they were screwing a set of twins and what Tom and I did to get even. Then I told her about the tulips, wooden shoes and windmills and the stinky cheese Ray bought and we made him throw it away.

By this time it was starting to get a little dark out and Sara had changed into some light weight sweatpants with a thin long sleeve T-shirt like top without a bra which made it difficult to look at her because the material kept rubbing against her nipples and they were staring me right in the eye every time I looked at her.

"They have a delivery service at the pizza place now. If you don't want to go out and eat later we can order pizza, but we shouldn't wait too long I heard that it takes a really long time to get your pizza, 'cause they don't have enough drivers."

"That sounds good to me. Why don't you order anytime you feel like it's time? I'm going to take a shower now. You cut the circulation off to my arms with your knees, I think."

"Oh! I'm sorry, baby, why didn't you say something?" she asked as she walked over and gave me a kiss.

"Because, while you were sitting on my chest with my arms pinned down with your knees, your robe was open, and the view was worth every ounce of pain." I grinned.

You're a dirty old man already at what….twenty-one?" She laughed. "See if I ever sit on your chest again."

"Actually I was thinking you might like to try it again later tonight," I smiled as I stripped and walked towards the shower.

"Wait!" she whispered. She picked up her robe off the back of the chair, walked over and handed it to me. "Mary Ann is still home, ya know; you might want to put this on."

"Haven't heard a word out of her in hours. She is probably asleep," I said.

"I don't care. She might not be, and she ain't seein' what belongs to me."

"You know you're starting to talk more like a Texan all the time," I said as I slipped into the robe.

She stepped up close on her tip toes and said, "Ride 'em, cowboy," and gave me a kiss.

I took a really long shower. It was the best shower I had since we left. I turned the water on as hot as I could stand it and let it beat down on my neck and shoulders and run down my back. I stayed in the shower until the water started to turn cold then climbed out of the shower and slipped into my own heavy white robe that my thieving little beauty had stolen from the hotel.

I came out of the bathroom, walked into the bedroom and dropped my robe while I got some clean underwear and T-shirt out of my drawer.

Suddenly I heard this gasp coming from the sink where Sara was brushing her hair. I turned to see her staring at me. "Cowboy, what have you done to Charlie? Where is he? I can't see him?"

"He is hiding, so you won't be pestering him for a while and he can get some rest for later," I said with a smile on my face.

"Maybe I should check just to see if he is okay," she said as she walked towards me.

"No, stop, he is fine, I promise," I said as I held out my hand for her to stay back.

"Besides I don't want you anywhere around him with that rat tail comb and brush you have in your hand."

"Okay, I'll take your word for it." She grinned and went back to messing with her hair.

I slipped on some sweats and a T-shirt, walked over, sat down on the bed, and lit a cigarette. *Damn; no smoke ring,* I thought as I exhaled.

"I called the pizza guy already; it will be a while before it gets here. Hope you're not really starving," Sara said.

"I'm fine. I can wait," I replied as I started going through some of the record albums to pick out some music to play. I was surprised at how many German albums I picked.

About an hour later there was a knock on the door. Sara picked up some money from the desk and headed for the door. I jumped off the bed and stopped her.

"You're not gonna answer the door with those nipples sticking outta that shirt like that," I said. "I'll pay for the pizza."

I snatched the money from her hand and pushed her gently back against the wall. She grabbed my hand and put it on her nipples.

I grinned at her and pulled my hand away. "You brazen little hussy!" I said with some distain, gave her a kiss; and then went to pay the pizza guy.

The knocking must have awakened Mary Ann; she passed through just as the pizza guy was leaving. I asked her if she wanted to join us for some pizza and she said no, she wasn't feeling well and was going back to bed. I didn't say it and I was sorry she wasn't feeling well but I was glad she wasn't going to be around this evening.

I set the pizza on the coffee table; Sara opened a can of coke and got herself a glass of wine. I thought that was unusual she usually drank beer with pizza.

"What's up with the wine tonight? You normally drink beer with pizza."

She smiled and said, "I think this is gonna be more of a wine kinda night."

I had no idea what that meant, but I liked the sound of it. We climbed up on the bed together and opened the pizza and dug in. Surprisingly we were both hungrier than we realized. It was a good thing Sara ordered a large.

After finishing off the pizza, we both sat back and lit up a cigarette. I exhaled no smoke ring.

"Damn it!" I said.

"What's the matter?" Sara asked.

"Tom can blow a smoke ring and I can't," I whined.

"You mean like this?" Sara asked as she simply exhaled a bigger smoke ring than I ever saw Tom blow.

"Damn, damn, double damn! How did you do that? This is embarrassing. My fiancée can blow a smoke ring, and I can't," I whined some more.

"Don't worry, sweetie, I promise never to blow a smoke ring when are in mixed company," Sara laughed.

"I know; it's all in the tongue. I think my tongue is deformed," I said.

Sara moved over close to me and started nibbling on my ear and kissing my neck.

"You may not be able to blow smoke rings with your tongue, but you sure know other ways to use it that would make anyone jealous if they only knew," she whispered.

I turned my head towards her and gave her a kiss and said, "I'll take that as a compliment."

Sara got up off the bed, walked over shut the door to her room and locked it. I think that was a clue. She slowly pulled her shirt up over her head and threw it at me. I took mine off and threw back at her. Slowly she slid the sweats down over her hips and down past her thighs let them fall to the floor stepped out of them and kicked them at me. I threw my sweats at her. She walked over, lay down on the bed, and pulled me down on top of her.

"Aren't you going to turn out the lights?" I whispered.

"Not tonight. I want to see your face."

As our pace quickened and our body heat began to rise, Sara had the opportunity to see exactly what she wanted to but looking down at me I had to wonder how much she could see through the sweat dripping down off her forehead and the wet ringlets of her hair hanging down in her face, before she collapsed over my body from a sheer exhaustion and pleasure like I had never seen her experience before. I know I was wiped out I could tell by her deep breathing and grasping for air that she was completely spent.

We lay perfectly still with her still on top of me and her face buried in my neck. Neither of us were able to breathe, much less talk, and I could tell her body had gone completely limp. Slowly both our breathing began to return to normal, but to my surprise I could feel her as she began to move again, undulating her hips, slowly as her muscles continued to spasm, tightening and then relaxing.

"Baby, are you okay?" I asked.

"Never been better," she whispered. "Was that lesson number four?"

"Ummm, almost, 3.5 anyway," I said

"OUCH! I cried as she bit my neck. "What was that for?"

"I was trying to give you a hickey," she whispered.

"Where did you hear about hickeys?" I asked.

"I was reading a book while I was in Switzerland, and this girl was giving her lover a hickey, and it kinda gave a description, but it was in German so I may have not got it all down right," she replied.

"I don't think you have to bite so hard. I think you have to suck more," I suggested.

"I'm not wasting good suction on your neck," she said.

"Okay, well that works for me. Just don't forget when you're giving a hickey and not."

She raised up, sweat still rolling down her forehead, looked me in the eye and said, "I missed you."

"I missed you too," I said.

She put her head back down next to me not bothering to roll over, within minutes I could tell by her slow even breathing she was sound asleep. I put my arms around her, kissed her cheek, whispered an "I love you," and fell asleep right where I was.

GERMANY
Chapter 93

It was the first Friday in April 1962; I was on the train bound for K-Town. It had been a typical week in the company, work, eat, sleep; and then do it all over again. The weather was really turning out nice this time of year. It was a good time to be outdoors. In weather like this you didn't mind working the gates.

Normally during this train ride I pretty much dozed off and caught 40 winks as they say. But this trip I had things on my mind. I was officially a short timer now; a double digit midget. I had a little over a month and a half left before I returned to the states. I was really apprehensive about the whole thing. I wasn't that crazy about going home but I hadn't been successful in talking Sara into renewing her contract with the government to stay and teach at least one more year.

Being a short timer meant one thing to most people, they were close to going home, but to me it also meant that I was now one of the oldest guys in the company. There were only a few of us left that had been there as long as I had. New guys had come in and replaced some of those that had left but it seems they all fit the mold so to speak. In the little over two years I had been there I could never recall a single incident between members of the unit; which is rare in any organization in the military.

Sara and I had had a great weekend last week after returning from our separate vacations. I think it was obvious to both of us how much we had missed each other even though we had not been apart any longer than normal; the fact that we were not traveling together seemed to be....wrong.

We didn't have too many more weekends together to look forward to until we faced the longest separation we had or would have since we first met. That was something I really wasn't looking forward to at all.

The train pulled into the K-Town Bahnhof before I realized we were even close. I got off the train, walked out and caught a cab to the BOQ. I paid the driver and walked up to the apartment. Sara met me at the door, with a big kiss; I could tell she was excited about something; she had that look on her face. She ushered me into the room and sat down on the bed beside me with my coke already in her hand. This was all leading to somewhere, I just wasn't sure where yet. But I had a sneaky suspicion I was going to find out.

I pulled out a cigarette but before I could get my lighter out, Sara was holding her lighter up to the end of my cigarette. I inhaled deeply and then exhaled; no smoke ring yet. Damn.

"Okay, what's going on? Did you wreck the car? The hotel in Paris called about their bathrobes? I can tell you're up to something; spit it out."

"I want to have a baby."

I choked on my coke, it came out my nose, and I dropped my cigarette in my lap and burned a hole in my jeans. And somewhere along the way I heard myself scream something like, "What the fuck did you say?"

Calmly Sara said again. "I want to have a baby."

"Oh, no! We've already been through this. No kids, not yet. You can't have a baby yet. You just gonna have to wait."

Sara moved closer to me and put her arms around me gave me a kiss. "Sweetie, I'm not talking about us having a baby, baby. I mean a baby like this," she said as she held up a picture of a litter of the cutest German Shepard puppies you would ever want to see.

"You know you almost gave me a heart attack. I'm gonna get you for this," I threatened.

"Promise?" she asked with a smile on her face.

I took the picture and looked at it. “Where did you get this?” I asked

“From the German newspaper. They are for sale in a village just down the road from here. I called and the man said he still had three left. “He is only asking 200 marks for them; that’s only about $50.00 dollars, and they are all registered with the German Kennel Club and have papers.”

She was really trying to sell me on this, so I knew she really wanted one.

“Who’s gonna take care of it while you’re in school?” I asked.

“I can come home at noon and take him out and be sure he has food and water.”

“You got this all worked out already, don’t you?” I asked.

She looped her arms through mine and leaned up, gave me a kiss and said, “Yes,” with that big irresistible grin on her face.

“And when do we get this “baby?” I asked.

“Do you have something to do right now? It’s still daylight outside.”

“You want to go now?”

“Yes, can we, please?” she pouted.

How the hell am I supposed to say no to that? I got up and finished what was left of my coke and said, “Let’s go.”

Our first stop was the commissary to pick up some dog food, and a bowl and another bowl for water and toy for him to chew on and some treats for when he was a good little doggie and didn’t pee on the floor. I could tell this was going to be an experience.

Sara drove like a German to get to this little village, just outside of K-Town. She had already got directions when she called to see if there were any puppies left so she had a pretty good idea of where we were going.

She finally found the house she was looking for and parked in front. I let her go to the door first to be sure it was the right place. After a short conversation with the man that answered the door she motioned for me to come on up. I got out of the car and the three of us walked around the side of the house and into a fenced area in the back.

There was the proud mother and father I assume in one pen and three little balls of fur with feet and ears in the other pen. The man opened the gate to the puppy pen and invited Sara and I in to meet the kids. Of course they were all happy to see us and Sara was delighted. Okay, I couldn't resist either; I bent down and petted the little shits. We did take some time in making a selection. This particular one caught both our eye. He had some great markings. He was brown with the black saddle back and you could tell he was going to look like Rin Tin Tin when he grew up, and he was a playful little thing. We picked him.

The guy explained to Sara that this was the first litter for this bitch and that it was customary to name the puppies by the letter of the alphabet depending on the order of the litter. In other words all these puppies' names would start with the letter "A." And since he had already registered the puppies with the GKC this one was named Asso something or other, don't ask I can probably say it but have no idea how to write it.

Sara paid the guy and we took Asso home. When we got back to the BOQ, Sara let Asso out of the car and let him run around and get familiar with the area and find "his" spot. In the meantime I carried all the stuff that came with Asso up to the apartment.

A short time later Sara came in with Asso all tucked up under her arms, talking to him just like he was a baby. She put him down on the floor and let him sniff around and get used to the upstairs toilet; while she fixed his water bowl and put a little food in the other bowl.

I was sitting on the bed smoking a cigarette, Sara came over and sat down beside me, lit a cigarette and we watched the latest addition to the apartment check everything out.

"What did that guy say this mutt's name was?" I asked.

Sara punched me in the ribs. "He is not a mutt. I don't remember what the name was right now. I'll check later."

"Well, I don't care what his name is on that paper but no one, not even a dog, deserves a name like Asso whatever. I think we should name him Fritz."

Sara thought about it for a few minutes and then said, "I think you're right, let's call him Fritz. I like that."

"Okay, Fritz it is then. Come here, Fritz," He didn't listen; he was too busy walking around in the closet.

We just sat back on the bed and watched Fritz become familiar with his new home Sara seemed to be very content just sitting there watching him. After about 30 minutes of constant wandering around, including checking out Mary Ann's side of the place Fritz came back to our side. He sat down on the little throw rug around the coffee table, looked up at us, with his floppy ears hanging over his eyes, his tail wagging and his tongue falling out of the side of his mouth and let out a couple of barks as if to say, "Okay, I like it here; you guys will do."

Sara laughed, all right we both laughed and Fritz ran under the coffee table and tired to jump up on the bed. Sara couldn't resist picking him up and bringing him up on the bed with us. He was giving her kisses all over her face and every once in a while he would look over at me as if to say, "Who are you?"

Sara gave Fritz to me she had to go to the bathroom. Now that I was the center of his attention I figured we might as well get something straight right from the get go.

"These are the rules. When I'm here I sleep in the bed; you sleep on the floor. If you have to go out you go tell her. Don't be telling me. I ain't running you up and down three flights of stairs just so you can go pee. And no paddling in your water dish; I don't want water all over the floor. Leave my socks alone, and don't even think about walking or chewing on my boots or shoes. Got it?"

I felt better after we had our little talk but all I got for my trouble was a wet tongue all over my face until Sara came back then he wanted to go back to her. I could tell this guy was gonna be cutting into my time with Sara. I think I was jealous already.

I woke up Saturday morning to some whispering coming from Sara's side of the bed. I opened one eye and could see Fritz standing on his hind legs licking Sara's face and hear her telling him to wait a minute and she would take him outside.

She had taken him outside several times before during the evening and once just before we went to bed but I knew that it was probably not safe to just jump out of bed without looking before you leaped. Sara slid out of bed, threw on some sweats and picked Fritz up and hustled him out the door and down the stairs.

I sat up in bed and surveyed the area. Sure enough there was a little spot here and a little spot there and one really ugly, brown-lookin' spot over by the desk. I fell back in the bed. I wasn't awake yet if anyone asked.

I dunno how long they were gone but Sara and Fritz finally came back to the room. Sara put Fritz in bed with me while she cleaned up his mess. He didn't waste any time making sure I was awake. I hid under the covers but he was ready to play, He kept trying to pull them off me or stick his nose under there with me. Sara thought it was so cute she had to get her camera out and take a picture.

Sara and I finally got our showers, one showered the other kept Fritz entertained and out of trouble. I played with him while Sara fixed us some toast and eggs on the hot plate. She brought it over and set it on the coffee table. Naturally Fritz thought it was for him and had his nose stuck right up there with the bacon and eggs. Sara gently kept pushing him down and telling him no and pointing to his food dish. But he wasn't having any of that. But to my surprise Sara made him keep his distance while we ate.

All day Saturday was devoted to Fritz, reminding him what was off limits in the apartment and then taking him on walks around the area outside so he could learn those surroundings and know where he could "go" and where he couldn't "go." Sara had gotten a leash and a collar and we took him for walks down through the woods to the picnic table where we rested and smoked a cigarette and let him check out the area.

We kept him outside most of the day, even took him for a ride in the car down to the snack bar. Sara kept him in the car while I went in and got us some hamburgers. Keeping Fritz out of the bags until we got back to the apartment was an adventure. He could smell that food. When we got back and put it out on the table he sat and looked at us. I was surprised, I figured he would be up on the table again but it appeared he had already learned he was not allowed to do that. I thought that was amazing for a puppy only about 10 weeks old. Sara couldn't resist, she had to give him a French fry for being such a good boy.

After lunch we took Fritz back outside and walked down towards the Guest House. It was becoming more obvious that Fritz was going to be a very smart dog. He was already walking well on the leash and not trying to move to the end of the leash, just keeping pace beside Sara.

I'll say one thing this dog was wearing me out. By the time we got back to the BOQ we were all tired. Sara and I lay down on the bed, and Fritz curled up on the little rug under the coffee table; it wasn't long before we were all having a late nap.

By the time we got up it was dark out. I know Sara and I were both still tired but I didn't get that impression from Fritz. He had managed to pull himself up on the bed and was going between the two of us licking us in the face.

"You wanna go out?" Sara asked; something she had been doing to get Fritz to learn that meant go out and take care of business.

He jumped off the bed and walked towards the door. I was totally amazed; this was the smartest dog I had ever seen. We hadn't had him much more than 24 hours and already he was smarter than some full grown dogs I had seen. Sara got up and got his leash and took him down for a walk.

I reached over and got my cigarettes off the record player and lit one up. No smoke ring. I could see where Fritz could be a lot of work and trouble for Sara but by the same token I couldn't help but wonder if she hadn't decided to get one now because she knew I was leaving shortly and she wanted something else in her life to keep her busy and spend time with.

They walked back in the door and as soon as Sara took his leash off Fritz came running over and jumped on the bed to give me a kiss and let me know he was home. I could imagine what this would be like in a few months when he was much bigger. You could tell by the size of his paws he wasn't the runt of the litter.

Sara fixed us some sandwiches; we ate, smoked a cigarette and then just sat back and listened to some music. Fritz sat at the foot of the bed. I guess he was listening too. I think all the fresh air had worn us all out, even though we had a nap Sara and I were both ready to go to bed; I took Fritz down one more time before we called it a night. He wasn't in any hurry and I just wanted to get back upstairs. Finally he found a spot and did his duty and we hustled back up to the apartment. Sara had already crawled in bed.

I walked in and took Fritz's collar off and heard Sara say, "Hurry up, big boy, I'm waiting on you."

"Are you talking to me or the dog?" I inquired.

Sara laughed, stuck her finger out from under the covers and wiggled her index finger at me in that come her motion. Then she lifted the sheet up to show me she was stark naked. I decided Fritz was on his own for a while. I got undressed and crawled in bed next to Sara.

"Aren't you going to turn out the lights?" she asked.

"Not tonight, I want to see your face," I grinned.

"You see my face all the time," she said.

"But I never get tired of looking," I replied as leaned down and kissed her gently.

GERMANY
Chapter 94

On Friday 13th of April I was working the main gate at Patton Barracks when I got a message to stop in and see the first sergeant the first chance I got but definitely before I took off for K-Town. Oakley had delivered the message as he was heading back over to Patton Barracks.

"What's this all about?" I asked.

"Hell if I know; Top just stopped me in the mess hall and told me to tell you," Oakley replied.

I didn't have a clue but considering it was Friday the 13th I couldn't help but wonder if it was bad news. I wished Oakley hadn't told me so early, now I would be thinking about it all day.

As soon as I got off, I went straight to the Orderly Room before I turned in my weapon or anything else. As I entered the Orderly Room, Top was standing at the Clerk's desk.

"Sammy, glad you made it; I was about to take off for the day. I have something for you I figured you would want to know as soon as they came in," Top said.

He walked into his office motioning me to follow him in. He walked around behind his desk, picked up a stack of papers, and handed them to me. I guess I looked like I didn't know what they were because Top said, "They're your orders, Sammy; you're going home."

This should not have been a surprise. I knew I was short. I knew I would be getting orders at some point, but this was only April. I stood there kinda stunned and began reading the orders. Basically they said I was departing Heidelberg by train on 18 May for Bremerhaven, Germany, for further departure on or about 19 May 1962 by boat, the USS Maurice Rose for the United States and separation from the US Army on or about 25 May 1962.

I don't know where my mind went from there, but I was brought back to reality by the first sergeant calling my name.

"Sammy, you okay, son?"

"Yes, sir, I'm fine," I said. "I just wasn't expecting these orders so soon, I guess."

"It means you're really short now, Sammy; you're on your way home."

"Yeah, I guess it does. Says here I will be leaving Heidelberg on the 18th of May for Bremerhaven."

Glancing down at the calendar on his desk Top followed his fingers across the page and then said, "Looks like you will be pulling your last day of duty on Friday the 11th of May. That gives you a week to clear post and outprocess here."

"That is only about a month from today," I said mostly to myself.

"That's about it. Sammy," Top said as he walked around his desk and headed out of his office, "you can still re-enlist for your own vacancy, you know."

I followed Top out of his office and out of the Orderly Room. Top went on up the steps and out the door. I stopped at the arms room and checked my weapon. I was still in a daze. I just wasn't ready for this yet. The armorer was jumping in my shit for being late turning in my weapon, but I didn't even hear what he said, just another voice in my head.

I walked up to the room, walked in, and sat down on my bunk.

"Hey, what do say, lover?" Rizzo hollered. "Got a cigarette?"

I set my cigarettes and lighter down on my footlocker, which was an automatic invitation for Rizzo to help himself. I still had my orders in my hand.

"Are you going to K-Town tonight?" Rizzo asked.

"Huh?" I said.

"Are you going to K-Town tonight?" Rizzo repeated.

That brought me out of my daze. I had to get ready to catch a train. Sara would be waiting on me.

"Yeah, I'm going. I gotta get moving. I'm running late," I said. I started changing clothes and getting ready to leave. I didn't know if I wanted to take my orders and show them to Sara now or not. I didn't even know if I wanted to tell her about them.

I had to hustle to make the train to K-Town. I just barely got seated before the train started moving out. I was still trying to decide if I should mention or tell Sara about my orders this weekend or maybe wait. The more I thought about it, the more I decided that nothing was gained by waiting; I might as well tell her now and get it out of the way.

I grabbed a taxi to the BOQ and upon arrival was greeted by his majesty Fritz. Sara had him outside and they were standing just outside the door. When I got out of the taxi I could see Sara bending down and talking to him and pointing in my direction. She finally got him to look in my direction and let him go and he came running over to me and jumping up on my legs. I'm glad he wasn't grown yet. We had to stop this jumping up on people before he got any bigger.

"Hey, Fritz, hi boy," I said as I patted him and scratched him behind his ears. He seemed to like that. I walked over to Sara with Fritz trotting right along beside me.

"Hi, sugar," I said as I leaned over and gave her a kiss.

She put her arm around my waist and the three of us went back into the BOQ. Fritz was handling the stairs like a real pro already; he knew exactly where to go.

"How was your day?" Sara asked as we entered the apartment, and she took off Fritz's collar.

"My day was basically pretty normal. I did get a surprise this afternoon after I got off, though," I said, sitting down on the bed and lighting a cigarette.

"Oh, really? And what was your surprise?" Sara inquired.

She got me a coke and came over to sit beside me on the bed. Fritz hopped up on the bed and stuck his nose between us like he was supposed to be in on the conversation too.

"I got my orders for going home," I said, as I attempted to blow a smoke ring.

"But you don't leave for almost two months yet, right?"

"According to my orders I leave Heidelberg on the 18th of May by train to Bremerhaven and then sail by boat back to the states for discharge on or about the 25th of May. Top told me that my last working day if I didn't take any leave beforehand would be Friday, May the 11th."

We sat quietly on the bed smoking a cigarette. Fritz didn't like the smoke so he moved off to a corner of the bed and lay down. I felt like I should say something but didn't know what to say. I had told her all there was to tell right now.

She leaned over and put her head on my shoulder. "I don't want you to go."

"I don't want to go either, but I sure as hell don't want to stay if you're not going to be here," I said.

"Are you mad at me?" Sara asked

"No, I'm not mad at you," I lied. "Why should I be?" Actually I was mad at her; I was mad because she wasn't willing to stay, get married in Germany, and give the Army life a try.

"I don't know. You sound like you are," she said.

"Sorry. I don't mean to sound that way. I guess I just wasn't ready to get my orders yet, even though I always knew I would be getting them. I just didn't think it would be this soon."

"I didn't think you would get them this early either," she replied.

"You wanna go out to eat?" Sara asked.

"I'd like to get a shower first. I was running late leaving Heidelberg. Do we have time for me to get a quick shower or will the club be closed?"

"It's Friday night; they should be open late enough. Go get your shower," she said.

I walked into the bathroom, Fritz thought he should go with me but I made him stay outside this time. I got the water going and waited for it to get hot. I really wanted to take a long hot shower but knew I didn't have time for that. I was a little upset with myself because I knew I had been a little short with Sara for something that we had already talked about and decided. I guess I was being a little selfish too. I was going home; she would be home a couple of months after that and all would be well again. That's just the way it was going to be.

I climbed out of the shower into my stolen heavy white robe, opened the door and almost stumbled over Fritz; he was lying at the bathroom door waiting for me to come out. We walked back to the bedroom together and he ran and hopped up on the bed and seemed surprised that I didn't come over to the bed also. When I went to the dresser to get some shorts he had to come see what I was doing. He was a curious mutt.

I got dressed. Sara had already changed. Now the trick was to leave Fritz by himself. I let Sara handle that; I went down and got the car started. She came down a few minutes behind me and climbed in.

"How did he take it?" I asked

"It was a little hard, but he is getting better; he is used to me leaving in the morning and then again at noon, so it's not quite as hard to leave him, and he does really well by himself."

We arrived at the club; the dining room was still open and had a few customers yet. We found a table for two near the far wall. The waiter brought us menus, Sara ordered a glass of wine and I got a rum and coke while we looked over the menus. We really didn't need to look at the menu long we pretty much knew what was on it already. I was in a fish sorta mood, so I had the fried shrimp with fries and hush puppies. Sara had a steak.

Our salads came right away and we made short work of those, I guess we were both hungry. Between the salads and the main course we had a cigarette.

"So do these orders change anything right away?" Sara asked.

"Nothing changes until I get on that train for Bremerhaven; then I'm gone," I said.

I felt like there was still some bitterness in my voice, and I didn't want there to be any. I didn't want any friction between us now. I needed to get over it and just accept the fact that I was leaving.

They brought our main course and we mostly ate in silence. The shrimp was good. I don't think I had had any shrimp since the last time we were here, and it had been a while. Sara commented the steak was good so we had a good meal even if it was a quiet one.

We smoked one more cigarette after we finished eating, then paid the bill and left. The trip back to the BOQ was a quiet one. I parked the car; we got out and walked into the building and up to the apartment. Fritz met us at the door with tongue and tail wagging.

I grabbed his leash and told Sara I would take him down for a walk and turned around and walked back out. We hustled down the stairs. Apparently Fritz needed to get out in a hurry and sure enough he did, He barely made it out the door but he did make it and that was what counted. We walked around the building and down the trail towards the picnic table. I sat down and lit a cigarette. I couldn't figure out what was bothering me, nothing really or totally unexpected had happened. I got my orders a little earlier than I expected but other than that nothing else had changed.

After I put the cigarette out Fritz jumped up on the bench next to me and licked my face like he was trying to tell me something. He seemed to sense that things weren't like they should be.

"You ready to go back to the apartment?" I asked Fritz.

He jumped down and looked back at me like "Well, are we going or not?" I stood up and we headed back to the BOQ.

By the time we got back to the BOQ, Sara had taken her shower and made herself comfortable in her robe and customary towel around the head. "You guys were gone for a long time; I was beginning to think you got lost," she said.

"We walked down to the picnic table and had a cigarette," I replied.

"Did you get it out of your system?" Sara asked.

"Get what out of my system?" I asked.

"Whatever is bothering you?"

"Sugar, I don't know what's bothering me, and I don't know what to tell you. Whatever it is I'll get over it; in the meantime, just kinda bear with me, okay?"

She walked over, put her arms around my neck and looked me in the eye. "I know what's bothering you. Let's get comfortable and talk about it, okay?"

"Define comfortable," I said.

There was a glint in her eye that pretty well told me what she thought comfortable was. We walked over to the bed, she pulled the covers back as I got undressed and after I climbed in she turned the lights out, kicked Fritz out of her spot and climbed in beside me.

She rolled over on my shoulder and put her arm and leg across my body. We lay there in silence for a while. Then she said, "I know you don't want to go home, and I know you're only going because of me."

"We already talked about this and decided that was the best thing for us to do," I said.

"No, I decided it was the best thing for us to do. You never did really agree," she said.

"Well, I may never have verbally agreed, but I came to the conclusion that you were probably right, and it would be the best thing to do. I know that you would probably want a wedding with your mother and daddy there, probably a bunch of other people that wouldn't be able to come here, for one, and I suspect your teaching future is in the states not here."

"But where is your future? What are you going to do? What are you going back to?" she asked.

"I don't have any answers to any of those questions. But something will come up; it always does," I replied.

"So you're all right with going home?"

"As long as I know you're going to be there I'll be fine with it."

She reached up and gave me a kiss and snuggled in a little closer. I felt Fritz jump up on the foot of the bed and rest his chin on my feet; so I guess we were all ready to settle in for the night now.

GERMANY
Chapter 95

The rest of the weekend we just spent hanging out at the apartment and playing with Fritz. He was fast becoming the most popular guy on the block. People in the BOQ that had been there as long as Sara who never said more than hello to her were now stopping in the hallway and stairways to pet Fritz.

Every time we took him out for a walk he was always stopping and making friends. The kids in the area loved to play with him and he loved to play with them. He would chase anything, a ball, a stick, a rock, a brick; if you could throw it, he would chase it.

Sara and I didn't have much time to ourselves; Mary Ann was home all weekend for some reason that she didn't explain and we didn't ask. We played some cards, took turns going out for something to eat and taking Fritz for a walk when he needed to go out.

By the time the weekend was over I felt better, I guess I got over the initial realization I was actually going home in just about a month. Sara and Fritz drove me to the Bahnhof Sunday afternoon. After Sara pulled up in front of the Bahnhof, I leaned over and gave her a kiss. Fritz leaned forward from the backseat and gave us both a kiss. I opened the door and started to get out when Sara grabbed my arm.

"Are you okay?" she asked.

"Yeah, I'm fine. Why shouldn't I be?"

"We didn't get a chance to talk anymore since Friday night," she said.

"I'm okay with things now; I think the realization that I was actually going home hit me there for a while, but I'm good with it now."

"Okay, I love you, Rick."

"I know, and I love you too. Now I have to go and get my train."

I leaned over and gave her one more kiss before I climbed out of the car. Fritz hopped up in the front seat and hung his head out the window. I scratched him behind the ears and he wagged his tail and his tongue at the same time as I said goodbye.

Monday evening after I got off work I was in my room changing clothes before going to the mess hall when Roach came in. He had taken a couple of days leave the week we got back from our leave.

"Hey, Bones, I hear you got your orders."

"Yeah, I got 'em. Are you going to the mess hall?" I asked.

Roach nodded his head and we walked out of the room. We didn't say much until we got our trays and sat down at a table.

"You have any idea what this shit is?" I asked, pointing to the alleged food on my tray.

"It's some kinda pasta shit, something the new mess sergeant came up with. I hear it's really not bad."

I took my fork and tasted this…stuff. It wasn't bad. It was noodles, with chicken in some kinda cheese sauce and some other spices that I had no idea what they were. I'm sure there was a name for it, but I didn't know what it was.

"I heard you had a great leave. Tom said you got drunk as a skunk in Copenhagen and ended up in bed with two women," Roach said.

"I guess he left out the part that he was in that same bed. And that I was too drunk to do anything with one woman, much less two," I replied.

"That's not exactly the way I heard it, but I believe you. All in all how was the trip?"

"To tell ya the truth, I really like traveling with Sara better. Tom said he learned something traveling with me and got into more than just going to the clubs and chasing women. DeLaney was a little lame, and Ray, well, he was just Ray," I laughed.

"So what have you been up to? Seems like it's been a month or two since we got together just to bullshit," I said.

Roach pushed his tray back, lit a cigarette. "I took a couple of days the week you got back and went on a trip with Bobbie Jo and her parents. We went to someplace down around Munich. We stayed at some Military Retreat called Walker Hill."

"Garmisch, you went to Garmisch. Sara and I went down there the first trip we took with that other couple," I said.

"Yeah, that was the place, pretty nice place; beautiful mountains."

"We were there in December. There was snow on the mountains, and they were really nice," I said.

I lit a cigarette, and Roach and I sat and talked until they ran us out of the mess hall so they could close it up. We walked back over to my room, no one was around; I sat down on my bunk and Roach sat on my footlocker.

"How many days you got left, Bones?"

"I figured it out on the way back Sunday. As of today I have 19 working days left. My orders say I will sail out of Bremerhaven on 19 May and arrive stateside on or about 25 May for discharge. When Top gave me my orders he looked at his schedule and said my last day of work would be about 11 May, which is a Friday, and I will start clearing post and outprocessing the next Monday, 14 May."

"Damn, you are short, ain't ya?" Roach stated.

"Shorter than I would like to be. Sara won't get home until sometime in July," I said.

Roach looked at his watch.

"It's almost time for me to start getting ready for work. This is my last midnight shift; then I have a seventy-two-hour break; let's you and me go down and check out some of the old places we used to go. I haven't been downtown in months."

"Sounds like a plan to me, but you gotta promise me you won't get drunk. I'm too short to be getting in any trouble now," I said.

Roach chuckled. "I promise; that ain't as much fun as it used to be anyway." Roach lit a cigarette and walked out the door.

The following Thursday night Roach and I grabbed a taxi and headed for the Westhof Bar. We had one quick drink, then went on down to the Hauptstrasse. On the way we crossed over Rohrbach Strasse, and both chuckled and laughed about each of our experiences on Rohrbach.

We continued on up Hauptstrasse; there were a lot of people on the streets. Roach and I guessed that there were tourists in town, and sure enough, there were about three busses parked in the Park Platz. We stopped in at a couple of the usual tourist traps that served large mugs and in some cases glass boots of beer and they all had the oompa bands There were some obvious tourists around but nothing really interesting; at least not to me. We wandered through and then moved on out and went down to one of the clubs near the old bridge that catered to GIs. We hit the Rendezvous Club first this place was always packed and was a big hang out for the guys from the company. Tommy Hackett and I had spent more than one evening in this place. It wasn't too bad for a Thursday night so Roach and I had one drink and then moved on up the street to the Kit Cat club. This place wasn't as lively as the Rendezvous but they pumped up the music anyway to draw in the customers. We had one more drink there and then moved on.

We returned to the barracks, walked over to the Patio by the Enlisted Club and had a drink. The Patio wasn't crowded and we pretty much had the place to ourselves. We sat and just talked about first one thing then another. We got back to the barracks and returned to our own rooms around 11:00 pm. I was in bed by 11:30 and asleep shortly there after.

Friday evening came and I was, as usual on my way to K-Town. I thought about a couple of things that had been said in the night before; about Roach and I going our separate ways. He staying in Heidelberg and me going; somehow that didn't sound right. I should be staying too. I wondered if last night would really be the last time we would be able to get together.

When I opened the door to the apartment, Fritz greeted me waging his tail and jumping up on me. Damn he was getting big already I thought. Sara came over and while her tail wasn't wagging her tongue was. She put her arms around me and gave me a big kiss.

"Hi, baby, how was your trip? Did you have a good week?" I could have come and picked you up if you had called. Fritz is being a pest this evening; he keeps biting my toes while I'm trying to grade papers."

"The trip was boring as usual. I'll tell you about the week later, and it sounds like Fritz wants your attention. But now he is going to have to fight me for it, because I want your attention, too," I said.

"If you will take him out so I can finish grading these papers, I'll be sure you get all the attention you want when I'm done," Sara replied.

"Okay, you got a deal." I looked at Fritz; he was sitting at our feet, waiting, looking up at us as if to say, "Okay, when is my turn?"

"You wanna go out?" I asked.

His ears perked up, he could hold them both up now and he looked bright eyed and alert.

"Where is your leash?"

He knew what I was asking, he walked over to the door and sat by it and looked up at the hook on the wall were we hung his leash. Sara had been doing a good job in training him.

We walked down to the picnic table I sat on the end of the table; took the leash off Fritz which was really a violation of the area leash law but I knew he wouldn't go far and he surely wasn't going to bite anyone. We were there about 15 minutes; Fritz came back to the table and jumped up in my lap. That was his way of telling me we could go back now. I hooked his leash back to his collar and we headed back up the trail to the BOQ. Fritz made one more stop just before we went in and then raced up the stairs and was waiting on me at the hallway door.

We got back inside the apartment, Fritz headed for his water dish as soon as I took his leash off. Sara was finishing up her last stack of papers. I kicked off my shoes, sat on the bed, and lit a cigarette. No smoke ring yet. Damn it. Fritz lay down at the foot of the bed. He had already got too big to get under the coffee table.

Sara came over and sat down beside me on the bed. "How was your walk?" she asked.

"It was fine; Fritz checked everything out and made sure everything was in its place." I laughed.

"You said you would tell me about your week. Did something happen?" Sara asked.

"Not really. Roach and I went out last night and went downtown," I replied.

"Oh, really, anything exciting happen?"

I told Sara about making the rounds of the different clubs then going back to the Patio by the enlisted club sitting out there and bull shittin' for a while.

"It wasn't anything exciting, but it was good to just be able to get out with Roach and talk for a while. We hadn't done that in ages," I said.

Sara made us some sandwiches. She gave Fritz a dog biscuit so he wouldn't be sitting there expecting us to give him some of our sandwiches. We ate and talked about first one thing then another. We finished eating and smoked a cigarette. She told me Fritz was becoming a bilingual dog. She had been giving him commands in English and German and he was beginning to understand them both. I thought that was pretty cool. But then thought it might be embarrassing having a dog that understood more German than I did.

"I'm tired. I think I want to take a hot shower and go to bed," I said.

"I'm tired, too. Why don't you go take your shower, and I'll take Fritz out one more time and then get my shower when I get back."

I got up and got undressed as she put the leash on Fritz, and they went out for a last walk tonight.

The shower felt good. I could feel the tenseness leaving my body but had no idea why I was so tense to begin with. I stayed in the shower until I heard Sara return.

I stepped out of the shower in my stolen heavy white robe. Sara was already pretty well naked and headed right for the shower as soon as I came out. I walked over, pulled the covers back and crawled in bed. I didn't even feel like a last cigarette. I was asleep before Sara even got out of the shower.

We spent most of Saturday going to the PX and the Commissary but our first stop was the cafeteria for brunch. Mary Ann was home so we talked her into babysitting Fritz for a few hours while we took care of the shopping. She didn't mind, making some comment about Fritz being the best male company she had in the past couple of weeks. Sara and I just looked at each other; we didn't bother to ask what that meant.

Fritz was happy to see us by the time we got back. Mary Ann apparently was too, she said she had someplace to go and left almost as soon as we got back. Sara put the groceries away and I took Fritz for a walk since Mary Ann hadn't told us the last time he had been out.

We decided to go to the club for supper. We left Fritz by himself. He didn't seem too happy about that but he was used to being there alone when Sara was working so we figured he would be okay.

The dining room was fairly crowded for some reason but we got a table without much of a wait. I ordered the steak and Sara had fish. That seemed to be our two mainstays at the club, we both had one or the other every time we went; but those were things you really didn't get anywhere else.

"Did you decide if you want me to take some time off?" Sara asked.

"I don't want you to put yourself in a bind for time you may need later. I'll be off starting the week of the 14th of May to clear post and process out. From what I hear that really only takes about a day, maybe two at the most, so I'll have most of that week with nothing to do but pack, and that's not going to take me long. Since I have to leave Heidelberg on the 18th by train maybe if you took off on the 17th we could stay in Heidelberg that night, and you could take me to the train station on the 18th. How does that sound?

"I can do that. I can drive up on the evening of the 16th if you want," Sara said.

"That's sounds like a good idea to me."

Our food arrived and we ate without too much talking. Afterwards Sara had one more glass of wine. We smoked a cigarette while she drank her wine and I sipped on my ice tea. We paid our bill and drove back to the BOQ. Fritz was happy to see us. I took him out one more time while Sara got her shower. She was out of the shower by the time we got back, dressed in her heavy white stolen robe and a towel around her head. I let Fritz off his leash and I went into the bathroom and took a shower.

When I got out of the shower, Sara was already in bed but not asleep. Fritz was lying in my place. I had to roust him out so I climbed over Sara and crawled under the covers. I couldn't help but notice that Sara was naked under those covers. And I couldn't help but smile when she rolled over in my arms and buried her face in my neck.

Sunday was a lazy day from start until time to take me to the train station. We ate in and took Fritz out for a long walk and sat down at the picnic table for a long time. Neither of us seemed to have much to say or didn't know what to say.

It was a quick good-bye at the train station. I think we were both just getting really anxious about my leaving. I had 15 working days left. Three more weekends together before I left.

GERMANY
Chapter 96

I can't think of a time that when a guy went overseas that he didn't have a short-timer's calendar at one time or another. Some started their calendars as soon as they arrived and others waited until they got down to a certain point, maybe 100 days or 30 days left before they started marking the days off their calendar. I had started one shortly after I arrived but after meeting Sara I kinda forgot about it.

As I was cleaning out my wall locker I found the one I had started many months ago. I never even got it completed down to one day. Now I was down to 4 days and a wake up and then I was on my way home. I really didn't need a calendar to tell me that. It seems there is a time during your tour that when you look back; it seems like you just got here, and time has just flown by but then you look ahead and it seems like the day you're due to leave will never get here. I could look back and feel like I just got here yesterday, but I couldn't look ahead and think my departure day was never going to get here. Maybe that was because I didn't want to leave.

It was Monday, 14 May, I was officially off the duty roster and relieved of all duties except to start and complete my out processing. I had pulled my last tour of duty the previous Friday; in keeping with tradition of the company I was assigned to Gate #1 at Campbell Barracks as my last duty assignment and wore my real leather gear instead of my patent leather. Also in keeping with tradition and as I had watched so many others that had left before me do, when we were relieved of duty that day I took off my leather MP gear attached it to a straightened out coat hanger and let it hang out the back of the ¾ ton truck we took back to Patton Barracks. I watched it bounce and tumble along the cobblestone streets, I could almost see the polish flying off of each piece. I thought of the time I picked that gear up from the supply sergeant and all the time and effort I put into making that leather shine until I could see myself in every piece of it. Now the next 'cruit coming in would have to figure out for himself how to make it shine just like I did. It was kinda hard to watch it being torn up like that.

I don't know why they gave you so much time to out process. Not that I minded having the time off, but it could all be done in one day, two at the most. I had to go to Campbell Barracks and get my clearance sheet signed off on by someone in G-2. I never did understand that; I never handled any classified documents or had anything to do with anything in the intelligence area. Everything else was done at Patton Barracks. I stopped by the Provost Marshal's office and got DeLaney to sign off on my clearance papers, then walked over to the dispensary and got the medics to initial off. The only thing left was the Central Supply Point and turn in my field gear and then the company supply room. But you didn't want to do that until the morning of your departure because you had to turn in your linen and blankets. My last stop was Personal and Finance; that took all of about 45 minutes. All that was left was packing my duffel bag, the supply room and signing out of the company one last time.

I was halfway tempted to go catch a train to K-Town for the next couple of days but I decided against it. Sara would be down here on Wednesday evening, the 16th, and I had just seen her yesterday. I figured I could wait a couple of days.

Our last three weekends together had been pretty low key. But then all our weekends were low key when we weren't traveling. With Fritz traveling really wasn't an option, at least not an over night trip. But that was okay; Fritz kept us entertained. Every weekend I saw him he was bigger, his markings were really starting to show and he was going to be one beautiful Shepard. And he was the smartest dog I had ever been around. Sara had been teaching him some basic obedience stuff, like sit, down, stay, heel and so forth and he could respond to all the commands in English and German. Sara would give him one in German and I would give him one in English and he never missed a lick. And he was good on the leash, when you took him out. He never went out to the end of the leash and tried to pull you along; he stayed next to you except when he needed to take care of business and then he might need some leash to find the place he was looking for.

Sara always took him out as soon as she got home from school. Of course the kids in the area were home from school too and they had a field across the road from the BOQ they played ball on but when they saw Sara come out with Fritz they would all holler at her to bring Fritz over so they could play with him. She would let him off the leash and he would run over to play with the kids. They would play keep away as long as they could with a ball but if one missed it and Fritz got it then they had to catch him. Of course they never could catch him; he would wear them out and then strut around like he was king shit with the ball in his mouth. Finally when they were all too tired to chase him anymore he would go drop the ball at one of the kids feet and wait for him to throw it so they could play some more. It was good for Fritz, he got lots of exercise and it was good for Sara and me when I was there, because Fritz was ready to eat and sleep after that workout.

Roach came by the room after work and we went to the mess hall. We joined Tom and Hobbs at a table with Harry, Rizzo and Dietz at the next table over. This turned out to be like a roast. Everybody had something to say about Bones. Of course most if it wasn't true. Okay, well some of it was. Even Top who had been working late came over to the table and made a comment or two about the skinniest 'cruit he had ever seen come into the company two years ago. Top only stayed a few minutes and he told me to be sure I signed out on Friday before I left otherwise I could be considered AWOL and they would have to send the MPs after me and bring me back. I told him he shouldn't put ideas like that in my head. He smiled and patted me on the shoulder; he knew I really didn't want to leave. Don't ask me how he knew that but it didn't surprise me; the guy seemed to know everything about everybody in his company; which is probably why he was the best first sergeant I ever served under.

After we left the mess hall, Roach came by the room and we talked while I packed my duffel bag. Tom came by, followed by Hobbs so the gang was all there. Rizzo and Dietz had to work the midnight shift; Harry and Hobbs worked day shift tomorrow and Tom and Roach were on break.

"Hey, everybody, listen up," Roach hollered above everybody else. "Tomorrow night at the club out on the patio we are gonna throw Bones a short-timer's party. Pass the word. It's open to anyone else in the company that wants to drop by."

"What time?" Hobbs asked.

"We should start showing up probably around 1800-1830 so we can get a couple of tables," Tom said.

"Can I bring my girl?" Rizzo inquired.

"Only if you promise to bring your own cigarettes, Rizzo," Roach replied.

"I can do that, but I'm out right now; anybody got one?"

Four guys threw something at Rizzo besides cigarettes. I was the only one to toss him a cigarette.

"Hey, thanks lover; I'm gonna miss you." Rizzo grinned.

By this time I pretty much had my duffel bag packed and sat down on my bunk. I slipped out of my shoes and lit a cigarette of my own. I exhaled and out came this huge smoke ring. "Yo, hey…ya'll look! My first smoke ring!" I shouted. Everyone applauded. I was so proud of myself. I tried to blow another one but never got close the rest of the night.

Tuesday morning I slept in and missed breakfast. About 0900 Roach and Tom came in and woke me up. "Get your ass outta bed, Bones," Roach said.

"What's the rush?" I asked still half asleep.

"We are getting outta Dodge for a while and going over to the snack bar," Tom said.

"Why?" I asked.

"Just to hang out. Now come on, let's go," Roach insisted.

"I gotta take a shower and brush my teeth," I said as I reached for my cigarettes.

"Hurry the fuck up before someone catches us, okay?" Roach complained.

"Just because you're relieved of duty doesn't mean we are," Tom chimed in.

I climbed out of bed and grabbed my shaving kit and towel and headed for the showers. The hot water beating down on my neck, shoulder and back began to make me feel human again as usual. I cut the shower short, walked over to the sink, shaved and brushed my teeth. I hustled back to the room and threw on a pair of slacks and a shirt, slipped on my shoes and the three of us were off to the snack bar.

"Did you guys eat breakfast?" I asked.

"Yeah, we ate," Tom said but that was a long time ago. I'm hungry again already.

I looked at my watch; it was right at 1100 hours. "The mess hall will be opening up in about 30 minutes," I said.

"I don't wanna eat in the mess hall. Do you, Roach?" Tom asked.

"Not really. How about you Bones?"

"I don't care, but I'm getting hungry talking about eating, so let's do something," I said.

We decided to grab something at the snack bar. The place was beginning to fill up so I told Roach to grab me a hamburger and fries with a coke. I'd stay and hold our table for us. I gave him a couple of bucks and he was off to get in line behind Tom. While they were standing in line I lit up a smoke and tried for another smoke ring, no luck again. I finished my cigarette just about the time they got back to the table.

"So when do you actually leave, Bones?" Roach asked.

"Sara is coming down tomorrow evening after she gets off work, and we are gonna spend Thursday together. Then she is going to take me to the Bahnhof Friday evening. My train leaves at 1800."

"How come you're going home by boat?" Tom asked.

"I have no idea; that's what my orders read."

"I thought everyone was flying these days," Roach said.

"I wish I was. I'm not crazy about taking a boat, and the guy at Personnel when he saw my orders and it said USS *Maurice Rose*; he said that was the slowest boat they had; it takes at least one day more than any of the other ships to get home."

"Be sure to give us your address before you leave," Roach said.

We finished our burgers and fries, got a refill on our drinks, sat back, and smoked and joked for a couple of hours. Finally we went back to the barracks and played some pool until it was time for supper.

I went back to the barracks after we ate, lay down on my bunk, and went to sleep. I couldn't have slept more than 30 minutes it seems before Roach was shaking me and yelling, "Wake up, Bones, you shithead. You're missing your own short-timer's party!"

I sat up and looked at my watch, it was 1900 hours. I had been asleep about an hour and a half. I reached over and grabbed my cigarettes and lit one up. I slipped on my shoes and Roach and I headed out for the club. As we entered the gate to the patio we could hear the guys over in the corner raising hell already. They had taken over three tables. I got a big round of applause when they spotted me and Roach walking through the patio gate. I probably would have been embarrassed but I knew most everyone on the patio and I had been through a few of these since I arrived there so I felt pretty comfortable with it all.

The roast from the night before in the mess hall continued for a while. Finally everything settled down, and those that could got into some serious drinking. Those that had to go to work on the mid-shift stuck with coke or whatever, and those with girlfriends got into them.

Roach, Tom and I just kinda sat and sipped our drinks and watched the others. Dietz came out of the club with two of the ugliest girls on the base. We had to laugh; Dietz was notorious for having the uncanny ability to find the ugliest girls in the area and hooking up with them. He always did that during Fasching. It got to the point no one would go down to Stadt Hall with him during this festival season just because he would walk off into the crowd and bring back all these ugly women to our table.

About 2200 hours, guys that had to work started drifting out. Actually I was ready to go to but not sure it would be a good idea since this was my party. About an hour later though most everyone was gone and the club closed in an hour anyway. We all walked back to the barracks which was about 30 yards away and everybody went to their rooms; by midnight everyone was either asleep or just passed out.

Wednesday morning I decided that Sara and I should do something special for the last couple of days we were going to have together for a while. I got the duty driver to take me over to Campbell Barracks and drop me off at the Information Station. I wanted to talk to Hans, our German interpreter. I asked Hans to give me some ideas as to the best hotels in Heidelberg. Hans was quick to recommend the Ritter St. Georg, which ironically was located on the Hauptstrasse, just a couple of blocks down from the Red Ox. I must have walked or driven by the place a couple of hundred times and never knew it was there or what it was. But then I never really had a reason to know. Hans got on the phone and made reservations for two nights for me.

I caught a ride back to Patton Barracks went back to my room. My area was starting to look pretty bleak. My duffel bag was packed, standing in the corner. All I had left was a change of civilian cloths, underwear and T-shirts and my shaving kit. I needed to go down to the cleaners this afternoon and pick up my uniform that I would be wearing on the train and stop by the Orderly Room and pay Top for half a month's service.

Rizzo and Dietz were asleep, and Harry was working. I walked down to Roach's room; he was lying on his bunk reading a book. "Hey, shit head, what kinda pictures you looking at in that book? Everybody knows you can't read."

"Fuck you, Bones."

"Nice talk, GI," I said.

Roach put the book down and sat up on his bunk. "Give me a cigarette, Bones," Roach said.

"Shit, you're gettin' as bad as Rizzo; I'm gonna take you both as dependents on my next tax return," I said as I tossed him a cigarette.

"I looked for you in your room earlier. Where you been?" Roach asked.

"I went over to Campbell to talk to Hans for a few minutes," I replied.

"What did you want with Hans?"

"I wanted him to tell me the best hotels in Heidelberg. I was looking for a really nice place for Sara and me to stay when she gets here this evening."

"Did he hook you up?"

"Yeah, old Hans is a good man to know sometimes," I laughed.

Tom came in. "Hey, Bones, what's up?"

"Not much. I'm just getting shorter by the minute," I replied.

"Give me a cigarette, will ya, Bones?" Tom asked.

"Holy fuck, do I look like a fuckin' vending machine? I can't believe you guys are all out of cigarettes already; it's only the middle of the month," I snarled.

"I'm not out, I got some down in my room, and I just don't wanna go get 'em right now," Tom mumbled as he lit his smoke.

"Okay. I'm going to the mess hall and eat since I missed breakfast this morning. Then I have to come back and go pick up my uniform from the press room. You guys going to eat?"

I'm goin, but first I'm going to get some cigarettes outta my locker before you blow a gasket again," Tom said.

Roach got up, walked over to his locker, and got out a pack of cigarettes. "I'm going," he said.

"Ya'll are some lazy bastards, ya know that?" I said.

We all laughed as we walked out the door. We stopped by Tom's room on our way to the Mess hall. The place was crowded; we should have waited for the lunch bunch to clear out. We found one table way in the back, and Charlie Waters joined us, so it was a full table. Charlie had just about given up on his Rizzo impersonation, but every once in a while he couldn't resist a, "What do say, lover?"

We pretty much ate in silence. Charlie had to wolf his food down he was on duty and had to go relieve another gate so that guy could come eat. The three of us finished up about the same time, slid our trays towards the center of the table and lit a cigarette. I didn't bring mine out until the other two had theirs going already.

I finished my cigarette, grabbed my tray and headed for the kitchen window to empty my leftovers and drop off my tray. Roach and Tom were right behind me.

We left the mess hall, walked back to the company, they went to the day room and I went to pick up my uniform. I took the uniform upstairs and hung it up then went back down to the day room and joined in a few games of doubles ping pong. The first sergeant came in and jumped in a couple of games. He was a terrible player but he made the game fun. Roach was only slightly better; but Tom and I were pretty evenly matched and had some down to the wire singles games in the past.

I finally decided to go back up to my room and wait for Sara. I figured if she called before she left that would be the first place someone would come looking for me and if she didn't call that would still be the first place they would come looking. I kicked my shoes off, lay back on my bunk, and promptly fell asleep.

It seemed like only a few minutes but was actually about 2 hours later Oakley was shaking me, telling me to wake up that there was a woman in a blue car waiting for me downstairs. I think he sounded like he was the only guy in the company that didn't know I was seeing Sara. And he may very well have been he usually had his head up his ass about most things anyway.

I slipped on my shoes, grabbed my shaving gear and little bag of clothes and hustled down the stairs. Roach, Tom, Hobbs and most everybody else were outside talking and joking with Sara. I caught hell when I came out with all the wise cracks and shit. Once I got in the car I leaned over and gave Sara a kiss and then we really got the heckling. The guys surrounded the car and sat on the hood and wouldn't let us leave. Sara was laughing and telling them to get off the car or she would run over them. Finally they cleared a path and we pulled away from the company.

"Where are we going?" Sara asked.

"Down to the Hauptstrasse to the Ritter St.Georg," I said.

GERMANY
Chapter 97

We found the hotel without a problem and even found a parking place only a couple of spaces away from the front door. We went in and as usual I let Sara do all the talking; things always went much better that way. I had told her we had reservations in my name on the way down so they were expecting us.

Our room was on the third floor overlooking the Hauptstrasse. It was a very nice room, well lighted and spacious. There was no air conditioning but there was a large ceiling fan that seemed to circulate the air rather well throughout the room. We opened the window and could hear the sounds of the street below but surprisingly they weren't overwhelming.

Sara began to unpack her two little bags, one with some change of clothes and the other full of all that other stuff women just can't seem to do without. I took my shaving kit out of my little bag and put it in the bathroom. I think more out of habit than anything else Sara had packed the cooler so we had some cold cokes with us in the room. I opened one up, slipped off my shoes and sat down on the sofa. Sara came over and sat with me and we lit a cigarette. I exhaled trying to blow a smoke ring but didn't, she exhaled and blew one just to piss me off I think.

"I thought you said you weren't gonna do that?" I whined.

"I said I wouldn't do it when we were out in public," she grinned.

"Humph, I'll have you know I blew a really big one just a couple of nights ago," I bragged.

"Oh! Good for you baby," she said as she leaned over and gave me a kiss.

"But I still think I have a deformed tongue," I said.

"I told you, you may not be able to blow a smoke ring with that tongue, but you can do some other amazing things with it," she said as she leaned in to give me a kiss, putting her hand on my thigh and squeezing.

"Okay, keep that up, and it will get you about anything you want, but do you really want it now? Wouldn't you prefer to wait until later?"

"Why not now and later too?" she whispered in my ear.

"Because you wear me out, and I'll want to take a nap and I don't want to take a nap this late," I reasoned.

"Are you sure?" she asked as she began to nibble on my neck and move her hand further up my thigh.

What the hell? I thought. *We can go eat later and sleep late tomorrow.*

"You don't play fair; you know that?" I said.

"Are you going to sit here and bitch about it or undress me?" she whispered.

"I'll shut up," I replied as I began to unbutton her blouse.

I woke up about 7:00 p.m. Sara was already up and obviously taken her shower, since she was sitting on the sofa and brushing her hair. I sat up in bed and grabbed my cigarettes off the night stand. "How long have you been up?" I asked.

She turned and smiled, "Not long, just long enough to get my shower," she replied.

I sat there on the bed smoking my cigarette and watching her brush her hair. I couldn't help but think how much I was going to miss this after I left. I finished my cigarette, slid off the bed and headed for the shower. I turned after I got the water going and hanging on the back of the door was my white robe with a note pinned to it. I walked over and unpinned the note and read it; "Don't forget where you got this. I love you," signed "Sara xoxo." I smiled put the note in the pocket of the robe, walked back to the shower, and climbed in.

By the time I got out of the shower Sara was almost dressed. But that didn't mean she was almost ready to go, she still had to go through that makeup-and-do-the-hair-just-right drill. I slipped on some jeans and a shirt, walked over, got a coke, and took a seat on the sofa. "What are we going to do tonight? Sara asked.

"I just thought we would go get something to eat and take a walk along the Hauptstrasse if you wanted to," I replied.

"That sounds good to me. Where do you want to go eat?"

"I don't know any place to go eat except the Bahnhof. This place has a dining room. Wanna try that?" I replied.

"That's fine with me," she said as she stepped out of the bathroom with all her make up on and her hair all done. She really looked good this evening. I stood up slipped my shoes on and we headed out the door and down to the dining room.

It was a very nice dining room, with soft lighting, and it was actually kinda cozy. We took a table in the far corner away from everything and everybody else. The waiter came over with the menus and took our drink orders. As usual Sara had wine, I thought I would try a rum and coke and then maybe switch to ice tea when the meal came.

I was planning on ordering my usual Wiener Schnitzel and Pomme Frites, but Sara said that in all the time we had gone out to eat in a German restaurant she doesn't remember me ever ordering anything different and said I should try something else just once before I left. She talked me into at least ordering a brat with potatoes instead of cabbage.

We took our time eating. The brat wasn't all that bad. Actually it was pretty good. It was just the cabbage that I never did like. We both had another drink after dinner and then went for a walk up one side of the Hauptstrasse and then down the other.

The stores were almost all closed and those that weren't already were about to; but we weren't looking to buy anything, mostly just out walking for the exercise and to walk off our dinner. We cut across the street to get back to the side the hotel was on and began walking back towards it.

When we got back to the room I opened the window over looking the street we had just been walking and watched those people still on the street moving back and forth. There was a movie theater just down the street and apparently it had just let out, the street had more activity on it all of a sudden. Sara came over and joined me at the window. We lit a cigarette and she rested her head on my shoulder as we both just watched the street below us, neither speaking, each lost in our own thoughts. You could just catch a portion of the moon behind one of the taller buildings down the street. It was a pretty, starry night out, not a cloud in the sky.

Sara moved back into the room and began to undress. I left the window open but pulled the sheer curtains together and they immediately began to billow in the soft breeze blowing into the room. By the time I was undressed Sara was already in bed. I climbed in beside her and she rolled over into my arms bringing one leg over mine as she usually did. I held her close and gently ran my hand up and down her back. We didn't talk; it didn't seem words were necessary. The breeze from the window was being blown over us by the ceiling fan, it was actually getting cool. I reached down and pulled up the light blanket, Sara stirred but didn't change positions. I covered her with the blanket. She moved her leg up higher across my body, muttered a soft, "I love you," and went sound to sleep.

When I woke up the next morning I was lying on my side with my back to Sara but she was snuggled up right behind me with her arm draped over my waist and her legs right up behind mind. I reached out and got my cigarettes and lighter. I tried not to wake her up but I guess I did, at least partially anyway, because she asked if I took Fritz out yet. I turned over, kissed her on the forehead and said, "Yeah, I took him out already and let him play ball with the kids across the street."

Without opening her eyes, she move closer to me and said "You're such a liar; Fritz is in K-Town with Mary Ann."

"If you knew that then why did you ask?" I responded.

"I just wanted to see what you would say," she said as she sat up in bed, stretched and letting the covers fall to her waist.

"How many times I gotta tell you not to do that in front of me," I said.

She looked down at me and just to tease me some more shook her shoulders back and forth. I grabbed her and pulled her down towards me, kissed her and said, "You better watch it, lady, or you'll get an EMHO."

"What's an EMHO?" she asked with a quizzical look on her face.

"I never told you what an EMHO was?" I asked, surprised.

"No, you never told me."

I pulled her down closer and whispered in her ear. "That's an early morning hard on."

She quickly sat back up with a big grin on her face and said, "I wanna see," and started to pull the covers down, but I grabbed her hand and said "NO! You can't see. If you're not going to use it you can't see it."

"But if I see it I'll probably wanna use it." She pouted.

"It's too late now. Anyway, it's not early morning anymore," I replied.

"I don't believe you," she said accusingly.

"Okay, go ahead and peek, but you're going to be disappointed."

She slowly pulled the covers up and peeked, saw that I was right and let out a big sigh of disappointment. "That's no fair; you should have told me about EMHO a long time ago."

"I couldn't tell you before," I stated.

"Why not?"

"I just thought of it," I said.

She hit me with a pillow and climbed on top of me and said, "Just wait and see if I ever tell you about HWP?"

"What the hell is that?" I asked even though I was pretty sure I knew already.

She leaned down and whispered in my ear. "That's hot wet pussy," then burst out laughing, her face began turning beet red. I couldn't help but laugh with her; she was so cute when she thought she said something really naughty.

I pulled her down, took her face in both my hands. "I love you," I said and then gave her a BWK. We wallowed around in bed for a while and got all tangled up in the covers and finally came up for air and sat back up and smoked a cigarette. When she was finished with her cigarette she hopped out of bed and headed for the bathroom.

I got out of bed, walked over and grabbed a coke then walked over and looked out the window through the sheer curtains. The street had come alive; all the stores were open and cars were parked up and down on both sides; people scurrying in all directions. I walked over to the nightstand got my cigarettes and looked at my watch. It was 10.a.m. I had about thirty-six hours left in Heidelberg and to spend with Sara. All of a sudden this whole thing really sucked.

Sara came out of the shower, "It's all yours," she said.

I walked in the bathroom and turned on the shower, waited a couple of minutes for the hot water to take over then stepped in. I thought about what we might do today. I didn't want to hang around the hotel room all day. We had almost already seen all there was to see in Heidelberg. *Oh, well,* I thought, *I'm sure we will come up with something.* We hadn't talked about it; maybe Sara already had some ideas.

"Are you hungry?" she asked as she sipped on her instant coffee.

"I could eat something. How about breakfast at the Bahnhof? We know what they have, and it's always good," I suggested.

"That sounds good to me," she replied.

We dressed, walked down to the car and headed for the Bahnhof. It was only about a ten-minute drive. It took almost as long to walk from where we parked the car as it did to drive over to the Bahnhof. We got to the restaurant and found a table near the front so we could look out over the street. We both ordered eggs and ham. Sara naturally had coffee, I had orange juice.

"What do you want to do today?" she asked

"I was going to ask you that. I don't have anything in mind until after supper."

"Oh, you have something in mind for this evening then?" she asked with a smile on her face.

"Yes, I do have an idea or two," I said.

"You gonna tell me?"

"Nope, I am not telling you now. You're just going to have to wait and find out later this evening."

"Is it a big secret?" she asked.

"No, it's not a secret; I'm just not telling." I laughed.

"Okay, so what are we going to do until then?" Sara asked.

"How about we go out to the Tiergarten?"

"Okay, do you remember how to get there?" she asked.

"No, but we can ask the waiter when we get ready to leave. I'm sure they can give you directions," I said.

Our food arrived; we took our time and just enjoyed our meal. Afterwards while Sara had another cup of coffee and I finished my orange juice, we smoked a cigarette. When the waiter brought us our check Sara asked him for directions to the Tiergarten. She thanked him, I paid the check, and we walked back to the car.

"I assume you got directions?" I inquired.

"Of course I did. It's pretty easy from here. It seems I recall it being a pretty easy drive when we went out there the first time two years ago," Sara recalled.

We found the Tiergarten without a problem and strolled around the place hand in hand and just enjoyed the weather, the plants and animals. We stopped a few times to just sit on a bench and watch the other people and a couple of times we stopped for something to drink at one of the little concession stands. We did a little reminiscing about our first visit there with Mary Ann and Barry. She couldn't help but bring up how Barry and I made idiots of ourselves trying to imitate the animals. I hoped she would have forgotten that part anyway.

As we drove away from the Tiergarten Sara asked, "What now? Are you going to tell me what you have planned for later on?"

"I thought we would go eat a relatively early dinner and then maybe go to a club or something," I said.

"I bet you have a club all picked out, don't you?"

"I might," I smiled.

We arrived back at the hotel and had to park a little further away but not that far. We got back to the room it was almost five p.m. when I looked at my watch. *Twenty-six hours;* I thought, *that's all the time I have left. I need to quit looking at my watch.* It pissed me off every time I looked at it.

"What time did you want to go eat?" Sara asked.

"I thought about 7 or 7:30 would be good," I replied.

"Are we going back to the hotel dining room to eat?" she asked.

"You have any better ideas? I'm open to suggestions."

"Last night when we were walking I saw a little café down the street that looked pretty nice," Sara said.

"Okay, we'll give it a try."

Sara began to get undressed, "I'm going to take another shower, I feel kinda icky after walking around the Tiergarten all afternoon," she said.

"You go ahead; I'll take one when you're finished."

"Sure you don't want to take one with me and scrub my back for me?" She grinned.

"No, you can't control yourself, and back scrubbing leads to other stuff," I replied.

"You're no fun at all," she pouted as she walked towards the bathroom. She left the door open on purpose just so I could see her slip out of her bra and panties. I was sure as hell tempted to go scrub her back.

GERMANY
Chapter 98

We arrived at the little café Sara had seen promptly at 7 p.m. We got a seat by the window where we could watch the people on the street. The place kinda reminded me of one of those little Bistros we ate in while in Paris.

I couldn't help myself tonight; I wasn't in the mood to try anything different so I stuck with what I knew; Wiener Schnitzel and Pomme Frites. I don't know what Sara had I think it was some kind of fish. We both ordered a glass of wine; I figured I could stretch it a little bit anyway and do something a little different. The place was a little crowded so service was backed up a bit. We really weren't in a hurry; we sipped our wine and smoked cigarettes. I tried a smoke ring again, but no luck as usual. I wanted to do at least one just to show Sara I could. I don't know what I did differently the other night that I actually blew one; but whatever it was I had forgotten it.

Our food finally arrived. Too bad I didn't find this place before; this was the best Wiener Schnitzel I ever had. Sara seemed to enjoy whatever that stuff was she was eating but it didn't look all that appetizing to me. We ate slowly and both ordered a second glass of wine. Wine isn't one of my favorite things to drink I probably shouldn't have had a second glass.

We finished our meal, passed on dessert as we usually did, finished our wine and smoked another cigarette. I paid the bill and we left the café about 8:45. I took Sara by the hand and started walking back towards the hotel.

"Are we going back to the hotel already? I thought you said you wanted to go to a club?" she asked.

"I do, and we are," I said as we passed the hotel entrance.

We walked up the street a couple of blocks then Sara saw the sign Red Ox. She quickly put two and two together. "You're taking me back to the beginning, aren't you? she asked.

"You catch on quick, don't ya? I grinned.

We walked in the Red Ox and I quickly went to the booth we had sat in before, as luck would have it there was no one sitting in it. We sat down in the booth and the waitress was right there. Sara asked the waitress to wait just a minute. "What was I drinking that night? she asked.

"You were drinking a beer, and I had a coke," I told her.

Sara looked at the waitress and ordered a beer and a coke. "You know what I like about you?" Sara asked.

"You want me to tell you right here and now?" I grinned.

"NO! Besides that; you always remember the little things. I wouldn't have remembered what I was drinking or what you had. That was two years ago," she said.

"You were wearing a short-sleeved white dress that buttoned all the way down the front with little green and yellow flower-like thingys on it," I said, "and a pair of white sandals."

"I still have that outfit; you should have told me. I would have brought it." She pouted

"I didn't think about it until this morning," I said.

The waitress brought our drinks and set them on the table. I lit a cigarette and exhaled....there it was my second smoke ring. Look! I said excitedly...there it is...my second smoke ring! Sara applauded and laughed and stretched across the table and gave me a kiss. "I'm so proud of you," she said.

I laughed; people around us must have thought we were crazy, getting excited over a smoke ring. I thought we were crazy getting excited over a smoke ring, but who really gave a shit.

We had a second round of drinks and reminisced about things. Somehow our memories always seemed to keep going back to Paris and that little fishing village in Spain.

"I can't believe I went skinny dipping on a public beach or anyplace, for that matter," Sara said.

"I can't believe you dressed up like a French hooker, even if it was just in our hotel room." I laughed.

"Well, she seemed to get your attention that evening. And I didn't want you looking at anyone but me."

"It was only because she looked like something out of an old movie. Trust me; you had my total attention the whole time."

We finished our second drink. I paid the check, and we walked out of the Red Ox. The first street we came to I turned and headed for the river. Sara already knew where we were going. We found a spot close to where we were that first night we met and sat on the grass. It was another great night; there was almost a full moon, stars twinkling and not a cloud in sight.

We sat quietly, just enjoying the view, the river, the stars, the moonlight reflecting off the river as it quietly made its way to wherever its journey took it. I put my arm around Sara, and she laid her head on my shoulder. I turned Sara's head up towards me and kissed her softly and gently laid her down on the grass. As we kissed my hand slowly began to explore her body.

Suddenly she pushed me away, "Oh, no you don't, cowboy, I don't put out on the first date," she said, "What kind of a girl do you think I am?"

"I'm sorry; I got carried away," I said apologetically.

Sara pulled my head back down to her and kissed me softly. "Take me back to the hotel, and then you won't have to apologize," she said.

We got up and walked back to the hotel. As soon as we got in the room, Sara excused herself and went to the bathroom. I lit a cigarette, walked over to the dresser and picked up a glass then walked to the cooler, scooped some ice cubes out of the cooler and grabbed a coke. I poured some coke over the ice in the glass and set it down on the night stand by the bed and then undressed and climbed in bed.

I had just finished my cigarette when Sara walked out of the bathroom. If I hadn't finished my cigarette already I probably would have swallowed it. I had never seen Sara look so beautiful before. She was wearing a toga type long gown draped only over one shoulder. The gown was made from a very, very sheer black material with gold sequins on it that seemed to make it shimmer. As Sara stood in the door way to the bathroom the light shined through the gown and revealed every curvature of her body. Sara walked over to the bed, climbed on top and moved over to me, leaned down, and began kissing my face and whispered in my ear, "Now where were we down on the river?"

I pulled her down closer to me and kissed her passionately our tongues intertwined together. I could feel her aroused nipples through the sheer material of the gown as she rubbed against my bare chest. As our kisses became more urgent and passionate she climbed on top of me.

She sat up, removed the gown and threw it on the floor; then leaned forward so that her breasts were only millimeters away from my lips. I found one and then the other erect nipple of her gently swaying breasts. I gently rolled her over on her back as I continued to kiss her neck and nibble her earlobes as my hands roamed freely over her body; stopping only to tweak her hard nipples between my thumb and forefingers. Her hands slid down my chest as she reached for me but I gently pushed them away.

"You just relax, and let me take care of things for a while," I whispered in her ear.

I reached over to the night stand and grabbed a piece of ice from the glass and put it in my mouth then lowered my head and began to kiss and suck her erect nipples. She jumped and squealed as the cold ice touched her nipples unexpectedly. As I continued to suck on one nipple and then the other my hand softly moved down her body making little circles over her tummy and around her belly button. I could feel her lower stomach muscles twitch and spasm involuntarily under my hands as they continued to move downward; followed by my lips with the ice held between them. I could feel her legs part as my lips traced the outline of her pubic hair and between the crevices where her legs and hips joined. Her hips began to move, rising and falling as I got closer. Her hands moved to the back of my head and her fingers intertwined in my hair as she pulled me down to her and thrust her hips up to meet me and I heard a deep groan come from somewhere deep inside her as my lips met hers. I felt her shudder as the ice melted between us. She moaned and pulled me up on top of her and cried out as our bodies fell into a rhythmic harmony and moved faster in unison as our passion reached explosion. As she reached her climax her fingernails dug into my back and her teeth bit into my shoulder. She clung to me for what seemed like an eternity; as if she couldn't let go. As her climax began to subside her body still involuntarily quivered and jerked in after shocks. I was spent and could only lie on top of her and not move, even though I could still feel her moving under me.

After several minutes of recovery she lifted my head to her face and kissed me tenderly. I looked down at her and smiled. "Lesson number four," I said.

"Don't tell me there is a lesson number five; I don't think I could take it," she grinned.

She put her arms around me and then suddenly pulled them back. Looking at her hands over my shoulder she let out a screech.

"Oh, my God, you're bleeding!" She pushed me off her and sat up and rolled me over to look at my back. "Holy shit, did I do that to you, baby? Why didn't you tell me to stop?"

"You were having too much fun." I grinned.

"Does it hurt?" she asked.

"I'll get over it. Besides, it was worth every scratch," I said.

"Don't move," she said as she jumped off the bed and ran into the bathroom.

I sat up, grabbed my cigarettes, lighter, and glass of coke. She came back with a cool washcloth and a hand towel. She climbed up on the bed next to me.

"Turn around," she ordered. She moved closer to me as I sat with my back to her and she dabbed the cool washcloth over my back.

"That looks terrible, baby; I'm so sorry," she said.

She got up on her knees and started to bend forward to give me a kiss when she saw the teeth marks on my shoulder. "Oh, my God, I did this too?" She moaned. She put her arms around me and hugged me resting her face against the back of my head.

"I love you, baby. I'm sorry I hurt you."

I turned around and put my arms around her. "That only means I did what I was supposed to do, and that is satisfy you," I said and then gave her a kiss.

"You certainly did that," she said. "Can I have a drink of your coke?"

"Get your own coke," I said.

She pouted and started to get off the bed. I reached out and grabbed her and pulled her back. "I was only kidding, sugar; you can have a drink of my coke," I said as I handed her the glass. I climbed off the bed and walked over to the cooler, grabbed a fresh coke and another glass of ice, went back to the bed and poured some fresh coke in both glasses.

"Where did you learn that ice thing you did? You never did that before," she asked.

"I saw it in a movie once. Did you like it?

She turned me around and looked at my back. "I'd say I did; wouldn't you?" she replied.

"It seemed to be working at the time." I laughed.

After we finished our cokes and cigarettes, we curled up in bed.

"I'm going to miss you terribly when you're gone," she said.

"I'm going to miss you more," I said.

"Nuh uh."

"Uh huh."

"You can't miss me more; there isn't more. I'll miss you the mostest," she claimed.

"Okay, how about I miss you just as much then?" I asked.

She slid down and put her head more on my chest and said, "Okay, that's all right." She pulled me closer to her, throwing her leg over mine. I knew she was getting ready to go to sleep. I leaned down, kissed her forehead, and just lay back and let her drift off to sleep.

It wasn't long until she was breathing deeply and steadily. I knew she was asleep.

I kissed her softly on the forehead and whispered, "I'll miss you the most, even if you don't know it."

I woke up the next morning when I felt a sudden rush of cool air over my body. I opened my eyes to find Sara sitting next to me looking under the covers.

"What the hell are you doing?" I asked.

"I'm looking for EMHO," she grinned.

I couldn't help myself. I burst out laughing. *Oh, shit!* I thought. *It's too early in the morning to be laughing so hard,* but I couldn't stop. Sara sat there, dropped the covers, and crossed her arms.

"Now you're making fun of me."

"No, I'm not, sugar; you just come up with some of the damndest things at the most unexpected times, and it just really makes my day when you do," I said as I pulled her towards me and gave her a hug and a kiss, still laughing even though I was trying hard not to.

"Don't give up. Sometimes I have an EMHO at different times during the day; and today isn't over yet."

"How do you get an EMHO anyway?" she asked.

"Well, they are all so known as a MPHO, which is usually why a guy gets one."

"Okay, what's a MPHO?" she inquired…

"I pulled her down to me and whispered in her ear. She pulled back and looked at me in surprise. "So other guys have them, and they really don't have anything to do with sex?" she asked.

"Afraid so, sugar. But they sure have a lot of staying power if you want to use it for sex. The guy just can't go pee before he has sex."

She sat there looking dejected. "And here I thought it was just something you had, and I had something to do with it," she proclaimed.

"You mean you never sat around with the girls and BS-ed about guys and such things?

"I never sat around and BS-ed with the girls about anything. I didn't have time; I had to get home and get supper ready and get my homework done and take a piano lesson."

I knew she had been raised in a very strict atmosphere, but it never occurred to me that she never talked to other girls, her girl cousins or somebody about boys. I had had my doubts when she told me she had never had a relationship with a man before except for that guy she said she never did anything with; but I could tell she was dead serious about what she was telling me now, and this made all the rest of it believable.

I moved over close to her and lifted her chin up so she could look me in the eye. "You know what? That innocence and lack of experience and knowledge just makes you that much more adorable in my eyes and makes me love you even more. I think I'm probably the luckiest guy around to have found such an innocent woman that is such a fast learner and can express her passion so profoundly when it's brought out of her."

She got up on her knees and put her arms around me. "So you're not upset with me because I'm such a dummy about some things?"

"I don't think you're a dummy about anything, just a very quick learner that enjoys her lessons," I said.

"That's because I have a great teacher who has a lot of patience with me, and I love him for being so good to me," she replied and then gave me a long, gentle kiss.

"Now what time to you leave today?" she asked.

"My train leaves at 1800," I said.

"That's six p.m., right?

"Right."

"So we should be at the Bahnhof at five?" she asked.

"At least by five. I don't what to miss my train."

"You're anxious to get away from me, huh?"

"You know what I mean," I replied.

"What time is it anyway?" I asked.

Sara reached across me to the nightstand and looked at my watch.

"It's almost 0900. Is that right? Is that how you say it? She grinned.

"That's right, that's how you say 9 a.m. Are you hungry?"

"Kinda, but I really don't want to go out. You may get a late EMHO." She laughed.

I had to laugh with her. "I might but I promise if I do you will be the first to know. I want to take a shower anyway, and then we can talk more about breakfast."

I got up and headed for the shower. I brushed my teeth at the sink while the water got hot in the shower. I stepped in, the hot water felt good as usual until I turned around and let it hit directly on my back then it stung from the scratches on my back. I turned back around and just let the water pour.

I was standing under the shower with my eyes closed when I felt these soft arms slide around my waste and soft lips kiss the scratches on my back. I looked back over my shoulder.

"Lady you're not supposed to be in here," I said.

"I know, but I was getting lonesome out there," she purred. "Besides you need someone to wash your back and lick your wounds."

I turned her around so she was under the water and I was standing facing her. "I tell you what. You can wash my back while I wash your…whole body."

I took the bar of soap and worked up lather in one hand and with the soap in the other I began to wash her; starting with her face, being careful not to get soap in her eyes, I washed each arm the started working my way down her body. As I reached her waist I got down on my knees and washed her thighs all the way around and as I washed her legs she washed my back. After I finished her feet I stood up, kissed her and told her to stay there and rinse off until I got back.

I stepped out of the shower grabbed my robe and put it on, then grabbed hers and walked back to the shower, opened the curtain and told her to turn off the water and step out. She stepped gingerly over the edge of the tub and I held her robe for her to put on. Then I got a towel and handed it to her.

"You have to do the towel around the head thing; I don't know how to do that," I said.

She turned around and stood on tiptoes and gave me a kiss. "Thank you, baby."

I walked out of the bathroom, grabbed a coke, went back to the bed shoved the pillows behind my back and sat back against the head board while I lit up a cigarette. Sara came out of the bathroom with her hair up in the towel; walked over and climbed up on the bed beside me. She lit a cigarette and set the ashtray beside her.

"So did you decide if you wanted to go eat or not?"

"I could eat something I think, but I really don't want to go far to get it," I said.

"We can probably still get breakfast in the hotel dinning room," Sara replied.

"Can you call down and find out?"

Sara got up and walked over to the phone and dialed. She had a long conversation with whoever was on the other end. Finally she hung up and came back and jumped back up on the bed. She took the towel off her head and began to brush her hair.

"Well? Are we going down to eat breakfast or not?" I asked.

"Nope, they are bringing breakfast to us. I ordered room service," she said with a grin on her face. "I ordered you ham and eggs with orange juice. Is that okay?"

"Sounds perfect. How long will it be?" I asked.

"The lady said no more than half an hour."

"I fired up another cigarette. "Do I have to get dressed?" I asked.

"I guess you could if you wanted to, but I don't plan on it," Sara said.

"You can just sign the ticket and give the guy a tip. Just like back home."

Almost 30 minutes to the minute there was a knock on the door. I opened it and a waitress brought a big tray in and took it right to the coffee table in front of the sofa. She set it down, she and Sara exchanged a few words and she started out the door. I slipped 20 marks in her hand and she thanked me and left.

Sara and I sat down on the sofa and ate. I had my orange juice and Sara had a big pot of coffee.

"Why didn't you have your little cup of instant coffee this morning?" I asked.

"I ran out. I forgot to put a new jar in the bag before I left," she said.

We finished breakfast about the same time, except Sara still had her coffee. I got up and walked over to the window and looked out through the sheer curtains at the street below. I stood there watching the traffic and the people. When I left Abilene, it never occurred to me that I might not ever see that place again the thought never crossed my mind. I guess I just always assumed I would. But I doubted that I would ever see this street or even this city again and that bothered me. I knew I would never forget it.

Sara came over and stood beside me. "What are you thinking?" she asked. I told her what I had been thinking about and how I felt about it.

"Maybe we can come back someday and visit," she offered.

"Yeah, maybe we can," I said but somehow I knew that was never going to happen.

I walked back to the bed and propped myself up on the pillows again and lit a cigarette. Sara came over and joined me. When she finished her cigarette she got up and went to the bathroom. I looked at my watch; it was almost noon already; six more hours. Actually only about four. I had to go by the company and sign out.

Sara came back out of the bathroom, she had her makeup on and her hair combed and fixed already.

"You're getting a head start on things, huh? That's a good idea. Did I tell you I have to go back to the company and sign out before I go the Bahnhof?" I asked.

"Yes, you told me," she said as she climbed up on the bed.

"So that means we should leave here about what, four p.m.?"

"That's what I was thinking. That will give me a chance to say goodbye to Roach and some of the others if they are around."

Sara got up and walked over and got a coke out of the cooler scooped up some ice cubes in the glass and then brought them back to the bed. She poured some coke in the glass for her and handed me the can. She was sitting on her knees on the bed with her legs spread slightly allowing her robe to fall apart at the waist. I had trouble looking above her waist but she wasn't saying anything; I couldn't help but wonder if she was doing that on purpose. I really didn't care, I could feel my breathing quicken slightly and the blood rushing to all the right places.

She just sat there staring at me staring at her.

"Remember me telling you how I sometimes get and EMHO later on in the day?" I asked.

"Yes, I remember that" she said.

"I think I'm getting one now," I said.

"Are you sure it's not just a MPHO?" she asked.

"Oh, I'm very sure," I said.

Sara reached down and pulled my robe apart. "Oh, my, what have we here?" It would appear you're in need of some attention." She grinned.

She untied her robe and dropped it off her shoulders and let if fall behind her. She moved over closer to me. She reached in the glass and pulled out a couple of ice cubes and put them in her mouth.

"What have you got in mind?" I asked.

She reached down and untied my robe and pushed it out of the way.

"I thought it would be interesting to see how well I learned lesson number four." She grinned.

Who am I to argue? I thought as she leaned forward and kissed me gently but wasted no time in moving her wet moist lips down my body.

Her lips followed the path of her fingers as she slowly worked her way down past my belly button and didn't stop until she found what she was looking for. Her pace was slow and steady and my hips found her rhythm and stayed with her, quickening only to meet her increased pace. She sensed the impending explosion rising within me and hastened her pace to meet the final eruption. She immediately moved to straddle me, quickly settling down over me and began to rock back and forth, leaning forward placing her hands on my shoulders. Her speed increasing as she began to reach her peak. Her hair was hanging in her face and there was a glazed, far-away look in her eyes, drops of sweat rolling down her forehead.

Suddenly she moaned, "Now, ohh, God, nowww!"

Her arms buckling, too weak to support her, she fell on top of me her body still twitching involuntarily. She lay still in my arms until her heavy breathing began to return to normal. When she had regained her composure she sat up, looked down at me, grinned and asked, "How did I do, coach?"

She was so cute I couldn't help but laugh. "Baby, you are without a doubt the best student I ever had or expect to ever have," I said as I leaned forward and kissed each of her still-erect nipples.

"Careful, cowboy, or we may have to practice lesson number four some more.

"Appealing as that thought is to me. I am afraid I will have to decline. I'm so sweaty now I need another shower."

"I have a better idea" She said.

"And what might that be?" I asked with raised eyebrows.

"That's a big tub in there; let's take a bubble bath together," she said.

"Do you have some bubbles?"

"There are some in there, sitting over the toilet. I saw them last night."

"You have to get up off me first."

Sara climbed off and led me to the bathroom. She got the water started add the bubble bath and we hopped in while the tub filled with hot water and bubbles. The tub was bigger than it looked; there was plenty of room for both of us.

Sara turned around with her back to me and leaned back against me. We just sat there and soaked. Occasionally she would turn her head and look up and give me a kiss or I would kiss the top of her head. Occasionally my hand my stray beneath the bubbles and she would slap my hand away.

"Stop that!" she would say.

"Why?" I asked.

"Because if you start I won't want you to stop, and I don't want to start something we can't finish."

I hated to admit it but she was right, it was just hard for me to keep my hands off of her. I wasn't sure what time it was but I had a feeling it was getting close to three p.m. and if that was right then we needed to be getting ready to leave for the barracks.

I climbed out of the tub and slipped on my robe and walked out to check my watch. I was right, it was a couple minutes after three already. I walked back in the bathroom bent down and gave her a kiss.

"It's a few minutes after three; we need to get ready to go to the barracks," I said.

"Okay, I'll be right out," she said. I walked out of the bathroom and began to put on my uniform. This was feeling more uncomfortable all the time now.

Sara came out of the bathroom after a few minutes. She had touched up her make up and re done her hair so all she had to do was get dressed. She dropped the robe and was walking around the room naked. She was driving me crazy and I couldn't help but stare because I knew this would be the last time for a while I would see her naked. She finally got some clothes on and broke my eyes away as I put on my shoes.

I checked all my pockets, keys, wallet, money; I had everything I should have in my pockets. Sara had her bags packed so we were ready to go. We walked out of the room and down to the desk. Sara took care of the checking out process. Once she was done we headed for the car. Repacked it one more time and then we were off for Patton Barracks.

It was only about a 10-15 minute drive, we rolled through the gate of Patton Barracks about five minutes to four. Charlie Morrison waved us through and shouted good luck Bones as we passed through. Sara drove down to the company and parked the car in the parking area on the side of the building.

"I'll be back as soon as I can," I said as I got out of the car.

I walked around the corner of the building and ran into a bunch of the guys, just hanging out smoking and joking. They all said something, goodbye, good luck, see ya stateside, something. I shook hands with them as I passed by. The Honor Guard was getting ready for Guard Mount they had a ceremony to perform this afternoon.

I walked down the steps to the Orderly Room, stopping by the pass box and sign out book. I turned in my pass and signed out. For destination I put Permanent Change of Station (PCS). Top came to the door of the Orderly Room, and it was just like he knew I was there. He said, "Sammy, come in. The commander wants to see you."

I must have had a startled or surprised look on my face I had never even met the fairly new company commander.

"Don't worry; you're not in trouble," Top said. "Just come on in and report to the commander."

I walked into the commander's office, came to attention, and reported. He returned my salute and told me to stand at ease.

"Specialist Shepard, I know you have someone waiting for you so I won't keep you, but I wanted to present you with this Honor Guard Patch and this certificate of appreciation for your outstanding performance of duty while stationed here with the 529th."

I stepped forward received the patch and certificate. "Thank you, sir," I said.

The captain said, "You're welcome," and shook my hand.

Top said, "Okay, Sammy, that's it. Go get your girlfriend and have a safe trip home. It's been a pleasure serving with you."

"Thanks Top; it's been a great tour. I want to thank you for all you have done for me while I've been assigned here."

I turned saluted the commander and left the office. I stopped by the armor's window and asked if Roach was on duty now; he said he had his weapon signed out, so he must be working. *Shit!* I thought. I wanted to see him before I left. I ran upstairs real quick and went to Tom's room. He was lying on his bunk.

"Hey, fart face, I'm on my way outta here; just came to say goodbye."

Tom got up and stuck out his hand. "Good luck, Bones; you got my address at home, right? and I'll be there in about three months."

"I got it, man; enjoy the last of your tour over here. I kinda wish I was staying, but I gotta go home, I guess. Do you know where Roach is working today?"

"I think he is working Patton gate. Who waved you through when you came on base?" Tom asked.

"Charlie Morrison waved us on," I replied.

"Okay, Roach has the gate, then. He told me at lunch that he was working with Charlie."

"Good. I can catch him on the way out, then," I said. "See you, Tom, be cool man."

"You got it; you take care, now, and don't fall overboard." He laughed.

I walked out the door went down to my old room. Rizzo and Dietz were there. Harry had just gone down to the latrine. I gave Rizzo a cigarette just for old-time's sake; he said, "Hey, thanks, lover."

I told Dietz to come see me when he got out, "But don't bring any ugly women along." He promised to leave the women at home. We all shook hands, and I was just headed out the door when Harry walked in. I said goodbye to Horse Face and told him to stay in off the scaffold before he fell and broke his neck.

I just hit the bottom steps when Roach came running in, we almost bumped into each other.

"Charlie Morrison just told me he waved you in a while ago. I was afraid I would miss you," Roach said.

"Tom told me you were working Patton Gate. I was on my way down there to see you," I said.

"Is Sara waiting for you?"

"Yeah, she is in the car around the corner," I replied.

"What time does your train leave?"

"1800 hours, and they are always on time. Let's walk around towards the car. I know Sara will want to say good-bye too," I said.

We walked around the corner and over to the car.

"I wish you didn't have to go, Bones. I understand why you do, but I wish you could have talked Sara into staying one more year. You know you would probably have made sergeant if you stayed."

"I know; I wish I could have talked her into it to. I happen to like it here," I said.

"Well, you know where I'll be for at least the next year or so, and I have your home address so we can stay in touch, anyway," Roach said.

We reached the car. Roach stuck his head in the window and gave Sara a hug. "I'm gonna miss this Boney shit probably almost as much as you will," Roach told Sara.

"I don't know about that, but I know he will miss you too."

Roach stood up, stuck out his hand, and we shook hands and gave each other a hug.

"Stay in touch, Bones; Bobbie Jo and I may come knocking on your door one day."

“That would be great. Be sure to let me know where you get assigned when you leave here, okay?”

“You got it,” Roach said as he opened the door for me.

I climbed in, Sara started the car and we moved on turning down the company street. Just as we turned the corner Sgt. Shire called the Honor Guard to attention and an order to present arms as we drove by. It may have just been coincidence that I drove by just as they were practicing, I don’t know but I returned their salute, and we drove on down the road past the company building and down towards the gate. I looked over my shoulder one last time at what had been my home for the past two years. Roach was standing out in the company street waving. I stuck my arm out the window and waved back. As we drove through the gate, Charlie Morrison came to attention and gave me a salute. I returned his salute and that was my last time through those gates. I felt kinda sick to my stomach.

Sara and I drove in silence to the Bahnhof. She parked the car I grabbed my duffel back and little tote bag out of the trunk and we walked inside. We checked the schedule against the number on my ticket but I knew my train left on track 6. I was about half way down the loading platform. We walked through the double doors down to the big sign that said track #6.

There were a lot of GIs around and I was pretty sure we were all going to the same place. It was 1740 already, I had 20 minutes to say goodbye but nothing would come out of my mouth. Sara was squeezing my hand tightly.

“Hey, if you squeeze much harder you’ll break a bone or something,” I said, trying to lighten things up a little bit; but it didn’t work.

Sara put her arms around me and whispered, “I love you, and I’ll be home just as soon as I can. I promise.”

“I’ll be waiting for you, and I’ll call you when I get home and get settled. Remember, it takes this tub of nuts and bolts I’m taking home a week just to get there, and then I have to get to Texas, so don’t get upset if you don’t hear from me for a couple of weeks or so, okay?”

“Okay, I won’t,” she said.

"Promise?" I asked.

I looked at the big clock over the doors. It was 1750. I noticed that others were starting to board and it was killing me just standing here like this, and I could tell Sara was upset too, she wouldn't look up at me.

"Okay, I guess I better go find a place to sit on that train before all the seats are taken," I said. I raised Sara's chin up to look at her face, and tears were running down her cheeks.

"Don't cry, sugar. I love you, and I'll miss you every minute we are apart."

I gave her a long, passionate kiss and a big hug. I picked up my duffel bag and headed for the train. I knew she was standing there watching me but I couldn't turn around now. I had to move on.

GERMANY
Chapter 99

Carrying my duffel bag over my shoulder; I pushed my way through the crowded isles of the train until I found a berth that wasn't taken. I set my bag down on one seat and sat on the seat across from it. There must have been a couple hundred cars on this train.

I took my hat off and laid it on the seat beside me and lit a cigarette. I wanted to look out the window and see if I could see Sara one more time but I knew she had left already. Neither of us were good at good-byes. I could have stayed on the loading platform with her a few more minutes but it was killing me knowing I had to get on this damn train. I just wanted to get on and get it over with and I know Sara hated standing around waiting for the final whistle to blow.

She had tried but couldn't keep tears from running down her cheeks when I kissed her good-bye that last time. I couldn't either but my tears only masked my sinking heart. Because at that moment I couldn't help but remember the story Marie told Bobby Ray and I about the man in the Tux in the little PX at Fort Huachuca and now I was him; leaving behind the one person in my life that really mattered.

It was all I could do to make myself get aboard this Train. I didn't want to leave. But like any good soldier and eventually like the man in the Tux; I followed my orders climbed aboard and left my heart behind.

The train began to pick up speed as it pulled out of the Bahnhof in Heidelberg. That rhythmic sound, that clickety clack of the train wheels on the tracks that I had become so accustomed to hearing traveling back and forth between K-Town and Heidelberg over the past two years had a different sound to them this time. Usually I was dozing off before we got out of the city but this time they seemed to keep my mind churning.

During the past three years I had found a life and a home. As I would come to realize later on I would never find another group of guys that all started out as strangers; yet ended up so close. I had found a family. Roach, Chuck, Tom, Rizzo, Harry, Dietz and all the others some became my roommates, some became my buddies, they all became my friends and some became like brothers.

More importantly I had found a woman I had fallen in love with. I often wondered if I would recognize the woman I would fall in love with when I first met her. What would she look like? Would she be tall or short? Would she be a blonde a brunette or a redhead? Love at first sight didn't happen for me. There was a lot of lust at first sight along the way; but that only lasted until the object of the lust was out of sight. Falling in love took a little more time but it lasted no matter if I was with her or not.

I popped open one of the cokes I had picked up when I passed through the club car a few cars back and lit a cigarette. I got up and shut the door to the berth; I just wasn't in the same happy mood as those other guys that were going home. As daylight faded into darkness I sat in the dark car and thought back about how far I had traveled and the things I had done since I left that small Texas town I had called home for so long.

When I left Abilene High I was about as dumb as a flat rock in a river bed and just about as slick. All my friends were moving on to the world of higher education. I know some classes would have come easy to me. I had a knack for some things. I could handle those but the classes that really counted in college I could never have dealt with. All I saw there was more of what I had been doing for the past 18 years or so, and I just couldn't see myself sitting in more boring classes and staying up all night doing homework and cramming for tests. I couldn't afford to pay for college, my family sure as hell couldn't afford to pay for it; a couple of junior colleges had offered some partial athletic scholarships but that wouldn't cover all my expenses and I was in no mood to work in some cafeteria or some place just to make ends meet. And basically I was just tired of books.

Sometimes I wondered how my life would have turned out if I had given it that old college try and gone on to college. But that thought never stayed with me long. Looking back, I don't think I have done badly for a guy with a 12th grade education. My short military career had taken me about as far as I could go in such a short time. I was ahead of some of my peers for promotion and was practically guaranteed a promotion if I had re-enlisted for my own vacancy in Heidelberg. I was kicking my ass for not doing that; but I had other considerations that I considered more important.

They used to say the Army would make a man out of you. I don't know if it made a man out of me but I know when I went back home a couple of times the guys I used to hang with still seemed like kids. And what were they doing with their lives? Not much; it seemed like they were waiting on life to do something for them.

And when I looked back and thought about all the things I had done with Sara in the almost three years we had been together I was kind of amazed. I wondered how many other guys my age could say they had done some of the things I had done.

I had ice skated in Garmisch in a 30-year-old Olympic skating rink. I visited Hitler's home in the Alps. I visited Vienna and waltzed along the tree lined banks of the Danube River and rode one of the biggest Ferris wheels ever built.

I traveled through France crossed the Pyrenees Mountains into Spain, and visited Madrid, Valencia and Barcelona; but with all the castles, palaces and museums we visited it was in a sleepy little fishing village we found paradise along the Costa Brava where Sara and I walked the beaches beneath the brightest moon and stars in the heavens and went skinny dipping at midnight in the Mediterranean.

I saw Paris and got dizzy driving around the Arc De Triomphe trying to figure out how to get off; walked the beautiful Champs-Elysees; ate breakfast at a side walk café. We went to the top of the Eiffel Tower, took a boat ride on the River Seine; and saw the Mona Lisa at the Louvre Museum.

I drove the Helmstadt Autobahn at the height of the cold war; climbed up on Check Point Charlie at the Berlin Wall and looked across into a ghost town that was East Berlin. I saw the Brandenburg Gate and The Reichstag.

I visited Tivoli Park in Copenhagen; tiptoed through the tulips in Holland and visited the city of Amsterdam with all its canals and the house of Anne Frank.

Maybe it wasn't around the world in 80 days but for a small town kid from Texas it wasn't bad. Of all the trips and all the things I got to see and do; none would ever have happened if I hadn't taken the opportunity to talk to that little brown haired, brown eyed school teacher from Philadelphia that August night in 1960.

I didn't have a clue when I invited myself to sit down beside her in the Red Ox that evening how she was about to change my world. It never occurred to me that this little girl; no not little girl, this young woman so mature in some ways but so naive and inexperienced in others would take my life and change it from the ordinary to the extraordinary and actually give it some meaning. I had no idea what it was like to actually care for someone and to feel that caring as it grew into a love that just got bigger and better. I never knew what it was like to have someone put their complete trust in me; to know that someone depended on me to be there and to take care of her and protect her. I never knew what it was like to feel and be needed.

It was the most exciting time in my life watching a woman, brought up in such a Victorian atmosphere shed her chrysalis like a monarch butterfly and become such a beautiful; passionate woman. Realizing for the first time in her life it was all right to have feelings and thoughts until now she had been taught to believe were wrong and inappropriate for a young lady; and that it was okay to act on those thoughts and feelings without having to feel guilty or sinful to have fun and enjoy the passions brought on by those feelings.

This was my life, my world for the past 2 years, 2 months, and 10 days. Something inside me told me that no matter what may lie ahead for me in the future or how long I lived, this time in my life would always be the core of all my memories.